An Old West star enjoys a quiet afternoon -- until a man shows up with a deal.

An office worker is haunted by a secret from his past -- until a man takes over his company's human resources department.

Four retirees prepare to live out their final days in peace and contentment -- until a man moves into an empty unit, bringing mystery with him.

He's the same man every time.

And he's not a man at all.

He's...

THE DEVIL YOU KNOW BEST.

THE DEVIL YOU KNOW BEST

Edited by R.J. Carter

Critical Blast Publishing
24 Hillside Drive
Holiday Island, AR 72631

Cover Art and Design by Bobooks
First Edition March 1, 2024

0 9 8 7 6 5 4 3 2 1

ISBN-13: 978-1-963-83503-8

DEDICATION

To the trio that made this happen:
To you.
To me.
And the Devil makes three.

CONTENTS

ACKNOWLEDGMENTS

It is the tellers of tales and the dreamers of darkness, who fearlessly reached into the shadows and dragged the Devil out of them, kicking and screaming, that made this book the success it is.

Te Lecturi Salutamus!

FOREWORD:
THIRD TIMES THE
HARM

They come in threes.

Celebrity deaths. Crucifixes on a hillside. Horror anthologies. We just feel a sense of unease if we don't have that closure a trio brings.

Of course, the moment I first saw the cover for The Devil You Know, I knew there would have to be two more. What I didn't see was how much interest there would be from writers trying to get into the mix. While we tried to corral things to another twenty stories, there were simply too many good stories to choose from, Hell had to widen itself to accommodate just a few more tales for this final sin.

The Devil takes on new and mysterious roles in this third collection. To be sure, he's still the consummate deal maker, heart breaker, soul taker we expect him to be – and if you need a reminder, just check out Dan Allen's "The Devil Takes His Time" or Kevin Lauderdale's "James and the Prince of Darkness."

But he's also a family man, as shown to us by Diana Olney ("Daddy Issues") and Sarina Dorie ("Meet the

Satans"). He has a penchant for hanging around the workplace, as we see in Jean Jentilet's "Human Resources" and Kristal Stittle's "Slow Day."

So thank you for coming back one more time. There are many tomes of evil out there for you to choose from, but as the saying goes (and if it doesn't, it should) – always go with *The Devil You Know Best.*

— R.J. Carter, Editor

INFERNAL LETTER

Donald R. Vogel

Dear Wormwood,

Never thought you would hear from ole Uncle Screwtape again, did you. The family is a bit concerned since your fall from grace and asked me to lend a hand. You know I've got your back, like the old days, but I never thought it would be to admonish you to cease and desist getting mortals to sell their souls. That, as we say, is a bit passé since the Boss prefers quantity to quality. You should know; that Tik Tok thing was your idea. Mortals are practically dancing with Mr. D., and yet you're backsliding.

Where once I would have guided you on how to get a sucker to sign on the dotted line, I now must warn you that the Unclean One has noticed your recent faux pas and is not pleased. I'm with Him in wondering what you were thinking by contracting with an evolutionary biologist. The title is hint enough: he's in the bag. His books on free will being an illusion were practically dictated into his ear by the Wonder Down Under. This signing strikes me as you trying a bit too hard to get back in His good graces.

Look at Job. That poor bastard had no choices. His Infernal Majesty's greatest trick was not convincing the world he didn't exist, but in duping Mr. Omniscience into torturing one of his most righteous creatures and calling it scripture. (If I may thump my chest a bit, predestination was my later innovation on the anti-free will movement. Ask Calvin, he's down here somewhere.) The beauty of it is in sowing confusion and indecision, not outright rebellion. The defiant seem targeted for redemption, ergo St. Paul, but the Punctured One says in Revelation that he will spew the lukewarm out of his mouth. See how this works?

I hope this isn't about competition with your cousin, Beelzebub. Not trying to fan the flames, but you should follow a bit of his example. Beelz is playing the long game. There may not be anything new under the sun, but he knew that Fascism wasn't dead yet. Give him credit for seeing the potential in an account everyone thought was depleted. In fact, you would do well to think about redeeming one of the oldies but goodies. Look around you. Plague is back with a vengeance. Even terrorism is taking newer and exciting forms. It's raining souls in both cases.

No offense, but you would be good at ignorance, if you do it as the Boss would: don't create more stupid, feed it. Intellectualize everything, to sow more pride in those who think they know better, and confusion in those who don't and just watch the division. Wow, I can see it now; they'll literally have their heads up their asses as punishment when they get down here. Forgive me for quoting the Other Guy, but the blind leading the blind always makes for good sport and soul stealing. Hmmm, maybe your recent signing can be of use after all.

I don't know about you, but I think we got the makings of a plan here. While your lackey is spewing science, blow the dust off some home spun wisdom for the dummies. See what you can do with "this too shall pass" or something like that. The Unholy Himself loves when mortals mistake aphorisms for holy writ. You're golden if you get His attention with a pivot on the signing and some creative bastardizations.

Listen to me, son, and we'll have you descending the ranks again in no time.

Disingenuously,

Uncle Screwtape

ABOUT THE AUTHOR

DONALD R. VOGEL is a fundraiser by profession, writer by aspiration, who lives in Long Island, New York with his wife and son. He holds a master's degree in English from Stony Brook University and has published both fiction and nonfiction in several literary journals.

RICKY'S HAND

Damascus Mincemeyer

'Ricky was of the devil. When he was on acid, he'd go back into the dark woods of Aztakea, and he would talk to the devil. He said the devil came in the form of a tree, which sprouted out of the ground and glowed. I tried to question him about it, but he said, "I don't like to talk about it. People think I'm nuts."'

— Mark Fisher,

Northport resident, age 17

What you're about to read is true.

Late in the evening on June 19, 1984, four youths walked into Aztakea Woods, a forested area skirting Northport, Long Island, New York. Seventeen-year-old Ricky Kasso led the band; the son of a history teacher and football coach at Cold Spring Harbor High, he'd earned the reputation among the teenage underworld as a waster, a minor drug dealer, a major troublemaker and, so he claimed, a willing servant of Satan. The year before, Ricky had been busted for digging into a colonial-era grave at a local cemetery and during a subsequent stay at the South Oaks Psychiatric Hospital in Amityville hinted at his association with a group called the Knights of the Black Circle. They were worshipers of The Devil, he suggested, a society hidden in plain sight throughout America's peaceful neighborhoods, quietly seducing innocent souls away from God in any fashion possible. Nobody believed him, of course. Doctors labeled Ricky 'antisocial but not presently psychotic', attributed his behavior to both drug abuse and a recent bout of pneumonia, then released him.

Accompanying Ricky that June night were fellow high school dropout Gary Lauwers and two other teens, Jimmy Troiano and Albert Quinones. After hiking into Aztakea, the four dropped acid and smoked some PCP; Gary used his socks and the sleeves from his denim jacket as kindling to ignite a campfire.

The murder happened near midnight. Some weeks earlier, Gary had stolen ten bags of angel dust from Ricky at a party, and though they'd allegedly settled the issue, Ricky renewed the quarrel. During the altercation he gained the upper hand, straddled Gary, and produced a knife.

"Say you love Satan!" Ricky commanded his prey.

Tearful, bloodied, gasping for breath, Gary instead whimpered, "I love my mother."

"*Satan*! Say you love *Satan*!'"

Desperate, Gary loudly professed his adulation for Lucifer. The admission did not save him. He was stabbed in excess of thirty times, his eyes were gouged out, his naked body covered with leaves and branches and left to rot.

Ricky was not quiet about the crime. For two weeks his homicidal boasts were whispered currency about town. To some he alleged that an approving Beelzebub manifested as a cawing black crow after the killing; disbelieving others were brought to view

Gary's decaying corpse before he and Jimmy made one final trip to bury the skeletal remains in a shallow grave.

Nobody who was shown the body squealed; an eavesdropping girl who overheard two teens discussing the matter eventually made an anonymous call to police. Ricky and Jimmy were discovered the next day sleeping in a car. Newspaper photographs of the arrest showed a wild-eyed, feral-looking kid. At his booking Ricky wore an AC/DC shirt. In his pocket was a scrap of paper listing the Dignitaries in Hell.

Two days after being arrested Ricky hanged himself in his jail cell.

Following his death, lurid headlines quickly dubbed him the 'Say You Love Satan Killer' and 'The Acid King of New York'. *20/20* soon aired a special episode about devil worship in America. Geraldo Rivera did, too. A frightened public raised questions: *was* a satanic cult operating on Long Island? Suffolk County law enforcement denied it; the Knights of the Black Circle were an exaggeration, they insisted. Just some delinquents causing mayhem. Besides, Ricky's deviant actions were caused by heavy metal music, horror films and too much television. Everyone knew that.

And thus from Northport the panic spread, fueled by ravenous reporters, the Moral Majority, bully-pulpit preachers and politicians alike. We were at spiritual war, they insisted. Evil was afoot on cloven hooves. The Lord of Lies lurked in subliminal messages in our records, in role-playing games, in ritual abuse in pre-schools. Armageddon had arrived. The End Was Near.

But of the Knights of the Black Circle, nothing further was mentioned.

Kim Gelardi had been on the phone with Emily Rameson for roughly an hour before her friend admitted, "I saw Gary's body, you know."

Sitting cross-legged atop the unmade covers of her bed, Kim groaned. The clock radio on the nearby nightstand was tuned to WLIR; 'Original Sin' by INXS had just finished playing, and the new Depeche Mode single, 'Blasphemous Rumours,' started in immediately after.

Kim twined the curly phone cord around purple-painted fingertips. "You're so full of shit, Em," she finally said.

Emily girlishly gasped on the other end of the line. "No! I'm *serious*. Melissa told Mila that she and Andy went with Jimmy to see it."

"And they just let *you* tag along? Little Miss Bookworm? Suuuuure."

Emily hesitated. "Well...okay, maybe I *didn't* see it. But Melissa and Andy did. For *real*."

"*Please*. Melissa will say *anything* to make herself sound cool. Mila, too. Remember when she swore she hung out backstage with Rob Halford at the Priest concert last month? Scuzz told me she didn't even *go*."

"*Scuzz*?" Emily giggled. "You mean Egan? You *still* hang out with him? Didn't you tell me he tried to talk you into sucking his dick at that party at Jones Beach on July Fourth?"

Kim winced at the memory. "Look, he was *really* wasted. But he apologized later. He's not that bad a guy, really. You just have to get to know him."

"He wears safety pins through his nose and listens to suicide music. I'll pass, thanks. And isn't sneaking out to that party what got you grounded in the first place?"

"Yeah, Steve threw a hissy. But whatever. Ask for forgiveness, not permission, right?"

Emily nervously laughed. "You're gutsy, Kim. If my stepdad was a cop, I'd be scared shitless."

"Here I thought you were scared shitless of everything anyway." Kim kidded. When Emily didn't say anything back, she worried the joke had slashed too deep and shifted the subject. "So you never told me where you're babysitting tonight."

Emily remained quiet. *Yep, hurt her feelings*, Kim lamented. After a beat, though, Emily said, "Bayview."

"Ahhhh. Swanky."

"Ha ha. They're named the Masons. Lisa and, uh, Edward I think. Lisa seems okay. Kinda on the snobby side. French lady, you know? I've seen Edward's picture but haven't met him. House is ritzy. Pool's fucking huge. Two BMW's."

"Yuppies?"

"*Totally.* It's pretty cool, though. I'm in their living room right now. Looks like the one from *Family Ties*, except waaaay bigger. Kid was already tucked in bed before I got here. Haven't even seen him. Hasn't made a peep the whole time, either. All I gotta do is sit on my ass, eat their food and watch TV 'til eleven."

"Rad gig," Kim fussed with the unsolved Rubik's Cube on her dresser. "Beats solitary confinement here in Alcatraz. Two weeks lockdown for a party is bullshit."

"Do the crime, do the time," Emily cracked before she abruptly hushed. After a full silent minute, she whispered: "Shit. I think someone's outside."

Kim set the Rubik's Cube aside. On the radio, Rockwell's 'Somebody's Watching Me' kicked into high gear. "What are you talking about?"

"I... I heard a noise. At the back door."

A mischievous smirk dimpled Kim's cute face. "You're so full of it, Em."

"*No.*" Emily's insistence was emphatic. "I'm *not* joking. I heard something." A pause. "There it is again. There's definitely someone out back. On the patio. By the pool."

Kim's smile faded. "Is the door locked?"

"I think so." Emily's breath quickened. *"Shit!* They're trying the knob. I'm scared, Kim."

She swore again, louder; Kim's lips curled. "If you're pulling a prank, so help me..."

"I'm not fucking pranking you!" Emily hysterically shot back. "They're in the house! They're in the—"

There was an ear-splitting crash, followed by Emily's sudden, frantic, high-pitched scream before the call disconnected.

Kim stiffened on the bed, staring at the phone's receiver; her knuckles were white, her hand was shaking. Almost mechanically she set the receiver in its cradle, her mouth suddenly sticky and dry, forehead damp with beaded sweat. *What the hell did I just hear?*

She flipped the radio off mid-song and for another few minutes sat perfectly still. It was eight forty-five. The midsummer sun was just setting, and in the dying light all the posters that usually brought her comfort seemed alien in the gathering gloom; those bands her Roy Orbison-loving stepfather hated, The Cure and Siouxsie, Subhumans and The Adicts, The Misfits' leering skull on the back of her bedroom door.

Kim's fingers wrung together. She envisioned the phone ringing and Emily giggling on the other end; they'd share a laugh and Kim would feel foolish for worrying. When nothing happened, though, Kim wondered, *What should I do?* Her stepfather was on-duty, and briefly she considered calling the Northport police station to ask for him, but the derisive sneer he'd likely lend in return made her think twice: *Your stupid friend is just pulling your leg,* he'd argue. *We don't have the manpower to waste sending someone out for a drive-by over some sick practical joke.*

Another impatient fifteen minutes slid by. It was Wednesday; in the living room, Kim knew her mother would be enrapt with *Dynasty* while polishing off the nightly glass of merlot. She also knew she couldn't get to either the front door or the house's rear exit without passing by the room and being seen. Her mother may not have appreciated the strict home rules any more than Kim, but she enforced them with the same impunity, which left Kim with few viable options. Sneaking out again so soon after her previous offense would mean weeks added to her current grounding, probably with revoked phone privileges.

"Fuck it," Kim tied her brown hair into a ponytail, slipped a pair of beat-up All-Stars on her bare feet and opened the bedroom window. There wasn't any screen; outside, the wind had picked up, blowing a gust that ruffled the curtains and chilled Kim despite the day's lingering warmth. Pocketing her keys and last twenty bucks, she exhaled an unsteady breath, grabbed the phone and started dialing.

8

Egan's '72 Dodge Demon was already parked and waiting by the time Kim reached the corner end of Laurel Road twenty minutes later. The car was a junkyard compactor's wet dream; rusted wheel wells, chipped green paint, hail-damaged hood, but its chrome cartoon devil-with-a-pitchfork emblem still shined impishly in the streetlight's glow as she opened the passenger's door.

"Thanks for doing this, Scuzz. I owe you one." Kim said after getting in. Slouched behind the steering wheel with the window rolled down, Egan's hole-filled Black Flag shirt was damp from the evening's heat, but he simply smirked, started the engine, and headed east on Route 25A.

"You don't owe me shit, Kimmy. This beats the hell outta sniffin' glue and watchin' Johnny fuckin' Carson. 'Sides, you know me. Always up for adventure."

Kim was rigid in the cracked leather seat, gnawing nervously at her nails, the final moments of the conversation with Emily re-playing in her head. *"Adventure's* not the word I'd use. Something seriously doesn't feel right."

"She's probably just out to get your goat," Egan assured her. "You know Emily. She's... *Emily.* Queen of the Weird."

"You used to say *I* was Queen of the Weird." Kim replied. Egan sniggered, lit a cigarette, exhaled a puff of smoke.

"Fine. If you're the Queen, then Emily's, like, the Duchess of York Weird or some shit. Point is, she's probably yankin' your chain. She knows you're secretly a wrinkly worrywart granny wrongfully incarcerated in the body of a seventeen-year-old punk goddess. We'll get there, find out everything's cool, then get lit on whatever Amontillado we find in the wine cellar. I mean, Bayview, right? You know those blue blood types are hoardin' the good stuff."

Route 25A led to Woodbine Avenue, where the houses thinned out and the tree line of Aztakea Woods began. Just seeing the forest in the car's headlights caused Kim to intensify her nail-biting. Even Egan squirmed in the driver's seat; trying to mask the unease, he randomly grabbed a cassette from the center consul and popped it into the tape deck. When Kim heard the Fad Gadget song 'Ricky's Hand' coming through the Demon's speakers, though, she couldn't restrain a groan.

"Turn it back off, Scuzz."

"Why?" Egan balked. "You love Fad Gadget. Frank Tovey's a mad fuckin' genius."

"Normally, yeah. But not tonight. *Please.*"

When he saw how serious she was, Egan finally relented, removed the cassette and fiddled with the radio dial until he found a rock station blasting Van Halen's 'Runnin' with the Devil.'

"Better?" He asked.

"Not much. But a little."

Aside from them, the road was empty in both directions. They were still driving by Aztakea when Egan glanced at the trees and slyly confessed, "You know, I saw Gary's body."

Kim skittishly laughed, partially from the evening's tension, partly from the allegation's absurdity. "I've seen you get queasy around moldy cheese, Scuzz. I seriously doubt you'd tramp through the forest to stare at some corpse maggots have made into a Happy Meal any more than Emily did."

Egan grinned. "You're a monster, Kimmy. That's why everyone loves you." But his lips quickly tightened before he stamped the cigarette into the ashtray. "I went to this party last spring. Cow Harbor Park. With Mila and that foreign exchange dude, Philippe. Everyone was high as astronauts, man, tripping out on mesc and dust. There was this kid there, gone out of his head, chanting all this fucked-up *Exorcist* shit, tellin' everyone he was gonna get in touch with the devil. I asked Philippe who the kid was, and he says, 'That's Ricky. Everyone knows Ricky.'"

Kim's muscles tensed. "You're still bullshitting me."

"I'm *not*." Egan's face was granite. "I mean, I didn't hang around long. They were breakin' into people's cars and shit. No way, man, got me enough trouble, you know? So I didn't put it all together until I saw the photos in the paper. Then I knew who that kid *really* was."

"Why didn't you tell me this before?"

"Didn't want you thinkin' I was some name-droppin' poseur tryin' to look cool. Trust me, *nothin'* 'bout Ricky was cool, not from what I saw. Dude was evil. Fucked-up evil."

Kim exhaled a relieved breath once Aztakea disappeared into the rearview mirror; ahead of them, Woodbine turned onto Bayview Avenue, and the waterfront space arose with chic boutiques, jewelry stores and homes of deluxe, old-world grandeur. The further they went the more out-of-place Kim felt; the anchored yachts and parked Mercedes' only made the Demon more conspicuous as it prowled the neighborhood's streets.

"Sure you know the right address?" Egan eventually asked. Kim removed the folded page she'd ripped out of the phone book before leaving home from her jeans pocket.

"Edward and Lisa Mason. 22A Bayview Avenue. That's who Em said she was babysitting for. I'm surprised they were listed."

Egan slowed the vehicle, ticking off house numbers as he drove. "Jesus, look at these joints. Feels like we're in an episode of *Lifestyles of the Rich and Famous.*"

"Champagne wishes and caviar dreams," Kim pointed to a two-story Craftsman-style home with Cape Cod architecture inlaid onto the hillside on the right-hand side of the street. "This is it."

Egan stopped the Demon but didn't kill the ignition; he was too busy scrutinizing the property's every detail the same way Kim was. From the street a set of stone steps ascended to a lawn lush with well-tended hedges and blooming rose bushes. The house itself was clad in gray-paneled exterior, with a low-pitched gable roof, an upraised wraparound porch, tapered columns and hexagonal tower on the western edge. A cement drive led to a multi-car garage, but when Kim followed the trail with her eyes, she frowned.

"Emily's Nova isn't here." She noted suspiciously.

"Doesn't mean anything," Egan asserted. "If they came home early she coulda left already."

Kim chewed the inside of her lip. "Maybe. I still want to check it out, though."

Egan shook his head, grumbled something inaudible beneath his breath, but parked the car at the curbside anyway. Kim was already five strides ahead by the time he caught up to her on the stone steps.

"What're you even gonna *say* to these people?" Egan huffed once they reached the porch. "'Good evening, Mr. and Mrs. Mason. Hate to disturb you, but did Jason Voorhees murder my friend in your living room tonight?'"

"That's not funny, Scuzz."

"Wasn't supposed to be. I just think you're upset and haven't worked all this through so much."

Kim opened her mouth, then closed it without saying anything. *How much have you thought this over?* She'd be the first to admit Emily could be a brat, but her brand of off-beat humor was never malicious. Would she go to such elaborate lengths for a joke?

She stopped just shy of the house's coral-colored front door. An arrangement of comfortable lounge chairs beside her on the porch provided an unobstructed bayside vista; above those were windows with drawn blinds, not quite enough to block what light came from the room beyond. Sucking in a breath, Kim forced down butterflies, stepped forward and rang the doorbell.

There wasn't an answer. Not to the initial ring, or the second two minutes later, or to either round of impatient knocks that left Kim's knuckles sore after that.

"Lights are on, but nobody's home," Egan jibed, though his mirth melted once Kim marched around the porch towards the side of the house. "Where *you* goin'?" He asked.

"Em said someone was at the back door," she answered. In her belly, those nervous butterflies had turned to clawing cats, and the sensation only worsened when Kim approached the rear patio. Like the front, the home's back lawn was meticulously kept, charming with a garden and gazebo and that enviable pool.

The door was already ajar. Light from within the house enabled her to see the entrance led into a kitchen. Rapping on the trim, she loudly called Emily's name, waited, repeated the action twice more, but her inquiries, like the earlier ones, went unacknowledged. Dissatisfied, Kim carefully nudged the door open wider and was about to peek her head inside when Egan's abrupt hiss startled her.

"The fuck you doin'?" He spat. "You tryin' to get us busted for some cat burglar bullshit?"

Kim's frustration boiled over. *"Look,* I just want to know Em is all right. If you want to duck out and go, then *go.* I'll find my own way home."

Weariness glossed Egan's cheeks. Twisting his lips, he sighed. "No... No, I'm with you. Shit, make it snappy, though, all right? Get in, poke around, get out."

Stepping inside the sudden air-conditioned coolness raised gooseflesh on Kim's arms. The kitchen was big enough to eat half her parent's house, and its decor defined elegance: hand-cut Italian tile, ornately patterned chestnut cabinets and polished black marble countertops; the wallpaper was of soothing, mottled sepia tones, and the rear wall was dotted with an arrangement of framed black-and-white photos. An island in the kitchen's center was topped with a floral arrangement, a bowl of fruit and, at last, evidence of Emily's presence.

"This is her purse," Kim remembered the day she and Emily went to the mall to buy it. Running her hand over the leather, she called out again: "Hello? Emily? Mr. and Mrs. Mason? Anyone?"

The house remained graveyard quiet save for the soft gibberish of a nearby television. Kim set Emily's purse down, then moved to the kitchen's exit; the vacant living room lay past, decorated with fashionable furnishings and a big-screen TV tuned to *St. Elsewhere.* Atop the oak coffee table rested a plate with a half-consumed bologna sandwich, an empty Coca-Cola bottle and a pack of Emily's signature menthol Virginia Slims.

"Look," Egan pointed to the floor. Just beneath the arched entranceway connecting the rooms were a dropped cordless phone and the smashed ceramic shards of a once-exotic lamp. When Kim took a second tenuous step, she noticed the nearest wall was marked with a smeared, reddish handprint, and for the first time that night her anxiety wasn't about Emily's safety, but her own.

Egan rapidly assembled the circumstantial puzzle pieces, too. Gently tugging Kim's arm, he said, "Y'know, I hate the fascist American military-industrial police state as much as the next Dead Kennedys fan, but I'm thinkin' we *really* should call your stepdad."

Kim's heart pounded. The tableau had jumbled her thoughts, but this time she didn't object. She'd just reached to retrieve the fallen phone when there was a clatter from the kitchen. Before she even glanced back the sound solidified into heavy footsteps echoing on that expensive tile; when a broad-shouldered shape draped in a hooded black clerical vestment appeared behind Egan, Kim screamed.

An attack came fast. The cloaked figure's leather-gloved left hand clasped tightly around a fiendish-looking crescent-bladed knife, and a response hadn't even registered on Egan's face before the weapon drove into his back. With the assailant's features shadowed by the robe's upraised cowl, Egan's stupid, surprised expression was all Kim saw, frozen on his chin while the knife plunged repeatedly through him. Blood trailed from Egan's mouth, his nostrils, down each arm; flailing, he clung to the edge of the entryway, leaving his own scarlet stain on the elaborate wallpaper on his journey to the floor.

"SCUZZ!" Kim shouted; shocked tears streamed involuntarily down her cheeks, and she almost gagged on the reek of metallic blood and loosened bowels coming from Egan's convulsing body.

Adrenaline took hold. With the robed attacker blocking access to the kitchen, Kim blindly backpedaled across the living room, through another doorway into a dining room. Egan's slayer was right at her heels, but unfamiliarity with the house slowed Kim's flight; she tipped over two chairs situated around the long dining table in an attempt to derail her pursuer and buy time. The ploy worked, but barely—the cloaked killer stumbled over the blockades, yet still rebounded faster than Kim would've liked.

A foyer extending to the front door opposed the dining room; seizing the opportunity, Kim bolted ahead, but a quick glance over her shoulder showed the murderer only six feet behind. Before she unlocked the door the attacker's free hand gripped Kim's right forearm and yanked her back.

Desperate, she pulled against the assassin's weight, but they were too heavy, too strong; instead, she lashed out, frenzied, in any way she could, hitting their chest, clawing at the blank pit under the hood. Two fingernails broke in the struggle, but she fought the pain and kept up the offensive; one of Kim's strikes tore the killer's cowl from their head, and once revealed, the repulsive goatish face beneath bewildered her. For a second—half, even—she thought the thing some monstrous, deformed creature, but a receding hairline above the horns betrayed the attacker's humanity, and with another scream Kim ripped the mask to the floor.

The robed man's face was sweaty, angry, but stunned; in the foyer's dimness, Kim saw cold, narrow eyes and thin salmon lips borne back over his teeth. He panted from exertion, but even the unexpected exposure didn't loosen his grasp.

"Fucking *bitch!*" The man spat as he slammed Kim against the door. The knife went up again; Kim braced for the inevitable, but a flash from outside interrupted the intended stab. Looking through the sidelight window, the man's fishy mouth tightened as a vehicle moved up the drive.

"Shit," he snarled. "She came back fast."

Jerking Kim away from the door, he delivered a sharp abdominal kick that doubled her over. Gasping, she couldn't muster any further resistance as the man lugged her down an adjacent hall. There was the fumbling of a deadbolt before another door opened and Kim tumbled end-over-end as she thundered helplessly down a set of stairs into the dark.

Kim crumpled to a halt at the base of the steps.

Time ticked by without measure; when she moved, a hundred agonized hurts screeched in unison. Her left wrist throbbed, her back, her temples. Something stung her eyes; after she wiped them, Kim's fingertips were daubed with blood.

"Fuck," she whispered. From above resonated the noise of heavy footfalls followed by the sound of something cumbersome being intermittently scooted across the floor. A minute later, muffled, arguing voices punctured the stagnant air:

"What were you *thinking*, Edward?" A woman barked. "The others will be down our throats if they find out about this. That Kasso burnout almost ruined everything for us as it is. Everyone's vigilant now. We can't risk the attention."

"What was I *supposed* to do, Lisa?" The fish-mouthed man's brusque tone replied. "They came right into the house. What was it you were telling me earlier today? 'Nobody will notice one missing babysitter from the 'burbs.' Looks like you were wrong as usual."

"And *you're* being a *bastard* as usual." Lisa's inflection became icier. "We can't allow this to disrupt tonight's ceremony. The celestial alignment will hold until dawn. The sacrifice can still be made." There was a pause before she resumed. "Here. Keys are in the boy's pocket. I'll move his car into the garage next to the girl's. We'll take them to the chop shop later. When I come back we'll prepare the incantations."

Edward didn't reply to that. Kim heard Egan's dead weight being dragged again; the back door opened, then shut, after which settled an eerie calm. When several uneventful minutes passed, Kim propped herself up, leaned against the wall and tried to gain a sense of her surroundings.

Two black velvet drapes partitioned the stairwell from the rest of the basement; soft amber seeped through the gap between each curtain, yet from Kim's position seeing anything further was impossible. She stood, took two wobbly steps, then swore once her tender limbs conspired to send her back to the floor. Afterwards, a hoarse voice floated from the hidden space behind the veil.

"Kim? K-Kim? Is...is that *you?"*

Kim's fear thawed once she recognized the speaker: "Emily?"

Ignoring the pain, she slung the curtain back; what lay beyond wasn't anything she'd anticipated. The amenities of an ordinary basement were absent: no washer or dryer or stored antiques, no den for entertaining. The chamber resembled a medieval nave more than anything; rows of flickering candles highlighted walls rich with detailed iconography of the sort one expected in some grand gothic cathedral but that upon closer inspection was rife with bone-chilling blasphemy. Cavorting monstrosities stared at Kim from every angle, inflicting unimaginable obscenities unto a host of suffering, damned souls, men, women, children, tormented, violated and butchered in endlessly wicked ways.

An intricate lattice of obsidian brick beneath Kim's shoes converted the floor into a vast pentagram, at the heart of which was an upraised altar shadowed by a life-sized grotesquery of a statue. Like Edward's mask, the sculpture's hideous features were comparable to a horned goat, only this head was attached to a voluptuously pregnant human form set upon cloven feet and studded with a viperous erect cock. A looping sigil topped with a double cross and encircled by a coiled serpent devouring its own tail was carved intricately into the thing's chest, and the entire statue, from horn to hoof, was coated with ancient layers of crusted brown blood.

This, then, was The Devil. Not some tragic Miltonian angel despairing its severance from God, nor some smirking lobster-hued trickster toting pitchfork and a quip. This was the true guide of Ricky's hand, the abyss writ in solid form, all the pain, cruelty, hopelessness and hate of creation condensed into a gestating belly and eager for birth. And it was here, Kim realized, that some assembled to beg and barter for influence and riches, and the understanding shook her.

Nauseated, Kim turned away from the altar. In the farthest corner Emily huddled, wrists bound with duct tape, her Bananarama t-shirt spattered with crimson, auburn hair gnarled; normally she wore glasses, but they were gone, and her bruised face was swollen so badly the left eye wouldn't open. Gauging from Emily's reaction once their gazes locked Kim judged her own appearance wasn't much better, but she shoved the thought aside and crouched beside her friend.

"How...how can...how can you be here?" Emily stammered as Kim attempted to unbind the duct tape.

"Scuzz and I came looking for you."

"I-It wasn't a babysitting job, Kim." Emily rasped. "I'm not sure they even *have* a kid. Mr. Mason...h-he was the one at the back door. I thought he was an intruder until he brought me down here. All this...all this was a trap..."

"I gathered that." Kim swallowed hard. "He murdered Egan."

Emily gasped. *"W-What?"*

Kim cursed in frustration; no matter how vigorously she twisted or tried tearing the tape, it stubbornly refused to yield. "We need to get out of here," she pulled Emily up with her. "Did you see another door anywhere?"

Emily was shivering. "No. I-I already looked."

"One way out, then." Kim guided Emily past the curtain to the stairs just as those heavy footsteps pounded again across the kitchen towards the basement. The unlocking deadbolt gave a resonant click, and once the door opened a gleam of light sliced the top of the steps, too dim to brighten the entire stairwell, but plenty for Kim to see Edward's cloaked shaped looming in the exit.

"Shit," Emily shrank back behind the drape. Kim followed suit, vainly searching for anything useful as a weapon; when she looked forward again, Edward had reached the bottom step, the knife that thieved Egan's life firm in his left fist.

"You're up and at 'em fast. Guess I didn't put you down hard enough." He stalked closer. "Trouble-making little bitch. Everything was going perfectly tonight 'til you and your maggot little friend decided to play party crashers. But we've waited too long for some gutter trash to destroy what we've worked for."

Kim jeered, "You know, I'd tell you to go to Hell, but I'm thinking that's exactly where you want to be. So I'll just say fuck you, asshole."

The remark was just a front to disguise Kim's palpitating terror, but it only incensed her malefactor. Edward lunged, threw Kim hard into the altar and readied the blade, but fatigue had taken its toll: Kim was only five-one and a hundred pounds, yet he labored to control her thrashing body.

One of Kim's floundering knees found the soft space of Edward's groin and he instantly yowled, slackened his hold and folded. Kim launched at him, tossing her entire shrieking frame atop his; the knife had slid from Edward's fingers once he'd collapsed, and now she snatched it, peppering him wildly anywhere the blade would go. Edward's screams swelled in the chamber until he dislodged Kim with a backhanded blow.

Kim's head swam as she stood. Emily was six feet away on the altar's opposite side; between them Edward writhed, blood pouring from punctures beneath his shredded vestment. Clutching his crotch, he wailed, *"You stabbed me in the dick, you fucking bitch! I'm gonna fucking kill you! You hear me? I'm gonna feed Satan your fucking soul in pieces!"*

Edward's agonized threats continued, but Kim tuned them out; her gaze inched instead to that iniquitous idol. In the candlelight its diabolic shape cast a jagged image over Edward, and Kim placed both hands firm on the statue's polished marble and pushed. The sculpture didn't budge, not at first; reading Kim's intent, Emily joined her, pressing shoulder to stone until the statue wobbled on its pedestal. Edward didn't even have time for another scream before the sculpture tipped over the altar's ledge and landed with sledge force onto his upper body; the sickening snap of breaking bones and flattening tissue churned Kim's stomach, and when she stepped around his spastic legs to grab for Emily, the sight of Edward's pulpy, squashed skull doubled the queasiness.

"I-Is he dead?" Emily asked as Kim sawed through the duct tape with the knife.

"Off to the land down under," Kim grunted. The process to liberate Emily's wrist was slow; sweat and blood slicked the blade, and twice Kim accidentally jabbed her friend's palm. After a fevered minute, though, the deed was done. "Let's go," she said.

Edward had ceased twitching by the time Kim led Emily towards the stairs. She'd only just pushed aside the dividing drape when a thick-headed mallet swung out from the area beyond and hammered into the wall. A woman blocked their path, tall with long black hair, a schoolmarm's austere face, cloaked indistinguishably from Edward in clerical robes and gloves.

Kim clutched the knife tight. With the confrontation's commotion she hadn't heard the woman coming down the stairs, and her appearance now set Kim's teeth on edge.

"This Lisa?" She asked Emily.

"It's not Elvira."

"Fucking *cunts,*" Lisa's voice was thickly accented and husky, almost masculine. "We wait so patiently for the proper lunar cycle to make our offerings. Two souls, male and female each, so that we may hold dominion in this world for another year. You will *not* be allowed to endanger that sacrifice."

"Oh, I wouldn't worry about your sacrifice, lady," Kim hefted the blade. "Old Scratch is probably roasting your evil shit husband on a spit over an open flame as we speak."

Lisa looked at Edward's corpse and scowled. "He meant *nothing* to me. My soul is given only to Lucifer. And soon so shall *yours.*"

She swung the mallet again, harder and faster, but anger diluted her aim and the intended killing blow drove into Kim's left shoulder. The impact made Kim howl, but when Lisa raised the weapon a second time, she still surged recklessly forward with the knife. One slash tagged Lisa's right ear, splicing across the cheek as the blade slit her open mouth into a ragged flap.

What happened next was a blur. Shocked by the sudden wound, Lisa staggered backwards, too close to the ritual candles. In a flash her hair ignited; before long the entire head was consumed and she dropped the mallet, screeching while she futilely tried to smother the flames with her hands. When the hood and top portion of Lisa's cloak caught fire she careened into the altar, her skin searing, bubbling, bursting, until finally she fell.

The blaze subsided, but the damage was done: Lisa was a featureless wreck, crisped to the muscle, opened pustules leaking yellow fat down blackened flesh. A sickly-sweet blend of burnt hair and fried bacon permeated the chamber, so powerful Kim wrestled the returning urge to vomit. That sepulchral stillness descended once more over the house, and for a moment Kim thought Lisa was dead until a hoarse, scratchy rattle crawled from the dying woman's throat.

"...*Ave Satanas...*" she sputtered, more grinding gravel than speech. The proclamation was her last act of devotion; after a feckless wheeze Lisa's charred head tilted back, her basilisk glare fixed permanently on Kim. Only Emily touching her uninjured arm broke the spell.

"Come *on,*" she pleaded. "Let's get the fuck *out* of here."

Kim tucked the knife into her waistband and covered it with her shirt before the pair retreated up the steps. The main floor was as she'd left it, chairs tipped and decorations askew from her earlier flight. A human-shaped scarlet spot now defiled the living room carpet, and a sidewinder trail of Egan's blood extended from the entranceway across that lavish kitchen tile to the back door and out towards the garage.

A clock near the refrigerator read 1:06 a.m. Beside that a phone was mounted on the wall, and Kim hastened to pick up the receiver. She was certain her babbling call to the police department seemed a lunatic's patter—kidnapping, murder, suburban satanic sacrifice, who *wouldn't* think that insane? The dismissive dispatcher acted like she was high, too, until Kim blurted out her stepfather's name. After that it was just a matter of waiting.

8

The red-and-blue disco strobe from police cruisers nearly blinded Kim as she walked through the open front door. Outside, the night's humidity had lessened, but still offered a muggy jolt after the house's air-conditioned chill. Next to her, Emily pointed to the driveway.

"There's your stepdad." She sounded relieved.

Steven Courchene was in his forties, well-built beneath his uniform, with the Grand Canyon furrows of a constantly aggravated man etched into his mustachioed face. He often reminded Kim of a balding Tom Selleck, and she teased him about it sometimes, too. Now, though, he didn't resemble Magnum P.I. as much as a concerned parent; he appeared between two parked cop cars, eyes desperately darting around the busy scene until they landed on Kim.

"Kimberly?" He ascended the porch steps. "What happened? How did you *get* here?"

"I-I'm *sorry.*" Kim blurted out. "I know I'm in trouble, but I *had* to...I had to come for Em. They...they killed Egan and were going to...they were going to…"

She couldn't finish the sentence. Just then another police officer emerged from the house and nodded to Steven. "You need to *see* this shit, Courchene. You're not gonna *believe* what we found downstairs."

Any residual doubt in her stepfather's expression vanished and he placed a palm on Kim's shoulder. "Look, everything's going to be okay. We'll need to take you to the hospital in a bit and get things sorted out. But for now the two of you should rest in my car."

Steven escorted the pair to his cruiser. Once Kim was in the back seat her beleaguered body relaxed and the evening's distress finally engulfed her. Everything poured out; tears flowed uncontrollably until a reassuring squeeze from Emily's hand to hers brought some measure of calm.

"Don't cry, Kim," she said. "We made it." Then, sweetly, "You saved my life."

Kim wiped the wetness from her cheeks but didn't say anything. The weariness was too much; even with the mounting police circus and flashing lights she felt exhaustion's oncoming embrace. The cruiser was just dark enough, the seat just comfortable enough, and despite the exterior ruckus, her head soon dipped into oblivion.

The car was moving when she awoke. Kim wasn't sure how long she'd dozed, but the passing scenery was still witching-hour dark. Emily slumbered beside her; in the front seat Steven drove silently, though when he heard Kim stirring she caught a glimpse of his eyes on her in the rearview mirror.

"W-Where are we going, Steve?" she asked, still groggy. "Is this the way to the hospital?"

Her stepfather remained quiet, even after she repeated the inquiry. Kim's unease began there, and deepened when Steven turned his cruiser onto an isolated gravel lane.

"You both caused a lot of bother tonight." He finally spoke. "Don't know how much of this mess we can sweep under the rug. If Ricky hadn't gotten impatient and did what he did to Gary things would be different. We never should've accepted a boy like that into the circle to start with. But he was devoted in his way. Maybe *too* devoted. He believed in the power. He just didn't understand how to keep his fat mouth shut. What's that saying? *Don't shit where you eat.* That's what Ricky did. Almost fouled all over everything, too. But we took care of that. Made sure he got strung up nice and pretty. Now we just have to do it again."

Kim's spine prickled. "Where are you taking us?" She demanded to know.

Steven ignored her. He simply stopped the car on the side of the lane, and as the headlights illuminated the forested wilds of Aztakea Woods Kim realized she had an answer.

Some distance in front of the vehicle was a small clearing where a bonfire's carnivorous teeth bit high into the night. From beyond the flames a stony visage insidiously familiar to Kim from the Mason's basement temple squatted half-lit in magma hues, only larger and vastly more imposing: those bat-like wings and clawed hands, the towering horns. Assembled around the idol were two dozen worshipers robed identically in those flowing black vestments. Many were masked as Edward had been; those uncovered were a motley mix: a few looked to be near Kim's age, some were old enough to be her grandparents, while still others bore the faces of Northport's upper-echelon elite—city council members and prominent business owners—their hands clasped and heads bowed in reverent chthonic chant.

Panic set in. Instinctively Kim reached for the door's handle, remembering too late that in a cop car there wasn't one.

"Wouldn't bother with that." Steven coldly reminded her. "Wouldn't bother screaming, either. Won't do you much good."

Kim slammed her fists against the vehicle's partition screen and yelled anyway: "Steve, you fucking *asshole!* What the *fuck* are you *doing?* Let us *go!*"

"I'm sorry it had to turn out this way, Kimberly. I really am." Steven opened his own door. "But you should've stayed home tonight. There are things out there some people were never meant to know about."

Steven met two unmasked worshipers at the edge of the gravel lane. One was tall and sallow-cheeked, with a crooked nose and graying hair; the other was a plump man Kim recalled seeing on TV dispelling rumors of cult activity in the city. Now he extended two fingers of his left hand in some sort of salute.

"The Knights of the Black Circle welcome thee."

Steven returned the man's gesture. "May the Fallen One bless us with his glory."

They said more to each other, but Kim couldn't hear it. Roused by the earlier shouts, Emily sat up, blinking and confused.

"What's going on?" she asked; once she spotted the bonfire, her voice trembled. "Oh fuck, what is going on?"

Kim studied her friend. "Are you strong enough to run?"

"What?"

"We've got one chance, Em," Kim's hand went to her waist, where Edward's knife was still concealed, unseen and overlooked even by her stepfather. Now the weapon was firm in her grip again.

Emily verged on tears. "What's *happening*, Kim?"

"Nothing good," Kim laced her fingers between Emily's. "Just be ready to haul ass, okay?"

Steven returned to the squad car, and Kim kept the knife low hoping he couldn't see it. His expression was stern as he unlocked the door. Once it was open, Kim noticed two sets of handcuffs in his grasp.

"Get out," he commanded. "You're—"

He said nothing further. Kim plunged the blade into Steven's left thigh, not as deeply or intensely as she'd hoped, but enough to allow the tiniest sliver of escape. Before her stepfather reacted, Kim wrenched the knife free and leapt from the cruiser, pulling Emily along with her.

Steven's cry was more surprise than pain, yet still sufficed to interrupt the black mass. Once the chanting stopped there was a pause where the only sound was the fire's crackling tinder. Then the pursuit began.

In her peripheral vision Kim saw the cultists break their formation, but she forced her attention forward and didn't look back. Steven's outrage sliced the air behind her, and soon bullets did, too; his revolver's opening report made Kim jump, but only quickened her tempo. A second shot went as wide as the first, and though she expected a third to follow it never arrived.

Emily kept pace beside her, their hands joined tight, but halfway across the clearing she was already gasping for air.

"Where are we going?" Emily sputtered between breaths. Kim thought about that. If even those closest to them filled The Adversary's clandestine ranks, where was safe haven to be found?

"I don't know," she admitted. "But wherever we go, we go together."

Twenty feet behind, the nearest robed pursuers closed in, daggers lustful for blood. Kim's lungs burned. Moonlight shone above their heads.

And both girls ran undaunted into the darkened forest.

ABOUT THE AUTHOR

Exposed to the weird worlds of horror, sci-fi and comics as a boy, DAMASCUS MINCEMEYER was ruined for life. Now he spends his days writing far-out fiction that's appeared in over 30 anthologies, including Fire: Demons, Dragons and Djinn, Hear Me Roar, The Devil You Know, The Devil You Know Better, The Monsters Next Door, No Anesthetic and Appalachian Horror among others. His first novel, By Invitation Only, is currently with The Rights Factory literary agency and awaiting submission to publishers. Hailing from St. Louis, Missouri, U.S.A, he enjoys reviewing books and movies for Critical Blast and spending way too much time on Instagram @damascusundead666

BETWEEN THE DEVIL AND THE DEEP BLUE SEA

Paul Barile

The last thing Lou grabbed as he was being pulled into the cyclone was Jophiel's harp, The last thing he left was a little piece of his heart.

Young Lucifer had no idea when he woke up that morning that it would be the last day he would spend floating on a cloud, eating grapes, and practicing the harp while his father, Apollyon, passed his days with other powerful angels discussing important matters.

Lucifer, Lou to his friends, fully enjoyed playing the harp and creating little songs for his one true love, the raven-haired Jophiel.

Jophiel would never notice Lou, no matter what he did, which made him love her that much more. She went about *her* day inspiring strength and goodness and kindness. Her eyes sparkled like ice crystals and her black hair fell past her strong shoulders in delicate ringlets.

Lucifer spent countless hours trying to hatch ways to get Jophiel to notice him, but she was in a league of her own. She was uniquely wonderful and just out of reach.

The elders – including Apollyon – spent their days discussing morals and ethics. They were powerful in this kingdom, but not so much beyond the kingdom. Apollyon vowed to change that. He would be the first angel to attempt to usurp the power of God and place himself on a throne at an equal height.

"I don't think so," God said when she heard the news.

She summoned Apollyon.

The angel strutted into the vast and glorious throne room where he refused the customary bow. God was amused at the petulance, and she smiled warmly.

"What are you on about, Olly?" she asked.

"I insist you abdicate your throne."

"That's not happening."

"I have the strength of a thousand angels behind me. Together we will force you to abdicate."

"Is it the power over the earth realms you seek, Olly?"

"Yes."

"Then you shall have that power."

"I knew you'd see things my way."

God shrugged.

"You'll have it on earth. You won't have it here."

God swung her arm around in the air in a circle that was growing around them and over their heads. As she moved her arms around a cyclone revealed itself. Steadily the funnel cloud grew and moved toward Apollyon. As the cyclone closed in, Apollyon called out for his son.

"LUCIFER!"

Lou ran into the room and was surprised to see the cyclone getting closer and closer to his father.

"DAD!" he shouted.

Lou ran quickly out of the room but came back – just as quickly - carrying something that glimmered in his hand. It was a harp that he held on to for life. He took his father's hand in his free hand and the two jumped into the eye of the cyclone before it closed up for good.

Lou and his father landed in a vast and arid land. It was a fallen angel, his son, and a stolen harp.

The heat did not bother them as much as it made their delicate porcelain skin turn deep red – the color of a dying leaf or an old brick.

"What happened, Father?" he asked.

"My bid for power was defeated. I will stop at nothing until I am on my rightful throne."

"What are we going to do?"

"I am going to go out there and fight everyone who crosses my path until I get an audience with God again. Them I will dispense of her."

"And me?"

"Who cares? You're useless. What are you going to do, *sing them to death?*"

"I can help, Father."

"You'll only slow me down."

With that, Apollyon took off across the scorched earth, leaving Lou to survive on his own with nothing but his wits and a harp.

Lou attempted to follow his father, but the elder angel was strong and swift. Lou was soft and slow. He didn't stand a chance. He began to walk toward the setting sun.

8

The Deep Blue Sea was always one heartbeat away from major label success. They were perennially considered an *almost* was. It wasn't that they lacked talent, they just never had any luck.

They'd land a big audition for a label and the drummer would get arrested. They'd get a slot opening for a national act and the guitar player would show up drunk. They just kept shooting themselves in the foot. It was almost as if their destiny was decided for them, and they were just going to play out the thread working dive bars and street fests for beers until their parents kicked them out of their respective houses or made them get jobs. The Deep Blue Sea was just about the best band that nobody ever heard of.

Byron Seltzer, the band's bass player, took each disappointment the hardest. He never gave up, but the sand was running through the hourglass, and he was running out of time.

8

It was a steamy Saturday night when Byron encountered Lou sitting on a stump, strumming his harp and singing for loose change.

"What's that you're playing," Byron asked.

"It's a harp," Lou responded.

"Yeah. I know it's a harp. But that song. What is *that?*"

"It's a little something I have been working on for about a thousand years."

"It always feels that way; doesn't it."

"No. Literally. A thousand years of scratching ideas together.

Byron noticed something peaking out from under Lou's poncho.

"Is that a tail?"

"Could be."

"So, what's the struggle with the song?"

"Do you know how hard it is to rhyme *Jophiel?*

"I can imagine."

"I'll get it. She's my muse."

"Are you in a band right now? Are you playing anywhere?"

Lou shrugged.

"Just this stump I'm afraid."

"Minimalism. I get that."

"My dad and I were recently evicted. I'm still trying to get my bearings."

"Seriously."

They looked at each other for a moment as if each expected the other to say something. Eventually Byron spoke.

"Well good luck…"

"Lucifer. You can call me Lou."

"Lucifer. Is that French?"

Lou shrugged.

"Good luck, Lou. If you get a chance, my band is playing at the Red Roxy. Come on out and I'll buy you a beer. Deal?"

Lou smiled. Byron walked away.

"A beer?" Lou called out.

"Okay two beers. You drive a hard bargain."

Byron walked away laughing to himself. Lou felt good like he'd actually just made his first friend.

8

The Red Roxy was neither *red* nor *Roxy*, but there was a nice sized crowd milling around waiting for the band to begin. Lou entered and looked around for Byron. He found a small stool in a dark corner and sat down. It didn't take long for Byron to spot him and – after a quick wave, Byron crossed to the bar, then over to where Lou was sitting. He carried two cold cans of beer.

"You came," Byron said.

"Sure. Why not?" Lou responded.

"We go on in a few minutes. If you stick around until the break, you'll get your second beer."

Lou took the beer and Byron turned to leave. He stopped and turned around and walked back to Lou.

"Trial."

"Trial?"

"Rhymes with *Jophiel.*"

Then he was gone.

Lou had never heard music like this. It was loud and aggressive, but at the same time jangly and loose. He settled in and let the percussion wash over him there in the corner.

When the band went on break, Byron came back with two more beers.

"That's interesting music, Byron. What do you call it?"

"I just call it three chords and the truth."

"You'll have to elaborate for me."

"It's Rock and Roll. You're not from around here; are you?"

"You have no idea."

They talked music for a few more minutes before Byron excused himself to go play another set.

After the show, Byron invited Lou to go out for breakfast with the band. Lou accepted because it was better to eat skirt steak and eggs with a bunch of strangers than it was to spend another lonely night sleeping on his stump.

As they finished their meals and washed it down with the dregs of the coffee pot, the drummer suggested that Lou bring his harp and come to the next band practice and jam with them.

"A harp may be just the elusive element that we've been looking for to make our music unique. People will have to notice us," the drummer said.

Everyone was surprised at this. He was the drummer after all.

"I only have one question," the drummer said. "Is that a tail?"

"Could be," Lou shrugged.

"So, you'll try?" Byron asked.

"Sure. I'll try."

The next day at practice Lou showed up with a harp in his hand and a song in his heart. They began to play, and it was good. It was natural. It seemed as though they had been playing together for years.

"Did you finish that new song?" Byron asked.

"I did thanks to you. I have it in my backpack."

Lou quickly showed the guys the changes and they immediately began to play, and it was perfect.

"I call it *All for Jophiel.*"

They played it a second time and it was flawless. They hit every note and it was beautiful.

"Let's record it right now," the guitar player said. "This is a solid jam."

They plugged in their guitars and put microphones around the drums and played the song for a third time. They looked at each other in amazement. The song had somehow gotten better, and they were playing with grace they didn't even know they had.

"Call Reuben," Byron said. "He needs to get this to the record label. Pronto."

Rueben came by and listened intently to the song while the band stared intently at him. When it was done, he gave his stamp of approval.

"This is a hit. This is solid gold," he said.

He took the tape to the record label and played the song for the suits. The decision makers who were famous for not liking anything – loved it. They absolutely loved it.

"This is a super smash with a bullet," one suit said trying to sound relevant.

They pressed a million copies of the record and sent them all over the world – to every record station that still played music. Every DJ who heard the song fell in love with it. They played it two or three times every hour on the hour just in case someone missed it.

The record began to sell at a rate so fast they couldn't print them fast enough. As quickly as they'd ship a case – there'd be an order for another case, and another.

The Deep Blue Sea, along with Lou, embarked on a whirlwind world tour. They went from Canada to Australia to Japan to East Moline. The more they traveled, the more powerful they became.

Every human being in the world heard of The Deep Blue Sea and everyone know *All for Jophiel* by heart. People sang along every time it came on the radio. They whistled it while they swept the floor or washed their cars.

8

One afternoon in Sandusky, Ohio, there was a knock at Lou's dressing room door. He opened it and was surprised to see his father standing there.

"Son?"

"Yes," Lou said unable to look his father in the eye.

"You've come a long way."

"I have."

"You have a lot of power."

"I don't look at it that way."

"You should be aware of it, but even if you aren't I am here now. I can help you navigate the immensity of your power and help you understand how to use it."

"And get kicked out of *another* heaven?"

"Son, listen-"

"No, Dad, you listen. I was just fine up there where we were. I had my harp and I had nice grapes – seedless grapes, Dad. Seedless. I had Jophiel. I was living the dream."

"She wasn't that into you, in case you didn't notice," Apollyon said.

"Well, I had my grapes, and I had my home, and all was well until *your* lust for power cost *me* everything – *everything*, Dad."

"What about your lust for power?"

"I have none."

"But you…"

"I make music. I love to make music. My music makes people feel good – great sometimes."

"Sure."

"It's the only power I want. It's the only power I need."

"Then you're a sucker."

"I'm okay with that."

Apollyon spun on his heel and stormed down the hall and out the door.

Later that night, the band took the stage in the packed arena. People were dancing and singing along when a beautiful woman with curly black hair and crystal-clear eyes appeared and raised her sword. Everybody froze except Lucifer.

"Lucifer?"

"Yes. Jophiel?"

"Is that my harp?"

"Yes, Jophiel."

"Did you steal it?"

"Yes, Jophiel."

"What if I want to back?"

"I will give it to you."

"You will lose all of this if you do," she said.

Jophiel swept her arm across the room. Lucifer looked at all the people in awkward poses with smiles frozen on their faces. The thought of giving this up broke his heart.

"What good is any of it if you are displeased with me," he said.

"The thing is," she started. "I don't need it right now, but if I ever do, I'll find you and come back for it."

"I'll be waiting."

"It's a really good song, Lou," she said.

Jophiel lowered her sword and dissolved into the mist that cooled the dancing crowd who had sprung back to life. As they began their next song Lou looked up and said a quick thanks to the heavens – to the woman upstairs.

Across the room the sound man and the lighting guy were watching every move, waiting for cues. When the lighting guy pushed the fader up to illuminate the stage, they noticed something they had never seen before.

They looked at each other for a moment.

"Is that a tail?" the sound guy asked.

"Could be," the lighting guy shrugged.

ABOUT THE AUTHOR

PAUL BARILE is the creator of Lucha Legends, a series of dual language books designed to teach young readers about Lucha Libre in both Spanish and English. He also writes the pulp series Jack Swagger as well as the Nicky Victory stories. In his spare time he writes essays, he plays bass guitar and writes lyrics for The Grudge Brothers and he travels small town Illinois looking for ideas for horror stories or essays. He also goes to a lot of Lucha Libre shows.

ONE NIGHT
AT TACO BELL

AE Stueve

Kyle Benson only knew pain.

He lay naked in the woods behind a Taco Bell on the edge of Oakview, NE just before the break of day. His whole body itched with tiny red bites. Placed purposefully between these bites were thousands of thin cuts just deep enough to bleed. Kyle could have told you about the unique blade that made all of these cuts, the way its dragonian bone hilt and ebonark steel made a terrible music of screams as his guard spun it through his three red fingers. He could have told you about the unique pain that the unique blade caused, the way the ebonark not only split the flesh but inflamed it as well, causing his skin to feel like it was not only being sliced and diced but somehow irradiated as well.

But Kyle could hardly speak. He could hardly think.

Since shoving open the secret cosmic manhole and climbing into our reality, all he could do was groan weakly and try with all of his much depleted might to keep the heady pre-dawn light from his eyes.

There were people nearby. Kyle heard them.

No one heard him.

It's warm, he thought, trying hard to move his head from left to right and failing. Not that it mattered. Everything was a blur. After what he had gone through, his senses were garbage. He sniffed. He smelled garbage. Waste was a distinctly human scent. Where he had been, there was no waste.

There was only pain.

Drained of all energy, he could not sleep, for the grass blades upon which he lay seemed bent on poking their way into the cuts that he didn't think would ever heal. While the light peeked over the trees and early morning gave way to afternoon, the creeping sun burnt his bites and blinded him with a brightness he couldn't remember having ever known.

Though, as the day progressed, the pain of his many, many injuries weakened and his hope that he might actually survive grew stronger. This did not, however, mean that the pain was bearable. It was not. On the rare occasion that he was lucid enough to focus on anything but his pain, he wondered if the sun had caused this increase in hope. The uncompromising brightness was terrible, but it was also reassuring. He had done what no one else had been able to do. He had escaped the darkness of his infinite prison.

Periodically he heard human voices somewhere nearby. None of them screamed. None of them whimpered. None of them begged. They chatted, and though he could not make out what it was they chatted about, he could tell they were happy. There was a lightness to their voices, a fullness, a contentment.

It was such a strange sound: happiness. It bred hope better than the sun.

When night fell, however; fear returned to fight hope. Kyle knew when it was full dark the guards he had escaped would be better suited to finding him. When the lights blinked out, they were at their strongest. They'd carry with them their bag of the 100-legged biting bugs they called 'fleshers' and if they did find him, they'd rain the evil little creatures down on his naked frame. They'd bring their ebonark blades. They'd bring their anger and, truly, their shame.

To be on guard duty when a prisoner escaped was to be a failure to the likes of them and, more importantly, to the likes of their king.

If they caught him, their revenge would be like nothing Kyle had ever known. And Kyle had known much in the timeless epoch he had spent imprisoned.

Kyle tried to call out once more. This mostly proved an act in impossibility. He could not yell. He simply didn't have it in him, not after his escape. There was also that distinct sour stench of abundant garbage somewhere close by. Though reassuring in that it meant there were people nearby, it was also nauseating. The paradox of being both nauseated and relieved was not lost on Kyle's slowly reforming self.

Now that the sun had set, his eyes no longer burned from the light, and he could make out the leaves hanging overhead. Seeing those little shadowy symbols of life as clear as he had since he'd been lying there did something to him, triggered something in him. He reached for one.

"Free," he scratched out the word softly. It sounded almost human.

He had done something no man had managed in billions of years, maybe trillions--time was strange where he had been held captive. He had crawled through nightmare tunnels inhabited by shit beasts and fought rabid shadowfolken that squirmed up from the darkest depths of the multiverse. He had outsmarted beings whose existence defied human reason, the spiderfolken, the roving feralities, and the stiltmen and wheelers. He had climbed the countless Stairs of Despair and reached the top, all the while the cries of the damned had pierced his soul. He had clawed his way through the sky barrier and torn apart the globulous insides of the Final Lower Demon. He had opened the Hope Gate from the *inside*. He could hear its comically benign creak as it swung on hinges older than time. Finally, he had climbed the Infinite Ladder, batting away armies of screechers and flying scrabbers until he reached the cosmic manhole. Comically, a necessity of cosmic maintenance had been his ultimate escape. Pain vapors needed ventilation and maintenance after all.

Now, though, he was depleted completely. Even if he could speak more than his one maniacal word of victory, he could not move. The guards were going to find him. He was going to be taken back. The darkness was rushing in. He suddenly knew it. He was going to be tortured once more for another eternity. Time was a joke, and he was the punchline. The torture was the sound of a trillion trilling cosmic laughs. His resolve, his hope, weakened in the darkness.

Until footsteps approached.

Kyle's eyes went wide.

A brief bolt of energy blipped through his muscles and he called out, "Help," with what little might he had. And though the word still sounded less human and more monster, to a man, it was clearly desperate.

"Hello?" came a confused, squeaky voice in response. "Is someone there?" The sound wavered, afraid.

"Help," Kyle said again. The word climbed to the precipice of his lips and jumped.

"Shit," a pimply-faced teenaged boy said, looking down upon Kyle and shining his phone light on him. In shock, the boy dropped a large black garbage bag. It hit the ground with a soft, wet plop. "What happened to you, bro?" he asked.

"Help," Kyle managed again. He couldn't focus on anything but the boy's voice. Everything around him moved like liquid and looked like a malformed reality. It was the shock of the bright phone light, it was the shock of the voice, and it was the shock of seeing another like himself simply existing. None of it seemed real. Kyle could not remember when he had last seen another person outside of the thresholds of torture, let alone heard them say anything other than "Please," or "No," or "Stop."

"I'll be right back!" the kid spat before backing up and disappearing.

Kyle followed the sounds of the boy's feet flying through the woods and onto what he assumed was pavement. He heard him enter a building and a bit later, heard him frantically explaining what he had seen to others as they ran back to Kyle.

"Here! Here!" the teen shouted as he shined his light once again on Kyle.

"What the hell?" came an older woman's voice. "Get him inside!"

The strange world, an emotionally infused mix of shock, wonder, and, yes, relief, spun up and flipped around as two sets of hands grabbed Kyle and pulled him through the woods.

"I've got a clean uniform in the back that should fit him," came the older woman's voice from behind them as Kyle looked up and saw a bright Taco Bell sign come into focus. The bell, the words, the colors, worked together to snap Kyle completely back to reality.

He groaned, taking it all in, righting himself from a perpetuity of wrong.

"Buddy, you okay?" came a third voice. This one was on his right. It was high pitched and nervous.

"Help," Kyle managed.

"Hurry!" came the woman's voice again. "Thank God the lobby's closed."

There was a new smell now, wholly different from the garbage one that Kyle had spent the day near. It was a salty, greasy kind of smell that reminded Kyle of something he had enjoyed once. Enticing and unhealthy, it pulled at him like an imaginary hand floating through the air, tugging at his senses, and, simply by existing, causing a small bit of his pain and fear to fade. As he was carried toward this smell, Kyle realized he needed to communicate something other than, "Help," to these people. He needed to communicate that he was deeply, *ravenously*, "Hungry."

As they ushered him into the Taco Bell, brought him some clothes, and cooked him up a few tacos, he learned that their names were Ronny, Jon, and Bernice. Ronny and Jon were two eighteen-year-old employees of Taco Bell while Bernice was their fifty-year-old manager. The lobby had just closed and the three of them were the skeleton night crew that rarely saw a lot of action if you did not count the hour or so between 1am and 2am when the bars closed. And nobody counts that hour.

It was 11:20pm when Kyle shoved a soft-shell taco into his mouth and savored the processed sensation of salt and something akin to meat and cheddar cheese and yes, an abundance of sugar.

"Do you need us to call anyone for you, honey?" Bernice asked, sitting across from him in the booth. Bedraggled and confused, with only enough flesh to keep his bones in place, Kyle looked like a meth addict.

Bernice knew that look well. She had seen it on her husband and son. Two years earlier, the meth had taken Troy and left her son a shell of what he once was. Seeing Kyle gave her some hope though. Her son, Jesús, had once looked like that. While he was not yet his old self, and she doubted he ever would be, he had survived and would continue to do so. How or why all of these thoughts unfolded in her mind while she studied the boy across from her was a mystery to Bernice.

Before she had time to ponder it longer, one of her employees spoke up.

"Like the police maybe?" It was Jon, the bigger one. He stood at the counter, wiping it down. All the lights were dimmed in the restaurant. Outside, the Taco Bell sign shined a soft light onto the parking lot, letting you know that the drive-thru was, indeed, open all night.

Kyle shook his head and sipped on the soda sitting on the table's edge so he didn't have to hold it. It was Mtn. Dew Baja Blast. It was the sweetest thing he had ever tasted.

"Do you need a ride anywhere?" Bernice asked.

"Like to the hospital maybe?" Jon added.

"Jon, shut the hell up," Bernice said. She turned a friendly eye back to Kyle. "What's your name, son?"

Kyle took a deep breath and took another sip. "Kyle?" he said. His eyes fluttered. Nothing made sense.

"That's a nice name," Bernice said. She offered Kyle a soft smile. She was far younger than Kyle's grandma had been the last time he had seen her, but nevertheless she reminded him of her.

"Last name?" Jon asked.

"Shut the hell up, Jon," Bernice snapped, this time there was far more anger in her voice. It made Kyle flinch.

"I'm sorry, hon," Bernice said, touching Kyle's hand as it rested on the table near his soda. He flinched from her.

Ronny came out from the kitchen, carrying a small paper bag of cinnamon twists, and sat down next to Bernice. "I found you," he said, offering Kyle the bag, "when I was taking out the trash to the dumpster."

"Thank you," Kyle said slowly. His throat felt better now that he had drunk something other than whatever poison his captors had been forcing down his gullet. His belly felt better now that he had eaten something other than the edible misery they had force-fed him for who knew how long. His body still hurt and itched, but with clothing on, even that was better. Still, he leaned back and hung his head.

"Seriously, what happened to you?" Ronny asked. His head was cocked to the side. He couldn't quite figure it out, but as he blinked at Kyle, he realized that this was not it for him. Being a night cook at Taco Bell was going to be a short chapter in his life and even if it was hard work, he was always, *always* going to remember it fondly. He shook his head and leaned back in the booth, eating cinnamon twists and dreaming of the future.

"Hell," Kyle said, pulling Ronny right out of the dream.

"What?"

"I. Escaped. Hell," Kyle answered slowly, each word its own struggling whisper.

"Shut up, that's not funny," Jon said. He had finished wiping the counter and made the sign of the cross as he approached the table.

"He obviously doesn't mean *Hell* hell, Jon," Ronny said. "Right?" he hid his nerves behind forced laughter.

"I do," Kyle said.

"What?"

The taco was working to give Kyle's body more energy. "You shouldn't stay here," he added. He thought he sounded nearly himself, like a person, not a prisoner, not a plaything, not a soul whose only purpose was to be tortured. Though his words were too weak, too soft. "Now that it's dark they might find me. They're stronger at night."

"Who?"

"Guards."

"What?"

"Guards. They'll take me... back."

"I'm calling 911," Jon said, pulling his phone from his pocket. "You need help."

"No," Kyle said. There was no urgency in his voice, no fierceness. "No more... people. You should leave."

"Why?"

"You're not safe."

"Are you going to hurt us?" Bernice asked.

Jon's fingers hovered over his phone, ready to dial. He blinked, taking in the sight of the bedraggled man sitting across from Bernice and Ronny. He looked like shit, all scratches, bones, bug bites, and oversized clothes. Bags of purple hung under his light eyes. Where he wasn't red with welts, he was the sickly pale color of tallow. His bones were sharper than Jon thought they should be, almost like they could cut through the brittle skin and tear the Taco Bell polyester Bernice had given him. Jon's brain told him that Kyle was weak. But his heart and his gut argued that he was strong. He was the strongest of everyone everywhere. Because of this, Jon suddenly wasn't afraid. He put the phone back in his pocket.

A pounding shook the entire restaurant and Jon's fear returned.

"They're here," Kyle said, tears running down his cheeks.

Ronny shot up on his knees and looked out the windows. "I don't see anything."

"You will."

The pounding sounded again. Dust from the ceiling fans sprinkled down on them.

"They always find me," Kyle said. He took a deep breath. "I thought... since I made it all the way out this time... maybe..." He belched and let his hands fall from the table to his sides.

"What?" Bernice said, covering her ears as the pounding increased in speed and volume. "We need to leave." The walls shook. The windows cracked.

"It's too late," Kyle said softly.

"We didn't do anything!" shouted Jon. "Why would they take us?"

"You helped me."

"What? You needed help!" Ronny shouted. "You were asking for help!"

"Sorry," Kyle said. "It was... natural to ask." The restaurant shook as though an earthquake hit.

Something outside growled. A dark iridescent form passed the window nearest them. Cooking instruments clanged to the floor in the kitchen as somewhere back there more pounding sounded.

"What's doing that?" Bernice asked, looking around. "We can't see anything."

"You will," Kyle said. "I think they... they take a minute to become corporeal here."

"What are you--"

Before Ronny could finish his question, Kyle's angry guards came into view in the bright glow of the Taco Bell sign in the parking lot. They were utter insanity formed into the semblance of giant men. Pustules of filth and hate popped on their rippling muscles of maggots. Bald pates rimmed with evil black horns topped these vile, slobbering creatures. The horns leaked gaseous ooze that encircled them and seemed almost alive. Their pig snout noses and insectoid eyes were mutilated masks of morbidity.

Searching. Always searching.

"Let us in," they said in unison with what could only be described as ungainly voices. "Let us in," they repeated and again their words emerged somehow wrong from their limpid lips. It was as though they were fighting to make human sounds flow from inhuman tongues. As they spoke, snakes emerged from the cavern of their mouths and licked their dull, tusk-like teeth. Orangish, chunky muck oozed like vomitous spittle from the corners of their lips and dribbled down their rocky chins onto unclothed bodies made of human misery and excrement. "Let us in," they said once more.

"Not fucking likely," Jon whispered.

Ronny squeaked an agreement.

Bernice held back vomit.

Kyle sighed. "You can't stop them." He sighed. "I'm sorry. They'll get in eventually. It'll be easier if you just open the doors. Maybe they won't take you if you offer me up."

"Holy shit, this is real," Bernice said.

The monsters crept around the building, pounding here and there.

"What do we do?" Ronny asked.

Kyle sighed. "Nothing."

"Why is it taking them so long to get in?" Bernice looked out the window as one of them punched at it with a hand of broken shark teeth. The window only cracked.

Kyle looked around as though surprised. "Wait," he said. "This is a Taco Bell." An idea hit him hard, a realization that only made perfect sense in that it made no sense. It was a paradox, this idea, and, as we all know, a paradox is God's favorite.

"How'd you guess?" Jon said sarcastically.

"Lots of love here," Kyle said, nodding. "Families, friends, all that. That sort of thing imbues a place with magical properties."

"What?"

"Love keeps demons out... for a while."

"How?"

"Demons... don't like it. It... it gives people hope," he said, blinking. "Wait."

"But they'll get through?"

"Yes," Kyle nodded.

"We can't run?"

"No, but now I'm--"

"And kill us?"

"No. They'll take us all to hell."

"We didn't do anything wrong."

"You're Christian?" Kyle asked.

"No, but that's what--"

"Nobody is *sent* to hell. That's bullshit. We're all... caught. But in here I'm--"

The door crashed open. The demons entered, bringing with them everything *wrong*.

Jon, Ronny, and Bernice cried out as one. Fear made them mad as they scrambled for an escape that did not exist. The demons were upon them with a swiftness that defied their size. The speed with which they worked would have been comical had it not been monstrous in a pure, undiluted way. It was like a scene from a movie that you only watch once not because it's bad but because it's disturbing. Within moments, Jon, Ronny, and Bernice sat wrapped in chains of pure pain. They whimpered and wailed until one of the demons snapped his thick fingers and metal plates flew from his side, smacking against the Taco Bell employees' mouths with a strange, squishy clank.

"You found me," Kyle said.

"You thought because you finally escaped to Adamah that we wouldn't?" one asked.

Kyle shrugged. "I hoped."

The demons had no answer. One pulled his ebonark blade from the sheath at its side. The other untied the string atop the bag hanging on a belt about his waist.

"I realized something when you were trying to get in," Kyle said, forcing himself up on wobbly legs. "Your powers, they're--"

"Shut up!" the one with the blade yelled. Orange slobber flew to the floor before him and burned holes in the purple and white tile.

"When it was daytime and you didn't know where I was," Kyle said, "I was certain I'd escaped. I was feeling... hopeful." He almost laughed now. "Then it got dark and I felt scared again. I felt *you.*"

"Human, you do not want to--"

"Stop," Kyle said as the demon with the bag attempted to shove his hand in it.

The demon stopped as though unable to control his actions.

"My hopelessness is not my own," Kyle said, "is it?"

The demons said nothing.

"It belongs to you. My weakness is not my own. It belongs to you. My fear is not my own. It belongs to you." He pushed his way out of the booth slowly.

"Bah," the one with the blade shoved it back in its sheath and reached for Bernice, Ronny, and Jon. "We're taking these three back with you. They will join you in the Pit of Despair."

"No," Kyle said. "You are not." He stepped toward them, grimacing and shivering. The demons effused a warmth that masked a cold that felt alive.

The demon with the bag wrenched Kyle into the air and held him so that its bug eyes stared directly into Kyle's.

"The pain I will inflict on you for this is—"

"You have no true power here," Kyle said, the full realization washing over him like the inviting scent of the bag of Taco Bell Cinnamon Twists. He laughed. It was his first real laugh in an amount of time that had no meaning on this plain of reality.

The demon backed up, dropping Kyle.

"We have all of the power," the other demon said, looking confusedly from his partner to Kyle. "We do!"

"No." Kyle climbed to his feet and reached onto the table, taking Ronny's discarded bag of cinnamon twists. He pulled one out and ate it. "You take the power from your prisoners. You," he paused, trying to turn his thoughts into words, "you... *siphon* hope, make us weak. When you're near, your power is strong. When it is night, your power is strong. When you are in your home, your power is strong. But here?" Kyle munched a twist. "Here in a place like this you are nothing."

He stepped closer to the demons.

The demons stepped back.

"My hope grew the further away you were," Kyle said. His words came out fast now, his lips having a hard time keeping up with the realization. "It, it, it took some time, but I am strong again. I am full of hope. You almost had me when you managed to get inside. Whatever it is... I don't know... *emanating* from you almost took me. But these people, this place," he motioned to the whole restaurant, "they helped me. I think I even let some of my own hope seep into them. I escaped hell." He stepped closer to the demons. "My hope is strong. I never would've made it this far otherwise."

The demons cowered, whimpering.

"You really have no power here."

"Stop," came a thundering voice from everywhere.

The demons cried out as one.

Silence fell on them as loud as the silence in the eye of a hurricane.

The door gently dinged open as a small skinny man dressed in a finely tailored black suit entered the Taco Bell. His black van dyke beard was the first thing Kyle noticed. It shouldn't have looked good. But it did. As did his matching hair slicked into a brilliant widow's peak.

"Aztoth, Ageroth," the man said, looking from one demon to the other.

Both demons knelt, bowing their heads.

"Yes, my lord?" one said.

"What are you doing here on the mortal plain?"

"Chasing an escaped convict who--"

"Silence," the man said.

He looked over the people in the Taco Bell. "You three," he said pointing at Bernice, Jon, and Ronny, "are not escaped convicts."

"No sir," Bernice managed to squeak out from beneath the metal plate over her mouth.

"But you," he pointed at Kyle, "are."

"Yes," Kyle said, nodding.

"No one has ever escaped to the earthly plain before," the man said.

"That's what Aztoth and Ageroth said... often," Kyle replied. "They bragged about it."

"But you did."

"Guess so," Kyle said.

"Interesting." He turned to the demons. "You two failed, didn't you?" he asked.

"Yes, my lord," one said.

"You know what that means," he said.

"Yes, my lord," the other said.

"Very good." He snapped his fingers and the demons blinked out of existence.

He turned to Kyle. "I would like to speak with you," he said.

"I'm not going back there."

"Voluntarily."

Kyle nodded.

"Do not worry, mortal. I would not think of bringing you back to hell. I cannot have you divulging your secrets to the masses down there after all, can I?"

Kyle stared hard at him.

"I do need to know how you did it though."

"What if I don't want to tell you?" Kyle asked.

"I'm sure we can... strike a deal."

"What about these three?"

"They are nothing to me. They can do as they please, *for now.*" He snapped his fingers and they were released.

"Fine," Kyle said. "But we should meet here, at Taco Bell. I'm not going anywhere with you."

"Very well." The devil sat down in a booth and motioned for Kyle to join him. He clapped at Bernice, Jon, and Ronnie. "We will discuss this over tacos."

ABOUT THE AUTHOR

AE STUEVE teaches writing, photography, filmmaking, and design at Bellevue West High and the University of Nebraska at Omaha. His novels, short stories, poems, journalism, and essays can be found online, on podcasts, and in print. To learn more about him, check out https://linktr.ee/stueveae

TO KILL THE DEVIL

Jonathan Garner

As I stood before one of the gateways to Hell, the plain wooden door, set in a wall of gray stone, looked less sinister than I'd expected.

Two years of intense research had led me here. Two years of studying old books, breaking into forbidden libraries all around the world, and trying to avoid assassins sent by secret societies of devil-worshiping cultists.

I stepped toward the door and ran face-first into a man who had appeared before me out of nowhere.

Another cultist. Great.

I jumped back and examined the man's dark-skinned hands for weapons. He had none.

When I raised my gaze, my mouth fell open. White-feathered wings grew out of the man's shoulders.

An angel.

"Why are you here?" he asked.

"Don't you know?" I replied.

He shook his head. "God has not sent me any messages about you."

"Then why are you here?" I asked.

"That's what I want to know from you."

"Then answer your own question."

"Fine." The angel crossed his muscular arms. "I'm Enos, the guardian of this gate. God put me here to observe, to watch for anything unusual. And you're pretty unusual."

I snorted. "I don't deny that."

"Your glow is murky. That tells me you know God, too, but aren't on good terms with him right now."

"My glow?" I examined myself. "I don't see anything."

"That's because you're not an angel. Now answer my question, and I might let you through the gate."

I sighed. "I want to enter Hell so that I can kill the devil."

Enos raised his eyebrows. "Well, I can honestly say that's an answer that I've never gotten before."

"So are you going to let me through?"

"Maybe. First I have a few more questions."

I gritted my teeth and tried to be patient. Offending the gate's guardian wouldn't help me any.

"Why do you want to kill the devil?" he asked.

"Because he's the source of all evil. Obviously. Don't you want to kill him?"

"Sure, but only God can defeat him, and someday he will. The devil's day of execution is already set, though its time remains a secret."

"I'm tired of waiting. I'll take the job off God's hands."

Enos narrowed his eyes. "And what makes you think you can kill the most powerful evil being in existence?"

I waved my empty hands in front of his face. "I know I can't do it with weapons from Earth. So I'm not bringing any. But I figure Hell probably has a weapon that I can use."

Enos shook his head. "None of the other angels are going to believe me when I tell them about you."

"Oh, I'm sure some of them will. They must have seen some of my handiwork."

"Such as?"

"I've killed a lot of people. I shot to death the deranged sword-wielding drug addict who I found chopping up my wife. Then I drove a truck over the dealer who sold him the drugs. Then I blew up every member of the gang that supplied the drugs."

"It sounds like you've been a busy guy."

"Yeah, I figured the only person left to kill is the one ultimately responsible for my wife's murder: the devil himself. He's had his claws in every homicide since Cain killed Abel." I leaned closer to Enos. "So, are you going to let me into Hell or not?"

Enos shrugged. "I suppose so. But I'll come with you to keep an eye on things."

"Won't an angel stand out in Hell?"

"I'll be invisible."

He swung the door open, revealing a swirling mix of fiery red and smoky black. Surprisingly, I felt no heat.

"Are you having second thoughts?" Enos asked.

I answered by stepping through the gateway. I braced myself for horrific, burning pain.

Instead, the temperature seemed comparable to Arizona in the summer. Unpleasant, but not excruciating.

When I glanced over my shoulder, the doorway was gone. My heart raced, and sweat broke out all over my body. What if I couldn't find my way back?

But I couldn't worry about that now. I still had a task to complete. And Enos had promised to accompany me. He would know the way back to Earth.

I began walking through the red and black fog, my footsteps the only sound.

Then a distant scream grabbed my attention. It sounded like a man experiencing unendurable agony. His screaming continued for at least a minute before ending abruptly.

Maybe the victim was a bad person who deserved whatever he got in Hell. But the one who deserved more punishment than anyone else was the devil himself.

Another noise reached me, panting like that of a large dog. Hot, malodorous waves swept over me.

I stopped. Through the haze, a giant shape became visible in front of me. At least six feet tall and inhuman, it resembled a grotesque hybrid of toad and cat, with warts and fur and big bulging eyes and a grinning mouth full of sharp teeth.

"Well, well, well," the toadcat said. "What do we have here? A newcomer to Hell." Before I could run, she bounded over and sniffed me. "What's this? You're alive, not dead. And that means I can't eat you."

Her smile turned into a frown. "That's not very nice of you. Why must you spoil my fun? I love to eat newcomers. Because they can't die a second time, they fully experience going through my digestive system and getting burned by my stomach acids. Then I excrete them and eat them again. It's such a lovely process. I'll do it repeatedly until they no longer scream and cry enough to make it worthwhile."

"My apologies," I said. "I'm looking for a weapon. I want something really nasty that's sure to kill any creature in the universe."

The toadcat hissed with laughter. "We're not in the universe, you dumb ape. We're somewhere else."

"Then I want a weapon that's sure to kill any creature that's anywhere, and I mean anywhere."

"Why should I help you? You'll be the one enjoying the pain of another, not me."

I scrambled onto her back and grabbed one of her large, pointed ears.

"Hey!" she whined. "That's not fair! I'm not allowed to hurt you in return. Not until you're dead, and even then only if you're sent to Hell. Though since you're here now, that indicates you'll be back later. And I'll have my revenge."

"Stop complaining and take me to a weapon like I described, or I'll rip your ear off."

She thought it over, her warty, furry tail flicking back and forth. "I know of a spear that can pierce through anything, even mountains or entire planets. Does that sound satisfactory?"

"Yes. Let's go."

She shambled through the red and black haze, grumbling under her breath. She grunted whenever her movements jostled me on her back and caused me to tug inadvertently on her ear.

After a while, the fog thinned, and a forest of sorts came into view. Thorns covered every dark tree, and branches sprouted green fungus instead of leaves.

As we entered the forest, a cacophony of groaning surrounded us. Men and women hung from some of the trees, nooses around their necks. They twitched and clawed at the ropes.

"Help us," they moaned. "Help us."

Pity stirred in my heart, but I buried it. I had to stay focused on my mission.

The toadcat giggled. "They're all guilty of strangling an innocent person to death in one way or another. They'll hang there for weeks, months, or years, always suffering, never dying, until the Hangman is finished with them."

"The Hangman?" I asked.

"Look ahead of us."

A black-cloaked figure shuffled toward us, resembling a Grim Reaper, but with no scythe. Its red eyes burned in its shadowy face, and it clutched a bundle of rope with long-clawed fingers.

It said nothing as we passed, though it watched us closely.

After we left the forest behind, a castle with many towers rose up before us. Its stones were dark red, and the mortar between them glowed like lava.

The toadcat carried me across the drawbridge that spanned the moat. Below us, hundreds of giant white snakes slithered in a circle around the castle.

At the gate, two living skeletons with swords barred our way.

"What is that thing on your back?" one asked the toadcat.

"I do not know," she replied. "But it is hurting me, and it wants the black spear that is kept in your armory."

The other skeleton examined me with hollow, dark eye sockets. "A pity that it lives. I so love to rip the skeletons out of dead humans and dwell in their spirit-bodies for a few centuries." She sighed and turned to her companion. "Go get the spear."

"Why can't they go get it themselves?" he snarled.

"I don't trust any living human, and I won't allow one to enter our castle."

With a growl, the skeleton vanished through the gateway. Several minutes later, he returned, carrying a black spear tipped with a foot-long dagger-like blade. I took the weapon out of his bony fingers.

The two skeletons watched the toadcat and me leave.

"I did as you requested," the toadcat said. "Now let me go."

"I will," I said, "right after I test the spear. Take me to the biggest, baddest monster you can think of, so that I can stab it and see what happens."

She roamed through a region of barren hills and stopped near the top of the last hill. Distant crashing sounds, like small rockslides, echoed through the air, followed by screams.

"On the other side of the hill," the toadcat said, "you'll find a creature that should be a good test for your spear. I'm not going any farther, because I'm scared of the huge, hideous thing. It sometimes attacks its fellow monsters if they get too close."

I slid off her back. "Okay, thanks."

The toadcat fled without another word.

I plodded to the top of the hill, sweat drenching my clothes. A plain opened up before me, with thousands of stone statues of people scattered across it. Among them prowled a creature that resembled a giant ape with green scales. It raised an enormous hammer over its head, then smashed a statue, and a human scream arose out of the crumbling stone.

"Hey, ugly!" I shouted.

The monster turned to look at me, then raced across the plain, its massive bulk shaking the ground. I waited for it to near the top of the hill. As its head rose above me, it lifted its hammer, ready to smash me like I was one of its statues.

Calmly, I threw the spear. The beast roared with dismay as the point pierced its chest. But the spear didn't stop. It drove straight through flesh and bone like a long, thin bullet and came out the back of the creature.

The spear clattered among some rubble, and when its point struck the ground, it started to sink into the plain.

The monster toppled to the ground and crumbled into pieces as if it, too, had been a statue. I circled the green mound and grabbed the spear before it could plunge out of sight.

I raised it high. Yes, if any weapon could kill the devil, this was it.

Now I needed to find my enemy, but I had no idea where to look. I would've asked the toadcat, but she was long gone.

Oh, well. Hell probably contained millions upon millions of demons and monsters. I could surely find another guide.

A distant discordant noise grabbed my attention. It sounded like ten thousand screams mingling together. Not a welcoming sound, but I'd investigate it to see if the creature or creatures responsible were of any use to me.

As I trudged across the plain, the screams grew louder. A city came into view, a haphazard collection of black-stoned buildings, castles, and towers, all of them crooked. Red-scaled humanoid demons crawled all over everything like cockroaches on trash. The humans, however, were the most horrifying sight.

Torture devices of every kind lined the streets, and through windows I could see them in the buildings as well. Humans tormented each other on racks and spikes, with whips and knives, in an endless display of sadism.

The demons watched, cackling, and occasionally they would release people from the torture devices, but only so those people could torture their torturers. Eventually the people would swap places again. Half the time they were overwhelmed by agony, and half the time ecstatic with cruelty.

I tried approaching several of the demons, but they scurried up walls and towers before I could get close to them.

"Leave us, living one," they snarled. "Come back when you're dead, and we'll let you join the fun."

I journeyed through the nightmarish city, my head ringing from all the screams. After several hours, I came out the other side, near a pass between two mountains. I sat down on a boulder, weary more in spirit than in body.

Enos appeared beside me. "Ready to go back to Earth?"

"No." I stood up. "But if you can tell me how to find the devil, I'd be most grateful."

"I'll do better than tell you. I'll take you to his palace. Just don't blame me for whatever happens afterward."

"Fine. And thanks."

I blinked, and not only had Enos vanished, but I stood before an impossibly huge palace of gold. Its walls and towers stretched thousands of feet above the ground, sparkling amidst the ever-present flames that flickered everywhere.

A staircase rose before me, a doorway at its top. As I started to climb, the butt of my spear bumped across one of the steps. The gold surface was scraped off in a line, revealing black underneath. Yet the gold quickly spread back over the blackness, hiding it.

I wiped sweat from my brow and kept climbing, trying to ignore my thirst, for I doubted Hell had anything to drink that wasn't poisonous in some way. When I reached the doorway, I peered inside. A maze of hallways awaited me.

While I pondered which one to try, a purple unicorn appeared, its eyes glowing green, its sharp teeth showing in a grin. Its horn was darkened near the tip, as if stained with the blood of people it had stabbed.

The unicorn clopped over to me, her voice like a cat's purr. "Greetings, human. The devil sent me to carry you through the palace. Climb onto my back."

Apparently I was expected. That didn't bode well for me, but I would not falter now.

Holding the spear tightly, I mounted my bizarre guide. She galloped down one hall, then turned into another. Most doors we passed were closed, but one stood open, and when a giant tentacle shot out and tried to grab me, the unicorn sped up and carried me to safety.

We traversed a seemingly endless series of halls, and for a while no more monsters sought to attack me. Then hundreds of bats, each with one large eye in their forehead, shot out of a doorway and chased us, their fangs glistening in their mouths.

The unicorn stopped and speared a bat with her horn. As she munched on the dead creature, the others flew away, and we continued onward.

Eventually I heard a deep, rumbling voice up ahead, sometimes speaking mockingly, sometimes roaring, and sometimes laughing.

Somehow, I knew it was the devil's voice.

We entered a hall with a high ceiling, and it led to a tall doorway surrounded by carvings of golden angels, as if this was a heavenly place instead of literally a hellish one.

"The throne room's through there," the unicorn said.

I slid off her back. "Thanks for bringing me here."

Her glowing green eyes examined me. "Maybe the devil will let me eat you later. I haven't tasted a human soul in almost a week."

She clopped down the hall and vanished around a corner.

I turned to face the doorway, and after a moment of hesitation, I stepped through it, expecting to find a throne room filled with more of the devil's creepy servants.

Instead, it was empty; just a vast expanse of pure, sparkling white, with a raised dais at the end of it. On a giant throne perched a creature that must be the devil, though not like any depiction of him I'd ever seen.

Even while sitting, he was twenty feet tall, with enormous gold-feathered wings and a white robe trimmed with gold. His face resembled that of a handsome man, yet his glittering eyes hinted at superhuman intelligence and cruelty.

"Welcome," he said. "I've been waiting for you. We have a lot to discuss, don't we? And as you can see, I've cleared my schedule for you. Now tell me: why are you here? I know, of course, but it will be so amusing to hear you attempt to explain it yourself."

"I'm here to kill you," I replied.

"Why? Because I'm too beautiful and wonderful and powerful, and you're jealous?"

"If you know so much, then you know why."

The devil smiled. "She screamed a lot. Your wife, I mean. You didn't get home until she was already dead. But I savored every scream, every groan, and every delicious fear she felt and agony she experienced."

My fingers clenched around the spear. "I'm going to drive this right through your heart, if you have one. And if you don't, I'll drive it through your head."

The devil snapped his fingers, and my spear vanished.

He chuckled. "Don't look so crestfallen. That spear, which could slay the mightiest demons in Hell, could do absolutely nothing to me."

I glared at him, trembling with impotent rage.

"But don't worry." He leaned forward, towering over me. "I'm not going to kill you. No, the best thing to do is to send you back to Earth, to be haunted by your heartbreaking memories for the rest of a long, weary life."

He stroked his chin. "But before I do that, I want to let you in on a little secret. You want to kill me, the devil. But I'm not the only devil. I'm just the big one. There are a lot of small devils inside of you. Every sin you commit is a devil." He grinned. "Come to me, my little darlings."

Something writhed in my chest. No, a lot of somethings. Then, bloodlessly, two-inch-tall creatures began crawling out of my chest. They were stereotypical devils, red, with horns and pointed tails and pitchforks.

Dozens of them crawled across my abdomen, with many more following, until hundreds swarmed all over my body, their laughter high-pitched and grating.

They gleefully recounted some of the sins I'd committed:

"I'm that time you shattered several windows of your fourth-grade teacher's house after you failed an important test you didn't even study for."

"I'm that time you wrecked while drunk driving at seventeen, and you switched places with your friend who was passed out, so that he got arrested instead of you. He still doesn't know what you did. He really thinks he was the one driving."

"I'm one of the many times you worked late out of greed and not necessity, leaving your wife sad, confused, and alone and yes, there's one of us for every one of those nights. I bet you'd give anything to undo all those wasted hours, but it's too late."

The devil gave a mocking frown. "You can't even kill the little devils inside of you, so how could you ever hope to stand a chance against me?"

More little devils kept crawling out of me, thousands of them, until they dragged me to the ground, like ants swarming over an injured bird. Sorrow, regret, shame, and other dark emotions overwhelmed me.

My mission had failed. The devil was still alive. And a seemingly infinite number of devils lived inside of me.

"Oh, God," I whispered, "let me die."

"Hey, tough guy," Enos said. "You wanted to kill the big devil, and you can't. But you can kill little devils. So start the slaughter."

I looked around, but the angel was invisible. Yet his words were tangible and true.

I grabbed a little devil and tore his head off. Then I grabbed another one and twisted him in half. The others began stabbing me with their pitchforks, but it hurt no more than being pricked by thorns. They could only afflict me, not kill me. I ripped apart hundreds of them, leaving their broken red bodies scattered across the throne room's white floor.

The devil no longer looked amused. His hands gripped the arm rests of his throne, and he rose to his feet, his golden wings unfolding and filling the room. Rage flickered in his eyes.

"You are beginning to annoy me, human," he said.

Enos appeared in front of me. "His life is not in your hands, devil. I'm taking him back to Earth. And there's nothing you can do about it."

I blinked, and I stood next to the angel outside the gate to Hell. When I examined my body for little devils, none were visible.

"Was that a vision or real?" I asked.

"It was real," Enos said. "Including the part about the little devils inside of you. Although you can't see them, they're still there. And if you don't want them to turn you into their puppet, you better spend at least as much time killing them as you do battling the evildoers outside of you."

I nodded.

Enos bear-hugged me. "I like you, human. You're a little crazy, but you're not a helpless lamb, like many of your kind. Just make sure you use your strength wisely, and you learn to balance justice with mercy."

"I will." I returned his hug, then stepped back. "Thanks for everything."

"Just doing my job."

Enos vanished.

I walked away from the gate with a different resolution than when I'd gone in. From now on, I would hunt down my little devils like the dangerous criminals they were, and with every one I destroyed, I'd remember the best thing I saw in Hell: the annoyed, angry face of the big devil.

ABOUT THE AUTHOR

JONATHAN GARNER is the author of the young adult supernatural thriller The Resurrecter and the editor of the poetry anthology Classic Poems About Spiders. He is currently working on his next novel. Learn more about his books, blog, and newsletter at https://jonathandgarner.com/

SLOW DAY

Kristal Stittle

The day was dreary, dull, boring, and mundane. Outside, a light drizzle was soaking the streets, the cars, the pedestrians, and the glass-sided buildings. The grey clouds hung low and uniform, thick enough to block out the sky but not dark enough to be spooky or interesting.

Inside one of the buildings was an office full of cubicles. The ceiling lights cast their low-wattage, yellowish glow onto the heads of two dozen workers tapping away on their keyboards. The people reflected the day. They weren't chatting or excited about anything. They weren't hard at work either.

I was sitting and staring at my screen, doing absolutely nothing. Recently, the company had hit an important milestone with our project, but then we came to a grinding halt. All the heads were busy, in meetings, planning the next phase, but grunts like me had nothing to do. We were just waiting on orders. There were only so many times I could play solitaire before it drove me insane.

I turned and looked into the cubical across from mine. Paul worked there, although he was currently asleep at his desk. I knew he would get in shit if he were caught. Although we all had nothing to do, we had to at least pretend we did. We were supposed to be revising our code, checking for any missed bugs, but there were only so many times you could look at the same thing. I had been looking at my section for the past three months. If I could kill it, I would. Instead, I ripped a page out of a nearby notebook and threw it at Paul's head. The man, who was ten years older than me and had remarkably less hair, awoke with a start. He snorted and grumbled as he sat upright, rubbing his eyes.

"Wha was tha' for, Jacob?" he mumbled, turning in his seat to look at me.

"You were asleep," I informed him. "If Mike came by, he'd tear you a new one."

"Mike's in a meeting until four. So's pretty much everyone else that would throw a hissy fit. You couldn't let me sleep until then?"

"You never know, someone might come down here to get something. Also, Fred would totally rat you out."

"Fair 'nough." Paul turned back to his computer, tapping the mouse with his hand to get rid of the screensaver. Both he and the screen would probably be asleep again in ten minutes.

I turned back around to my own computer knowing that Paul wasn't going to entertain me. It was only 1 PM but I had already exhausted all my usual battery of websites. There were other sites I would like to visit, but the company blocked them on my computer. At least they hadn't yet discovered the site I was using for solitaire. I hated the company. I didn't like writing the boring software code, the cubicles, the off-white walls, the blocked websites, or the dress code. I didn't even like the other people. They were boring, unimaginative, uninteresting, and many were decades older than I was. At twenty-five, I was the youngest person on the floor by far, creating a wide generation gap. What I really wanted to do was make video games. I had designed and programmed a few simple things, but nothing I could make any money off of. Currently, I was working on something that I should be able to sell; I just needed more time to work on it. If only the company hadn't blocked me from connecting with my home computer, then I could be doing it now.

I pulled my notebook to me and began doodling with a pen. I'm not a very good artist. The mini-games I had made had all their art done by my roommate. My roommate went to art school and also wanted to make games, but currently he was stuck working for his cousin's exterior house painting company. I doodled out some ideas to show him later.

As I sat there, sketching out a level design for the platformer game I was making, my stomach began rumbling. I wasn't hungry, I had eaten my lunch that day; it was my food's outward descent that caused the rumbling.

So, I got up from my chair and left the cubical, obeying nature's call. As I suspected, Paul was asleep again, drooling on his own arm. I could have woken him up as I went past, but decided against it. Maybe on the way back I would. Although I didn't particularly like Paul, if Paul got chewed out, he'd complain to me about it. Paul complained about nearly everything.

As I walked toward the bathroom, I glanced into other people's cubicles to see what they were up to. Fred was the only one I spotted actually working. Nicole was drawing a monster in a sketchbook that looked disturbingly real; far better than my scribbles. Andrew was chatting with someone through email. Danny had a word doc open and was typing furiously, probably writing another story. Trevor was putting together a model airplane to join the other five he already had decorating his desk. Everyone in the office had their quirks and hobbies, I wasn't an exception.

I left the cubicle area and stepped out into reception. Betina, the receptionist for our floor, was chewing bubble gum and typing away at her own computer. She probably had actual work to do, sending and receiving emails, setting up conference rooms and meetings. The woman was in her sixties but certainly didn't act like it. She was always chewing gum, wearing bright outfits and flashy make-up, and flirted with the men despite being happily married. She was the only person I somewhat liked in this godforsaken glass coffin and usually I would stop to talk to her. She looked busy today though, so I continued on to the bathroom.

Through reception, I passed the few chairs and the elevators. I then walked past the break room, a few meeting rooms, and neared the management offices. The bathrooms were next to the offices, which was annoying because Mike, my supervisor, would always see me as I walked down the hall and give me some extra, bullshit assignment. Today I had no need to worry because Mike was one floor up in the big meeting.

The door to the bathroom was a pale blue colour. Pushing through that led me to a small antechamber with another pale blue door to push through. The bathroom itself was painted white and the stalls matched the doors. The sinks were steel and set into a black, speckled, marble counter. The ceiling in the bathroom was actually interesting. It was high up, allowing pipes and duct work to be exposed.

I walked to the stall at the far end to do my business. It was my favourite stall, although I had no idea why. Maybe I just liked being far away from the entrance. Once the door was safely latched behind me, I pulled down my pants and sat on the toilet. Because it sometimes took me awhile to get going, I usually played games on my cell phone. When I took the device out of my pocket, however, it was dead. Considering I had charged it last night, I wasn't at all happy about this. I never had much luck with phones.

The ducts above hummed and rumbled, forcing AC air down on my head.

As I sat, waiting for my bowels to move, the door to the bathroom burst open with a mighty slam. I jumped where I sat, nearly spilling myself off the seat, due to the sudden crash. Considering the door was on a pneumatic hinge, it probably shouldn't have been able to open so quickly. Whoever had just come in probably broke the door in the process.

And did the air just get a degree warmer? Probably a warm draft from the hall.

A sound not dissimilar to a woman's clicking heels travelled across the floor. Had a woman just come into the men's bathroom? The sound travelled right up to my stall and stopped before it, but I couldn't see their feet. The owner of the footsteps politely knocked upon my door.

"Occupied," I informed whoever it was. The other stalls were clearly empty; I don't know why he, or perhaps she, didn't just go into one of them.

Whoever it was knocked again, louder this time. The stall door shuddered from the force.

"Occupied!" I called louder, my voice wavering. This whole thing was very odd and I admit to being a little scared. Having my pants around my ankles didn't help.

The air definitely got warmer.

"I have come for your soul," a deep and certainly male voice grumbled from the other side of the door.

I grinned. It must be someone playing a practical joke. "Very funny guys."

The temperature flared higher. Whoever it was outside my door slammed their fist loudly into it, the latch barely hanging on. I jumped again with fright, an uncomfortably high pitch "eek" escaping my mouth before I could clamp my hands over it.

Who would possibly play such a joke on me? Surely not Paul. I couldn't think of anyone. Danny maybe? Was Steve in on it? Maybe if I could make out their footwear...

Slowly, I leaned forward on my seat and looked beneath the door. They weren't the kind of shoes I was expecting. In fact, they weren't shoes at all. A pair of large, cloven hooves stood before my stall, attached to a pair of ankles covered in a coarse, dark brown fur. As I watched, the weight shifted from one foot to the other, causing a subtle movement to the feet that made me think they were real and not just custom boots. But how could they be real? A tail, or what I assumed was a tail, swung down near the feet. Before it lifted back up out of sight, I noted it was covered in a finer fur of the same colour as the feet and ended in a spade shape.

I tried to swallow, but my mouth and throat had dried up worse than a block of wood in the desert. Surely my bored mind was just overreacting, and I was seeing things that weren't true.

"Open the door," the heavy voice grumbled.

"Still occupied." Why I said that, I have no idea. Why my voice squeaked was a little more understandable.

"I'll break it down if you make me. And you *don't* want to make me." A heavy fist slammed into the door three more times, rattling the bolt lock.

"Who is it?" When I get scared, I resort to jokes. It's a quirk of mine.

"I have many names."

"Tell me one." Perhaps if I stall him long enough, someone else would walk into the bathroom, and they could call 911.

"Lucifer."

I shuddered at the sound, which managed to be both a growl and a hiss; like it was spoken by more than one voice.

"Ah, Lucifer, I've heard of you." My mouth was running on autopilot, for better or worse.

"I'm glad."

"So, what can I do for you, here in the public bathroom?"

"I've come for your soul."

"My soul?" I squeaked. I coughed once to clear my throat, although there wasn't anything in it that needed clearing. "What could you possibly want with my soul?"

"To bring it to Hell with me, of course."

"Of course. Why *my* soul?"

"You sold it to me."

"What? No I didn't." I think I would have remembered selling my soul to Lucifer.

The heat in my bathroom stall jumped into the Sahara Desert range. I also heard the sounds of billions of distance voices crying out through the ductwork and pipes in the ceiling. I clearly had just upset him.

"I don't remember selling my soul," I told him earnestly. Perhaps I had been a small boy, who was goofing off when it happened. How was I to know then that the devil was real?

"Here is the contract," the voice grumbled as the temperature dropped to more survivable levels.

The hooves stepped forward to where I could see them without having to lean down. The spade at the end of his tail swept in under the door and then out again, as quick as a snake tongue scenting the air. I instinctively tucked my feet further back from the door. A thick, powerful-looking hand reached under the door, its nails pointed and shiny black like obsidian. Clutched in the hand was a scroll of paper wrapped in an ink black ribbon with a broken, blood red seal. I pinched the edge of the scroll carefully between two fingers, trying my hardest not to touch the hand. As soon as I had a grip, the hand released the scroll and disappeared from my stall.

The paper was unlike any I had ever felt before. It looked old, slightly yellowed, but was very tough and coarse. It had been weaved out of a material I couldn't identify. Slowly, I unrolled the scroll, revealing the black ink upon it. The ink was like holes that had been cut into oblivion, not like something that had been merely scrawled upon the paper. I didn't dare run my fingers over the text, for fear that my eyes would be proved right and that I'd be sucked through them. The text it formed was unreadable, at least to me. I had always been terrible at reading other people's handwriting, and this was such an overly elaborate text that I could only make out a handful of letters. My eyes ran down the page to where I expected a signature in blood. There was a signature, but it was in a basic, regular blue pen, nothing strange about it at all. It wasn't my signature though.

"Umm, this isn't me," I told Lucifer. *Lucifer!* And I was telling him he made a mistake? Let's just say that it was a damn good thing I was sitting on the toilet.

Silence was the response, but I could feel the heat starting to rise.

"No really!" I bent over and pushed the paper under the stall door. "I can't read the signature, but I know for a fact that it's not mine."

"It isn't?" He actually sounded like he believed me.

"No. Who's is it? And what did he ask for?"

"Steven Evans. He wanted a regular bowel."

"Well, that makes sense." Relief washed over me as I realized he had the wrong guy. "Steve is in the stall at the other end."

"I fucking hate you, Jacob," Steve finally spoke up from where he had been doing his own business in silence the whole time.

"Steve!" Lucifer boomed, turning toward his stall, his hooves clicking along the floor. "I have come for your soul!"

"No wait, please!" Steve begged.

I listened as the stall door was ripped from its hinges and tossed to the ground.

"NOOOOoooooo!" Steve screamed.

A sound like tearing came from the ceiling above. I looked up, but couldn't see anything near me. A strange, red light was coming from over toward Steve, however. Again I heard the sounds of billions of distance voices. They were crying out in pain and ecstasy. From closer, over by Steve, there was a horrible crunching and slurping, a bizarre suction sound, and then a loud snap. After a strange zipper sound, the red light faded, and all other sounds silenced. I sat with bated breath, wondering what was going to happen next.

Lucifer was still here. I listened as he walked on his hooves to where the door had fallen. It scraped along the ground as he picked it up and slammed it back into place. The devil seemed to be cleaning up after himself. The hooves then walked back over to my stall.

"What's your name?" he grumbled.

"Jacob." I was squeaking again. Perhaps he was going to get rid of the witness?

"Is there anything I can do for you, Jacob?"

"What?"

"Is there anything you want? I can give you anything."

"Umm, no thanks."

"Are you sure?"

"I'd rather not go to Hell."

"How do you know you're not already?"

He had a point. I had no idea. I mean, I wasn't a saint or anything. Based on what I knew of religion, I was definitely on the hell list.

"I can make sure that game you're working on is a best-seller. And that woman you see on the bus a lot; I can make it so that you hit it off really well. Maybe baldness runs in the family, or... smallness."

"What if I asked to live forever?"

"I'd still collect your soul. That's how zombies are made you know."

"What did Steve get?" I was amazed at myself for even thinking about it.

"He made the deal when he was five years old. Poor kid had crapped his pants just one too many times at school. I gave him fifty years of the healthiest bowel you can imagine."

Steve had always been really regular, everyone knew. You could set your watch by him.

"Yeah, you know what? I really think I'm good."

"You're not that good." Lucifer's tail whipped under the door again with its snake-like quickness.

"Good enough."

"Suit yourself." The heavy hooves retreated from the bathroom.

I was finally able to take the shit I had gone to the bathroom to take. Although the entire time I expected Lucifer to come barging back in. After pulling up my pants and flushing, I exited the toilet stall. The rest of the bathroom looked just the same as it had when I first entered, as if nothing had happened there. I washed my hands in the sink and turned to Steve's stall. The hinges were a little bent out of shape. I walked up to the door.

"Steve?" Why I expected an answer, I have no idea. I pushed on the door, which wasn't locked anymore.

There was Steve, pants around his ankles, slumped over sideways with his head on the toilet paper roll, dead as a doorknob. He looked sad and pathetic.

"I hope it was worth it," I told his corpse. I then left the bathroom and went back to my own desk. Paul was still sleeping across the way. I could've called someone about Steve, but decided against it; let the next guy find him like that.

I did, however, pull my notebook over to me and write down the date and time. Underneath, I wrote and underlined the words "In case of emergency, call Lucifer."

ABOUT THE AUTHOR

KRISTAL STITTLE is a born and raised in Torontoian, although she's known to frequent the lakes and forests of Muskoka. Trained in 3D animation, she continues to paint and illustrate regularly while dabbling in photography whenever she's not writing. She's the author of the zombie Survival Instinct series, as well as Merciless, Yellow Line, and numerous short stories. You can check her Linktree (https://linktr.ee/kristalstittle) to find out where she is on the internet, and possibly see a picture of her cat.

THE DEVIL
AND
ANNIE OAKLEY

Tom Folske

It was a fine spring afternoon when Annie
Oakley decided to sit down for a spell in the
comfortable, worn rocker her husband had made her.
She watched the wind push the day lazily along from
the shade of her back porch. It had been just over a
year since Buffalo Bill had hired her to perform in his
Wild West Show. A woman in a wild west show was
ludicrous to some, but Bill had stood by her side,
especially after she outshot Wild Bill Hickock.
Although Wild Bill had been starting to go blind, he
did graciously admit that she would have topped him
at his best, though not by much he had to add. He
told her that after she shot an ace through the spade at
thirty yards.

Annie was peacefully alone for the day. Both Bills
and Frank Butler, her husband who also worked on
the show, had gone to meet with a Comanche warrior
whose skills with a bow and arrow and tomahawk
were supposedly unparalleled, even by the great chiefs
like Sitting Bull and Crazy Horse. Annie enjoyed the

quiet. She had just poured herself a glass of whiskey with a splash of lemonade that had been freshly squeezed that morning, and for the moment, was entirely content with the world.

That's when everything went completely black all around her, a black so absent of light that she was instantly cold. Cold as death. Annie could feel her breath frosting as she rose quickly to her feet, contemplating heading inside and grabbing her rifle, but knowing in her heart that it wouldn't help. She was, however, unable to think of a single other thing to do. When her hand reached the door handle, there was a tremendous cacophony of what sounded like wings flapping, wings too large to belong to any bird, followed by the ruffling of settling feathers, right before everything returned to normal.

Annie was still processing the event the had just transpired, when she heard a voice that as it spoke, began so vast, it seemed to be coming from all around her, as well as in her head, before it adjusted itself, with an almost undetectable smoothness, into a warm, soothing voice that could've entranced her for hours. It sounded close behind her.

"Phoebe Ann Mosey... Or is it Annie Oakley you prefer?"

Annie froze. Her Winchester was above the mantle, maybe twenty feet from where she now stood. She didn't answer the stranger as she again contemplated her rifle, as well as the chances of reaching the gun before whatever was there could reach her.

"Your rifle will have no effect on me," the voice said as it changed its cadence once again, this time into something friendly, neighborly, and unremarkably normal. "Besides, I am not here to hurt you. In fact, I have a proposition you might be interested in."

Annie turned around, feeling more anger than fear, knowing she could outshoot anyone and wishing more than ever that she had her gun. The only time in her life that she had ever truly been acquainted with fear, was when she had been a young, novice marksman, and the fear she knew then was that of starvation. Annie's father had died when she was only five, leaving her mother with seven young and hungry mouths to feed. This meant that Annie and her siblings had to grow up much more quickly than they ought to have, which is essentially how she became such a great marksman in the first place. She feared no man, however, though the hairs on her arms and the back of her neck stood up when she finally did turn around, just like right before a good thunderstorm, and there, half a dozen feet away from her, stood a short, thin, absolutely unthreatening man who appeared to be a salesman, dressed in a black suit and wire-rim spectacles. He had somehow just appeared at the bottom of the steps leading up to Annie and Frank's back porch, where moments ago, no one had been approaching for as far as Annie could see. This entity, who had appeared immediately after the darkness departed, she knew in her soul this was no man.

"Annie Oakley, as I live and breathe," the Salesman said with a slight chortle as he began charismatically up the steps, without invitation, and made himself comfortable in Bill's rocker. He gestured for Annie to sit down in her own chair, like they were old friends about to regale each other with news of friends and family, like it was his house and not her own. Annie contemplated going for her rifle one more time, before deciding it probably really would be useless anyway.

Annie took a seat next to the Salesman and was immediately overwhelmed by the smell of sulfur.

"Don't worry, you'll get used to it," the malodorous merchant assured her.

"What shall I call you?" Annie asked, knowing what this entity's God given name was, but reluctant to call him by it.

"I go by many monikers and appellations, No. 44, Old Scratch, Samael, Memnoch, others that you are well aware of, but presently, I have grown fond of the title of Old Nick, or just Nick, whichever you prefer."

"And why are you here?" Annie asked, now fully aware of the game that she had inadvertently been forced into playing, and of absolute belief in the nature of the person she was playing it with.

"You asked me my name, but it is your name that is arguably much more famous here in the west. People come for miles and miles to see you shoot, I'm told. I have come from much further away to see that very same thing."

"Talk to Buffalo Bill when he gets back. He can get you front row seats. Maybe he'll even give you a discount."

"Annie... Annie... Annie... I don't want the show. I want you. I want the world's greatest marksman for my ranks. I am here to offer you a deal."

Annie didn't reply.

"Okay, I have a rifle made of pure gold, the finest weapon ever crafted, one that never misses."

"No deal," Annie replied with a scoff. "That sounds gawdy as all get out. I value my soul more than gold sir, and why do I need something that never misses when I already never miss."

Old Nick looked forlorn, which brought the hint of a smirk to the corner of Annie's lips. She was starting to feel increasingly confident. He may have been the one to make the game, but she was beginning to see that he had to play by the rules... or at least he was choosing to play by them.

"A rifle that fires true every shot, that never has to be reloaded or cleaned could pique my interest," she offered, more for the challenge than the reward.

Old Nick immediately brightened up. "Okay," he said. "Here's my proposal…"

Old Nick stood up and produced a small figurine of a white dove, roughly the size of a hummingbird, seemingly out of thin air. He walked down the porch steps and set the dove figure on top of the base post of the railing.

"One hundred paces to shoot this dove," the Salesman explained.

Annie looked at the mysterious stranger expectantly, knowing this feat was far too easy and could be accomplished by a great many individuals.

"Fair enough, I was hoping you would instantly agree, but I am sometimes known as the Prince of Lies, a rather undignified and undeserving title, if I do say so myself, so your hesitation is understandable. The trick, is to shoot the dove backwards at 100 paces, using only that mirror."

Annie looked out across the arid terrain, and saw a full-size revolving mirror, like one a wealthy, highbrow woman, might have in her bedroom. It had appeared, also seemingly out of nowhere, at what she would have judged to be about 100 paces out.

Annie contemplated the Salesman's offer. The shot was hard, nigh impossible, and if she missed, it meant an eternity of infernal horror and suffering. Annie knew herself and her abilities. She had only drunk enough whiskey to calm her nerves,.not to sway her shot. She had never been an effeminate girl, despite being naturally pretty, but she did keep up a certain demeanor and appearance for the show, which meant she had grown accustomed to being in front of a mirror, especially lately. Ultimately, her decision came down to one factor and one factor only... She never missed.

"Challenge accepted," Annie told Old Nick confidently, almost like she was unperturbed by the matter, like she did when she was young, and she made people bet her a quarter that she couldn't shoot six cans off a fence in six shots. She made a lot of quarters that way.

Annie casually turned around and opened the back door, not forgetting to pick up her whiskey and lemonade in the process and take a swig. She walked as normally as she could, the liquor helping some, but her heart was racing, her stomach was twisting up, and her hands probably would have been trembling, had she not had such mastery over everything below her wrists. She had made a Faustian bargain and there was no going back.

Annie stopped in front of the mantle and gazed up at her Winchester. She had just cleaned and oiled the magnificent rifle earlier that morning, a task she performed every morning, and now it seemed to shine defiantly from its hand-crafted, cherry wood rack. It was as if the weapon were giving Annie its full support, like it was telling her they had this, and if they didn't, it would follow her to Hell to take out demons.

Annie carefully took the Winchester, her Winchester, her favorite and most trusted rifle, down from the mantle. The weight and structure of the weapon were perfect, divinely familiar, as the gun itself seemed to become another appendage, another part of Annie's anatomy, the instant it was in her grasp. She released the barrel, exposing the chamber and grabbed one cartridge out of the box of ammunition below where the gun had rested. She loaded the rifle with that single cartridge. She locked the barrel back in place and was about to go out and face her destiny, then turned around and looked at the box one more time. She grabbed one more cartridge, because although polite and well-mannered like spoiled cream that looks fresh, she didn't quite trust the Salesman.

Annie exited her house again, took one more swig of her whiskey and lemonade, just to calm her rapidly beating heart, and looked down at the Salesman, who smiled coyly up at her from just beyond the bottom step.

She considered shooting him right there, planting one right between his eyes, and if she had to make another bet that she could do it before the devil reached her, she would have taken that bet too. She didn't shoot him, however, instead she smiled politely at him, like Buffalo Bill sometimes instructed to do when certain investors came to the show, as she walked down the stairs in the most proper ladylike fashion, like this was all just part of the show.

"Are you ready?" Old Nick asked, a devious smile forming across his face.

"Are you?" Annie replied.

Old Nick gestured for her to lead the way.

"Most people can't even cut their own hair in a mirror," Old Nick told her as they walked. "They either go over or under too far, compensating the wrong way in what should be a simple task."

"I'm not most people," Annie told the Salesman.

They walked the rest of the way in silence, stopped only when they were about three feet from looking glass. Old Nick moved right next to Annie, almost touching her, so both their images could be seen in the mirror.

"One shot," he told her with a scoff, as if he had already won, as if the shot were impossible.

"One shot," Annie repeated, just confidently.

Annie Oakley took her gun, placed the barrel backwards over her shoulder, cocked her head away from the barrel to save her ear a little trauma, and stared intently into the mirror for over a minute. She then took the deepest, longest breath of her life, and as she exhaled, she squeezed the trigger.

ABOUT THE AUTHOR

TOM FOLSKE lives in Minnesota with his wife, four kids, and three black cats. He loves horror and writing equally. Tom has had over a dozen short stories published by various publishers, both online and in print. In 2024, Tom is slated to have stories featured in upcoming anthologies or magazines by Jersey Pines Ink, Theaker Quarterly Fiction, Celticfrog Publishing, Haute DIsh Literary Magazine, and House of Loki Press.

SERIAL KILLER

Martin Klubeck

The woods are lovely, dark and deep. But I have promises to keep, And miles to go before I sleep, And miles to go before I sleep.

— Robert Frost

"The Right Reverend Marcus Johnson has a very full calendar," she said with a practiced frown.

I, of course, knew that. Anyone running for Congress would be busy. Johnson was also leading one of the largest Baptist congregations in the country. And he was a husband and a father too. Busy would be an understatement.

"Yes, but I really need to talk to him. It's a matter of life or death," I said.

"Let me get you his aide-de-camp."

"If that's the best you can do."

"I'm sorry, it is."

The receptionist was more polite than I would have been. The lobby was full of people wanting to see the Reverend. There were reporters, local and district staffers, well wishers, job seekers, and parishioners. It was standing room only.

"I appreciate it," I said.

Perhaps it was the badge I flashed. It showed that I worked for the FBI.

It wasn't real.

8

Thirty minutes later she waved me to her desk.

"Mr. Amos can see you now. Through there, third door on your right."

"Thank you."

Security was light, but the door wouldn't open until she pressed the buzzer. The loud click of the lock disengaging let everyone in the waiting room know that I had gotten my golden ticket.

The hallway was pretty busy with people moving from office to office. I would have smiled at the hustle and bustle. I enjoyed seeing the liveliness of people engaged in passionate work. But I was a little preoccupied.

I knocked on the door and walked in without waiting for a reply. The room was sparsely furnished. A few filing cabinets to my left and two folding chairs were in front of a used surplus metal desk. One window, open enough to let a nice warm breeze in. Blinds blocked the sun. A mostly empty bookshelf. I noticed there were four copies of Reverend Johnson's autobiography. The only other books were a dictionary, a book on technical writing and another on marketing. They all had a healthy lair of dust. No pictures. None on the walls, none on the desk. No framed diplomas.

In contrast to the sparseness of the office, papers and folders cluttered the desk. The man behind the desk gave the impression he was eternally busy.

"Mr Amos?" I asked.

I closed the door behind me.

The man closed a folder, leaned back in his chair and looked at me. "Yes. Janet said you had a serious matter that you wanted to talk to Marcus about?"

"*You* could say that," I said.

"You said it. Life or death, right?"

Agitated, but only a little.

"Oh, that. Yes and no. More yes than no," I said.

If my banter bothered him, he didn't let it show.

I sat in one of the chairs and unbuttoned my jacket. I watched his eyes. He noticed the shoulder holster and gun under my left arm.

"I'm sure you know about the Corpus Delicti Killer."

"The serial killer? Yes, it's been in the news constantly. It's taken away attention from our campaign." He sounded disappointed. "But isn't it the *Corpus Killer?*"

"That's what some genius in the media shortened it to."

"Okay, yes. I know about it."

Uninterested.

"And you know that he's been targeting influential figures," I said.

"'He?' How do you know it's a 'he?'"

"Most serial killers are male, especially ones that use a gun."

He didn't seem convinced.

"We have eyewitnesses," I said. He raised his eyebrows, the exaggeration clearly asking for more information. "But eyewitnesses are notoriously unreliable. The only consistent description is that the person of interest is a male."

We sat for a few moments in silence.

"So I'm still not sure what Marcus, Reverend Johnson, can do for you."

"Actually, I'm hoping *you* can help me."

"I'm not sure what I can do for you," he said.

"We believe the Corpus Killer has killed three in the city over the last two weeks."

"Believe?"

He noticed.

"It's complicated."

"Well, I don't see how this concerns Marcus or his campaign."

"It's because of his victims, who he targets."

That look again.

"And...?"

"Sonia Weaver, an up-and-coming local radio personality, disappeared on the fourth. Witnesses saw her last with a middle-aged male."

He nodded at me.

"John Blare, a popular character by all rights, a week later. He was becoming well known for his philanthropy. The mayor awarded him the Key to the City for his volunteer work."

"I remember that one. I hadn't heard of Blare until then."

"Yes, it's one of the factors in our profile. The victims are all rather humble. They don't seek out the limelight. The last victim also fits that description."

"Any DNA? Fingerprints? Anything?"

Most people asked those questions as an accusation. But Amos seemed genuinely curious.

I shook my head. "Actually, we have nothing."

"Nothing? If the killer is using a gun, you should have a bullet at least? Don't tell me the killer is taking the time to dig the bullet out of the body or finding it if it passed through." Now he seemed a little angry.

"Good questions. Very insightful."

"Any answers?" Compliments didn't faze him either.

"Nothing. Technically, we can't even be sure there have been any killings."

"I'm confused. You said you have eyewitnesses."

"True. But we have no bodies."

"So, how do you know they're dead?"

"We don't."

"So what did your eyewitnesses see?"

"In every case, they saw a middle-aged man. Average height. We're pretty sure it was the same man. And he was with the victims, moments before they disappeared."

Amos nodded.

"For example, Sonia Weaver was on the radio. The person of interest found his way into her studio. Witnesses saw him enter. Witnesses saw him leave."

"Okay," he said.

"But Sonia didn't finish her shift. When the song ended, there was dead air. Her assistant tried to call her in the booth, but she didn't respond. She wasn't in the booth, but the assistant swears Weaver never left."

"Hmm."

"John Blare stepped into a bathroom at the Salvation Army and never came back out."

"And a middle-aged man was seen?"

"Yes, entering the bathroom right after Blare. The man left soon after, but Blare never did."

"And no bodies?"

"None."

"And the third victim?"

"David Wilson."

"I've never heard of him either."

"He was a grad student working at the institute for International Relations. He was assisting Professor Mike Coti on a research project."

"None of these people were prominent," he said.

"I didn't say prominent, I said influential."

He nodded.

"Wilson became Coti's top assistant. He was very influential in the professor's journal publications. The latest on the reestablishment of the Soviet Union has gained a lot of publicity."

"Okay. And you think Marcus is a major influencer? You think he's a possible target for this killer?"

"I didn't say that."

"You didn't need to. You said it's a matter of life and death, right?"

"Sort of."

"Well, how can I help?"

He leaned forward and pushed the papers to his left and right, clearing his work to give me his full attention.

Nice touch.

Now I leaned back. I wasn't in a rush.

"Do you believe in God?" I asked.

"What?"

"Do you believe in God?"

"Does that matter?"

"You're working for a religious man who is running for Congress. Why?"

"Because I believe in *him*. I believe he'll do great things."

"Okay. But Reverend Johnson's platform claims he does everything for Jesus Christ."

He nodded.

And flinched. Agitated.

"How do you feel about that?" I asked.

"What do you mean?"

"Do you think it will hurt his chances to be elected?"

"There are other people in congress who believe in God."

"Not from this part of the country."

He nodded.

"And none as vocal about following Jesus."

Another flinch.

"I don't think it will hurt his chances at all. I think it may help. People find him refreshing."

I nodded.

"How long have you been living in the city?"

It's a common tactic by law enforcement to change the line of questioning. It can keep the respondent off balance.

"Excuse me?"

No emotion.

"How long have you lived at 213 Holbrook Street?"

"A few months, I guess. Why?"

"And you worked your way from a volunteer staffer to the number one advisor in that short span of time?"

"Yes…"

I thought he wanted to say more, but nothing came.

"What did you do before volunteering?"

He didn't answer.

"You're pretty young to be retired. Are you independently wealthy? How could you work full time as a volunteer? I checked, and you still don't get paid."

Now *he* leaned back.

"I can't find anything about you before starting here."

"I like my privacy."

"Yeah, I noticed that."

I took my Glock out of the holster. I held it on my right leg with my finger on the trigger. He tried his best not to notice.

"You think I'm the Corpus Killer? That's absurd."

"No. I'm as sure as I can be that you're not the Corpus Killer."

"Then what is this about?"

"Do you believe in the Devil?"

Off balance. Finally.

"No."

"Really? I'm surprised."

"Why?"

"Your candidate believes in God, professes a love of Jesus Christ." *Is that a sneer?* "If you believe in God, don't you have to also believe in the Devil?" *And it becomes a small smile.*

"I never said I believed in God."

"Does the Reverend believe in the Devil?"

"I don't know. It's never come up."

"Doesn't he ever preach about the Devil?"

"I don't know, but he's a very positive person. He likes to focus on the *good news*, so maybe not."

"He has to know the Devil's biggest weapon is to stay anonymous. He wants us to forget about him; To not believe he's real."

"I think it's time for you to leave."

I nodded.

I stood up and pointed my Glock at his head.

Still as a statue. Who looks down the barrel of a gun and doesn't flinch?

"I told you, I'm not the Corpus Killer."

Did his lips move?

"And I told you I knew that," I said.

"Wait." He said it as a command.

"Do you believe faith can move mountains?" I pressed on.

"You seem fascinated with religion."

A new tact?

I didn't argue.

"Faith can do and be many things. Yes, I believe a person with faith can indeed move mountains. A person with faith can change the world. But too many people have twisted their faith. They are not on the right path. They are being misled and misguided. Faith can also be blind." *Babbling or stalling?* "A person blinded by faith might ignore those same mountains, assuming God will move them for him. People need leadership, a guiding beacon, steering their path. My work with Reverend Johnson will provide that path."

"There's a lot of truth in that," I said.

"Yes, yes. And trying to hurt me, or anyone, wouldn't sit well with your future."

"You mean the future of my eternal soul?"

"Yes. Exactly."

"But I'm not worried about my soul. How's yours doing?"

"My soul?"

Off balance, again. Two for me.

"Yeah. Are you worried about *your* eternal soul?"

He didn't answer. For the first time since I entered the room, I saw real emotion on his face. And instead of fear, it was anger.

"You won't get away with this," he said as he started to stand up. "I'm not afraid of guns."

"That's okay. You don't need to be."

I pulled the trigger. The gun bucked in my hand, the recoil sending the nozzle up toward the ceiling. A blinding light flared from the barrel.

But there was no sound.

"Faith can do a lot of things."

No bullet escaped the barrel. And no hole appeared in Amos' forehead. But his body, starting from his head down, exploded into a fine dry mist.

"Including sending your ass back to Hell."

The mist that, moments before, was Amos, burned up like the tiniest pieces of flash paper.

I returned the pistol to my holster.

Time to go.

ABOUT THE AUTHOR

MARTIN KLUBECK is the author of *The Adventures of Sir Locke the Gnome* and *The Timewarp King,* His short story, *"The Monster Next Door"* was published in *The Monsters Next Door* anthology. He is currently working on the first of his Goode Knight mysteries - they're just a little south of cozy.

THE CURIOUS AFFAIR AT THE ARKWRIGHT CLUB

Mike Murphy

Wine! *Hundreds* of bottles.

"This is *quite* a wine cellar!" Marshall Leibowitz remarked as he and the white-haired cork master, Frank Remley, walked down the slightly creaky stairs into the large, climate-controlled basement room.

"No other wine club can boast of vintages rarer than those here at Arkwright," Remley said proudly as the two men stepped onto the floor and looked out over the wooden racks.

"I would think not!"

"As a member, you will have access to *all* of these wines."

"Really?" Leibowitz asked excitedly.

"In a 'diplomatic' fashion."

"What do you mean by that?"

"We can't possibly partake of every vintage we have in the racks," the older man explained, "so, at our monthly meetings, the members vote for the wine that should be enjoyed at our *next* meeting. Whatever bottle gets the greatest number of votes is properly prepared and served then."

"I *really* hope I'm voted in. I've been waiting for an opening here ever since I moved to the city."

"I have no doubt you will be admitted at today's meeting."

"Seriously?"

"As a young attorney, you are just the kind of professional we're looking for as a new member," Remley told Marshall. "It is, of course, *terribly* sad that Mr. Raymond passed on."

"I had the honor of working on some legal documents for him. He was a fine man."

"But, without his death, there would not be an opening here at Arkwright."

"You *really* think I'll be admitted?"

"I'd say you can count on it," Frank commented. "As a member, you'll be expected to donate four hours a month of your time to the club's care and upkeep."

"That's *in addition* to the yearly dues?"

"It is," Remley said. "Is that a problem?"

"No, but isn't such a stipulation... well... excessive?"

"Not at all. Our charter has maintained that requirement since the club's founding in 1928 by Simon Arkwright. In this way, we save funds that would have to be spent on hired help, allowing us to invest instead in the acquisition of rare vintages. *Everyone* donates his time." Remley paused, smirked, and inquired, "Do you wish *not* to be considered for membership any longer?"

"Oh no. Certainly not!" Leibowitz replied, quickly dispelling the notion. "Any true wine connoisseur would be a *fool* to pass up the opportunity. I was merely taken by surprise."

"If you have physical limitations that prevent you from performing certain tasks, please inform the secretary after you are admitted. We don't wish to cause our members any bodily harm."

"I can do whatever might be needed."

"That's good to know," Remley told him. "Colonel Thrip, 88 years old and sharp as a tack, recently had to stop assisting with the club's upkeep. Bad heart, you know?"

"I'm sorry to hear that."

"But with him being the Colonel and having been a member in fine standing of Arkwright since the *Carter* Administration, we have waived that requirement for him." Frank gestured at the many wooden racks. "Perhaps you'd like to perform your service here, tending to the bottles? We need someone for that chore."

"I would like that very much, and it *wouldn't* be a chore." Leibowitz reached out and removed a random bottle from one of the racks. He blew the dust from the label and could not believe his eyes. "The '47? I've only heard rumors of its existence." He grabbed another bottle and was equally astounded. "How did you ever come across such rare specimens?"

"The name Arkwright carries great weight in the wine world. Anything can be had... for a price."

He carefully removed another bottle. "This one is empty," he said, confused.

"Yes, it is."

Leibowitz tapped on another couple of bottles. They were also dry. "Do the members save the empties as remembrances of vintages enjoyed?" he wondered.

"Not exactly."

"Then why. . ."

"There is *one* more thing you should know about Arkwright." Remley stepped forward and removed an empty bottle from a rack. "Our secret," he said proudly. He pulled the cork from the bottle's neck. The wine cellar began to violently shake. Dust fell from the ceiling, and many of the bottles dinged against one another.

"It's an earthquake!" Leibowitz exclaimed.

Remley was strangely, totally calm. "Don't be alarmed."

ȣ

"We have to get out of here! The whole place is going to collapse!" Leibowitz called.

"Just a moment longer," Remley told him.

"How can you know th–" And the shaking quickly stopped. "I'll be damned."

Still holding the empty bottle, Remley approached Leibowitz and brushed some dust from his suitcoat. "Are you alright?" he asked.

"Yeah," Marshall responded, "but my nerves may never be the same. You?"

"Don't you worry about me. I've been through this before."

"There have been other earthquakes?"

"That *wasn't* an earthquake."

"But the whole room –"

"Would you like to know what that was?"

"Of course."

Remley pointed to a door on the far wall. "Open it," he instructed the club's would-be member. "The answer lies there." Though he had taken a good look around the wine cellar, Marshall hadn't noticed that door when he first came down the stairs.

"How'd that get there?" he asked. "It wasn't there before the shaking started."

"True, but it is now," Remley teased. "Aren't you curious what's on the other side?"

"I *know* what's on the other side: Washington Street."

"I wouldn't be so sure," Frank told him. "Open it!"

"Why should I?"

"It's about time you learned Arkwright's secret. I don't share this information with just anyone, but I feel a certain... kinship with you." Together, they walked to the door. Leibowitz slowly reached out and clutched the doorknob. "You can't be hurt by what's on the other side," the cork master assured him.

Gathering his courage, Marshall turned the knob and quickly opened the door. This wasn't the snow-covered road he was driving on earlier. The sun was shining on passing pedestrians, and some birds were chirping happily. "This *isn't* Washington Street."

"I *know.*"

"Where. . ."

"Italy."

Leibowitz's brain heaved, and then he uneasily chuckled. He said, "I know what's happening: It's a gag you play on potential members."

"Not at all."

"Then how could we –"

"The proof is in the pudding," Remley said, and he took a couple of steps toward the threshold. "Follow me."

"Out *there?*"

"Where else?"

"We can't –"

"You will see some *amazing* things," the older man told him. "Come."

ϫ

Leibowitz was incredulous as he and Remley walked along. They truly were in Italy! "I've been here before – a few years ago – with my wife," he said, "but it looks... different."

"That's because we are in the Italy of 1971," Remley told him.

"What?"

"We have not only traveled in location, but in time." He gestured at the people passing by. "Notice the fashions," he remarked. "Hideous!"

"I don't understand any of this."

"It is the secret of Arkwright – the thing that makes us so special."

"Why is no one paying us any mind?" Marshall asked after looking around.

"They can't see or hear us."

"We're... invisible?"

"This is *their* time. We don't belong here."

"I can't buy that."

"No?" Remley queried before loudly announcing, "All Italian women are ugly and should be on leashes!"

Marshall anxiously grabbed his arm. "What are you doing?"

"Proving my point," Frank explained. "Did anyone react to what I just said?"

"No... No they didn't."

"And don't you think that remark should have bought me a *pack* of trouble?"

"Yes, if these people could. . ."

"I rest my case."

8

The wine shop was tiny, and the many patrons milling about made it seem even tinier. Frank guided Marshall to a particular display. "Did you stop here when you visited Italy with your wife?" he asked.

"It's a coffee shop now."

"Pity."

"Why are we here?"

"To acquire some fine vintages for the wine cellar."

"But no one can see or hear us," Leibowitz mentioned. "How are we going to pay?"

"We aren't."

"Stealing?"

"I wouldn't be concerned about breaking the law," Remley told him. "You weren't even *alive* in 1971. How can you be convicted of shoplifting that occurred before you were born?" Frank stopped at a display and began rummaging through the offerings.

"I can't do this," Leibowitz told him. "I've never broken the law." Smiling broadly, Remley held a bottle in front of Marshall's eyes. "Oh my God!" he exclaimed, touching it as gingerly as one would touch a newborn. "Is that *real?*"

"It certainly is."

"That vintage is impossible to find. I know. I've tried."

"It's easy to find in 1971," Remley said. "Take two bottles. I'll take two myself."

"I *can't.*"

"Don't you want to enjoy this wine as Arkwright's newest member?"

"I do," an ashamed Leibowitz admitted after a short pause.

"Then take a bottle in each hand and follow me back to the wine cellar."

"They'll see us."

"When we touch the bottles, they will become invisible as well."

"Are you certain?" Leibowitz asked.

"As long as the Arkwright wine cellar is in this time, we cannot be seen or heard." He shortly grew frustrated. "Do you want the wine or not?"

"Are you *sure* we can't get into trouble?"

"How do you think Arkwright has so many rare bottles in our wine cellar in the first place? I've done this dozens of times with absolutely *no* difficulty." He took down two bottles and held them close. "Well?" he said, prompting his traveling companion. Leibowitz looked around, sighed, and – against his better judgment – did the same.

8

The wine cellar started shaking again when Remley closed the door to 1971. Before long, it ended. Leibowitz took this to mean they were back in the present day. "Are your bottles alright?" Frank asked him, as he started putting his two in some empty slots on a rack.

Marshall glanced at the stolen wine. "Just fine," he answered, his mind conflicted.

"Put them with mine before anything happens to them."

"OK, but then I want some questions answered."

"*Later*. It's almost time for the vote on your membership."

8

"Congratulations," the tall, curly-haired man said to Marshall as he strode up to him in the club's common room. "Welcome to Arkwright."

"Thank you."

"Make sure to pay your dues on time," the shorter man beside him joked.

As he watched them walk away, Marshall heard a quavering voice say, "Mr. Leibowitz?"

He turned quickly and recognized the elderly, balding man sitting enveloped in the large wing chair from his many television documentaries. "Colonel!" he exclaimed happily. "I didn't see you there."

"That's because I've grown shorter and more frail over the years," Thrip suggested.

"Not at all. It's an honor to meet you in person," he told the older man. "My father has a collection of *National Geographics*. I remember reading about your African safaris. Fascinating stuff!"

"I'm glad you enjoyed the accounts, son, but those were *ages* ago," he responded. "I was wondering if you might be available for dinner. The meeting should be breaking up soon."

"I would enjoy that," Leibowitz replied. "Is this concerning a legal matter?"

"Yes," Thrip answered quickly. "How about Georgio's? Do you like Italian?"

Marshall chuckled slightly and answered that he did.

"Is something wrong?"

"Not at all," Leibowitz assured him. "I've visited Italy... *twice*. Isn't it difficult to get a reservation at Georgio's?"

"Not when you know the proper people."

"And when you're Colonel Reginald Thrip."

"I suppose my name *does* carry some weight," the older man agreed. "I'll get us a private room."

ᚻ

The walls of the room the teenage waiter led Thrip and Marshall to were covered in a vibrant fresco of an Italian village on a bright, sunny day. Music Leibowitz expected would be playing came faintly through overhead speakers – loud enough to enjoy but not to stifle conversation.

They had barely stepped through the archway than Georgio, the owner, was upon them. The corpulent, middle-aged man had doffed the jacket of his too-small three-piece suit some time earlier. A grease- and sauce-stained apron hung about his hefty waist. He gently took the Colonel's withered right hand in his own calloused one. "My friend," he jovially remarked, "it has been some time."

"It certainly has," Thrip agreed.

"I will be waiting on you *personally* this evening."

"Excellent." The Colonel gestured at Marshall. "May I present Mr. Leibowitz, Arkwright's newest member."

Georgio grasped Marshall's right hand and shook it heartily. "Congratulations, sir," he said. "A pleasure."

"Nice to meet you," Leibowitz returned.

The owner showed the two of them to the room's only table. "Do I *dare* bring our paltry wine list to men of the prestigious Arkwright Club?" he asked.

"Just get us a bottle of my usual."

"Yes, Colonel," Georgio replied, walking briskly away and calling over his shoulder. "I'll bring your antipasto momentarily."

ರ

"What legal matter did you want to discuss, sir?" Leibowitz asked as they settled in.

The older man was embarrassed, but answered, "I... uhm... lied about that."

"I'm sorry?"

"I wanted to speak with you about Arkwright. I had to feign the need for some legal advice to get you alone for a time. I apologize."

Marshall was very confused. "What do you want to talk about?" he inquired.

"Right up front," Thrip admitted, "I should tell you that I was one of the two people who blackballed your membership."

"May I ask why?"

"I didn't want a fine young man like you to get involved in a godforsaken club like Arkwright."

ರ

"Your antipasto," Georgio announced as he placed the laden plate on the table between his two customers.

"Thank you," said the Colonel.

He plucked the chilling wine from the standing ice bucket one of his waiters had brought and showed them both the label. "It is to your liking?" he asked.

"Very good," Thrip commented.

"Shall I open it for you?"

"No thank you."

Georgio placed the wine back in the ice and inquired, "What would you gentlemen like for your dinners?"

"A steak for me," the older man said. "A *thick* one, medium rare, with all the trimmings."

"Wonderful choice." The big man turned to Leibowitz. "And you, sir?"

"The same."

"Medium rare too?"

"Please."

"I will place your orders with my chef. If you require *anything*, just ask."

As Georgio walked away, Thrip said, "They make an excellent steak, Leibowitz. You'll enjoy it."

"I'm sure I will," Marshall agreed. "Can we get back to Arkwright now?"

Thrip slowly removed his glasses and rubbed his tired hazel eyes. "Of course."

"You called it 'godforsaken.'"

"I did, and being a Christian, that *isn't* a word I use lightly."

"Why has God forsaken the Arkwright Club, Colonel?"

"It has a *terrible* secret."

"Time travel?"

"You *know* about that?" Thrip asked, amazed.

"Mr. Remley demonstrated it to me earlier today. We went to 1971 Italy."

"Then it may be too late," the Colonel said. He pounded table. "Damn it! I should have acted earlier! If Remley's taken you on a time hop, it means he considers you a likely donor."

"Donor?'" Marshall repeated.

"Did he convince you to bring anything back to the present?"

"Just a couple of bottles of wine."

"Wasn't that against your morals?"

"Well... yes," Leibowitz admitted, embarrassed, "but he assured me no harm would be done."

"That's what he tells *everyone*. That's what his predecessor told me so long ago." Thrip leaned closer to his dinner guest. "Didn't you wonder how the time hop was possible?"

"No. I... I didn't," Marshall replied, surprised that he hadn't. "I suppose I was astounded by the trip."

"Remley counts on that for his donors."

"That's the second time you've used that word," Leibowitz said. "Tell me, Colonel, how is the time travel possible?"

Thrip sighed heavily. "The club was founded in 1928," he began, putting his spectacles back on. "It was a modest success. Simon Arkwright was a connoisseur of fine wines. He hoped to instill that love into the people of Boston and, in doing so, become incredibly rich." He leaned back in his chair and asked, "You know what happened the following year?"

"The stock market crash."

"Even for the well off, the wine club was a dispensable luxury. Membership plummeted, and Arkwright was faced with bankruptcy. The story goes that he turned to an unusual source for help."

The pentagram completely drawn on the rug of the club's wood-paneled common area, Arkwright read the incantation. Almost immediately, there was a clap of thunder, and he was no longer alone. "It's you," he said to the devious-looking man who had appeared in a puff of smoke before him. "It's really you!"

"Why are you surprised?" his visitor asked in a voice like a hiss. "You called me, and I answered. I am always ready to talk business."

"You know what I want?" Simon asked.

"Yes: The most successful wine club in the country."

"In the world!"

"Even better," the Devil said, smiling. "I can provide you with that."

"In this economy?"

"You will have to turn members away," he hissed. "I will want something in return."

"What?"

"What do I always want?"

Simon swallowed hard and said, "I understand."

"We'll start with yours, and we'll work out an agreement for me to get many others."

8

"Souls?" Leibowitz asked Colonel Thrip after Georgio brought them their dinners and wished them a pleasant meal.

"Precisely," he agreed, cutting half-heartedly into his steak. "As part of their agreement, Simon was given dozens of empty bottles, all of which – when the cork was removed – would transport him and anyone else in the wine cellar to the location and year on the label."

"That's what Remley and I did this morning! It was an Italian wine. The cellar shook like an earthquake."

"I know," an embarrassed Thrip said. "I am one of those who sold my soul to Arkwright."

"How?"

"Simon bested me in a battle of wits," the older man recalled, "and I mistakenly agreed to the arrangement."

"There must have been some document you had to sign."

Thrip chuckled slightly. "You're thinking like a lawyer. It's a verbal agreement." He took a swallow of wine to fortify himself and continued. "When Simon fell ill years ago, he groomed Remley to be his successor and carry on his... arrangement. The full power of the deal with the Devil now rests with Frank Remley."

"Are you saying that I. . ." Marshall started, alarmed.

"I don't believe so, but the time hop he took you on shows that he thinks you can be added to his list of donors. Some of them were told the story of Arkwright and the Devil. They laughed it off."

"How could they?"

"If you had heard it from anyone but me, wouldn't you have thought it a fiction?" the Colonel asked him.

"What are the rules of the deal?"

"I'm not sure."

"Then how –"

"I've seen the ledger Remley keeps – a list of all the members whose souls he's earned for Satan. He's blatantly updated it in front of my eyes, knowing that there is nothing I can do to change my destiny."

"And he wants to add my name to that ledger?" Marshall asked.

"I believe so," Thrip replied. "You must be very careful in your dealings with him. He will get you to give your soul away before you know it."

"I'll be careful, sir" Leibowitz assured his dinner companion. "Where does Remley keep this ledger?"

"Tucked away behind a loose brick along the south wall of the wine cellar."

"We'll have to get it."

"What good will that do?"

"It will show us who's loyal to Remley and can't be counted on for help," Marshall explained. "You and I can –"

"No, no," Thrip interjected, turning pale. "I'm sorry, but I cannot."

"Colonel?"

"I am a weak man. Not only old and infirm, but weak in spirit and, especially, in character."

"You?" Marshall asked. "That's not possible. I read all about –"

"My exploits among animals are legendary," Thrip continued, "but I am a coward when it comes to people."

"All I need you to do is keep Remley occupied while I go down to the wine cellar."

"I cannot."

"Colonel –"

"Please do not ask me again!" Thrip cried, his eyes welling. "So many before you have lost their souls – men I might have been able to save – but I was afraid. My condemned soul and I have to live in shame with that fact."

8

In the dim light, Leibowitz struggled with the brick. "Come on, come on," he murmured. After what seemed like an eternity, it came free. He put it down at his feet and reached into the hole in the wall, withdrawing the ledger. He flipped through the handwritten entries. This was most of the membership! There were precious few men he might rely on.

He heard the sudden voice behind him. "What are you doing?"

"Mr. Remley," he said, turning slowly and hiding the ledger behind his back. "I didn't see you."

"Obviously," the cork master replied. "Did you forget that no member is allowed down here without my company?"

"I... I guess I did."

"Such an offense is grounds for dismissal."

"Then I'll be going," Marshall said, taking a couple of steps.

"Not with my ledger you won't," Frank insisted. "Who told you about it?"

"That's none of your business."

"I underestimated you," Remley told Leibowitz, pacing before him. "I thought you would be an easy mark – another soul for the taking."

"You were wrong."

"I will not allow you to ruin what I have built here. My deal has made me *very* wealthy. You saw in our time hop how easy it is to take what we want."

"I shouldn't have listened to you."

"Who got hurt by what you did?"

"*I* did. I'm ashamed of myself."

"I still feel that kinship with you," Remley said, leaning into Leibowitz's personal space. "I'm offering you the opportunity to remain a member here. Hand me that ledger and never mention it to anyone."

"I can't do that."

"There's one factor of my bargain that no one else knows: I am allowed to bring back *anything* I wish from the time hops."

"Really?"

"Money, jewels, artwork. Whatever I touch is mine. I have accumulated a sizeable nest egg that I am willing to share with you. You could retire immediately, never work another day in your life. All for a mere soul."

"*Definitely* not."

Remley slowly removed a revolver from his coat pocket. "I tried to reason with you," he continued. "Now I'm *ordering* you: Put the ledger back where it was." Leibowitz reluctantly did so. "And the brick." Marshall picked it off the floor and eased it back into the hole.

"Happy?" he sarcastically asked.

"*Happier*," Remley clarified. "We're not done yet."

"No?"

"You're too honest – a threat to my pursuit of wealth. It's time for us to take another time hop together." He withdrew an empty bottle from the wooden rack before him.

"Where to?" Marshall asked.

"That's a surprise, but for you, it will be a one-way trip. I'm going to leave you there to fend for yourself."

"Put down the gun, Remley."

"Colonel!" Leibowitz exclaimed as the elderly man joined them.

"Thrip," Frank said. "I'm surprised you made it down the stairs."

As the Colonel walked into the dim light, the gun in his right hand became visible to the other men. "I'd watch your mouth," he remarked, pointing it at the cork master.

"So, the great Colonel Thrip has a weapon. However, unlike your much-ballyhooed safaris, your would-be prey is *also* armed."

"It seems we have a stand-off."

Remley held the bottle high in one hand. "Ready for a time hop, Colonel? Mr. Leibowitz will not be returning from this one... and neither will you."

"You forget that I'm armed."

"You don't have the *courage to* shoot a human being. I've known you for years. Simon knew you. You're weak, a coward."

"Even a coward has his moment," Thrip said.

"And *this* is yours?" Frank asked, amused.

"I can't allow you to do to him what you did to Miller, Norton, Lawford, and the rest. I should have acted long ago, but I didn't. For that, I am ashamed."

"And how will a coward like you stop me?"

A shot rang out. Remley collapsed onto the floor, a bullet in his right leg. As he fell, he dropped the bottle, which rolled away, and his gun. He screamed in pain, clutching at the flowing wound. Leibowitz scooped up the revolver. "Even a coward can have *one* moment of bravery," Thrip told the bleeding man before turning to Marshall. "We'll have to smash all the empties. That will prevent any further time hops."

"You *can't!*" Remley called through gritted teeth.

"Do you care to see if I have a *second* moment in me?" The Colonel turned to Leibowitz, who was standing in the dim light, staring transfixed at the bottle. Thrip walked slowly towards the young man, keeping an eye on Remley. "Are you alright, son?" he asked.

Leibowitz defiantly strode to the cork master. "Is *this* where we were going?" he screamed at him, waving the bottle in his face. "Is this where you were going to *leave me?*"

"Damn right it was!" Remley answered.

Thrip gently took the bottle from Marshall's shaking hand. In shock, he read the label to himself: "Germany, 1939."

ABOUT THE AUTHOR

MIKE MURPHY has had over 150 audio plays produced. He's won The Columbine Award and twelve Moondance awards. He's written two short films, *Dark Chocolate* and *Hotline*. His screenplay *Die Laughing* was a semi-finalist in 2020's Unique Voices Competition. His TV pilot script "The Bullying Squad" was a quarter-finalist in 2021's Emerging Writers Genre Screenplay Competition. Mike's blog: audioauthor.blogspot.com.

THE DEVIL TAKES HIS TIME

Dan Allen

The Devil came a-callin' for Chester, and Lord knows that scoundrel had it coming. Dirty lowdown coward abandoned the South in her time of need. Left his brothers bleedin' and a-dyin' behind a wall while the Yankees advanced, slaughtering everyone they found. He coulda stayed. Others did, and fought for the Southern Cross and died for the cause, like a man. But, no. Chester ran like a weasel. A coward if there ever was one.

The Devil paid no mind to burstin' cannon shells and flyin' bullets. He walked straight through the battle and never flinched. Couldn't no one see him 'cept for Chester, and there weren't no mistakin' who he was.

Chester knew the Devil. He knew him well. The way he appeared to float but managed to leave cloven hoof prints, the way he vanished only to reappear yards away, and the way he smelt like the morning-after remains of a campfire. Yes, Chester had met the Devil before. He owed the beast a debt, and renegers pay double.

The Devil came dressed all fancy, fit for a funeral. A black suit and vest covered a crimson shirt. Dark round glasses hid burning ember eyes, and perhaps as a tribute to the founder of the feast, he finished the look with a black stovepipe hat. Chester heard the whisper down low where can't no one hear and a chill went down his back. A life saved is a life owed, and the Devil come to collect.

Chester skedaddled along a creek, and before he reached the tree line, he turned. Far behind, the Devil wandered down the row of rebel soldiers, touchin' one here and there. Then, a second later, a musket ball left a little round hole in their foreheads. Smoke come out of those holes. Smoke first, and then the blood flow right behind. Oh, how the Devil took his time.

Chester ran and ran pretty near as fast as possible, and when he reckoned enough dust was put behind, he slowed to catch his breath. The fightin' had been here a day or two before, and the stench choked the air from his lungs. Here, the flies were the victors and ruled the ghostly battleground. They feasted on congealed blood, and then the nasty creatures landed on his face, teased his nostrils, and walked over his lips. Chester wiped his mouth and spat. It was enough to make a grown man lose his breakfast.

Now, Chester was familiar with death, and dyin' was why the Devil was on his trail. To be clear, it was Chester's own damn fault. He shoulda never have messed with that woman, but he always had a weakness for curly blonde hair and an oversized bosom. Oh, what a glimpse of cleavage could do to that man. Of course, he didn't know she was married at the time.

Devil whispered in Chester's ear, down low where can't no one hear, no one but Chester. Devil say," Go get your gun, son. Get your gun and shoot that man of hers down. Shoot him down dead before he gets you first."

So, Chester got his gun, and the Devil followed him, always just a step or two behind. Devil whispered in his ear and pushed him along. Chester didn't see the horned beast but knew he was there. He heard the clod-clop, clod-clop of hoven hooves against the cobblestone and smelt the sulfur sparks. Chester climbed up the steps of his lover's porch and pounded on the door, but it was the little woman with the blonde curling hair that shot him down. Surprise, surprise. A woman can hate her husband, but that don't mean she'll let somebody else take him. No siree.

That's how dumb ol' Chester done got himself killed, or woulda had the Devil not whispered in his ear and offered the dead man a deal. "You can have five more years, Chester—five more years in exchange for your soul. Now get on up, boy. Get on up out of that pool of blood and walk away."

Well, five years passed faster than a poker dealer's shuffle, and now Chester found himself amongst bloated stinkin' carcasses with the Devil close behind. And just when Chester stopped chokin' on the stench, the skies opened up, and it started to pour. The rain came down in buckets and barrels, and Chester couldn't tell if it was night or day. Wasn't long before the mud was well past his ankles, and Chester slipped and fell. Now covered in muck, he crawled on his hands and knees through the field of unburied dead. Chester slid deeper and deeper into the quagmire and looked around for help. He was up to his armpits in it now, and he stretched his neck to keep the sludge away from his mouth.

The Devil took shelter beneath the only tree still standing and patiently watched. He coulda ended this quick, stepped on Chester's back, and put him under.

Wouldn't have taken but a second or two, but the Dark Prince appeared to have no interest in gettin' dirty. No siree. That old Devil just shook his head and smiled.

Chester lunged forward, grabbed a dead man's leg, and pulled himself out. Exhausted, he closed his eyes and let the rain pound the slime off his body. At least the downpour chased away the flies and temporarily masked the smell of death.

Next mornin', Chester helped himself to a dead man's horse. He figured it wasn't stealin'. The man had no need for it anymore, anyhow. So, Chester kept movin', and the Devil followed, always a shadow or two behind. Finally, Chester cracked the whip and rode that horse until she broke.

Devil whispered in his ear, "Whatcha goin' do now, boy? Your horse done died."

Chester paid no mind. He'd been a runnin' from somethin' or other his whole damn life, and this was no different. Chester made it as far as the Mississippi and snuck aboard a riverboat. And as the boat pulled away, Chester took a look behind. He heard no clod-clop, clod-clop on the boardwalk and smelt not even the slightest hint of sulfur.

Chester smiled, figgerin' he'd finally shook himself free. He took the last of his money and tried his hand at gambling. The whiskey did its damage, and Chester got careless. He never saw the Devil touch the cards. Not long after, Chester done got himself cleaned out. Later that night, he cried in his beer and watched the big paddle wheels go 'round.

The Devil slid in behind and whispered in his ear. "You can't outrun me, boy. Ain't no one ever did, and ain't no one ever will."

Chester braced himself, expecting the worst. Perhaps the Devil planned to rip his still-beating heart from his chest or maybe take his head with the flash of a single fingernail. But instead, the Devil got nice and close, so close that Chester could feel burnin' hot breath on the back of his neck. Then that ol'son-of-a-bitch gave him a good push and sent Chester overboard headfirst into the giant churning wheel. The Devil left him for dead, or that's the way it looked.

The wide wooden slats cracked Chester's head and split it open. The next bent him in half, busted a few ribs, and sent him to the water. The third drove him into the bottom. He drifted semi-conscious through the muddy river as the paddle wheeler continued rollin' and turnin' along and left him far behind.

Perhaps the cold water revived him, or maybe it was one of them good angels, but Chester started a-chokin' and a-coughin' and soon found himself crawlin' up the riverbank. The next few days were a blur. He stumbled through the midday sun and collapsed again. Homesteaders headin' west found him, made a bed in their wagon, and nursed him back to life. They fed him hard beans and jerky. It might have been dog or gopher, but Chester had an inklin' it wasn't beef. Later, when Chester was healed enough to ride, he rewarded those homesteaders for their hospitality by stealin' a horse. He figured he was a dead man anyway, so what difference would it make if he swung from the end of a rope?

He picked up a day's work here and there, things like diggin' post holes and plowin' fields. Of course, he did a little more thievin', too. But that was more like stealin' chicken eggs than robbin' stage coaches. Finally, after a couple of weeks' ride west of the Mississippi, Chester's wounds got the better of him, and he collapsed in the saddle. The horse must've wandered for days, for he ended up in Pawnee territory. Probably somewhere in the flatlands just before the foothills of the great mountains.

Chester woke on his back, lookin' up at the stars. A fire blazed nearby, and a woman sang words he didn't know. Although she might have been a coyote 'cause she sure sounded like one. The woman blew smoke in his face, and Chester had some sort of spirit dream, hallucinations, and the like. Sometime later, he hooked up with this native woman, and they became married. There wasn't no ceremony or nothing like that. They just said it was so. His bride, Makawee, was nothing to look at, but neither was Chester. At least she had all her teeth. He didn't. And she could easily take him in a wrassle. If love is blind, they were proof it works both ways. Not sure how they communicated, at least while the sun was up.

They settled on a godforsaken plot of land with more dust than grass. Chester tried his hand at dirt farmin' while Makawee went about the business of child makin' and homesteadin'. She built a sod shelter for them and a little corral for the livestock. With only one horse, they didn't need nuttin' bigger.

The Devil, he sure do take his time, but eventually, he came for Chester. He came to claim what was his. And when he came, he touched a blanket here and there. The running face sickness took Makawee down shortly after the twins were birthed. Poor woman lay covered with the dots, leakin' pus and smellin' worse than her own sick up. A merciful God took her quick, else Chester might've needed to finish it himself. He wasn't born into nursing. Didn't have the stomach for it. Woman, child, or horse, if somethin' got too sick, then it's best to put a bullet in its brain.

Makawee's passin' hung over the homestead like a bad moon. Life had changed without the woman around, and there wasn't a man alive who could've worked hard enough to replace her. Chester tried; Lord knows he tried. But some things are written in the wind. They are meant to be, and the Devil was a waitin'.

In the meantime, Chester made do best he could, cookin' an' scrubbin', but he wasn't meant to be no mother. He taught them boys to chore soon as they could walk, but still, Chester carried too heavy a load. He could barely feed himself, let alone two youngins. Lord knows he tried. He worked himself skinny, and at night, he prayed. "Oh, Lord, help me. Help me care for these boys." But only the Devil heard his prayer. He had already put his mark on this man, and Chester was his to do with as he pleased.

The Devil lingered, biding his time. Perhaps he thought Chester hadn't suffered enough, or maybe he just enjoyed the chase. When the weather turned cold, the Devil whispered in Chester's ear. He spoke real low so only Chester could hear and he planted a suggestion. It was a dark and ugly idea, but Chester mistook it as a sign from above.

Next mornin', he woke them boys, dressed them in their best, and marched them to the top of Lookout Ridge. And there they stood each a side of him, all tall and proud, leaning over the edge. Far below, the prairie dust carried whispers of the Devil's advice. Chester put a hand on one son's back and, with the slightest pressure, he made a choice.

The other son screamed and tried to pull away, but Chester held him by the ear and tried to explain. "There now, boy. With only one of you, I'll be able to manage just fine."

But the other son would have none of it. No, siree, that wouldn't pass. The child acted out. Kickin' and a screamin' and trying to punch his father. Chester didn't take kindly to the ruckus and gave this son a little push as well.

A chill passed over Chester, and he'd felt that chill before. The eyes of darkness were watchin', and Chester scanned the valley for those familiar glowing embers. But the Devil wasn't that far away. He stood just a step or two behind, where he'd been all along.

Later that night, Chester sat on his little porch and looked at the stars, ashamed and uncertain of what he had done. The silence in his hut roared louder than a waterfall. He missed his children, but most of all, he missed Makawee, and he lowered his head and prayed.

"Oh, Lord, bring her back to me. I need her. I'll do anything. Please. Please."

Of course, the Dark Prince was the only one there to hear Chester's plea and whispered in his ear. Low and soft so only Chester could hear. "If I do this, both your souls are mine."

Chester sobbed and nodded. That was all the Devil needed, and he vanished into the ground. The Devil already owned Chester's soul, and Makawee's wasn't available for the takin', but the Devil seemed happy enough to oblige. Perhaps he wanted to participate in a grotesque circus of the bizarre. Something evil and twisted.

The Devil dug through the dirt, and he found Makawee's rotting corpse. Then, the Devil made himself at home.

Just before dawn, Chester felt a gentle hand on his face. A familiar touch and he opened his eyes. Makawee put a finger on his lips, crawled under the sheet, and then let him have his way. Just before the deed was done, Chester heard a coyote howl and smiled, having heard that song before.

The lovemakin' was good, and Chester tried to make it last. In his mind, he went over all their best moments, all his memories, and he slipped into a daydream. But something wasn't right, and the warmth was gone. He smelled the putrid battlefield and the bloated, sun-baked bodies of the dead. Beneath him lay Makawee, one eye missing and her skin peeled from her cheek. A worm crawled out of her mouth, and the Devil laughed, and then he pulled a rib from Makawee's chest. He snapped it off quick and stabbed it into Chester. He plunged it in deep. The Devil stuck Chester straight through the heart and then twisted.

Chester lay, bleedin' out beside his decomposed Makawee, and the Devil leaned in close. The Devil, he whispered, soft and low so only Chester could hear. "Be careful what you wish for, boy. Be careful."

ABOUT THE AUTHOR

DAN ALLEN is Canadian and lives in Ontario. When not writing, he travels the world with the love of his life, seeking out diverse cultures and fascinating people. He enjoys sailing, eating new foods, and exploring ancient civilizations. He has survived three expeditions to the Mayan ruins in Central America, explored the Canyons of the Ancients in Southern Colorado, and visited the Pueblo cliff dwellings at Mesa Verde. In addition, he recently returned from traversing the Inca trail from Cusco to Machu Pichu. This past summer, he enjoyed a mystical experience at Stonehenge that requires further analysis. Dan's short stories appear in numerous magazines, anthologies, and podcasts. Visit www.danallenhorror.com to see a presentation of his published work. Follow him on Facebook and X at @danallenhorror. You can write to Dan at contact@danallenhorror.com

JAMES AND THE PRINCE OF DARKNESS

Kevin Lauderdale

"James?"

"Sir?"

"I am in a bit of pickle, James."

"Indeed, sir?"

"I seem to have sold my soul to the Devil."

"*Indeed*, sir."

Careful readers will not have missed my valet's emphasis of that particular "indeed." James rarely emphasizes, and when he does, it indicates an enterprise of great pith and moment.

Diabolism is not the usual topic of conversation to be found at my breakfast table. Ordinarily, as I peruse my copy of the *Times* and examine the morning post, James stands by ready to assist, and he and I engage in a spirited discussion of the news of the day. Anyone sharing my toast and marmalade can expect yours truly, Reggie Brubaker, to be up to snuff not only on the weather, but also which horses at Kempton Park are worthy of a solid turf investment.

And as you sip your Lapsang souchong, while looking out of my breakfast nook's window upon the most fashionable view in London (you can see the Ritz from my apartment on Piccadilly), James will be similarly well-versed on The Foreign Situation and prepared to discuss the exclusion of gnomes at the Chelsea Flower Show.

It was not so on that day.

"Yes, James," I said. "Sorry to impose, but I'm afraid I may need your help on this one."

"As you say, sir."

"You were a dashed good sport about helping me to get out of my engagement to that fairy princess. And I certainly appreciate your assistance with the ghost of Lord Sandwich. Not to mention that you played an integral role in finding my periwinkle tie only yesterday. Stout yeoman's work all around, I say."

"You are too kind, sir. Perhaps, if you would inform me of the particulars of the situation."

"Ah, yes. Well…" I took a large sip of tea to fortify the inner Brubaker. "It started last night at my club. Ox Cartman was having his stag night. He's marrying the daughter of Judge Bowles. You remember Bowles, James? The one who dunned me a fiver for jaywalking in Drury Lane."

"Ah, yes," said James. "'The Hanging Judge.'"

"Exactly. In any case, Ox had downed a bottle of champagne and was taking on all comers at billiards. Well, that is my game, so I could not let the challenge go unmet. But, hark the sequel. He won. Twice in a row, in fact. Thus, completely emptying my pockets of all available brass. After meeting such a Waterloo, I decamped to the club library."

James nodded sagely, and I continued, "I am ashamed to admit, James, that I paced about, idly running my fingers along copies of Dickens and *Wisden*, muttering aspersions against the good name of Cartman, all the way back to those ancient forebears of his who were the first porters. I accused old Ox of having... well the phrase I used was, 'the Devil's own luck.' And then, after some business with a brandy bottle, I said that I'd sell my soul for that kind of luck."

"Ah," said James. "The operative phrase, I believe."

"Quite so. I would have sworn that I was alone in the library, but no sooner had I spoken that o.p. when I caught a whiff of sulfur. I turned around, thinking I had somehow missed some bloke there, and he had just lit up a cigarette. Well, there was someone there. Most definitely not an invitee to Ox's stag party."

"How so, sir?"

"To begin with, his clothes. All red velvet: jacket, trousers, waistcoat, and tie. Vermillion with black piping. Not the thing, James. Not at all. Clearly not from a Savile Row tailor. Oh, also, his skin was bright red, and he had horns and cloven hooves."

"*Indeed*, sir?"

"That's the second time, James. You're making me a bit nervous."

"My apologies, sir. Please go on."

"Well, he said his name was Mr. Nick, and he could provide me with exactly what I had requested."

"I believe I can see the rest clearly, sir. In your... impaired state—"

"I was not at my best, James, that much is so."

"You signed."

"In blood, James."

"*Indeed*, sir."

Third time. "Oh, is it that dire?"

"Infernally. What next, sir?"

"Well, then I went back and beat Ox for three straight games. Then I cleaned out Dicky's pockets in darts, and Flippy's at pitch penny. All told, I cleared ten bob. Not bad for a night at the club." I took another swig of tea. "But, in retrospect, I'd rather still be able to call my soul my own. My actions as a younger man, particularly during my college days, may not guarantee me admission into Heaven, but such uncertainty is preferable to reserved seating in Hell. But you have an idea, eh James? Surely, you can get me out of this."

"Possibly, sir. You did say, 'the Devil's own luck'? That was the exact phrase?

"Yes. Important, is it?"

"Possibly. I may have an idea, sir. Give me half an hour."

I did so.

8

Half an hour later, I had changed from my gray silk pajamas into gray flannels and the aforementioned periwinkle tie.

I met James in the sitting room.

He handed me a card. "If you will be so good as to read from this, sir."

I glanced at it. "What's all this, James?"

"My assumption is that you wish to break the contract."

"Yes."

"Then we shall have to open negotiations."

I read from the card. "'Beelzebub, Prince of

Demons, Lord of Flies, and Prince of Darkness, I call upon you to appear—'"

There was the whiff of sulfur, and Mr. Nick stepped out from behind the left side of my Chinese silk screen as if he were the Villain in a Christmas panto on stage at the West End. He was still wearing the egregious red velvet outfit.

"Ah, Mr. Brubaker," said Mr. Nick, his voice silky like the skin of a snake. "What an unexpected pleasure to see you so soon."

I nodded. "Allow me to introduce my valet, James."

"Indeed," said James simply.

The Devil sniffed in James' direction. "Do I know you?" he asked. He squinted. "You seem vaguely familiar."

"I am unaware of any previous acquaintance," said James.

"Hmmm," muttered the P. of D. "Yes, vaguely... Oh, well. It is of no consequence." He turned to me. "Well, Mr. Brubaker, I imagine you've had second thoughts about our agreement. Seller's remorse?"

"Exactly," I said. Was he going to offer me a way out? Perhaps conversion to a lease with option to buy? That's how my cousin Alfred came to own his cottage in the Cotswolds.

"Too bad," Mr. Nick said flatly. "Our contract is unbreakable."

Damn, I thought. Appropriately so, at least.

James coughed the cough of the perennially discrete.

"Yes?" I said.

"Yes?" said Mr. Nick.

"Perhaps I might offer a suggestion."

"I don't know why," said the Author of Sin. "I feel neither the inclination nor the compulsion to negotiate." He turned to me. "You've signed, Reggie—I may call you Reggie, mightn't I? I feel I know you so well. And we will be spending a great deal of time together in the future." I nodded weakly, and he continued: "Excellent. You have signed and that is that. You did receive the luck you requested, didn't you?"

"Yes," I said.

"Quid pro quo," said Mr. Nick. "My half of the arrangement was satisfied, so now it's up to you. I'm in no hurry. Even if I say so myself, my terms are very generous. We didn't stipulate luck for last night only. You may continue to enjoy your wonderful luck until you die. Possibly decades from now, due to old age, in bed, surrounded by a loving family." He grinned a horrible grin, and I saw, for the first time, his teeth. (The light had been dim in the club library.) They were twisted needles of ivory, spirals that, clearly, once they clamped down into something, would be nearly impossible to pull out. "And then I'll take your soul."

James asked, "If you are not open to negotiations, then why are you here?"

"It amuses me to see mortals squirm."

James said, "Merely for the sake of thoroughness, allow me to ask the—"

"Oh, that's good," said Mr. Nick, clapping his hands together. "In how many fairy tales and short stories in *The Strand* has someone been undone with 'You never asked for it' or 'You didn't say I couldn't'?"

James continued, "Will you, Satan, please cancel Mr. Brubaker's contract with you?"

"No."

"He offers to return the luck you gave him."

"No."

"I'll throw in the ten bob I made last night!" I added.

"No," was the Fallen Angel's steely reply. He turned back to James, "Why are you negotiating for Mr. Brubaker? Are you his barrister as well as his valet?"

"No. However, as a valet, I endeavor to give satisfaction."

"Well, go ahead then. I enjoy seeing valets squirm as well as mortals."

"Why do you need all these souls anyway?" I asked.

"Hell is endothermic," said Mr. Nick.

I turned to James. "It requires heat to function," he elucidated.

"Precisely," said Mr. Nick. "Why do you think dead bodies are cold? Your heat is in your soul. Have you ever been stuck in a lift with two or three other people? You know how hot it gets in there. Same principle applies to Hell. The more souls in Hell, the warmer it gets. Hell is very large, and I like it *hot*."

"Perhaps," said James, "Mr. Brubaker could give you something else in exchange for canceling the contract. You would not get his soul, but you would be remunerated for your time."

"Oooo," chortled Mr. Nick. "Are we talking about *your* soul?"

"No," said James.

"Not willing to give that much satisfaction, eh?" He turned to me. "It's so hard to find good help these days."

James said, "It is simply a case of you having nothing that I require."

"Nothing! You are a *servant*, James! You are at the beck and call of this imbecile." He turned to me, and, with a half-nod, added, "No offense intended."

"Quite all right, old man," I replied with a toss of a hand.

"You cook his meals, do his laundry, and, apparently, get him out of all the assorted scrapes he bumbles into. And from even what little I've seen of him, that part alone must be exhausting."

"I find that being in Mr. Brubaker's employment provides infinite diversion and amusement."

"That's right," I said. "Just last month, we went to Cannes."

Mr. Nick said, "How would you like to live in Cannes all the time, James? Or, better yet, be one of those American oil millionaires? Go anywhere you wish, any time you wish. Not be dependent on this one." He nodded towards me. "Wealth, James. I can't imagine that what he pays you goes very far. In exchange for your soul…" He straightened his back as if to salute. "I could make you King."

"'To be a king and wear a crown is a thing more glorious to them that see it than it is pleasant to them that bear it,'" said James.

"Good Queen Bess," said Mr. Nick. "Didn't have any luck with her either." He pointed at my dinner table with a scarlet hand. "Simpler tastes, eh? Then how would you like a valet of your own? Have someone else bring you the filet mignon and fresh, warm bread."

"'The sky is the daily bread of the eyes,'" was James' retort.

"Reduced to quoting Transcendentalists like Emerson? That's truly pathetic. Fine, you like being a servant. I could help you with that too. I could send some of my lesser demons to be your underlings. Sous-chefs, things like that. I'm sure there's aspects of your position that even you find tedious. They could bring in the logs for the fireplaces. There's no need for you to get your feet dirty trudging about filthy London."

"'London, thou art the flower of Cities all,'" said James with an unabashed sincerity that deeply moved me.

"William Dunbar now. Of the Scottish poets, I much prefer... *Burns.* Okay, cut to the chase: How about women." Mr. Nick looked around my flat. "I can't imagine there are very many of those flitting in and out."

"'Sufficient unto the day—'" began James.

"Enough quotes!" said the Devil with a snarl. "Even I can cite scripture for my purpose. Well, here is a quote for you: 'It is better to reign in Hell than serve in Heaven.'"

"No," said James. "I am quite satisfied with my present situation. Besides, I have always doubted the sagacity of that statement."

"Then we have no deal. Mr. Brubaker's soul remains mine."

I said, "I thought everything was negotiable. Or is R.J. Wolverhampton, the author of *The Thinking Man's Guide to Modern Business Practices* mistaken?"

"Well, of course, there is cancellation and then there is nullification," said Mr. Nick. "The contract can always be *nullified.*"

Bluebirds arose and filled the sky of my heart.

"But only if both parties agree."

Bluebirds dropped from the sky like damp socks.

Mr. Nick continued, "That is part of every

contract. It will not be said that the Prince of Darkness cheats."

James said, "Mr. Brubaker was not in his usual state of mind at the time he signed. Is there a mental impairment clause that would nullify the contract?"

The Chief Deceiver smiled. "Well, true, anyone who would wear periwinkle with gray flannels…"

James said, "Gentlemen who pair red velvet with hoofs are hardly in a position to comment." Mr. Nick's eyes glowed white hot, but James added, "And who sport a tail that has clearly not been brushed in a week."

His tail whipped in front of him, Mr. Nick examined it, then pushed it away. "No such clause! The contract is unbreakable!" He snorted angrily. "Unless both parties agree. Standard details of null-and-void. I do *not* agree."

"Have you ever broken a contract?" James asked.

"Never."

"I think you may wish to in this case."

"Why?" asked Mr. Nick.

"To avoid the following: Would you care to shoot dice with Mr. Brubaker?"

"What do you mean?"

"To 'roll the bones,' I believe is the vernacular. If you win, things stay as they are. If Mr. Brubaker wins, you tear up the contract, and his soul is again his to do with as he sees fit."

The Devil smiled. "Counteroffer: If I win, I take Mr. Brubaker's soul now, and—Wait! Oh, wait, wait. Oh, you are a good and faithful servant, James." Mr. Nick spun around, his velvet jacket flapping and his hands clapping. "No, no. Mr. Brubaker is extra lucky. He has the Devil's own luck. He's guaranteed to win.

A clever notion, though. Good try."

"Would he win?" asked James. "Even against you?"

"Well, I am, of course, preternaturally lucky."

"Hence the phrase, 'the Devil's own luck.'"

"Hence the phrase," the Devil agreed. "Hmm, an interesting question. I've never tested my luck against that of a client's. Perhaps the dice would land on their points, with no resolution. His enhanced luck and my supernatural luck might just cancel each other out."

James said, "Possibly, but I believe not. You see, I believe that you are now less preternaturally lucky. I believe that you are now *unlucky*. Any luck you had is now gone, transferred to Mr. Brubaker."

"What? Preposterous!"

"Yes, your agreement with Mr. Brubaker was for 'the Devil's own luck.' Your luck, specifically."

"That's a mere expression. What you suggest is impossible. I'd know."

"What else have you done since you saw Mr. Brubaker last night?"

"Just going to and fro in the earth, and walking up and down in it. It's early yet. I rarely get started looking for souls until after lunch."

"Then you have not yet had time to realize your mistake. Shall we test it?"

James pulled a pair of dice from one of his pockets and gave them a casual shake.

What I don't know about James' past would be enough to fill half the volumes of the British Library. Had he spent his youth as a riverboat gambler on the Mississippi? Was he able to roll seven the hard way at will?

"No," said Mephistopheles. "His luck versus my luck means that the odds are already fifty-fifty. That would prove nothing."

Visions of James in a seersucker suit and straw boater sipping a mint julep dissolved before my eyes.

Mr. Nick said, "We need something more random."

"I believe I have just the thing then," said James, who produced from my sideboard, a silver, dome-covered tray. He removed the cover to reveal one of my best Wedgwood bowls containing half a grapefruit. Beside it lay a serrated grapefruit spoon.

The Devil picked up the spoon (Hooves for feet, but hands like anyone else you've ever eaten breakfast with). He circumspectly turned the bowl and then dug in to—

"Ow!"

He had been hit in the eye with a squirt of juice.

"Try again," said James, "just to be sure."

The Devil examined the pinkish-red fruit again, turned the bowl to a new configuration and—

"Ow!"

"Twice," said James. "I'd call that bad lu—"

"Don't say it," said the Devil, his face turning from bright cardinal to deep maroon.

"Oh dear," said James, "and I do believe there is a loose thread on your jacket."

The Devil began to whip his head around rapidly. "Where? Where?"

"Behind you. Where your tail separates your jacket's center vent. Does your tail dress left or right?"

The Devil spun around trying to look behind himself, and he appeared for a moment like the family dog chasing its tail.

"This does not seem promising," said James. "I suspect you could not make it to the lobby of this building without something untoward befalling you."

"Oh, do you? Well, we'll see about that."

With a huff, Mr. Nick stormed out of the parlor, opened my front door, sashayed through and—

BUMP! CRASH! THUD!

"James, did the Devil just fall down our stairs?

"Only one flight, sir."

I shall not transcribe the curses and oaths that followed.

Suffice it to say that the Devil reappeared in my parlor accompanied by his signature whiff of sulfur. His jacket looked rumpled, and I would swear that one of his horns was askew.

"What have you done to me?!" he demanded of James. "Are you some other Archangel in disguise?"

"No, just a man."

"Then how did you—"

"Nothing," said James. "You did it to yourself. You gave Mr. Brubaker the luck of the Devil."

"You're out of luck, Nick," I said.

The Dark One spun and scowled his ice pick grin at me.

"Um, *Mister* Nick?" I ventured timidly.

"What you say is both ridiculous and impossible," said the Devil to James. "Give me those dice!" James handed them to Mr. Nick, who looked at them carefully then jostled them in his scarlet palm. "These seem ordinary enough."

"They came from my Monopoly set," I said.

"Very well," said Mr. Nick. "We'll each roll one.

Highest number wins. If I win, Reggie here dies and comes to Hell immediately. If he wins, the contract is null-and-void. I don't get his soul, and whatever luck I gave him returns to me." He threw me a die.

I rolled a five.

Mr. Nick rolled a four.

The Prince of Darkness held out a rolled-up piece of paper, and we three watched it glow from within until it became a cylinder of embers, then a column of ash. Then it crumbled into a pile that singed my Afghan rug.

I felt a momentary tingle as my enhanced luck left me.

Mr. Nick held his tail close to his chest. "Never speak my name again. If either of you ever say something that draws my attention... Next time, I will not be so easily mollified."

With that, he turned and twisted into himself, disappearing with a whiff of sulfur.

"James," I said. "I need a whisky."

"Indeed, sir." He moved to the sideboard and poured me a tumbler.

I sat down in my armchair. "That," I said, "was remarkable."

James stood beside me and handed me the salver. "Not really sir. He gave you luck, but it wasn't his own."

"I don't really follow you, James."

"Millions of people must have wished for 'the Devil's own luck,' and I'm sure he's given luck to more than one person in exchange for a soul. You had only that extra luck granted to you last night. Magical as it was, it was never all of his personal luck. At no point was he without all of his preternatural luck."

"But how do you explain the grapefruit?"

"A particularly juicy variety, just arrived at the greengrocers from Florida this morning."

"The loose thread?"

"I do not know if there was one or not. As you noted, sir, it was distinctly evident that he had not used a Savile Row tailor. That, combined with the showiness of his ensemble, told me that he was insecure in his choice of outfits. I played upon that insecurity. There might have been a loose thread, and he knew it."

"The stairs, then?"

"A liberal application of butter. Do watch your step, sir, until I am able to remove it."

"Wait, so then I wasn't preternaturally lucky myself?"

"None of those things had anything to do with you, sir. You still had your enhanced luck. In order to trick him into nullifying the contract, I did not need to convince him of your good luck, just him of his bad luck. And that was easy enough to manufacture."

"So, you lied to the Devil?"

"I am sure that is not counted a sin, sir."

"But the dice? How did you know they wouldn't, um, land on their points?"

"Oh, sir. Have you ever known dice to do that?"

"No," I said. "Ah, so my luck was stronger than his there at least. I was guaranteed to win, eh?"

"No, sir, they might have still fallen in his favor. That was a calculated risk."

"A calculated risk!"

"I am not a theologian, sir."

"Fair enough. James, it may be better to reign in Hell than to serve in Heaven, but it is decidedly best to holiday in the south of France. If you take my meaning."

"I believe I do, sir. I shall arrange for tickets to Cannes immediately."

I raised my glass. "Here's to a place that is warm... but not too warm."

ABOUT THE AUTHOR

KEVIN LAUDERDALE'S work has appeared in several of Pocket Books' Star Trek anthologies, the journal *Nature*, and a handful of genre / "new weird" anthologies.

HUMAN RESOURCES: A LOVE STORY

Jean Jentilet

Looking back, I guess things were pretty far gone by the time the companywide email ordering us all to adjust our calendars for an all-hands went out.

Everyone reported to Chadwick Tower's central atrium at the appointed time, grousing about the interruption but filing into the neat rows of folding chairs nonetheless. I sat in the row closest to the refreshments table. Drew Lindsey sat next to me like always. I don't know why. We weren't friends. I've never believed in friends at work. I never went to group lunches or happy hours. How happy could an hour be if I've just spent nine of them with the same people?

"Bro, what's up with that?" Drew pointed at my left hand resting in my lap. "Lyme disease?"

I looked down. The skin around the heart-shaped splotch between my thumb and forefinger was puffy and red.

"Mosquito bite?"

It had been so long since I'd thought about that heart-shaped splotch that even I believed it was a mosquito bite. For a few minutes, anyway.

Drew looked away. "Get some calamine on it. It's gross."

The chatter around us tapered into silence as Milton Chadwick, III—Executive Vice President at Chadwick Analytics for three whole months by that point—fawn-walked up to the podium. Milty (or Wee Milty, as we called him behind his back) was the grandson of CA's founder, the original Milton Chadwick, aka Milty Prime. (We called Wee Milty's father Mid Milt. We didn't really talk about Mid Milt. He left the family business after getting lost in the Port-a-Pots at a music festival when Wee Milty was a baby.)

"Hey, everyone. Thanks for making time."

We all played along with smiles and nods, except for Drew, who crossed his arms over his chest with a dramatic sigh.

"I know there's a lot going on with the end of the fiscal year coming up." Milty spoke with the stilted, uncertain cadence of a third grader reading a book report. "But I wanted to share some updates, and get some face-to-face in. So, let's get to it. First things first. Today is an exciting day for Chadwick Analytics. As you all know, Deke Upton retired recently, after thirty-five—wow, really?—years as our Director of Human Resources. There was a lot of interest in Deke's position." From the back of the room, Lil Cosgrove cleared her throat. Lil was HR's only other employee, and had been Deke's assistant for most of his thirty-five years at CA. The thanks she got for her service was food poisoning from the club store sushi that the company served at Deke's retirement party. "It was a tough decision, but we're happy to welcome our new Director of Human Resources, Old Sc—

wait. Sorry, wrong notes. I'm getting a little conflustered…"

One of the interns that followed in Milty's wake like beer cans behind a Jet Ski during spring break cupped his mouth to Milty's ear. Milty pursed his lips and nodded.

"Sorry. Please, welcome our new Director of Human Resources—Lucifer, but he also goes by Luce, if that's easier for people to remember. That's not… that's not a problem. Luce! Come on out! Meet the whole crew!"

The hard tap of footsteps echoed from the stairs behind the podium.

"Is this a joke?" Drew muttered. "Did he say Lucifer? Is this a skit or something?"

Lucifer emerged from behind Milty, tall and ruddy in an immaculately tailored suit and thoughtfully waxed Van Dyke. No horns, no tail. Just hooves. The last time I'd seen him, he was in full regalia: horns (the big ones that could gore a grown man, not the little ones like on the cans of potted meat), cape, tail, pitchfork, skin redder than a Santa suit, yellow eyes. Different times, I guess.

Half-hearted claps bounced around the atrium. I touched the back of my hand.

Drew jabbed an elbow into my side. "Is this dude actually wearing boots that look like hooves?"

"Um…sure."

As Milty droned on about the pizza party we would get if we kept our numbers up—no more sushi, harharhar—Lucifer's eyes slid past me and settled on Drew.

"You think he heard me?" Drew asked.

"Yeah." I inched away from him as much as the tight rows would allow. "I think he might have."

ꝸ

After the meeting, Lucifer stood chatting with Wee Milty to one side of the refreshment table, mug in one hand, chocolate frosted in the other. Lil had stopped the progress of the line to flirt over the last cruller with Owen, the daytime security guard, whose whole job seemed to be sitting at the front desk and reading on his phone while the bank of monitors in front of him cycled endlessly around the building through offices and halls and elevators. Sometimes, he looked up and pretended to check badges. On good days, he would grunt in a way that could be interpreted as "good morning." All this movement and talking with Lil was a side of him I'd never seen. He plated the cruller and handed it to Lil with a little bow. I just wanted to get my donut and get back to my desk. I slipped my hand under the plate and took the first donut I touched: jelly filled.

"Gross," I muttered when I saw that oozing purple eye. Owen and Lil shot me identical annoyed looks.

"Jelly-filled." I raised my plate, but they had already gone back to their donut game.

My donut and I caught an empty elevator back to the tenth floor, where I sat in my cubicle and ate and put my mind to not scratching the back of my hand. Scratching wouldn't help. Scratching would only draw blood. That, I knew from experience.

ꝸ

In high school, I was in love with a girl named Michelle Miller. She knew I existed, but I thought about her a lot more than she thought about me. I'm pretty sure she didn't think about me at all unless I was actually standing in front of her, and even that was probably hit or miss. I didn't let that get in my way. One stop at the local esoterica shop, and I had everything I needed: grimoire, candles, salt. I locked myself in my room, made a circle of protection (which is harder to do than the movies make it look), lit the candles, and chanted the invocation that promised to raise the devil himself. Nothing happened. Not the next day, or the next week. My mother complained about the house smelling like rotten eggs and patchouli, and I had to move furniture around my room to hide the wax that wouldn't come off the floor.

It was two weeks later when I came home from school and there he was, sitting on my bed with his horns and cape and tail, flipping through my sketch pad, his pitchfork propped against a bedpost.

"Word on the street is that *you* are looking to make a deal," he said, without looking up.

I stood with my backpack dangling from my shoulder. Should I kneel? Bow? I kept talking. "I... like I said. I want Michelle Miller to love me.

He tossed my sketch pad to the foot of the bed. "No, you didn't say that. You said you wanted her. That could be taken a lot of ways, and if I was in a *mood*, you would get whatever interpretation of that I found most entertaining. But I'm not in a *mood*, so I'm giving you the opportunity to clarify."

"I want her to love me." In hindsight, I think I just wanted to have sex with her, but my brain was too awash in hormones to know the difference.

He stood and walked to the window, hands clasped behind his back, tail twitching. "A lot of people change their mind once they find out that this is not a matter of me waiving my hands and solving their problems. I can't engage in direct manipulation. I can't *make* her love you. I can't make her *do* anything. I don't like it, but rules are rules. Rules keep us right. It's a basic law of the universe. Direct manipulation catastrophically disrupts the continuum. Collapses it right back into formless firmament and all that jazz, which no one wants. But what I *can* do is give you the tools to make it happen. Tempt her to do something she wouldn't be inclined to do otherwise—open her eyes, if you will, to your potential by providing you with something that you could not obtain on your own."

"Like what?"

His cape spun out like a tutu as he turned away from the window. "You'll need to speak to her. Make eye contact. With her eyes. And…" He waved his hand up and down my body. "Tighten it up. Presentation is important."

"That's it?"

He sighed and shook his head. "No, that's not it. That's free advice that you could have gotten from a hundred magazines." He nodded towards my desk. There in the middle of it was a plain white envelope sealed with a little red dot of wax—nothing fancy, no sigils or anything.

"What's that?"

"The contract for your review. Note questions or changes in the margins. Blue ink,

please. I do reserve the right to deny my services if your suggestions are unreasonable. And then there are two front row tickets to the Buff Boys—Michelle's favorite band, correct?"

"They're not a real band, but yeah. She loves them."

"Hm. Well, you got in just under the wire. I have contracts with everyone in the first three rows. I almost had a moment of shame." He shrugged. "If you can't make something happen with that…"

I opened the envelope and slid out the tickets. Front and center.

"Thanks."

But he was gone. No snap of the fingers, no puff of smoke. Just gone. His pitchfork jittered, then it was gone, too. I checked under the bed and in the closet. I looked at the tickets again. The Buff Boys. Front and center. I read the contract over my usual after-school toaster pastry. It was a lot of words to say what he'd already told me—no direct manipulation, and in exchange for these tickets, my immortal soul would be available for any task that Lucifer (or authorized agents thereof) saw fit, in perpetuity. The contract would go into effect once I used the tickets for their intended purpose. It all seemed straightforward to me, though I did have to correct the spelling of my name in a few places.

Michelle didn't say no. Not to the concert. She even kissed me afterwards, and promised we could catch a movie that weekend. When I got home, there was another envelope on my desk, with another red dot of wax. I opened it. The notary public seal of Beelzebub glowed white between Lucifer's signature over his printed name, and a picture of Michelle and I in the front row of the concert embedded into the paper over my printed name. The deal was done. I barely slept that night, thinking about Michelle and how things would be. The next morning, there was the heart-shaped splotch on the back of my left hand. I scratched it raw for a week until I understood what it was—a reminder of my obligations.

You can figure out the rest. Michelle and I didn't go to that movie. She was busy that weekend, and every other weekend for the next year and a half. I tightened up, bought a new wardrobe, got a cool haircut. I looked her in the eyes when I asked her to prom, and she looked me in the eyes when she laughed in my face.

The heart-shaped splotch faded to just a half-shade darker than my skin. Barely there. But it never went away, and I never stopped feeling cheated. Lucifer and I had unfinished business. I had available credit on my soul, and I knew exactly how I wanted to spend it: paid vacation.

It's amazing how fast a dentist's visit here or a trip to the DMV there can add up. My fiancé, Bri, and I had been planning a trip to Koh Samui all year. Had our flights booked, hotel reserved, everything. Then I found out that Bri was also planning a trip to Sicily with her ex. After that, I needed a few days to drink, in the course of which I cancelled her half of things but kept my own. I was going, and she wasn't. That was the best revenge I could imagine. Then my appendix burst. I realized I didn't want to go Koh Samui alone, but then, my car broke down, and I got distracted with that for a week as the repairs became more and more elaborate. When I finally got back around to cancelling the rest of the trip, I'd missed all the refund deadlines. That same day, my original time off request was flagged because I was out of PTO. Flat broke. I appealed, but by then, Deke was mobility scooting into the sunset. Lil managed to pull her head out of the toilet just long enough to deny the appeal.

But Lil wasn't the final word anymore. Once my donut haze wore off, I scheduled a meeting with Lucifer in his Appointly. His calendar was nearly full, which was strange—I thought most people would be more reticent—but I found a spot. That night, I dug that old contract out from under my passport in my firesafe, and went through it, line by line, highlighting and tabbing and taking notes.

I was going to get my PTO. One way or another.

8

The HR suite was tucked into the back corner of the second floor of Chadwick Tower. Its waiting area was lined with molded plastic chairs in the oranges and yellows of old sitcoms and carpeted with an industrial nap the color of bad olives. I reported early for my appointment, my contract under my arm. Lil, her dust-gray curls tight around her face, greeted me with a smile from behind two monitors, our pastry table kerfuffle apparently forgotten.

"How's life on the tenth floor?" she asked.

I smiled back. She knew why I was there. She knew what she had done.

"Good, Lil. How's it down here with…" I glanced towards the opening in the corner that led down the hallway to the Director's office.

Her smile went stiff.

"There's always an adjustment with new folks. He's with someone at the moment, but I'll let him know you're here."

She tapped something into her computer, her fingers poking out of carpal tunnel sleeves on each forearm just enough to do her job. I settled into a chair the color of soggy autumn leaves and browsed on my phone for mindfulness techniques. The itch of my mark had become a constant distraction, but on top of the leaky faucet clacking of Lil's keyboard, it was unbearable. Ten terrible minutes later, Drew blustered out of the Director's hallway, cheeks flushed and eyes narrowed.

"That prick," he hissed as he stormed past.

A moment later, Lucifer appeared, perfect smile in place. People say he has too many teeth or that his teeth are all fangs or that his mouth is filled with blood. I'd only seen him with that perfect pitchman smile. A dentist's nightmare. No one's kid was going to college on those teeth.

"Phil! It's been month of Sundays, hasn't it?"

"It's been a while," I agreed.

"Well, come on back. Let Lil get back to her shows."

Lil scoffed and tapped harder at her keyboard.

I followed Luce back to his office, which was nice in that it had a window and some real shelves and a door that closed but was otherwise just as small and utilitarian as every other office in the building except for maybe Milty's. He settled in behind his desk, where a laptop, a phone on a charger, and a framed picture of a blonde-haired boy kneeling next to a rust-colored puppy and staring into the camera with darkly gleeful eyes were arranged in a perfect semicircle around a neat stack of papers. He motioned me to the only other chair in the room, which seemed to be made from the scraps of plastic jack-o-lantern candy buckets.

He patted his chest. "Can I just say that you've come quite a long way? Sartorially, I mean. That tie is sharp."

I tugged at my collar. "Thanks."

He sighed and kicked his feet up onto his desk. Cowboy boots today. No exposed hooves. "I'm not usually one for footwear, but I love these. The weather around here is so moody, it makes my hooves crack. These protect, and they look good, if I do say so myself." He laced his fingers behind his head. "Anyway—you wanted to discuss your PTO?"

"That's right. My PTO." I tried to remember where I had planned to start my argument. "And actually, I wanted to bring up an…an unresolved issue that—"

"Let me stop you there." He held up his hand, palm out. "I know where this is going. My policy has *always* been that if you're able to pronounce the incantation, with intent—which you did—then you're able to make the contract, and that contract was very clear. It always is. So, let's move on. About that PTO…"

"I don't think I want to move on."

I ruffled the pages of the contract. Maybe he hadn't seen it. Maybe he didn't realize that I was prepared.

"Phil, the world is full of people that think I didn't give them what they paid for. I'll tell you what I tell everybody: I have quite literally the best lawyers in creation drafting my contracts." He jabbed a finger at my yellow-flagged pile. "There are no loopholes. You're welcome to pay an attorney of your choosing five hundred an hour to tell you the same. Or we can address your current concerns regarding your PTO. Sound good?"

Every clever argument I had dreamt up, every point I had sticky-noted, disintegrated. I nodded.

"Great." He relaxed back with a leathery creak. "And close your mouth. I can see your fillings."

I closed my mouth.

"So that PTO—you're fresh out."

"Right." Back to the realm of the possible. "I didn't realize how close I was to being out, and I have a trip planned that kind of snuck up on me with a lot of personal situations. So now, I either take it unpaid, or lose all my deposits. It's a lot of money. To me, it's a lot. I appealed it, but then Deke left, and Lil denied the appeal, but I think she was delirious or something. The sushi—"

"She might have been delirious, among other things, but she made the right call. For once." He shook the mouse squatting on his desk and clicked around, grunting all the while like a doctor poking at a tender abdomen. "Mmhmm. So, I'm betting that you've never read your employee handbook. Hmm?"

"Maybe not." Definitely not.

"As I thought. PTO is transferable. For example, there was a nice story in the company newsletter when Mike Gottlieb in facilities gave some days to his wife in travel services so she could have an extra paid week of maternity leave." He arched an eyebrow. "What a prince."

"What good does that do me?" I scratched the back of my hand before I realized what I was doing.

"I can't just give you more PTO because I like your tie. Rules are rules. You know that. But, if you could find *someone* with plenty to spare who might be willing to give you a day or two—or ten—then bing-bang-boom. It's just a few days, right? Ask a friend."

"I don't—"

"Have any friends?" That smile again, with his tongue crouching behind his teeth. "The one that was just here. Smells like baby oil and cheap beer. What's his name? I've seen you two chatting." His forehead wrinkled with concentration.

"Drew? I never really smelled him, but he just left as I was coming in."

"Yes, Drew Lindsey." His face relaxed. "That's right, sorry. You can't smell souls yet."

"Souls have a smell?"

"Sure do. Each unique. It's a foolproof way to identify people trying to... hide from me, I guess, is what they're trying to do. Yours is cinnamon-ish, with a touch of the old brimstone, due to your status."

I lifted my arm and sniffed. "I don't smell anything but my dryer sheets."

"Well one, like I said, you can't yet. You're still flesh and blood. You don't get the nose for it while you're topside. And two, you can't smell yourself anyway."

"Oh. So, you're saying Drew has that much PTO to spare?"

"I can't get into the specifics of anyone's PTO status with you. Confidential." He slid his feet off the desk. "I'm just saying, use your resources. You find some days somewhere; I'll push it through ASAP."

"That's it?"

He blinked. "That's it."

Sticky notes flaked off my contract and onto the floor like dandruff as I stood. "Thanks for the tip. I guess."

"Phil, I'm here to help. But rules are—"

"Rules. They keep us right. I know."

Back out in the waiting area, Lil had a game of solitaire going on one monitor, and an old movie on the other.

"You look about as happy as your friend," she said.

"He's not my friend."

Her front-desk smile didn't move, but her eyes went wide and then her eyelids fluttered and she turned her head—just a quarter turn—like she'd heard something and was listening for it to happen again.

"Everything okay?" I asked.

She crinkled her nose. "Everything's fine."

8

I started bringing in donuts and coming in early to start coffee in the various breakrooms around the building to see who came in early. I stayed late to see who stayed late. If anyone had ten days laying around, it was the in-at-7:30-out-at-6:00 crowd. It was the easiest way I could think of to jump start some good will, and after a few days, it started to work. I cringed on the inside at the nods and waves in the hallway, but I always nodded and waved back. If I could put together a strong pool of fifteen or even ten people that I could work my case up with, then I could put together at least a few days. Maybe even the full two weeks.

I didn't believe for a second that Drew had any spare days, but on the off chance that he did, that would be one less comfort zone I had to leave. He worked on the far end of the cubicle field from me, but the breakroom was close to his desk, so I had a good excuse to pass him a few times a day with some friendly small talk. I noticed a row of wrestling figurines standing guard on top of his monitor, their plastic faces pulled into permanent scowls, muscly arms raised in threat, so I caught up on all the news in professional wrestling and formed a hundred fake opinions about it. It was important to seem sincere.

On one particularly late day, I happened upon Drew at the elevator on my way out. In ten years, I had never seen Drew Lindsey before eight-thirty or after five.

I nodded at the elevator door as it slid open. "Walk you down?"

"Sure."

In the filth-glazed stainless-steel doors—Mike Gottleib wasn't doing his job—I watched Drew's reflection as the elevator clunked and creaked on its way.

Finally, I said, "The PTO policy around here is bullshit. Did I tell you what they did to me?" Drew shook his head. "So, I told you about the whole Bri-Koh Samui thing, right? Well, now I'm supposedly all out of PTO. They flagged my request after I'd made all the deposits. All nonrefundable. Bullshit, right?" Drew nodded. A good sign. "I appealed, but then Deke left, and Lil denied it, and now…"

"You've got to be sweet to old Lil." He grinned. "She'll hook you up. How do you think I got the cube near the breakroom?"

"Maybe. But she can't like, breach policy. Luce said she—"

"Luce? You're actually on terms with that asshole?" He pressed the heel of his hand to his forehead. "I have two theories about *Luce*. It's either a performance art thing, like a college friend of Wee Milty's or something. *Or* it's a test by the higher-ups. See how well we fall in line. You know." The elevator eased to a stop and dinged. Drew fired up his vape pen. "Like those prison experiments back in the day."

"I guess that's possible." I'd find another time to bring up the PTO. Maybe when he was in a better mood.

The elevator door trembled open. Earbud guy slipped out and vanished. I followed Drew out. The garage seemed stale, and too dark, like walking through a dirty screen. The back of my hand prickled for my attention. I ignored it.

"Look—speak of the devil. What does that sign say there? That one." Drew waved his vape towards the row of executive parking that abutted the elevator alcove, cement ballasts at one end to discourage the peons. Each spot was reserved with a little metal nameplate screwed into the wall: President, Executive Vice President, Vice President of Blahblahblah, Vice President of LaDeDa, and Lucifer. No title. Just Lucifer. In the same boring sans serif as the other titles.

"Lucifer," I said. "But that's his name, not his title. His title is—"

"What, Prince of Darkness? Are you *serious*, Phil? Is it something in that shitty coffee you make? Why is everyone being so casual about this? The company is transparently messing with us. Think about it: if the devil—oooh, booga booga scary—actually existed, why would he be *here?* In HR, of all places? Does the devil—the mythological creature, not the prick up on second—strike you as being good with people?"

The itch on my hand worked towards my wrist. I put it behind my back. "In a way. Sure."

"Whatever." He sputtered out a stream of smoke. "He's a prick. I don't like him. My last merit increase still isn't showing up in my checks and he's trying to tell me it was because Deke forgot to cross a T or something, so it's going to be another two cycles. The actual devil could just mumbojumbo and make it so, right?"

"Rules," I muttered, to myself more than Drew. "Rules keep us right."

"Same bullshit he said. Prick. This whole thing's a joke, and a dumb one." He smirked and tucked his vape back into his pocket. "I got a joke of my own."

He went to Lucifer's nameplate, hands fumbling at his belt buckle. On the ground behind him, in the center of the parking space, a glowing red circle popped up from the ground. The sound of Drew's zipper opening, then the quiet splash of piss on concrete, echoed around the garage.

"Do you see that?" I asked.

Drew looked at me over his shoulder, his mouth moving, whatever words were coming out of it lost under the sound of the air crackling and sparkling in tiny buzzing bursts like miniature fireworks displays. The circle spread to cover the whole parking space, stopping sharply at the faded yellow lines marking the space's boundaries, then went a white so bright that for a second, I didn't know if I was dead or blind. When the brightness receded and my eyes adjusted, Drew was gone. Fire bounded the parking space on all four sides, then rushed towards the center, filling the whole space but still respecting the yellow lines. Flames licked the ceiling. A beaming white square appeared at the center of the parking space where the red circle had been. It grew longer and wider as it rose up from the ground, odd shapes sprouting from it at odder angles. When the flames sunk back into the concrete, there were no scorch marks or ash. Just a car, silver and seamless, as if carved from a single hunk of metal. I blinked again and for a millisecond, I was aware of pure, solid blackness. One single slice of nothing. I felt nothing. I knew nothing. It might not have been a millisecond. It might have been forever, except that when I opened my eyes, everything was exactly as my mind had left it. The driver's door opened, and Lucifer stepped out. He tilted his head back, nostrils flaring. He went to his nameplate, kicked a tire, then turned and looked at me, right in my eyes, his lips curled in a snarl.

"God*damn* it."

୪

Lil was long gone. It was just Lucifer and me in the HR suite, probably the entire building. I stood in the doorway as he paced back and forth behind his desk.

"I guess we have ourselves a situation, here."

"*We* have a situation? I think *you* have a situation." I wasn't going to follow where he was trying to lead. "Drew and I were just talking. You're the one that disintegrated him."

"Metaphysical inaccuracies aside, Drew was interfering with the use of a reserved parking space, which is subject to disciplinary action up to and including termination. Section ten, sub A, sub sub two. Sub sub three, whenever the revision comes out. We had to add some language for ADA compliance."

"You went a little beyond termination."

"I didn't know he was there! If he hadn't been trying to show off—"

"Wait, what? You can tell me what I had for breakfast a week ago, but you don't know when someone's using your parking space for a urinal?"

He paced. One lap. Two. "I'm not omniscient. You watch too many movies." Three laps. Four. "I want you to understand that what happened to your friend—"

"He's not my friend." I tucked my hands into my pockets and watched him. Back and forth. Back and forth. For once in my life, finally, I had the upper hand. "But I can be, like when his family starts asking questions when they realize he never got home from work. What do you think I should say when his mother wants to know where her son is? Where's my baby boy? We had a Mother's Day brunch planned. Where is he? I know what I'll say. I'll say, well, he was minding his business when out of nowhere, the Lord of the Flies over here—"

"Beelzy's the Lord of the Flies. I hate flies."

"—tore into his parking space like a bat out of Hell. Pun intended. Sorry for your loss, Drew's Mom, but at least there are some deep pockets to sue. The deepest."

"It was an accident, which wouldn't have happened if—look, things are hectic and I'm low on manpower. Some things have been automated. Some…routine security measures, for example." He threw up his hands. *Whaddaya gonna do?* "I took my boots off to let my hooves breathe for a little, forgot to put them back on, was coming back to get them. I was in a hurry. I had dinner plans. It was so late in the day, I wasn't thinking about people still heading out. About all the possibilities, all the keys floating around. I'm not used to things being so…delicate."

I patted my pockets out of habit. "Keys?"

He tapped the back of his hand. My mark went hot.

"Got an itch you can't scratch lately?"

"I thought the mark was just a reminder that we had a deal."

"What?" He tossed his head back and laughed. "Who forgets they have deal with me? No, it's like a club wristband and a key in one. It moves with your soul, that's why you can't scratch it. When you part ways with your body, the grunts see it and know not to send you into gen pop with all that miserable wailing and gnashing of teeth nonsense. Otherwise, under normal conditions, the key aspect only activates when you've been given a specific assignment of a time sensitive nature. It gives you some limited access to…safe shortcuts through the continuum for those still embedded in their mortal coils. Sadly, today, timing was everything. Drew shouldn't have even been able to see my parking spot."

"I badged him in without knowing it?"

"Something like that."

"But I don't have any kind of assignment, as far as I know, much less a time sensitive one. Which means it wasn't supposed to activate. So, are we not under normal conditions? Is that what you're saying?"

He pinched the bridge of his nose. "We'll have Mike look at it. It'll be fine."

"Mike Gottlieb has a key?"

"We're dancing near confidential territory here, so let's get back on track. I'm sorry about your friend—"

"Still not my friend."

"—but everything is under control. I trust you'll exercise discretion here?"

"Keep quiet, you mean? Maybe. If you tell me why there's a shortcut or whatever to Hell out in the open where anyone could just fall in if someone waves a hand in the wrong direction. That's terrible PR all around."

"Okay…" He came around to the front of the desk and sat on the edge, crossing his legs just above the hooves. "It's not technically Hell, but that's not the point. Let's think this through. Does anybody's life get easier if you post this on social media, or whatever it is you're planning?"

"My life gets a whole lot easier, actually."

And then, there it was. The one people talk about. The smile with too many teeth.

"How do you figure that?"

I shrugged. "I need ten days of PTO. You find my ten days, and I don't even remember who Drew Lindsey was."

He dropped his arms and went to pacing again. "I can't do that. Rules are—"

"Rules. They keep us right. Yeah, I know." I straightened up and stuck out my chest. There had to be respect points for bowing up to the devil, there in his very own office. "But these aren't *real* rules, are they? These aren't basic *laws of the universe,* right? These are just dumb, mean corporate rules. You're the Director of Human Resources. You can wiggle them."

He threw his hands up over his head, claws extended. "All the rules are real!"

The air throbbed. My eardrums quivered.

"Sorry about that." His voice fell with each word until it was back to normal. Again, he paced. "Okay, as a good faith gesture, I'm going to be as honest as I can be with you, Phil. Milton—Milty Prime, as you all call him—has had some concerns about transitioning to Milty's leadership, and I share his concerns. At this moment, it's to my advantage to ensure the continuation of Chadwick Analytics unencumbered by problematic attention or entanglements, legal or otherwise. For example, a wrongful death lawsuit. And if it's to my advantage, then as one of my contractors, it's also to your advantage. Think of your future, here and *later*, which can be as pleasant or unpleasant as I want it to be. So, let's play nice, shall we? I'll make you an offer: I will find an exception that I can support *within* company policy, but you might need to put in a little sweat equity. You've been here a while. Maybe it's time for a promotion. Make the increased PTO accrual retroactive? Then, we'll be square, and you *will* exercise discretion. Deal?"

"I don't like using the word 'deal' with you. But sure, I get my days, my lips are sealed."

His claws retracted as he extended his hand and we shook. Heat tore up my arm from the webbing between my fingers. He turned back to the window.

I took a step out the door. "Okay, then. I guess I'm heading out." Curiosity snuck into my brain on the back of my victory. I had to know. "So, you didn't actually answer my question—did your little shortcut malfunction because we're not under normal conditions? What kind of conditions are we under, exactly?"

He turned his head just enough that I could tell that his mouth was starting to look too big again. "If I tell you that, Phil, then the last sound you hear will be your mind tearing itself apart like a cheap hotel sheet as it descends into a madness that will make actual Hell seem like a mercy. Is that good enough for you?"

"It's going to have to be, huh?"

He didn't answer.

"Have a good night," I said, and closed the door between us.

8

The next morning, two emails from HR were waiting in my inbox. The first was companywide, a list of gentle reminders: please have all time-off requests submitted two weeks prior to the requested time, please observe all designated parking guidelines, and restrooms are located near the elevators on all odd-numbered floors.

The second email was just for me:

Re: Time-Off Request-Paid Status Approved

All ten days. I could relax.

Still, passing Drew's cubicle on my way to the breakroom was like seeing an animal carcass forgotten on one side of the road while its guts were on the other side after a midnight tango with a yellow-jacketed trucker. But as I got into the weeds of planning finer and finer points of my trip, I nearly did what I'd told Luce I would do: forget who Drew Lindsey was.

Two days before the official start of my vacation, Drew's cubicle was no longer empty: Wee Milty stood in the middle of it, turning this way and that, baffled by the world of the common grunt. An intern stood to his left, tapping furiously into a phone; Lil was to his right, gunmetal curls wobbling as she shook her head and muttered something at the stenographer's pad resting in the crook of her elbow. I tried to slide past the whole mess, but Milty spotted me and waved me in. I shoved my left hand into my pocket.

"Phil, right?"

"Phil. Yep." I flashed my teeth.

Milty nodded at Drew's empty chair. "You're friend flaked on us, huh?"

"He's not my...." What was the point? "Yeah, looks like it."

"Yeah." Milty gave The Rock's dome a swipe with his forefinger. On the back of his hand was a red splotch shaped like a dollar sign. Same place as my heart. Of course. "So, I know it's not really your job, but do you think you could get his stuff boxed up for Lil so she can get all that where it needs to go? Within the next day or two? Definitely by the end of the week. We need the desk. Gotta keep the ship afloat." He stuck out his hand and balled it into a fist. "Thanks for your help."

I made my own fist, and decided as I did that I would put in my notice if Wee Milty exploded his fingers, but he didn't. Just bumped, winked, nodded, and walked away.

Lil bopped my shoulder with her steno pad. "You know he's considered not re-hireable with a no-call no-show, right?"

So much for Drew being sweet to old Lil.

"That's none of my business."

"Just thought you'd like to know. Maybe you can pass it on? If you happen to talk to him."

And with another bop—more like a swat—Lil followed Milty and the intern to the elevators.

8

I just kept a hot plate, some protein bars, and a stress ball at my desk. Drew had the wrestling figures, pictures, some printed memes, and a plastic cow that mooed and shot brown candy balls from its ass when squeezed. I was out of boxes before I even opened his desk drawers. The supply closet next to the breakroom was usually just full of things like pens and rubber bands, but I hoped there was a box or two in there so I didn't have to schlep ten floors down to the mailroom.

I scratched absently at the back of my hand as I peered around the nests of rubber bands and bundles of pens.

"Phil! Hey, Phil!"

I stopped at the sound of my name. The voice was muffled but familiar. I peeked out into the cubicle field. Heads down all around, click-clacking away. No one in the breakroom.

"Phil! Can you hear me?"

I still couldn't place the voice, but I followed it anyway, to the back of the closet, where there were no shelves. Warmth spread out from my mark, killing the itch and engulfing my entire hand. A small red circle—just like the spot in Lucifer's parking space—popped out from a spot waist high in the wall. Soft heat rolled from my hand, into my arm, through my body.

"Who is it?" I asked.

"Seriously, bro?"

"Drew?"

"Yeah." There was a muted shuffling sound. "Do me a solid and get me out. It's hot in here and it smells like ass."

"Drew? How?"

"Just get me out!"

"How'd you know it was me?"

The shuffling stopped.

"I smelled you."

"What?"

"I can't explain it. I just got a whiff of chai and this weird eggy smell and I knew it was you."

"But I—" I bit down in the rest of the sentence. What could I say that wouldn't be awkward? I saw

Lucifer's parking space swallow you? Sorry, I didn't realize I my hand would open a poorly secured portal to Not Technically Hell?

"Phil?" His voice was thin and watery.

"Yeah, sorry. Hold on. Let me see."

There were no hints of a secret panel or any other way to get to Drew—no hinges, no knobs, no seams. I touched my fingertips to the wall, hoping they would feel something too subtle for my eyes. My hand glowed white—that same intense white as the parking spot when it went nuclear. It was almost hot, but pleasant. The wall disappeared with a smell like rotten garbage and burning tires.

Drew stood on the other side of the place where the wall had been for a long moment, blackness at his back, toeing at the closet floor before committing a full-footed step. He looked like himself. No soot smeared across his cheek, no holes in his gut or his skull where some underworldly surgery had been performed. Just Drew. Tie loose, hair mussed.

"Thanks, man." He took a step towards me, hand outstretched.

Tensing up in anticipation of a bro hug, I took his hand, but there was something wrong with it. It *gave*. He backed away, smile shrinking, eyes going wide, tremors stuttering down from his head and into his shoulders, then into his chest.

"Drew?"

Another step back and he was through the half-closed closet door. I threw it fully open and there he was, whole body vibrating like a tuning fork. Back he went, fainter with each step, through cubicles and oblivious co-workers like so much mist. By the time he reached the elevator, all I could make out was the white of his eyes and teeth and underwear, and then he sunk into the wall.

In the supply closet, the wall was solid again, smooth and flat. It might have never been otherwise, but the stink it had unleashed lingered. Warmth snaked around my fingers. I looked down.

My mark was bleeding.

8

It's hard to focus while you're wondering if the spirit of the co-worker that you just let out of Not Technically Hell is going pop through another wall and start pointing fingers. It stuck in my mind the rest of the day and kept me up most of the night. Drew reappearing. Drew disappearing. What had happened to Drew, where had Drew been, what was next for Drew? Should I give Luce a heads up? Did Luce already know?

At two in the morning, I woke up having to use the bathroom, which made me think about Drew again. I couldn't go back to sleep. I went through my itinerary to distract myself and it worked for a little while, but by four, I gave up, got dressed, and went to the office. At the security desk, Owen's first shift counterpart sat with his eyes closed and his head resting against the neck pillow tied to his chair. The monitors in front of him shuffled through their rounds.

I started a pot of coffee. The morning song of alerts and alarms from phones and computers fluttered around the cubicle field as the early birds drifted in. By the time I got back to my desk, there was a new email waiting for me.

From: Human Resources

Re: Time-Off Request-Paid Status Revised-Denied

"What the fuck?"

It was the standard HR form that came back from every request, from sick days to desk assignments. But there it was, halfway down the screen: the dates of my vacation in one box; time off approved in the next box; paid status denied in the next box; signed by LC in the last box.

LC.

Lil Cosgrove.

Lil Fucking Cosgrove.

8

Under the pensive flicker of depleted fluorescent tubes in the elevator down to HR—Luce trusting Mike Gottlieb to address anything more consequential than a trash can was maybe the most confusing thing of all—the full extent of how screwed I was hit me. I shouldn't have complained about the jelly filled.

My hand tingled as the elevator opened onto the second-floor hall. A red-orange light seeped through the doors of the HR suite, casting ominous shadows everywhere, but it barely registered. By then I was so angry that I would have waded through a lake of blood with buoys of bodiless heads to get answers.

The waiting area was empty—Lil wasn't at her desk—but the walls pulsed with radiant red circles, a thousand little shortcuts to Not Technically Hell. I kept it in my pocket and headed down the hall to Luce's office, calling as I went. Spots popped out of the floor, the walls, the ceiling.

"Luce? Hey, Luce? What's going on out here? Do you know?"

"Phil?"

Lil's voice drifted out from Luce's open office door. I slowed down. Everything was wrong.

"Lil?"

"I'm here," came that sweet front-desk voice.

"Is everything okay?"

Her head popped out of the office door, curls bouncing. "Everything's great. Come on in."

Luce wasn't in his office. His desk was barren of everything but the picture of the blond boy and the dog (in a different frame than I remembered), and Lil's steno pad.

"I guess you're here about your PTO." She motioned to the chair in front of the desk, but I shook my head and leaned against the door frame. The déjà vu made me queasy.

"Luce and I—"

"Lucifer is gone now, as I'm sure you've gathered. I'm the new Director of HR. I think you're one of the first to know."

"Okay," I said. "I mean, congratulations. But the thing is, Luce and I had an agreement."

"Yes, I'm familiar with your arrangement with *Luce*." She smiled then, and she looked...not younger. It wasn't that. Not *younger* but *ageless*. She could have been thirty or eighty or anything over or under or in between. She was all of them at once. Her carpal tunnel sleeves were gone; her bare forearms were crowded with a mess of crisscrossing red lines and circles.

I ignored the fire in my hand.

She moved towards me. "It's a new day here at Chadwick Analytics." She spread her arms wide. Red spots popped out of the walls, a whole summer's worth of red-orange fireflies. "We're starting fresh. Don't worry. There'll be an all-hands to go over the changes."

My throat narrowed. I opened my mouth, not sure I would actually be able to make a sound.

"Is this....my fault?"

"It has nothing to do with you." She dropped her

arms to her sides. The walls went corporate beige again. "Yes, your friend's misfortune—"

"He wasn't my friend."

"—provided an opportunity for improvement, but changes were coming. Everything changes, Phil. I'm sorry things didn't work out for you—you are a valued member of the Chadwick Analytics team—but I had the proof and you didn't. That's why cultivating relationships with your co-workers is so important. You didn't even think about the security team having access to the garage surveillance footage, did you?"

I shook my head. Owen. Wordless, motionless Owen. Flirty, cruller-stealing Owen.

"Because you don't think about them at all. Neither did Luce. It's not personal. You just ended up on the wrong side of the roll. Blame Luce—I tried to tell him, but he wouldn't listen." Lil's curls cascaded over her shoulders and down her back, going from gray to silver to black on the way. "If it's any consolation, I'd like your input on ways we can revise our leave policy to be a little more…flexible. Maybe situations like yours could be avoided in the future."

"I…" I straightened up, ready to ease back down the hall and right out the building. "I mean, okay. That sounds good. Yeah. Let's do that." I didn't want to do that. I would be happy to never breathe the same air as Lil Cosgrove again.

"I'm glad to hear that you're willing to work with us. I'll make a note to follow up with you. Get you on my calendar." She smiled again and grabbed her steno pad off the corner of her desk. "Is there anything else I can help you with?"

"No."

Her eyes sparkled. "Great! But if there ever is anything, you know—my door is always open."

"I know." I was already halfway down the hall.

Back at my desk, I typed up my resignation.

8

So that brings me here, to a beach in Koh Samui in a light drizzle that hasn't stopped since I got off the plane.

I saw Luce earlier. I was here, under my tree, when down the beach he came, whistling, messenger bag over his shoulder. He was in shorts and a t-shirt, nubby tail and nubby horns, hooves caked with sand. He dropped the bag between my feet and sat next to me under the tree.

"What's this?" I asked.

"That," he said, "is the official, original, formerly recorded contract for your soul. Which I have cancelled. All yours to do with as you wish."

"My soul? Or the contract?"

"Both."

I opened the bag and slid out the contract. Across the top, in the same bold and bright white letters as Beelzebub's notary stamp: DO NOT ENFORCE – REGISTER OF SOULS– DO NOT ENFORCE

"Why?"

He sighed. I got a whiff of tequila.

"Well, simply put, the end is nigh. I tried, truly, but the dissolution of consensual reality has reached a tipping point. At the current rate of collapse, I'd say the laws of physics go off the farm in about nine months, give or take. Without getting into the math of it—which no one follows anyway—there's maybe three months before things get very unpleasant in this corner of the universe. I'm getting squared away before that happens and my ass loses track of my asshole. You were top of mind, what with everything. You know."

I slipped the contract back into the bag and pulled the bag into my lap. Nothing felt different. "Actually, no, I don't know."

He knocked his hooves together. Sand fell off in wet chunks.

"What's your first memory, Phil?"

"Getting into a rock fight with a neighbor kid, but they weren't rocks, they were cat turds." I could still smell the soap my mother scrubbed me with when she realized what I had done.

"Mine is of waking up at the bottom of a crater in the middle of the desert, no idea why I was there. All I knew was my name. Before that, it was sound and light. A sense of being." He drew shapes that didn't make sense with his forefinger in the sand as he talked. "Lil's is of wandering in a field next to a great wilderness. She could hear voices from behind the trees, but she couldn't get through to them. Couldn't even step into the shade without losing her breath."

"Lil? Cosgrove?"

"Just Lil. Lillith, if she's feeling fancy." His smile then was one I'd seen before, in the mirror, the night Michelle laughed in my face. "I've never trusted anyone the way I trusted her. Not even Beelzy. Then Milty got his claws into her."

"Wee Milty?" He wasn't my friend, but I felt like Drew was there next to me, jaw dropping next to mine. "How?"

Luce's grunt told me that he couldn't believe it either.

"The whole Chadwick line has been mine since… Charlemagne-ish, I think. I found one of them wandering in the woods, starving. The deal developed over time, as those generational deals do. Needs change over centuries. Even mine. I had their souls, but what I really needed was reinforcements. Topside. In exchange for me providing them with opportunities to gain insights that their competitors wouldn't have, they built their HQ over the largest hellmouth in the western hemisphere. Though just to be clear, hellmouth is a misnomer. It's not Hell. It's a complex nexus of several adjacent chaos realms, which if you actually express as a quadra—"

I yawned, wide and loud. "Lost me."

"Anyway, Lil wanted to live like a human again for a little while, which I don't get. You're all so awkward and you always look like you have to vomit. But that's what she wanted, and I needed someone I could trust. The hellmouths are touchy areas." He waved his hand over the sand, erasing all his work. "Fundamental reality is a realpolitik situation. Myself and certain other parties have a mutual interest in keeping things stable. They like order because order enables peace. I don't care about order, and I definitely don't care about peace, but the only chaos I can abide is *my* chaos. If it's not *my* chaos, then I'm no better off than I was when I woke up at the bottom of that crater, and I've worked too long and too hard. So, we worked together *on this one thing.* I want to emphasize that it was just *this one thing.* But entropy's a bitch, and things were getting particularly dicey at the hellmouths—which are my purview. That's where Lil came in. She was supposed to keep an eye on things, let me know about any new activity. Then a couple months ago, reports start coming in from everywhere that all this weird elder god dark energy—those guys are fucking nuts, by the way, steer all the way clear—was breaching agreed dimensional boundaries, and it was concentrated at the Chadwick hellmouth. Turns out, Lil was doing some direct interference of her own. Which, as you know, is against the rules."

"Rules keep us right." I pictured Drew rolling his eyes.

"More than you know. Deke was a rules man. He wouldn't play with Wee Milty. He wasn't planning to retire for another five years, but one morning he woke up with the idea in his head that he was done. An idea that Lil had put there, while he slept and dreamt of a beautiful woman whispering in his ear. She did that, and other things like that, but the Deke thing was the red flag. And each time she did, a little crack started. Little cracks get magnified as they spread through the continuum. They become big cracks, and next thing you know...sorry about your friend." He shrugged. "Lil was my blind spot. Living with humans again for so long did something to her. Once Wee Milty and the others turned her against me..."

"Owen?"

"Owen. Mike Gottlieb, which was kind of shocking. Wee Milty wanted a better deal and once he figured her out, that was it. The parking garage thing gave them leverage against me with Milty Prime, who *really* resents the fact that the Chadwicks would be a family of dirt farmers if it weren't for me, even though he won't admit it. And, well...here we are. I can't fix the plumbing if I'm not allowed on the property." He drew a smiley face in the sand with a dollar sign on its forehead and a gun to its temple. "And if I put my finger on the scale to fix it—"

"It all falls apart anyway." I went cold, even with my soul there in my lap.

"And much faster since I displace more energy than she does. Quite a pickle, isn't it? At least I'll get the satisfaction of seeing the looks on their faces when they realize what they've done. Except for Lil, obviously. There's no hiding from the collapse of creation, but I can keep it as easy on her as possible for as long as I can."

I pulled my soul closer. "But it's her fault."

"It's not *all* her fault. Besides, she's the mother of my child. What do you want me to do?"

I remembered the picture of the blond boy and his dog.

"Your child? The Anti...you know."

"You can say it, Phil. It won't hurt my feelings."

"The Antichrist?"

Luce sighed. "He's disappointed that he's not going to get his time to shine, but he'll be okay. As okay as any of us."

"How bad is it going to be?"

He kicked a clod of sand towards the water. "Very bad, for a little while, but I wasn't lying—you'll be insane way before the real shit goes down. There'll be havoc, then silence. Perfect silence. The sound of every piece of energy in the universe, of the very idea of existence, just blinking out. Time will end. There'll be eternity. There'll be a flash, time will start back up, and round and round we'll go, from the top, second verse, same as the first. Like always. You won't remember any of it. I don't even remember it. I only know what I know because they just show us the highlight reel once in a while to remind us of how important the work is." A streak of sunlight cracked through the clouds. "Look at that. Old Sol making it out today after all."

"So why this?" I nudged at the messenger bag.

"Because you puffed up to me in my own office. Didn't go behind my back. I respect that. So, when your physical form succumbs to the loss of cohesion between its cells, you don't have to hang out in the void with me for however many eons. You can just go find a corner somewhere. Go to sleep. And when you wake up, you'll be throwing cat turds at the neighbor kid again. And again and again and again, until someone figures out where the brakes are. Which is definitely above my paygrade." He hoisted himself back to his feet with a groan. "Maybe next time, things'll go better with Michelle, huh?" He winked and started back the way he had come.

I called after him. "I'll see you later?"

"Later...." His voice rolled across the sky. "Much, much, much later..."

And then he disappeared into the rain.

ABOUT THE AUTHOR

JEAN JENTILET lives in North Carolina with a miniature pinscher and a Shih Tzu who occasionally grant her leave to go on long walks and write dark fiction. Her stories have appeared in *parABnormal Magazine* and *Samjoko Magazine*, as well as the anthologies *The Monsters Next Door and Crybaby Bridge: A Collection of Utter Speculation.* Her work has been featured as part of D&T Publishing's Emerge series. Jean's thoughts about horror movies and David Lynch can occasionally be found at 25yearslatersite.com. Ever in search of the perfect cup of coffee, Jean also enjoys throwing axes and making furniture.

DADDY ISSUES

Diana Olney

"I'm gonna make you a star, sugar."

The second the club owner opens his mouth; I want to bite his tongue off.

It would be like a kiss, but better. Hard and then soft, an embrace deep as nightfall, warm as sunshine, desperate as first love. And just as sweet, too. With one quick snap of my jaw, the flavors would bloom, a sanguine bouquet flowering in every shade of red from the roots of the severed muscle. The body would struggle, naturally, but I'm always up for a challenge. I am more than judge, jury, and executioner—I am an artist of death, and the gallows are my canvas. At my hands, this lowly worm would go out with a bang, a boom, an aria, the primal refrain of his death rattle rising into an eleventh-hour elegy far more eloquent than the way he's still wasting his breath, blowing smoke into this decrepit dive night after night.

But it wouldn't be wasted on me. One look at this guy, and I know he could feed my demons for a month.

And they know it, too.

"You already look the part..."

As the scumbag drones on, flicking his silver tongue behind a flash of nicotine-stained teeth, I barely hear a word he's saying. My demons are hellbent on drowning him out, swarming my skull with susurrant demand.

Go on, take a bite.

No need to wait.

Believe me, I'm tempted. I stiffen my spine, holding myself back, and an involuntary shiver rolls through my vertebrae, sending pinpricks of anticipation into every nerve in proximity. My snaky companion says something, another half-assed pick-up line, surely, but he can't hook me. I'm already ten steps ahead of him, reveling in the bacchanal of his stillborn screams like a Bathory slipping into a freshly drawn bloodbath. I close my eyes, just for a second, imagining the vibrations singing through me, showers of silent-film terror macerating pound after pound of flesh while my demons follow, picking at the scraps like a pack of vultures.

But we wouldn't stop there. No. We'd slice, incise, filet, butterflying the flesh into wings wet with dew, lapping up the juices until our mouths ran red. Then, we'd wash it down with a chaser—bourbon, neat, on the house. A quick palate cleanser before moving on to darker, more extraneous cuts.

Hearts take a while to harvest, especially the black ones. All that debauchery gets embedded deep, too close to the bone to extract in one go. Livers are worse, thanks in part to the popularity of Speakeasies—an exorbitant trend propagated by the allure of exclusivity, not the scarcity of booze, which has never been scarce in New York, not even when it was illegal. The liver I had yesterday was a gamey brick of cirrhosis, and removing it was a royal pain, like pulling teeth with rusted pliers. And don't even get me started on souls. Last month, I had a date who clung onto his for a full hour after I tore his arms off.

I don't partake of the souls, personally. I've had a few samples, here and there, but human spirits never sit well with me. My dad, on the other hand, can't get enough of them. Granted, he doesn't inhale his meals the way I do. The complexity of the soul is meant to be savored, he says, and he prefers to take his time. He does have eternity, after all.

But we'll get to him later. Back to business.

"...you've certainly got the legs for it."

The creep is still talking, spinning his sticky web of propositions. I shift in my seat and drain the rest of my martini, the easiest alternative to tossing the drink in his smug face. Or worse. I'm trying to stay civil, but I swear, this grinning pestilence is practically begging me to drink him in, to crack his flimsy, liver-spotted shell open like an egg and liberate him from the weight of all the stale sin clogging up his arteries.

But I don't do it. I don't do any of those things.

Instead, I just nod.

And I smile. That's a requirement.

But my smile can't hold a candle to the one spreading like wildfire in front of me. The club owner, Fast Eddie, they call him—though I've yet to see him do anything but take his time—beams like a hungry blade, yellow teeth slicing through a cloud of cigar smoke in a freshly-sharpened scythe. His build is just as lean: a long, lazily coiled length of rope wrapped in tailored cashmere—Hugo Boss, I believe, with gold-plated Cartier cufflinks. The predators around here love their labels. Across the room, the wolfish Manhattanites are flaunting their Armani wool blends, leaving me with the serpent whose latest skin cost more than my entire wardrobe.

"You'll have to audition, of course," Eddie continues, chomping on the end of his Cuban, "but let's wet your whistle first, eh? You can wet mine too, if the mood strikes you." Right on the punchline, he erupts into guttural, hacking guffaws, rollicking in a squall of smoke-strangled laughter.

I force a courtesy giggle. Nope, never heard that one before. Not since prohibition ended, anyway. Either this scumbag is taking the Speakeasy front way too seriously, or he's living in the wrong century.

Then again, so am I.

Keeping one eye on my slippery mark, I shoot a sidelong glance around the room, delving deeper into my surroundings. I know the reputation of this place, but I'm a first timer, as they say.

The club, aptly named the Gilded Cage, is what I imagine the insides of the behemoth that swallowed Jonah would look like if the belly of the aforementioned beast was redecorated in the Byzantine era, host to handful of glitzy soirees, then promptly abandoned. The main room is a hollow rib cage of sprawling, vaulted ceilings with a beveled spine that stretches all the way to the stage, drawing the eye to a tattered velvet curtain that I assume used to be red, but now falls somewhere between brown and a muddy, blood-splatter ochre. Flanking the curtain, twin faux-marble columns stand at attention, boasting gold leaf filigree that sets the scene for the rest of the decor. Every inch of the Cage, from floor to ceiling to furnishing, is dipped in gold—or was, until the paint started to peel, exuviating from the grayed alabaster bones of the room like the patchwork decomposition of flesh from a corpse. Before the club began to rot, the bar was up in the balcony, the remains of which have been reduced to the architectural equivalent of a tumor: a jagged, stair-less protrusion jutting precariously from the wall above the entrance. The current bar is almost as much of an eye-sore, crammed in like an afterthought beside the stage and partitioned by beaded drapes that, while clearly hung this century, are missing more than a few of their golden tendrils. The "secret" bar is a must, if you want to call your watering hole a Speakeasy, but this one keeps its secrets about as well as a streetwalker in crotchless panties.

On the bright side, at least the girls here are better dressed than that.

As if following my train of thought, my tipsy companion leans in closer, sliding halfway out of his chair to size me up. Through the spill of smoke, I can see him taking measurements, calculating waist size over profit margin. "But don't worry, the audition is just a formality. Especially for you. Believe me, baby," he adds with another chortle, "I know a star when I see one."

I nod again, straining to temper my disgust. I've seen what happens to stars in this place. First, they rise, then they fall, crashing and burning straight into the ground. It doesn't matter how bright they are when they walk in the door. Fast Eddie is the Pied Piper of the underground sex trade, singing empty promises like pop medleys into any ear that will listen. The local ladies see through his act, but that's not who he's after anyway. He wants new blood: the young, the soft, the naive, the baby-faced runaways and doe eyed Lolitas with no attachments or baggage except high hopes for their big city dreams. Those are the stars of the real show, the divas of the steamy melodramas that unfold behind the scenes. But he doesn't throw them to the wolves right away. Like any businessman, Eddie knows how to break in his merchandise. He gets them hooked on booze, coke, dope, molly; whatever vice gets his starlets to shine for the crowd, soaring so high, they don't see it coming when he knocks them down—down from the stage and into perdition: dark, moldering tenements wrought of terror and tears and the sweat-soaked fever dreams that only living nightmares can bring. And they stay there. The girls always stay, because by the time they open their eyes, they have nowhere else to go.

"Don't be nervous. You're gonna be right at home here...?" An inflection slides surreptitiously up to my ear, slick as diamondback scales. "What did you say your name was again, doll? Melissa? Mercedes?"

I cock my head. Shit. Looks like I tuned out again. "Melanie," I correct.

"Melanie. Of course," Eddie whispers, slow as black-strap molasses, pouring the syllables into a languid stream of saccharine. From his lips, the name sounds suddenly obscene, a lascivious echo of whatever lewd fantasies he's currently coveting. He should enjoy them while he can. If he wags that tongue much longer, he's going to get a sneak peek into my secret desires. "A beautiful name, for a beautiful girl," he adds with a wink.

"Thank you," I tell him, slipping back into character just to keep my skin from crawling. Of course, my name isn't actually Melanie. My real name, this lizard-brained creep couldn't even pronounce, let alone remember. Maybe he would, if I was famous, like my mother, but not everyone back home is blessed with infamy of the legendary Persephone. May she rest in peace.

"I just call 'em like I see 'em." Eddie leers, skirting his gaze along the curve of my hourglass frame before coming to rest on the empty tumbler on the adjacent table. "Care for a refill, Miss Melanie...before we get down to business? You look like you could use a little more liquid courage."

I cross my legs defensively. "Sure."

As Eddie's sharp edges cut through the labyrinth of close-knit tables en route to the bar, the house lights dim, and I watch his latest acquisition drift on stage, wafting like an errant breeze from behind the tattered velvet curtain while the boozehounds below lap at her heels. She's a meager offering—once a woman, now barely a girl, switchblade-skinny and pale as death. Platinum hair, porcelain skin spiderwebbed with scars and cigarette burns, half of which are too faded to be Eddie's work, tell-tale signs of a broken home. But wherever she came from, she's not any better off now. Her attire—kitten heels, pencil skirt, and a steel-boned corset that could make Bettie Page's submissive heart skip a beat—looks almost as uncomfortable as the forced smile she's wearing. When she steps into the spotlight, regret emblazons the hand-painted mask of her make up like a half-hearted apology, running into the margins of her expression in a harried scrawl that makes a terrible mockery of the beauty she was born with.

But to me, she's still lovely—in a fixer-upper, *Pretty Woman* kind of way. Just my type, actually.

With a shaking hand, my new crush white-knuckles the microphone, anchoring herself in place as she introduces her opening number, but I don't catch her name. Her song, however, makes a big impression.

Her ballad is the voice of heartbreak: cracked, atrophied, worn down to a flinty, vibrato whisper by one too many nights spent in the chokehold of addiction, a gasp of shallow breath hanging from the noose of a fallen halo. It's a hard story to tell, and it doesn't have a happy ending. But the audience doesn't mind. To them, her lament is little more than foreplay, a commercial jingle advertising a product for sale. And around here, damaged goods aren't a throwaway—they're a kink. So, it's no surprise when tonight's tear-jerker soundtrack draws a rabid crowd, pulling the wolves out of the walls by the second verse.

I grimace, dropping my stilted smile like a bad habit while I listen to the catcalls roaring over knock-off Bettie's anthem. She won't last long, this one. Not if Eddie and his lecherous patrons have their way. Best case scenario, she'll have a fighting chance, once I take him out of the equation. That's what I'm hoping, anyway. Call me a hypocrite for my own depraved appetites, if you must, but in situations like this, you have to fight fire with fire, and right now, I've got the only other match in the city.

Light him up lighthimup yesyes do it.

Now.

No, not yet, I tell my demons. Patience is a virtue, even for us. Eddie is the only name on my list tonight, but if I'm not careful, he'll drag his hapless pets right down with him.

And this one is teetering dangerously close to the edge.

On stage, Bettie's voice breaks, splintering like a broken mirror, the notes of her swan song raining down in a hailstorm of silver shards. Before I can stop it, sympathy follows, spilling down the latitude of my marrow and filling my slender frame like a champagne flute. Poor girl. I don't want to think about what kind of horrific encore awaits her—here, or in the tortuous halls of my father's house. I may be a born-and-bred Daddy's girl, but it's a complicated position, and like sweet Bettie here, I've got a laundry list of "Daddy issues." The difference is, I keep my baggage close to the chest, rather than on my sleeve. That's where most mortal women make their first mistake, showing vulnerability to those who prey on it.

But I digress.

The bottom line is: being inhuman doesn't make me immune to humanity. I'm too close to it, stuck rubbing elbows with the wretched and damned night after night, side effects of which may include: second thoughts, empathy, compassion, and in the rare instances when I let my guard slip, the Mother Teresa of all buzzkills—a guilty conscience.

Oh, and the occasional one-night stand.

Of course, Dad doesn't know about any of that. And I'm not about to tell him. As cliché as it sounds, he wouldn't understand. All my inner demons come from mom's side of the family—even the ones that share his love of suffering.

Don't get me wrong, I don't mind working in the family business—it is the oldest in recorded history, after all—but I'd be lying if I said I approved of the politics. Over time, the rivalry between Upper and Lower Management has become a glorified pissing contest, a race of who can meet their quotas faster. And my father will do anything to get ahead. Bribery is his ace-in-the-hole. At least ten percent of his intake, he lines up in advance, buying souls long before their expiration date. Though to his credit, it's almost a fair trade. Those men—and handful of women—live very, *very* well before they have to pay up.

And then there's me.

Dad has hundreds of collection agents, but I'm the only one who cuts corners—among other things. However, it is worthy of note that the names on my list are done deals already. My charming friend Eddie, for instance, has a tumor in his head the size of a golf ball, and he doesn't even know it. His doctor must either be blind or completely incompetent.

It would be a stretch, though, to call this a mercy killing. Mercy is not a part of my father's business model—that's the competition's angle. I'm fine with that, usually, but tonight, I can feel myself slipping.

Not for Eddie, of course—it's his victims that worry me. I'm not here to save souls, but in my humble opinion, these girls don't deserve to be demon-fodder any more than they deserve to be sold into the skin trade. And that's what will happen to most of them, without intervention—be it divine or a six-month stint in rehab. But I'm not even allowed to make suggestions. At the end of the day, the best I can do is try to up the stakes in their favor.

On the bright side, the easiest way to accomplish that is simple: do my job. Follow Dad's orders. Plus, a girl's gotta eat, one way or another, and nothing feeds me and my demons better than a buffet of all-you-can-eat villainy.

Speaking of, it looks like dinner is about to be served.

Just as Bettie finishes her ode to melancholia, Eddie manifests, brandishing a freshly lit Cuban and a double martini. I keep my composure, folding into my coquettish guise without skipping a beat. But my demons make it hard to keep it on.

Herehere herehere heis givehimtous giveusfleshboneblood and—

Meat yes meat wewillskinhimandeat it raw.

The masses are getting restless.

I shake my head, scattering whispers like ashes to the wind. But this time, my demons will not be subdued so easily. I blink, and a cold, creeping sensation slithers behind my temples, winding through gray matter like a tendril of poison ivy. Within seconds, the branch swells, spreads, growing limbs, claws, and teeth, so many teeth I can see as much as feel them, rows and rows of ravenous jaws sprouting forked tongues and needle-sharp canines, an orchard of mouths gnawing in insatiable madness on the walls of my skull.

Aka: an instant migraine.

"You okay, babydoll?"

A pertinent question, despite the unsavory motives of its source. My demons and I usually get along better than this. Then again, I did skip breakfast today, which may have put a kink in the bond of our usually symbiotic relationship. But I'm not about to let civil war break out, especially not this close to dinner. I nod absently to Eddie and slowly rise from my seat, straightening myself into a decisive, pre-sharpened pinnacle that pulls every tendon, tissue, and ligament in the lithe musculature of my frame to the tautness of piano wire. This vessel may look young, but I've had it a long time, long enough to be fluent in the deepest forms of body language. None of which is meant for Eddie, but he enjoys the view anyway, gazing into the rift of my plunging decolletage with a stare that says he already has my cup size memorized. I don't try to stop him. I—

Fuckingpig sinnerparasitemonster.

Gut him.

Jesus.

No. He's dead already.

I don't argue with that one.

Stifling a bitter laugh, I step forward, stilettos stamping between the cracks in the tile floor with surgical precision as I close the gap between myself and my mark. He has no comment, for once, but my demons do. Once I stretch to my full height, standing eye to eye with the beanpole silhouette of my mark, a prickling, bee-sting tremor assails my anatomy, festering in the infinitesimal spaces where flesh marries bone. I cringe, quietly cursing the hair-trigger nervous system of this form. In nature, pain serves its purpose, providing intel on the integrity of the flesh, but in my case, it's a blatant overreaction. Thanks to

Dad's defense team, this structure is fortified against blades, plagues, bullets, radiation—and immolation, of course—essentially everything except actual acts of God, so unless the big guns upstairs try to smite me, which hasn't happened once in all my years traipsing topside, most of the aches and pains are just overkill.

Fortunately, the discomfort doesn't last, a sure sign that my rebellious co-pilots are about to acquiesce. As my muscles continue to harden, sheathing my bones in layers of adamantine armor, the show of dominance sends the right message to the Alphas, dampening the cacophony in my head to a dull roar of white noise.

Music to my ears.

Eddie passes me my martini and arches an intrigued eyebrow. He isn't afraid. Not yet. To him, I'm just another strange, feral thing to be tamed, a pet in need of a master.

"Thanks," I tell him, then raise my glass and down the drink in one voracious, frat-boy-with-a-beer-bong gulp. There's a chance Eddie spiked it, but that doesn't concern me much. Hell, a little extra kick might be just what I need to keep the edge off my nerves.

"Bravo! Looks like it's about time for that audition, eh?" Eddie exclaims, grin cocked like a rifle. "I've got a private room backstage. VIP only." He pauses for a strategic exhale, the smoke from his Cuban an uninvited hand caressing my cheek. "Care to join me?"

"I'd love to," I tell him. And this time, I mean it.

୪

"Alright, my little star," Eddie sneers, sipping top-shelf whiskey from a cheap glass. "Are you ready to sing for Daddy?"

Hell.

No.

The answer is electric, an automated message whipping through my synapses. At last, my demons and I are in agreement. Despite a private affinity for karaoke, the kind performed for a built-in audience too biased to heckle off-key renditions of *Rebel Yell* and *Sympathy for the Devil,* I am not going to sing. And I am not, under any circumstances, going to call this walking disease "Daddy."

But snaky Eddie here isn't the first to ask. Over the years, I've had quite a few dates make the same request. Maybe it's my big blue eyes, or the fact that the size-zero skin I inhabit might have been jailbait before I moved in. Which for the record, was my father's suggestion. At the time, I thought he just missed his little princess, but lately, I've begun to question his motives. Thanks to me, he's damned a record number of pedophiles.

Either way, I never do it. I may have a few "Daddy issues" outstanding, but I'm not going to work them out by chanting his name while a scumbag with a penchant for kiddie porn spanks me. That's just pathetic. And kind of blasphemous.

Plus, I don't even swing that way.

But I don't tell Eddie that. Naturally.

"Sure," I lie. I lie—and I keep smiling. I smile big and bright, licking a streak of artery-red lipstick from my teeth while my one-man audience gets comfortable, ensconcing his wiry silhouette in the arms of a weathered loveseat that has never heard the name Martha Stewart. A two-second glance around me elicits a rush of pity for whoever did the original interior design; I'm sure this space used to be glamorous, but from where I'm standing, the "VIP Room" has suffered even more neglect that the main hall of the club, falling into a state of hopeless, moldering disrepair that would be a challenge for the most skilled Extreme Remodel crew. The walls, once gold like the rest of the Cage, are barely standing, stripped of their upscale status and riddled with open cavities sepulchered in cobwebs and black mold. The smell doesn't help the aesthetic either. Had I not been raised in the deepest bowels of iniquity, every breath would be a dry heave, fouled by the miasma of sour sin in the air.

"This is...nice," I tell my host.

We both know it isn't, leading me to believe Eddie doesn't bring clients back here until they're completely hammered, or too worked up to care about the integrity of the environment in which they get their rocks off. When I look up, the mirrored ceiling breaks my gaze in two, splitting my reflection right down the middle. In the periphery, the cracks branch out like tributaries, veining the corners of the ceiling like broken vessels in a bloodshot eye.

Eddie follows my gaze, and for the first time, I detect a hint of insecurity, a chink in his well-ironed veneer of chauvinism. At the edge of his angular cheekbones, the hook of his lip is slumping, creeping down by degrees, as if his dime-store politician's smirk has finally reached the end of its run and is now attempting to slide right off his face. "The room needs a bit of TLC, I know," the greaseball admits, voice crackling with uneasy static. With a shaky hand, he sets his whiskey on the withered remains of an end table, barely touched. "But we're fixing her up. Come spring, this will be a palace fit for a Queen." He takes a puff of his Cuban, then retreats into a dense partition of smoke, curtaining himself while he spackles his bruised ego. He recovers quickly enough. When the fog clears a moment later, he's ready for the next address, his easy expression a portrait of razzle-dazzle lacquered in an oil-slick finish. "But you don't need creature comforts, do you my dear? Because you're already a Queen, aren't you?"

"Indeed, I am," I croon, matching his silky tone. Technically, that was my mother's title, but at this point, I might as well try it on for size.

"That's what I like to hear." Eddie inhales another swill of smoke, then bursts into laughter, mouth agape like a trap door, and there's that tongue again—lolling, teasing, daring me to come inside. Beneath the facade of my flesh, my demons perk up, salivating like Pavlovian dogs.

It's time.

Bleed him dry.

Soon, very soon, I assure them, soothing my pets like a mother placating an impatient child. But my promise is far more sincere than the white lies mortals feed one another. I'm starving. And so are Dad's infernal subjects below. I can feel them, sense them, their twisted masses steeped in sinuous whispers, the susurrant hiss of a snake pit bound tighter than knotted entrails.

Meanwhile, their next meal is still laughing. For a second, I give in and laugh along with him, tittering acidly under my breath. But only until he starts talking again.

"Well then, Queen Melanie. Shall we proceed? I can't wait to see what you've got for me." Eddie snickers, malfeasance threaded like razor-wire between every word, sharpening, tightening, corseting his rhetoric into a treacherous net.

I lock eyes with Eddie, returning his barbed grin. I know exactly what he's hoping to catch.

Little does he know, the hunter is about to become the hunted.

"So," I step closer, looming over my prey. "You wanna hear a song?"

8

When I open my mouth, I don't sing.

But my demons do.

They don't even need a warm-up. In a visceral fit of hysteria, they scream from my throat, screeching, howling, wailing like an air-raid siren at the end of the world. Not that they have any interest in apocalyptica. Like me, my diabolic minions have but one single purpose:

To eat.

And eat we shall.

Eddie is not given the chance to scream. Or a chance to go for the loaded forty-four magnum—the one he thinks I didn't see—taped under his seat. Before his tipsy lizard brain can tell his arm to reach for the gun, the wrath of Hell is upon him, bursting from my eager lips in a swarm of metastasizing entropy. My demons are starving, and they know who's on the menu. Thrown from his pedestal, Eddie gasps, pitches forward and falls to the floor, cowering before their horrendous glory.

And they are *glorious*. Even to my disillusioned eyes, my infernal counterparts are a sight to behold. Their aesthetic is the anatomy of nightmares: a black, monstrous tempest writhing with claws, wings, and teeth, every razored filament and snapping jaw bound by synchronized bloodlust. Their voices, a cacophony: no words this time, only the sound of violence, sharp as a dagger, final as a death rattle. I watch, enthralled, as the cloud descends on our quarry, subsuming first the flesh, then the orifices; torrents of rabid, Cimmerian shadow diving into the slack-jawed "O" of Eddie's almost-scream like an inhalation of smoke from one of his beloved Cubans.

When the remains of his cigar falls to the floor, cast aside like unwanted scraps by the voracious crowd, my insides jitter with laughter.

But the real fun is just beginning.

My armies make quick work of our prey. Eddie thrashes, limbs akimbo in useless, flailing defense as the last inches of his face vanish behind a cloud of beating wings, never to be seen again. There is no time for goodbyes. In a matter of moments, the Gilded Cage's infamous proprietor is stripped of everything he holds dear: his power, his ego, his custom-tailored designer suit—and the skin beneath it. As my throat begins to clear, releasing the last of the horde, I beam with pride while my demons emancipate Eddie from his time-worn flesh, revealing the veritable spread of delights beneath.

I move in, breath bated in anticipation, and hunger flickers through me like arson, a Molotov cocktail igniting desires too long suppressed. Emptied of my demons, I am a well of appetites: a bottomless gluttony catacombed into deep, needful hollows, every recess of my being a hungry mouth to feed.

On the floor, a cracked, fetal sob twinges somewhere in the fray, muffled by a chorus of chattering teeth and tearing flesh. It sounds like Eddie wants to say something. Words are lost to him, but I'm impressed he's still trying, bloodying his already mutilated vocal cords with such arduous and futile labor. Intrigued, I lower myself into the shallows of the bloodbath, leaning over the heap of skinless gore. His new ensemble is appropriately macabre, the black shroud of my demons corseted to every edge of his ravaged frame. But the clouds will part for me.

Sensing my presence, the horde recoils, parting like a curtain to unveil the fruits of their labor. In the wide, lip-less hole that used to house Eddie's sycophantic grin, a few stragglers linger, roiling in the wet, red dark like worms. I inch closer, my hunger an inferno aching to spread.

I am not disappointed.

I take the tongue first. Once the last of my demons scatter, I strike, clenching my fingers around his jaw. I show no mercy. As the horror of my intentions tears through him, I pull, rip, distend, stretching the opening as far as it will go. There is just enough room. Bone fractures with a procession of jarring cracks as I bind my prey in a savage lip-lock, a kiss forged from pure desire. The vibrato of his agony fills my throat with music, deep and satiating. But I am not done yet. As his tongue lashes, sensing the threat, I latch on at the base, pinching the muscle between my teeth. Then, I bite down, slicing through villiform threads of sinew with a snap of serrated canines. Blood geysers from the wound, drowning the final permutations of a scream. Beneath me, Eddies heaves, bucking in agony, but I hold steady, my fingers collaring his throat in iron. Keeping a firm grip, I pull my head back just as the severed organ goes limp, sliding in like a shelled oyster. Closing my eyes, I press the morsel against the roof of my mouth, reveling in aphrodisiacal streams of nectar, then tip my head back and swallow, consuming it all.

That's it.

Yesyes drinkitdown.

From the sidelines, my demons chitter with mirth, enjoying the spectacle. My main course, however, doesn't react so well. In the chokehold of my embrace, Eddie quivers and warbles with wordless anguish, begging to be released.

But that was only the first course.

As I dive in for seconds, inhaling the hemorrhage blooming from his speechless mouth, I savor every lie, every secret, every scintilla of vice, each one as precious as a rare gem. The tongue was an indulgence, dessert before dinner, but these are the sacraments I need. Like a fine wine, the offering fills the empty spaces inside me, whispering promises only the dead can keep. And yet, the vessel refuses to expire. Desperately, ravenously, he clings to life, clutching ragged breaths like rosary beads.

It is too late for prayer now.

Not that Eddie had any Gods to begin with. When I taste his organs, I am awash in blasphemy, bright as flame and black as ink, ribboning through each morsel that graces my lips. I would thank him, if my mouth wasn't full. When he said he'd make me feel like a Queen, he wasn't lying.

The feast is my coronation.

There aren't many leftovers. The brain, I bequeath to its cancer, watching as consciousness sinks into a thick marinade of rot and terror. The heart, I sample, tasting the soft beat through the bars of its broken cage. But in the end, that stays too, as sustenance for the soul. Though it may not keep for long.

By the time I'm finished, even my demons are satisfied. At last, my mind is quiet. Content. Calm. So calm, I don't notice the embers smoldering in the background, quietly cooking up a five-star meal of their own.

Maybe Eddie's does. But he doesn't say a word.

I would have caught the fire sooner, had it not been for the highly unusual—and combustible— circumstances of my upbringing. Being raised in a twenty-four-seven inferno, one becomes accustomed to the ash, the smoke, the rolling heat waves and mile-high walls of inextinguishable flame. I can be knee-deep in the molten rapids of a literal lake of fire, and I'll barely feel the heat. In fact, this body is completely fire-proof, thanks to Dad and his team.

But I'm digressing. Again.

Long story a beat shorter: I fucked up. I smelled the smoke, but didn't see the flames. Didn't see the glaring, greedy tongues of wild vermillion that shot up like weeds from Fast Eddie's discarded cigar and onto the flammable remains of the wall behind me. A total rookie mistake. And now, it's too late to fix it.

Or go running home to Daddy.

The blaze is already rampant, devouring the south wall and surrounding furniture like a fat kid plowing through a box of girl scout cookies. But I can't just leave. Dad will be livid if I flee, allowing his property to go up in smoke with the rest of this dilapidated club. And it wouldn't be any less miserable a fate for poor Eddie—his soul would burn eternally in the ghost of this room, just as it would in the ever-lasting conflagration below. Hell would have him, eventually, but it could take fifty years to scrape his spirit out of the wreckage, and that would be bad optics for my father's end-of-year reports.

Dad doesn't like to lose, likes it even less when it reflects badly on him, and lost souls are a major embarrassment. These days, hauntings are getting scarcer, but there are a few outstanding criteria that guarantee spiritual displacement. Drama, mainly. It's all about making an impact, going out with a bang brutal enough to throw off the soul's trajectory. With time, a wound on the world may heal, but in the afterlife, violence always leaves a permanent stain. Which does not bode well for anyone in this building.

"God damnit."

Out of ideas, profanity seems the only course of action. My demons are napping, too deep in their post-banquet slumber to hear my distress. Meanwhile, the blaze ignores my outburst entirely, carrying on uninterrupted. Beside me, another searing tongue curls itself around the emaciated flute of a standing lamp, inches from reaching the ceiling. Two of the four walls are now engulfed, their brittle, worm-eaten innards acting as ready-made tinder. This club is going to be a funeral pyre within the hour. And not just for Eddie.

I glower at the budding inferno, raking a hand over my forehead. Personally, I don't give a shit about Eddie's afterlife, as long as it's appropriately heinous, but he isn't the only one in danger of becoming spiritual kindling. Beyond these walls, sorrow lingers, a shadow lying in wait. But it does not wait in silence. Even now, I can hear it, crying out like mourning, like a widow bent in anguish over a casket, a concerto of tangled heartstrings ruing the day they locked their dreams inside the Gilded Cage.

But they won't be caged much longer. Their quarters are just down the hall, behind the padlocked door Eddie claimed was a dressing room. He didn't want me to find his pretty pets, but soon enough, the flames will.

Unless—

I shake my head, banishing the thought before it sinks in. I can play the victim till the end of days, batting my lashes at all the Hell-bound lowlifes on Dad's hit list, but not the hero. Even dressed to the nines in distressed damsel finery, I'm still just a wolf in a nice outfit. A predator. A monster. The one and only Daughter of Darkness.

End of story.

Of course, this story is a long way from over. Which is made all the more apparent when, as if on cue, the floor begins to shake, rippling with fitful shivers of imminent bedlam.

"Fuck."

None of this is a surprise, but in my beleaguered state, the disruption still throws me for a loop. As the tremor builds, rolling like a wave beneath me, I gasp and pitch forward, teetering in the six-inch stilettos strapped to my feet. Spitting an additional slew of expletives, I recover just in time, stumbling into the single non-flaming wall in the room while loudly cursing my choice of footwear.

On the bright side, I'm now a semi-safe distance away from the fault line.

In the seven- or eight-foot gap between my disheveled stance and the withered husk of my dinner, the quake makes its mark, drawing a long, jagged line in the hardwood. My pulse quickens, beating in time with the ruckus as the crack bursts open, stretching into a sickle-shaped gash that bears a striking resemblance to the Glasgow smirk Eddie wore back when he still had lips. But at least this one isn't as chatty. A few disgruntled tremors later, the quake dies down, descending gruffly into the abyss like an petulant child sent to bed before dinner. The floor, however, keeps smiling, grinning up at me almost smugly, as if it knows what's coming.

No.

No no no no.

At least my demons are awake now. Roused from their slumber, they trash with worry, pricking my nerves like some bizarre internal form of acupuncture. Not that I blame them. Sensing the impending disaster encircling our shared body, they know we're about to incite some serious wrath.

I frown, nervously biting my blood-stained lips. Hell hath no fury like a woman scorned, but my scorn was only supposed to take out Eddie, not the entirety of his moldering empire. That's a lot of souls Dad will never get a taste of.

Maybe I could devise a way to diffuse the situation, if I had a moment to think. But I don't. In my line of work, judgment is always punctual, and my meal break ended a while ago.

He's coming.

He'scominghescoming.

Right on schedule, a fresh burst of thick, sulfuric smoke fills the room, hazing my vision in swirling obsidian. I sway like a pendulum, struggling to keep my balance while my eyes variegate with defensive tears. But I don't back down. Showing weakness now would be like throwing gasoline on every flame in the vicinity.

Shielding my eyes with the back of my hand, I creep forward, plunging through the acrid smokescreen. I get close, but not too close, stopping just shy of the outermost crack. Then, I lower my gaze, facing off with the grinning Hell-mouth. Inside, doom approaches: a stark, insidious stretch of black juxtaposed by the red-hot depths like a shadow on the burning face of the sun.

He always has to make a big entrance.

Across the room, the unblinking eyes of my fileted victim flare like headlights, reflecting the fevered effulgence of the encroaching blaze. At this point, I doubt he's lucid enough to feel conscious fear—the mind doesn't function so well without a steady supply of blood and oxygen—but the sheer, unvarnished horror in his eyes suggests that if there is any life left in that wretched soul of his, it's telling him to be scared to death.

He should be. He's about to meet my dad.

8

At this point, I'm sure it's no secret who my father is, despite how rarely I call him by name. In my defense he has many, *too many,* and very specific opinions on each of them. He'll answer to "the Prince of Darkness," for instance, but has complained for centuries of the inaccuracy of the title, since there's no one sitting on the throne but him. When he wants an ego boost, he endorses "Satan," as well as the legions of mortal worshippers and heavy-metal burnouts who hail the moniker from their various dark, sweaty dens of misbehavior. He doesn't often go by Mephistopheles—it's a bit of a mouthful for the modern tongue—but he still makes his fair share of Faustian bargains. The list goes on. Though as far as I know, he's never had any complaints about his Christian name, Lucifer.

I rarely address him using any of the above. The world will never stop inventing new words for evil, but at the end of the day, he's still "Dad" to me.

For the most part.

As the smoke disperses, coiling around his limbs like a mist of gray pestilence, I can finally see his infernal glory in vivid detail. Historically, Satan has always been a shapeshifter, but he hasn't done many wardrobe changes lately. Style, he says, is almost as timeless as sin, and I'm sure the editors of *Vogue* and *Forbes* would agree. From the neck down, he could be a wildly successful mob boss or drug kingpin, perhaps even a Wall Street executive—the difference is negligible, since they often shop at the same stores. Either way, his attire is flawless, sheathing the tower of his build in an armature of matte black that looks less like fabric and more like a second skin. Who knows, maybe it is. His silhouette is so dramatic, even the flames pale by comparison, the delineation of his outline standing out like a masterpiece against a backdrop of amateur artworks, a Caravaggio amongst sloppy, crumpled caricatures.

I sigh, shifting my focus from my father's debonair portrait to the encroaching disaster. For obvious reasons, Dad is entirely unfazed by the inferno. He is, however, supremely pissed off about it. He just has a unique way of showing it.

For a full five minutes after his arrival, he doesn't say a word. Eyes honed to sniper-precision, he shoots a round of dirty looks around the room, firing silent, scathing bullets into the flaming walls, the mini bonfires of furniture, and the miraculously un-immolated body on the floor. By the time his regard circles back to me, the fire has spread, burning the black of his stare like coal. Gaze unbroken, he inhales a sharp sibilation of smoke through his teeth, square jaw clenched in an attempt to bite back his fury. Then he raises a many-ringed hand, not in greeting, but to smooth back a single rogue strand that has escaped the plateau of his otherwise immaculately slicked-back hair, an imperfection that I know from experience isn't accidental, but premeditated, planned precisely to add one more infinitesimal layer of tension to this moment.

My father learned ages ago that whether you're a man, a God, or the Antichrist, power is all about presentation, woven like fine thread into the carefully curated optics and subliminal messages of body language. To keep power, you can't just close a single fist around it, you must embody it entirely. Especially if someone else wants it. That's when the sleight of hand really comes in useful. Manipulation is a tried-and-true tactic, hence the two-faced stand-offs and twisted, Machiavellian plots that dominate every conference room in the city. These moves topple empires without ever entering the battlefield, and my father, ancient, bloodthirsty being that he is, invented most of the playbook.

heishere heishere.

Beneath my skin, my demons scatter like roaches exposed to light, hissing in fear as they search for sanctuary. But I don't follow their lead. Unfortunately for Dad, his scare-tactics don't work as well on me. Our third wheel on the floor, however, looks appropriately terrified. Granted, his face—or skull, if I was to accurately describe the flesh-to-bone ratio of his countenance—is stuck that way now. In his glass-eyed gaze, some lights are still on, but it's hard to say if anyone is home.

I'm sure Dad can tell. Without visibly moving a muscle, he comes closer, drifting in with the clouds of smoke, some of which I suspect did not originate from the fire or the chasm—when the Devil gets heated, he really smolders. The floor groans beneath him, dissenting as he alights onto the rotted hardwood. He studies me a moment, taking in my impassive expression. Then, at last, he speaks.

"What. The. Hell." A dramatic pause, and then, *"Have you done?"*

This time, his aim is right on target. If his stare is a sniper, his voice is a shotgun, every word a hollow point shattering the airwaves like sheets of glass. Wincing, I shrink back against the wall and instinctively cover my ears. Which accomplishes nothing. The echo of the blast is subcutaneous, piercing like shrapnel. My body may be fortified against earthly hazards, but my father's unholy bravado is about as unearthly as it gets.

"Oh," Dad groans. Seeing my reaction, his eyes go wide, the onyx of his pupils mirroring my distress in disarming duplicate. Sometimes, he forgets he's addressing his own daughter, not some misguided Archangel out on a crusade, hoping to heat up the cold war between Heaven and Hell.

"Sorry, princess," he says, lowering his tone an octave. "I got a little worked up there. You know how stressful this time of year gets. I just lost another village to those damned missionaries. Well, not damned, but…" he trails into a sardonic laugh, a resonance like steel scraping bone. "You get the idea."

"That's okay," I mutter, rubbing my temples. "I just wish you'd inoculated this vessel for migraines."

"Ah." Dad sighs. "Well, we're still working on that one. The human mind is resistant to advancement. You know this."

My gaze trails onto the catatonic ruins of Fast Eddie, dead-eyed and motionless. "True."

"But let's not get off topic. You've made quite a mess here," the Prince—sorry, *King*—of Darkness declares, his cadence a firm hand reminding me who's in charge. Preparing his judgment, he discharges another round of scrutiny into fire, which has officially reached critical levels: eighty percent inferno, a meager twenty percent breathing room. "We need to talk," he adds flatly. An order—not a request.

I nod, but I'm already distracted. Through the roar of the blaze, the laments of its soon-to-be-victims are still seeping in, looping like melancholic Muzak in the background. Sounds like the songbirds are having a rough night. Little do they know, it's going to get astronomically worse.

But I'm trying not to think about that.

Dad doesn't comment on the noise. "So…" he presses, arching a poignant eyebrow in my direction. "Are you going to tell me how this happened?"

I purse my lips, mulling over a slapdash list of excuses, when all at once, it hits me: yes, he wants an explanation. He wants one, but he doesn't need one. He's the Lord of the Underworld, for God's sake— not that I'm dragging Dad's nemesis into this equation, except to say that much like Him, my father has eyes everywhere. Eyes that have surely already provided the explanation he just demanded. Ergo, what he's really asking for is a confession.

Which suddenly, I don't feel like giving. Sure, I screwed up. But if memory serves, I've made less than ten mistakes over the course of the last century. That, I think, should earn me a little leeway. Or better yet— a vacation.

Not that the "boss" would ever approve one. He's got plenty of other reapers—deathless, devoted underlings who would fill in anytime. But to him, it's a matter of principle. And control. I may be immortal, but I'm not supposed to have a life. I'm supposed to be a workaholic, just like Daddy.

Of course, I'll never get my way by being insubordinate. Hell, look what happened to him.

"Yes, of course, we can talk," I say finally. I force a congenial smile, slipping into the dutiful daughter routine. "But why don't we do that..." I extend an arm, making a sweeping Vanna White gesture towards tonight's offering, which I imagine is starting to get stale, "after—"

I stop short, cut off by a violent, thundering blast, furious as my father's tempestuous baritone, followed by a jarring sputter, like a misfired engine or a hacking smoker's cough, reminding me briefly of the fateful cigar that sparked the first of the flames. And oh, how they've grown. The backdraft has reached its breaking point, and I'm right in the eye of the storm. But I don't get a chance to return its gaze. Before I can blink, the blaze starbursts, detonating like an atomic bomb in my vision. And just like that, the room vanishes, receding into the red.

Then it starts screaming.

The sensory overload hits like a sledgehammer. My head spins, whirling with vertigo. Through the blinding anarchy of scarlet, orange, and vermillion, there are no landmarks, save for the scintillant flurry of airborne embers, taunting me like will-o-the-wisps. I have no idea how Dad is faring. I'm sure he'll get what he came for. He wouldn't let a soul that wicked slip away.

But I can't let myself dwell on it. In tandem with the panicked shrieks rattling the bars of the Cage, an internal alarm is blaring, demanding action.

Run.

run run runrunrun.

My reaction is instantaneous.

As I follow the rising siren's song of screams, tearing through molten curtains of flame that turn my silhouette into a living torch for about thirty seconds before disintegrating into bursts of fuming cinders— having a fire-proof vessel does have its perks—I don't think about what I'm doing. I don't think, period. My body is already miles ahead of my mind, and at the rate we're moving, it's impossible to tell when the two of them made this decision.

I may not be human, on paper, but that inherent fight-or-flight instinct is hard to erase.

But once I make it into the hall, which is now mid-extreme-remodel, draped in billowing sheets of crimson, it is clear this is not a retreat. My thoughts may be lagging behind, but my feet know exactly where they're headed. As do my hands, which instinctively shatter the scalding hot padlock on the door, snapping it like a twig.

There is no pain. There is only the sound of terror, swelling in sonic desperation. Behind the door, the songbirds are crying havoc, pouring their dying hopes into a distress call that no one in this ice-cold city will answer.

Except me.

I am here. And I'm not leaving without them.

Hell has enough broken hearts already.

My father, though, deeply disagrees. As my hand turns the doorknob, he howls in the distance, adding an explosive, powder-keg of a solo to the symphony of discord.

"Melinoë!"

Fuck.

He must really be livid. It's been almost a century since he's called me anything other than princess.

8

From the street, the club looks nothing like I remember. Finally living up to its name, the Gilded Cage shines like a great, empyreal beacon, crowned in lambent spires that illuminate the starless night halfway to Heaven. Ironic, considering where its owner is headed.

But that is of little concern to me.

My attention is here, on the flock of dazed, leggy songbirds milling around the sidewalk. The crowd is a tableau of shock and awe, glazed with a wide-eyed, burning wonder that summarizes the evening's pyrotechnic events far better than I ever could. I don't often use this term, but it really is a miracle they're all still standing. They'll have a few new scars, but remarkably, none of the ladies will need skin grafts.

"Hey," the bird nearest to me croons, tilting her swan-like neck in my direction as her trembling fingers struggle to light a cigarette. I sense she's fumbling with words as well, straining to find a clear line of dialogue in the haze. She looks at her unlit Lucky Strike, then back to me, knitting her soot-smeared brow in thought for a moment before settling on a simple, "thank you."

That's good enough for me.

"No problem," I tell her, lying through my teeth. There are a myriad of problems coming my way, a chain of repercussions to my frivolous heroism that could topple like dominos any minute. But I won't trouble this girl with all that. In her short time on this earth, she's had more than her fair share of troubles already.

Poor, sweet Bettie. I barely know you, but in the depths of my dark, hollow heart, I know you deserve so much better.

Cigarette held tight between the pout of her lips, she regards me quizzically, puzzling over the woman-shaped enigma standing before her. For a split second, recognition simmers in her steel blue eyes, and I see her place me, spotting my face in the crowd during her big number earlier in the evening—a crowd that never left the building.

I don't say anything, no comment always being the best option, but quietly, I worry she might call my bluff, tossing my innocuous guise of smoke and mirrors to the wind. Which would be a total disaster. As much as I'd love to come clean, it wouldn't be worth the mess. In situations like this, the truth goes one of two directions: up or down. My money's on the former. Mortals always confuse demons with angels, no matter how many times the world tries to set the record straight.

Admittedly, it was me who just wandered into a gray area. But I intend to stay there. After the night I just had, the last thing I want is to start a new religion.

Across the street, a fleet of fire trucks and aid cars burst onto the scene, pouring gallons of too-late salvation onto the inflamed building. Around me, the survivors gasp, swaying in their charred frocks and broken stilettos as they watch the fire begin to fizzle. For a blaze of glory, the Cage's death throes don't last long. Downstairs, on the other hand, the inferno is just getting warmed up.

Beside me, one last flame leaps to life, kissing the end of Bettie's dangling cigarette. Snapping her Zippo shut, she inhales deeply, the pearling smoke adding a pale chiaroscuro to the ashfall veiling her face.

"So," I venture, curiosity overpowering my fried nerves. "What's your name, hon?"

My companion doesn't respond right away. Following a plume of smoke, her stare drifts across the street, sweeping back over the smoldering ruins of her former prison. Her expression is dubious, wary, as if she doesn't trust what she sees.

I want to tell her it will be alright, that the nightmare is over, that she is safe. But I don't. She's heard that song and dance before, and I'm not a fan of covers.

She takes another drag, then turns back to me. "Candy," she says, spitting the name in the center of a near-complete smoke ring.

I cock my head, thrown by the sudden shift in her composure. Candy is a sweet indulgence, but hers starts to sour the moment she breathes it into existence, twisting revulsion like barbed wire around her features. But there's something else there, too, and it only takes me a second to place it. That barricade she just put up is more than just bitterness—it's a wall, a dam holding back a raging river.

I heave into a sigh, bending beneath the weight of revelation. This girl wasn't the one I heard sobbing tonight. Aside from her broken-hearted Nancy Sinatra routine, she doesn't show her pain. She swallows it.

She's been drowning in it for years.

If I could, I would dive in with her. But if I'm being honest, a part of me is already there.

Instead, I take a baby step toward her. "Candy, huh? That's your *real* name?" I ask gently. I'll laugh if it's Bettie.

That gets her attention.

"Oh! No." Her eyes spark, cloudy baby blues

226

flashing with sudden clarity, a warm glow lightening her expression. But under the surface, the damage is still there. "Sorry, stage names are hard to shake," she palms her cheek with her free hand, like she's trying to cover the cracks. "It's actually Dahlia."

I lower my gaze, eyeing the scrawny wisp of her silhouette. I bet she was a beautiful flower once, before she came to the city. "That's a gorgeous name. Don't change it."

Lowering her cigarette, Dahlia smiles—a real, unscripted smile, bright and pure as the golden beams of daybreak that are inching tentatively into the smog-choked sky behind her. When she looks at me, a thousand words flicker between us, the shape of a story we both know by heart already. "Thank you," she says again, and I can tell she means it.

"Don't mention it," I reply, returning her grin. Hope looks good on her.

Yes yes she looks delicious.

Well, look who's awake. I was starting to think I was living with a bunch of narcoleptics.

We are here we are here we are—

Starving.

I scoff under my breath. My demons will have to go hungry for now. Dahlia's soul may be succulent, but it's not on the menu. And I'll make sure they don't forget it.

Before my minions have a chance to complain, a low, uneasy rumble interrupts their chatter, shuddering through my nerves like the bass of a cranked stereo. Luckily, the girls don't react. They aren't sensitive enough to pick up the signal, but the source of the disruption is closer than they'd ever guess.

But I'd better not incite a panic. Keeping my trepidation to myself, I survey the periphery, then hone in on ground zero. The rescue team is still toiling away, scouring the ruins for jaws and teeth to match with dental records, but as my eyes trail over the debris, I don't see any cause for alarm. Eddie's degenerate followers will yearn for revenge, but they can't haunt me unless I let them. I don't scare easily, and of all the vengeful spirits I've pissed off lately, there's only one who poses a threat.

Dad.

His wrath is coming. Maybe not today, or tomorrow, or next week, or the one after, but sooner or later, it will find me. Behind the scenes, Hell is preparing to break loose, and when it does, the Devil will take me down, dragging me back home kicking and screaming. Then, he'll decide my punishment, which could be any number of gruesome horrors. Maybe he'll stick me on level two, parading my underage vessel like a dangled hook to further torment the rapists and pedophiles. Or, if he's feeling especially cruel, he'll chain me to a desk, where I'll spend the next year crunching numbers.

But he'll have to catch me first. And until that happens, I am officially on vacation.

Without a second thought, I turn away from the ashes of the Gilded Cage and observe the flightless birds lingering on the sidewalk. A few of the girls have already departed, swept up by aid cars or nosy newscasters. The rest seem unsure of where to go from here. Amidst the dull roar of the city, whispers dart through the thin crowd like mothwings, a nervous flutter waiting for someone to flip the lights on. Their faces are somber, stained by smoke and shadow, some of which will never come off. My pretty new friend, however, hasn't lost her radiance.

But she could, if she isn't careful. Her smile is fresh, fragile, a sliver of hope still in danger of spreading too fast and shattering her whole epilogue to pieces. Nonetheless, it's the closest I've ever been to a happy ending, and I'm going to make sure she gets to keep it.

Come Hell or high fucking water.

ABOUT THE AUTHOR

DIANA OLNEY is a Seattle based author, but she is most at home in the shadows, wandering the paths between nightmares and dreams. She writes in many shades of fiction, including horror, fantasy, science fiction, and LGBTQ dark romance. Her stories and poems have appeared in *Dark Horses Magazine* and anthologies by Hellbound Books, Crystal Lake Publishing, Worldstone Publishing, and Critical Blast. She is also the creator of *Siren's Song,* an original comic series due to be released this year. Visit her website dianaolney.com or find her on Facebook for updates on her latest terrors.

MR. DAMAGE

Ray Zacek

A fiery dragon rippled over his bicep, vivid in crimson, emerald green, and blazing orange, his lucky dragon tattoo. Painfully acquired over hours in the chair in the tattoo studio, but the artist at Bangkok Best, named Narong, assured him good luck would always follow him. Always. Luck never never fails, Narong insisted with a wide grin. Whatever vagaries or vicissitudes might befall him, and these were inevitable in life, dragon luck would come through when he most needed it.

And now was when Chris Zucco needed that luck.

He sat in bankruptcy court. In Re: George C. Zucco, aka G. Chris Zucco, debtor, Middle District of Florida, Tampa Division. Waiting for his final hearing, the honorable judge so-and-so presiding; Chris forgot her name. Middle-aged blonde woman with a no-nonsense demeanor. Chris' financial fate rested in her hands. She had a lengthy court docket to work through that morning and looked harried. That, Chris Zucco concluded, worked to his advantage. He surveyed the church-like chamber. High ceiling, dark brown wood panel walls, rows of seats like pews, all filled, everybody silent. Chris waited. And waited.

Played the daily Wordle on his phone and scanned social media until his case was called by the court clerk.

Chris Zucco stood and approached the bench …

Months earlier, behind the financial eight ball, he had filed Chapter 7. This required him to attend something called a 341 hearing to answer questions from the court-appointed trustee and any creditors who showed up. And they did. Several po-faced lawyers for people to whom Chris owed money; his debts were legion. Chris Zucco represented himself, asserting he lacked the funds to hire counsel.

"Honest," he said to the trustee. "I'm *literally* out of pocket." He turned the pockets of his razor-creased khaki pants inside out for dramatic effect.

A creditor lawyer smirked.

Divested of assets and unemployed, Chris Zucco owned *nothing* for the trustee to liquidate. Absolutely. Zero, nada, niente, zilch. He swore to that fact, filing disclosure forms with the court under penalties of perjury.

"How are you living," the trustee asked, a diminutive woman with a helmet of black hair and an assembly line approach to her job.

"Marginally," Chris said. He smiled. "One day at a time. Moment by moment. Almost like Zen, you know. I strive for that kind of equanimity."

The trustee remained unamused, uncharmed by his upbeat attitude, and furrowed her brow. "How are you paying your expenses?"

"There's not much expense."

"But how are you *paying*?"

"Family. Friends. I have many loyal friends. I live with my girlfriend. But that's kind of iffy." A small shake of his hand indicated uncertainty. "Until she's tired of supporting me or I can get back on my feet, whichever comes first. *Ha ha*.' Nervous laughter, followed by a sigh and a quick mask of despondency, almost but not quite tearing, *suggesting* tears, and glad he had taken acting lessons in New York.

"I'm trying to stay positive in the face of adversity."

The trustee remained indifferent and noted, "Your financial disclosure doesn't list any vehicles."

"Sold the Lexus over a year ago," replied Chris. "Other vehicles were leased. Repo'd or returned to the dealership."

The trustee leveled her gaze at him. "How did you get here today?"

"My girlfriend loaned me her car." He paused a beat for effect, and added, "It's a twelve-year-old Toyota Corolla."

The trustee's job was to liquidate available assets to pay creditors, but the trustee summarily called it quits, concluding this was a *no asset* case. Attorneys for creditors objected: Mr. Zucco has concealed or transferred assets yada yada yada. But, of course, they couldn't *prove* it. They filed objections with the court, issued subpoenas, deposed him, hammered him, investigated, dragging on the case for months, but ultimately found nothing. Nada, niente, zilch.

Chris gloated: *This is Florida, the Sunshine State, bitches, and you got 1,350 miles of coastline upon which you can go pound sand.*

At his final hearing in front of the bankruptcy judge, his lucky dragon smiled and farted furious flames upon his adversaries.

The judge concurred with the trustee, overruling creditors' objections, and granting a discharge. That legal abracadabra meant his debts vanished. Erased.

Wiped the fuck out. Meaning Chris Zucco won the contest, ridding himself of a towering dogpile of accrued debt--including old income taxes. Stiffing the IRS proved icing on the red velvet cake.

Bitches, you can't touch me. Chris suppressed a grin leaving the courtroom. Creditor attorneys cold-shouldered him as they passed down the hall. He waited for the next elevator to the lobby to avoid them, taking in the panoramic view of the city and Tampa Bay from the windows. Black vultures cruised on the rising thermals and congregated on the top of the federal courthouse. The next elevator all to himself, he descended; the doors susurrated open to the lobby with its shiny marble floors. Chris strolled past security guards and metal detectors and paused outside on the steps to bask in the radiant Florida sun. Gorgeous day. He had parked Amber's ice blue Toyota in a metered space on Polk Street a block away near the Si-Am Thai restaurant and the glitzy marquee of the old Tampa Theatre. The Hub Bar on the corner beckoned and Chris wanted a drink but demurred. Previous substance abuse had contributed to his current predicament. Don't court DUI, he counseled himself. Keep things low risk. For the time being. There'll be ample oppo to celebrate.

He was about to scooch into the driver's seat of the Corolla when a white panel van pulled alongside. Its brakes screeched. Panel door slid open and a blonde amazon tasered him and dragged him into the van and slammed the door shut with the finality of a guillotine. G. Chris Zucco involuntarily urinated and convulsed as the van sped away.

8

"Wake up!" The blonde slapped Chris Zucco. "Wake the fuck up!"

"Whaaaaaa?" He drooled. His cheek stung. A rack of high-intensity lights overhead blinded him; he squinted. Groggy, head throbbing, grimy, sweaty, Chris found himself stripped to his jockey briefs and lashed to a folding chair on a bare concrete floor. The woman slapped him again. The smirk on her face and glint in her eyes telegraphed that she enjoyed this.

"Stop!"

"He wants to talk to you," she said. A hard, unpretty face. Eyes green and mean, like a snake. Spiky white-blonde hair, chin weak. She wore a black sleeveless t-shirt and cayenne red yoga pants. Silver rings pierced her nose. Tats latticed her muscular arms, a black fleur-de-lys prominent.

"Who wants to talk to me?"

"Mr. Damage," she replied. With a sharp turn on her heels, she strode away, pushing through the curtain of PVC strips.

"Who's Mr. Damage?" Chris called after her.

She didn't answer. Chris' eyes adjusted. He hurt. Zip ties cut into his ankles and wrists. He found himself in an enclosure of vinyl strip curtains. Chris smelled paint and motor oil and urine from his jockey shorts. An industrial fan whirred overhead. An ominous and continuous whoosh.

The woman reappeared through the curtains, scowling, carrying a small melamine bowl. She held the bowl by his mouth.

"Swallow," said the woman.

"What is it?" He stared into the bowl. A bubbly brown liquid, grayish taupe chunks floating on its surface.

"Shrooms. Now open your fuck'n mouth."

Chris balked but she pinched his nose and pressed the rim of the bowl to his lips and teeth. Chris slurped. The liquid proved warm and savory, and he swallowed the soup and the mushrooms, almost choking. He felt the warm pungent concoction plunge like effluent into his empty stomach.

"Tastes funny," said Chris.

"Turmeric. He swears by it." Taking the empty bowl, she turned away.

"Who swears?"

"Mr. Damage," she replied with an exasperated sigh, and stalked out of the enclosure again with a mannish stride.

"Hey," Chris called after her again. "Hey, hey, hey. Talk to me. What's going on? Why am I here? Why are you doing this? Did someone *hire* you to do this?"

He shouted until his lungs ached. No answer. Nothing. Silence except for the minatory sound of the fan overhead. He tugged the zip ties that bound his wrists and ankles. to no use. A lengthy nylon rope at his waist also lashed him to the chair, which was bolted to the concrete floor. He perspired under the harsh lights. How long he waited, he could not calculate. Half hour, forty-five minutes, an hour, more than an hour, eternity. His stomach rumbled. He burped, the taste of turmeric in his mouth. Stomach cramps assaulted him, twisting his gut into painful figure 8's. Chris groaned.

A gravel voice. "The bellyache goes away."

Chris looked up. The vinyl curtains parted. A scrawny, scraggly-bearded rodent in grease-stained gray coveralls stepped into the disclosure. He lugged another gunmetal gray folding chair.

Chris studied him, genuinely confused. "Do I know you?"

"I lost weight."

He unfolded the chair in front of Chris and sat.

Steel toe work boots planted firmly on the concrete floor, skinny body loose and relaxed, almost feline, a wide derisive grin on his face. A gold cuspid glinted. This freaking clown with foul sauerkraut breath had to have been hired by one of his disgruntled creditors, Chris reasoned. Several suspects came to mind. Barry Schaumberg, who carried grudges like forget-me-nots; Fat Ellis, that Aussie sluggard and former pro-wrestler; or possibly Petrus, who had hired that smirking lawyer at the 341 hearing.

His weight-loss-bragging captor said, "Pleased to meet you, hope you guessed my name. My bitch only told you twice."

Chris swallowed. His stomach churned like a turbine. "Oh, right, right, right, Mr. Damage." He summoned resolve; Chris Zucco was a smooth operator who could talk his way out of a sunburn, and that lucky dragon would come through again. Had to!

"Okay, Mr. Damage. Let's talk. Who're you working for?"

"I'm self-employed," Mr. Damage said, affronted. Then, distracted like a kid with ADD, he reached out and stroked Chris' upper arm. "Nice tat! I *like* that. I covet that. Where'd you get it?"

"Uh, Thailand," said Chris. The fingertips caressing his arm felt a little too cosy for comfort. "Pattaya Beach. I was in the Navy. But look, look, look, tell me who hired you to do this."

"Nobody hired me. You owe me."

"Owe you for *what*?"

"Put on your thinking cap, Zucco!" He withdrew his hand and glared. "Mr. Damage. *Mr. Damage.* I worked on your car! The fuck'n Lexus."

"Oh, yeah." Chris nodded. Grey matter sizzled.

Mr. Damage Auto Body & Collision Repair. A garage in east Tampa, near Gibsonton, the old carny town. Chris had taken the Lexus LX there after a fender bender. Mr. Damage did expert work and came highly recommended. The guy was an old hippie, a stoner, plump and mellow, and easy-going about payment. But he was a scarecrow now, neither plump nor mellow.

"You must be ... *Don?*"

"I'm known as Don." He leaned back in the chair, relaxed. "I have had different names in different times and places but in the sweet here-and-now I am Mr. Damage, and you, Chrissy, owe me two grand, two hundred and fifty-seven semolians."

"That's not that much," said Chris. A pittance compared to his other debts.

Mr. Damage brushed this aside with a wave of his hand. "Like they say, the principle of the thing."

I should've paid him out of the insurance check, thought Chris. *But I didn't, fuck me!* Now he had to think fast to placate the crazy old hippie and extricate himself from this bloody mess. Chris took a deep breath.

"I'll level with you, Don. I'm broke. Flat broke, man. I just got out of bankruptcy! Did you know that?"

Mr. Damage nodded. "I knew that."

"That's where I was, coming out of the federal courthouse downtown when you, uh, grabbed me. Your timing is not good. Simply awful. Are you kidding? I don't have any money."

The blonde reappeared, snorted with contempt, and pulled out a small semiauto pistol from under her t-shirt. She brandished it and pulled back the action to chamber a round. "He's fuck'n lying!"

"No! No! I swear! Believe me, Don! Mr. Damage, believe me. You saw what I'm driving. A *Corolla* for fuck's sake! I lost the Lexus, lost every cent I had, lost the house in south Tampa. *Lost everything!*"

The blonde leveled the muzzle of the pistol at Chris' face. "Open your mouth."

Chris shuddered. "Whoa! Let's not do anything rash. No, don't do this! Don! I get back on my feet, give you my word, *I'll pay you.*"

The blonde seethed. "I said open your fuck'n mouth." She jammed the barrel against his lips, chipping a tooth, crushing Chris' lip.

"Wait," said Mr. Damage. His face remained impassive, stony. He placed his hand on the blonde's wrist, his bony fingers caressed her pale skin, his touch dainty. His voice conciliatory. "Ashley, Ash, baby, wait. Back up. Not before the Reveal."

"Shit," said Ashley. She scowled but lowered the weapon and replaced it under the baggy t-shirt in the waistband of the yoga pants at the small of her back. She stepped back and folded her arms across her chest, subordinate but sulky, and stood by the curtain of vinyl flaps.

I can manage the situation, Chris thought. Copious sweat burned his eyes. The coppery tang of blood filled his mouth. His pulse raced. *My luck is going to hold. My luck is going to hold. My luck is going to hold.* His stomachache had subsided. He felt no pain. He felt dizzy, but confident and, oddly, almost euphoric. Sure, sure, sure, he could talk to Don, and they'd work this out. Reasonably. Focus, focus, focus! This was business. The art of the deal. The luck of the dragon. Chris Zucco would walk out of here with a win.

"Talk to me," said Chris. "We can work this out. Give me two weeks. Two weeks and I'll pay you what

I owe you plus. Starting a new job. Sales. And that, sales, you know, is my *forte*. I can finagle an advance. Or I can borrow from family. So, what say you, Don?"

"Nope," replied Don.

"What? *Why*? Why, Don?"

He announced, "Because I am a Scythian."

Chris looked at him, stupefied. "What's a Scythian?"

His smile was serene and knowing. "Ancient nomadic warriors of the Asian steppes north of the Black Sea. In a past life, I was called Dakkar, and I was a shaman. *This* was given to me *to know.*"

"Oh," said Chris, hiding his incredulity. "Uh, who gave this to you?"

"The shrooms. They told me." He went on. "Shrooms are conscious entities, and they can impart knowledge, if they so choose, if we approach them the right way." He sounded professorial and wagged his bony finger for emphasis; then Mr. Damage nodded. "I made supplication. Crawled on my belly like a serpent. Ate dirt. Humbled myself before their glory. And the shrooms granted me a revelation of past lives. The Scythian one, the best. And so, long story short, I live *this* life Scythian-style. According to an unsparing code."

Unsparing. Chris didn't like that word. A negative word, a discouraging word. Got to navigate past unsparing, he resolved, and anchor in a safe harbor. Chris thought: humor the guy. Play along with his delusion. Let him wax eloquently. Establish some affinity. Reach an agreement. Go free.

"That is cool, Don. That is, absolutely, cool beyond cool, Don. Uh, Mr. Damage. Or should I call you Dakkar? But listen to me. Listen. I. Can. Pay. You. I *will* pay you what I owe you, bruh. Given time, time, a little time is all."

A wry smile of disappointment crossed Mr. Damage's face. "You don't believe me. About the Scythian life."

"Sure, I believe you. I do," said Chris.

Mr. Damage remained unconvinced. "Didn't expect you would," shaking his head. "You must *see* to believe. The shrooms you ate should be starting to work now."

"Work?" said Chris. A twinge of panic fluttered, like a tiny dark bird taking to wing. The wings created a ripple; Chris trembled. "What, what do you mean *work*? Work how?"

"You're ready for the Reveal." Mr. Damage kicked off his boots and peeled off his black compression socks. Then he stood. "Mr. Damage, Don, Dakkar. Only names. Names of the meat suits I've worn at different times. But, ah, meat don't last, the way of all flesh. What is beneath, what is essential, what is eternal, is the Spirit in the Sky."

"Huh?" said Chris. The ripple became a wave engulfing him with silt like stark terror as the overhead fan roared like a buzzsaw.

Mr. Damage stood. He towered. As if he had in that instant, gained height. Looking up rendered Chris dizzy. Behind this monstrous being the vinyl flaps waved like the sea of grass over the steppes.

When Mr. Damage spoke, his metallic voice echoed. "Each soul is a spark from the primordial fire. At the beginning of time, she was. The Flaming One, Goddess of Fire at the Heart of the Universe. She created this all, everything that exists."

Mr. Damage stripped off his gray coveralls. He wore nothing underneath. Chris watched, eyes bulging, as Mr. Damage transformed. Scrawny limbs, sunken chest, scabby scars, pale skin, and purple veins became scaly and magma red, pulsating, daimonic.

His eyes blazed darkness and dripped ichor. The balls of his feet clip-clopped on the concrete as he circled Chris.

Chris Zucco screamed. He twisted in the chair bolted to the floor.

Mr. Damage traced an evil vulture talon feather-soft along Chris' upper arm. "The tat. *Exquisite* dragon. I'll take it. The tat instead of the money you owe me."

Chris blurted out: *"No! No no no! Don't do that!"*

"Scythians take trophies. Ash, bring me the blade." The woman vanished like a wraith into the icy vinyl curtains.

"No! No, I'll pay you! Double, triple, quadruple what I owe you! I've got money. A bundle. Money's offshore, in the Caymans."

Mr. Damage chortled. "In the Caymans?"

"Yes! Yes! Wire transfer, wire transfer. Twenty-four hours."

"Never fuck with a Scythian," said Mr. Damage as Ash handed him a gleaming surgical steel scalpel. Then she stuffed a rag inside Chris' mouth, wrapped hurricane tape around his face like a shroud and applied a headlock, immobilizing him. Chris choked. Ash looked up at Mr. Damage.

"Take the money instead," Ash said. "We need money, numbnuts."

"Shut up. Money's nothing. Money's shit. I want the dragon. My lucky day it came to me."

Chris Zucco howled as Mr. Damage, eyes shining in ecstasy, pressed the cold edge of the blade to taut, quivering skin.

Bright red blood pooled on the concrete and Chris Zucco slumped unconscious in the folding chair, a wad of cotton bandage taped to his arm. Ash stepped behind him and whipped out the small caliber Bersa pistol, attaching a suppressor to its threaded barrel. Without a particle of compunction, she pointed the pistol at the back of Chris' head and squeezed the trigger. The pistol rattled twice, double tap.

"Did I tell you to do that?" Mr. Damage, dismayed, sat naked on the concrete, the strip of skin with the beautiful dragon tat in a dry, clean paint tray in front of him.

Ash scoffed. "It's what I do. Clean up your fuck'n messes."

"I planned to let him go."

"Like hell," said Ash. "That was never gonna happen."

"Insolent thing, aren't you?" Mr. Damage glowered. "Think about which tit you want in the wringer."

"Oh, bite me," she said and went to fetch plastic sheets and tarp for disposal of the body. Her fealty never faltered – Mr. Damage was, after all, a ferocious and charismatic shaman, and she remained in his thrall. Of all the men she had known in her luckless life, a cruel, alcoholic father back in Gretna; her drug-addled mother's abusive boyfriends; her own abusive boyfriends and former fetish partners; Mr. Damage stood out, the Scythian devil she knew and loved best. For that revelation, Ashley Robichaux needed no shrooms.

ABOUT THE AUTHOR

RAY ZACEK is a former fed, flaneur, and writer of horror, noir/crime, and dark fiction living in Tampa, Florida. His stories have been published in two previous Critical Blast anthologies: *The Devil You Know Better,* and *The Monsters Next Door.* His work has also appeared in *Tule Fog, Shotgun Honey, All Due Respect, Denver Horror Collective, Deadman's Tome* and *Out of the Gutter.*

Follow him on Facebook:

www.facebook.com/profile.php?id=100086806883340

THE DEVIL WITH POMPOMS

Robert Allen Lupton

Everyone is dead except me, of course, or I couldn't write this. Shame on me. I've written one sentence and it was a lie, or at the very least, inaccurate. I would have been more accurate to have written *everyone human who was involved is dead except me.* A situation that will soon be rectified.

One of the lessons I learned as a child was that no matter how fast you are, someone is faster, no matter how strong you are, someone is stronger, and most importantly, no matter how smart you are, there's always someone smarter. I did it again. I lied. I was taught the lesson that there will always be people faster, stronger, and smarter than me, but I didn't learn it. I only thought I did. If my friends were still alive, they'd agree with me.

The day after I graduated from High School, my alleged girlfriend and cheerleader, Martha Carson, told me she was going to college out of state and since long-distance relationships never worked, adios muchacho, and have a nice life. I was despondent at first, but it was the summer of love, 1967, and five of my friends, Greg, Kevin, Mikey, Tate, and Brian crawled into my Ford Econoline van and the six of us, four badly made fake IDs and twelve cases of beer left Ponca City, Oklahoma for the promised land, otherwise known as San Francisco, enticed by the lure of forgetfulness, free love, and free drugs. That's another lesson I'd conveniently forgotten, free stuff costs the most.

Interstate 40 had just been completed and it followed old Highway 66 across West Texas, New Mexico, and Arizona. We ran out of beer outside Los Angeles. We gassed up in Palm Springs, California, and Greg, who was the biggest, armed with fifty dollars and a fake ID, walked into the liquor store next door. Mikey followed him inside. The sign said Pearl Beer cost ninety-nine cents a six-pack, so fifty dollars would buy twelve and a half cases. The woman's name tag said Rowen and Rowen lifted the eyeglasses on the chain around her neck and inspected Greg's ID. She eyed him through red rheumy eyes and then glanced at Mikey. A driving license didn't have a photograph. She fingered the ID for a moment and tapped it against her oversized hook nose. "Ponca City, huh, you little shits are lucky I was born in Tulsa, otherwise I keep your fifty bucks and flush this piece of crap down the toilet."

She stuffed the fifty into a pocket on her large Hawaiian-style dress covered with palm trees, coconuts, and dancing women wearing fewer clothes than they do in the lingerie section of a Sears catalog. She lit a cigarillo, one of those little cigars with a plastic tip, and said, "Welcome to California."

It took us two trips to carry the beer. We iced down two cases and headed down the road listening to Gracie Slick on the eight-track player. We all wanted somebody to love.

We played the Beatles next, and then Johnny Rivers. A sheriff pulled us over near Bakersfield. I gave him my real driver's license. He looked it over, walked around my van, and said, "Open the back door, Jimmy. I ain't seen no one from Ponca City since we kicked their asses in the state semifinals back in 1958."

He tapped my ID against his hooked nose and put on the glasses hanging from a lanyard. He smiled at the cases of beer, empty and full, and sneezed at the stench of six unwashed male bodies in a confined space. "Well, you Okies ain't smugglers, or if you are, you're the stupidest I've ever seen. You boys gonna drink all that?"

Brian, always a smartass, said, "Yessir, the drinking age is 18 in Oklahoma."

The sheriff took a cigarillo from the shirt pocket of his Hawaiian shirt festooned with semi-clad hula girls. "Don't bullshit a bullshitter. My Mom lives in Enid, I know the drinking age, and besides, you ain't in Oklahoma anymore. I'm off duty or I'd run your redneck asses in just for the hell of it. Get the hell out of my county and when you go home, pick a different route."

Brian started to say something, but Tate pushed him back into the van. "Sir, yes sir. Thank you."

We had five cases of Pearl left when we got to Haight Ashbury. I'd never seen so many people in my life. None of them were as clean as we were and we were on the downside of disgusting. Kevin said, "I stink and y'all stink. Find a place to stay. I ain't sleeping in this van another night."

I didn't find a place to stay, but the third time I circled a large park, a station wagon pulled out of a parking place right in front of me. I wheeled right in. The driver in the station wagon waved at me, a cigarillo in hand. A plastic doll did the hula on the dashboard.

We slept in the park. I'd like to say that several beautiful young women showered us with free sex and drugs, but the only thing we got showered with was a rain squall at sunrise. I can't speak for the others, but, I stank like a wet collie.

We took turns changing in the van. A woman walked across the street with a sign in her hand. She walked around my van, looked at the license plate, and said, "I grew up in Oklahoma City. Where you boys from."

"Ponca City. We just got here last night."

My boys are off to summer school at Cal Berkley and I've got two rooms to rent. A hundred a month, each, money upfront."

She didn't look old enough to have kids in college. She was gorgeous and her hooked nose offset her eyes perfectly. We huddled for a bit and bitched to each other about California prices. "Yes, ma'am, we'll take them for a month."

I handed her five twenties and two fifties. She shoved the twenties under the coconuts on her Hawaiian print blouse and the fifties behind the frames of her horn-rimmed glasses. "Hose yourselves off before you come inside. I'll get you the keys. My name is Brenda. If you need anything, let me know. I've got good connections."

She caught me staring at her breasts and smiled. It wasn't a good smile. It was a Snidely Whiplash tie you to the railroad track kind of smile. "Anything. House rules are simple. Don't piss me off. You won't like it if you piss me off."

We wandered around Haight Ashbury the next day in groups of two. Six is a good number for team sports, but it's not good when you're looking for girls.

Girls were everywhere, but so were the boys they were with. Everyone had someone, except for us. Greg and I tried to talk to several people, but they were too stoned or too occupied to bother with a couple kids from the Midwest. The only girl who even responded asked, "You got any acid?"

Greg said, "Sulfuric or Hydrochloric?"

She just walked away.

We went back to Brenda's that afternoon and sat on her porch. She came outside and I offered her a Pearl.

"So, how was your day?" She snickered, "You didn't get lucky or you wouldn't be here."

Tate and Brian joined us. Brian replied, "Not sure that I want to. This place smells worse than a Fort Worth feedlot. The people stink. There aren't any public bathrooms and the stinky people act like the world is a toilet. Cats are more hygienic. The girls we met won't talk to us because we don't have no drugs."

Brenda finished her Pearl and sat up straight. "So you're not impressed with our little town?"

"Nothing wrong with it that a good fire or a firehose wouldn't fix. I can't believe people live like this on purpose."

Mikey and Kevin took off their shoes and sat on the steps. Greg said, "Your feet stink."

Kevin laughed. 'Not in this town they don't."

Brenda took off her glasses and lit a cigarillo. "It's too bad your road trip isn't working out. I can help with that. I've done the best I could for you so far, but I guess it hasn't been enough."

I shook my head. "No. ma'am, renting rooms to has been plenty."

"That's not what I mean." She exhaled cigarillo smoke through her petite hooked nose and gestured at her blouse. 'I would have thought you'd have figured it out by now. I gave you enough hints, but when an eighteen-year-old boy has one thing on his mind, well, he has one thing on his mind.'

Kevin stared at her. "She's got the same nose as that old lady that sold us the beer. She's smoking the same kind of little cigar and she's got the Hawaiian print top and her glasses are on a string and she said she was from Oklahoma and ..."

Brenda finished her Pearl. "Good for you, Kevin. I sold you the beer. I pulled you over so the real sheriff wouldn't and I held a parking place for you for three days. It took you long enough."

Tate thought about it. "Ma'am, you don't look like a male sheriff."

She smiled and her face darkened. Shadows drifted rapidly across her skin like storm clouds dancing over the moon. Her face faded in and out of focus, the only constant being that sharp hooked nose. The sheriff's face morphed into the old woman from Tulsa's. It became younger and the eyes of the girl who'd wanted some acid looked at us. The flickering slowed to a stop. "I can look like whoever I want. I got tired of waiting on you, so I decided to take things into my own hands."

Greg went pale. "Demon! She's a demon."

"No such thing as demons," I said.

Brenda ground the cigarillo out on her cheek. It didn't leave a mark. "Well, actually there are, but I wouldn't send a demon to make a deal with you boys. I don't delegate everything."

Greg dropped his beer. "She's the devil!"

"Now that wasn't so hard, was it? That's me. No sympathy, please."

"Supposing we believe you, whatcha want, our souls."

"Not exactly, those will be mine anyway. All of you will commit a mortal sin before you're twenty-five years old, but I'll give you a chance to keep your souls."

"Why didn't you just appear to us in Ponca City?"

"I might have known you in Ponca City, but a girl has to have some secrets. This is too nice a job to rush. Besides, I crave entertainment. Eternity is so damn boring."

"I'm not doing nothing bad," stated Tate.

"Except for your grammar. Tate, your father will develop lung cancer. You'll help him die. A mortal sin. Now, boys, here's the deal. All of you are mine, sooner or later, but I'll give one of you a chance at redemption. A contest, damn, I do love a good contest. The first one of you to make it from here to Bakersfield alive gets a get-out-of-hell-free card. The contest starts at sunrise tomorrow. No rules. Bonus points if you kill each other."

Kevin walked into the yard. "I don't believe this crap. I'm not going to play. I'll sleep in the van."

Halfway across the street, a Volkswagen van ran him down. Brenda's face flushed red and a hint of horns poked through her hair. She snarled. "That's not how this works. No one says no to me! Any more questions?"

Any questions or objections we had died with Kevin, so none of us said a word. I don't know where the others slept that night, but I lay awake under the van. I must have drifted off because when I got up to drive to Bakersfield, all four tires were flat. I kicked the door. Brenda walked across the street and handed me a cup of scalding hot coffee. "Better get started, Jimmy, everyone else left at sunrise."

"They slashed my tires."

"Well, actually I might have done that. Seemed only fair."

"You didn't say you were gonna be involved in the contest."

"Didn't say I wouldn't be. Now finish your coffee. Don't break the cup. It's an original Thomas Frye, England, 1751."

I grabbed my Boy Scout backpack and locked the van. No one was gonna steal a van with four flats, but I figured it was even money that a troop of hippies from Illinois would move in long before I saw the streets of Bakersfield. My choices were the bus station or hitchhiking. I picked the bus station. No doubt every broke and hungry free love reject would be hitchhiking home.

The problem was that I didn't have a clue where the bus station was. I tried to ask people in the park, but they ignored me. I found a gas station and figured I could buy a map. A beautiful young girl walked out as I walked toward the door. She handed me cola and a bag of Twinkies. Her blonde hair was tied with a Hawaiian print bandana and purple-tinted granny glasses were balanced on her hooked nose. She couldn't be a day over eighteen. I looked closer and she was Martha Carson, the head cheerleader at Ponca City High School who'd broken up with me less than two weeks ago. Her hair and makeup were different and I'd never seen her braless in the daylight, but it was her, but I knew it couldn't be her.

"Really, now you're Martha?"

She laughed, it was a scary laugh, a Boris Karloff, it's-time-to-die laugh. "Girl of your dreams, Jimmy, but you can still call me Brenda. Told you I might have been in Ponca City. I'm coming with you, but I'm just here for the show. Can't wait for the finale.

You don't need a map. I know the way."

"Why would you help me?"

"Jimmy, there's just something about you. You're my favorite, for now anyway. I'll keep track of the others and keep you posted. What's the plan, Stan?"

"I'm going to the bus station. You won't lie to me, will you?"

"I'd say no, no matter whether I'm going to lie to you or not. Are you stupid, of course, I'll lie to you. I'm the devil. It's my job. Take the Number 20 bus. It'll take us to the big dog, the Greyhound Station. The next bus to Bakersfield leaves in 45 minutes. Brian already has his ticket."

Brian was at the Greyhound Station. "Better kill him," whispered Brenda. She licked my ear. "He'll kill you. Only one of you gets to Bakersfield alive." She rubbed my thigh. "I choose you, but I only help those who help themselves. Kill him!"

I remembered what happened when people said no to Brenda. I followed him into the restroom, caught him at the urinal, and shoved his face into the pipes. I pulled him into a stall and shoved his head in the toilet. Then I threw up. I washed and went back to the waiting room. Brenda handed me a small bottle of Listerine. "Sissy, that wasn't hard was it. Your first mortal sin took less than a day. Welcome to the home team. It gets easier every time."

"There won't be a next time."

"What, you think this bus is going to take you to Bakersfield without anything going wrong? Silly boy, where's the fun in that. Fasten your seatbelt, Jimmy, it's going to be a bumpy ride."

"You stole that line from Bette Davis."

Brenda patted the seat next to her. "Maybe she stole it from me, or maybe I gave it to her. I'll never tell."

Brenda was now clothed in Martha's cheerleading outfit. Her legs were longer than I remember. I sat down, but I stayed as far from those tan legs as I could. I pouted, not proud to say it, but I did. The bus pulled into traffic and was broadsided by a garbage truck.

Tate was driving the truck and another Martha Carson was riding shotgun. I crawled out a window and reached to help my Martha, I mean Brenda, out, but she wasn't inside the bus. She was right behind me. Tate and the other Martha abandoned the trash truck. His Martha pointed at me and handed him a tire iron. "Kill him, Tate. You know the rules."

Blood dripped from Tate's forehead where he'd hit the windshield face first. He wiped his face with his shirt. "I don't want to kill him, he's my best friend."

"I'll be a better friend than he ever was. Kill him."

I glanced at my Martha. "What the hell, Brenda? Why are there two of you? Are you helping him or are you helping me?"

"Call me Martha for now. One of my names is Legion, for I am many. There are as many of me as I want there to be. As for helping, I really don't do that. I'm more of an agent provocateur. I push people. I keep them motivated as much as necessary."

"I'm not killing Tate."

The eyes on her blemish-free cheerleader face turned black and her voice turned cold. "Your call, but someone's killing someone. I'll wait with Tate's Martha while you two sort this out. Don't take too long. Greg and Mike are still out there."

"He's got a tire tool. Can I have a flaming sword or something?"

"Flaming swords are for archangels, not for little boys from Oklahoma. You'll put your eye out. Here comes Tate."

I ducked the tire iron and confronted Tate like a man. I ran. I ran around the bus, dodging injured people. I jumped over broken glass and pooled motor oil. Tate slipped on the oil, fell, and dropped the tire iron. I didn't turn and fight him, I crawled back through the bus window and hid.

The inside of the bus was a charnel house. Dead people were visible through the smoke. The stench of blood and feces was overpowering, but the smell had a sharp undercurrent, diesel fuel. Smelled like farm equipment from back home. Diesel was leaking.

The bus was a death trap. Stupid! I hadn't tried to hide in a burning building, but this wasn't much better. I turned toward the window, but Tate was already crawling inside. I moved as far away from him as I could and tried to open another window, but with the bus upside down, I had to lift the large window rather than slide it down. It was too heavy.

An old man lay on the floor next to me. His dead hand still gripped his walking cane. His pipe was clenched between his teeth. When I jerked the cane free, his arm shifted and uncovered a Zippo lighter. I shoved the lighter into my pocket and then pounded the window with the cane. They broke at the same time. I kicked the window a couple times and crawled outside.

Tate grabbed my foot. He didn't hit me with the tire iron. He tried to pull me into the bus. I kicked him in the face, squirmed free, and slithered across the wet pavement. My shirt and pants were soaked. I touched the damp cloth and sniffed. Diesel fuel. Leaking fuel spread from under the bus.

Suddenly I had a plan, not a good plan, but a plan. I stripped completely and stood there naked as a centerfold and clicked the Zippo. I may not know much, but I knew that lighting a Zippo while I was wearing diesel-soaked clothes was a bad idea.

The Zippo didn't light. I pounded it into my fist, clicked it open, and blew on the wick. Tate was almost out the window when it finally lit. I cupped the lighter in my hands for a moment, stepped back, and tossed the Zippo onto the puddling fuel. True to the advertisement, the Zippo didn't go out. It splashed in the diesel and kept burning. The flames moved in slow motion, Tate reached for the lighter and I ran. There was a crackle and then a whoosh behind me.

Tate staggered forward in flames. His Martha walked into the fire and took him by his burning hands. She hugged him and I swear that the flames lifted her and Tate up into the billowing smoke cloud, but Tate's body was still standing there burning. I ran.

I dove for cover when the bus exploded, just like actors do in the movies, and the force drove me forward. For the briefest second, it felt like I could fly. Maybe so, but I couldn't land. I skidded across the asphalt while pieces of bus, Tate, and the old man rained down around me.

Brenda stopped my skid with one foot. "Well, Jimmy, nicely done. I didn't bring any marshmallows. I'm shocked to see you naked and afraid. Presumptuous of you to strip down in front of me. We're not in high school anymore. I would have thought you'd have at least bought me dinner first."

I coughed and spit out black gunk. I ran my hands through my hair and someone's brains. My chest and legs were covered with scrapes and road rash. "Can you heal me and get me some clothes?"

She smiled. "Healing's not really my thing, and as for clothes, there are suitcases from the bus scattered around. Pick something nice. You should hurry. People saw you blow up the bus and the police are coming."

I found a pair of Converse All-Stars, two sizes too big, tube socks with yellow stripes, blue jeans, and a Hawaiian shirt with dancing hula girls. I looked at Brenda and pointed to the shirt. "Really?"

"Yes, really. You might want to think about stealing a car or something. Hear those sirens?"

I tried to blend into the crowd, but that wasn't as easy as it sounded. I was dressed like an old man on a Hawaiian vacation and Martha, who was Brenda, or Brenda who was Martha, not sure I ever got that straight, followed me waving her pompoms and cheered. "Truck, truck, steal a truck. Go, Jimmy!"

The spectators took up the chant and I joined in to hide in the crowd. We clapped, shouted, and danced around the flaming bus. "Two bits, four bits, six bits, a buck. Our boy Jimmy's gonna steal a truck."

We stopped chanting when the first fire truck pulled up. Two more were right behind it. The firemen dismounted their vehicles and in a choreographed display unloaded their equipment and surrounded the flaming bus. The chief used a megaphone to order the crowd back and then shouted. "Fuel Fire. No water just yet. Just keep it contained until the fuel burns up, then we'll flood it."

In the melee, I slipped away unnoticed. Martha hit me with a pompom and pointed to the red pumper fire engine. She softly chanted, "Truck, truck, gonna steal a truck."

I was pretty sure that sealing a fire truck was a direct road to hell, but I figured that my ticket had already been punched. The fire crew was busy scurrying around the site. I climbed into the empty cab. Heavy duty transmission for a big truck, fourteen forward gears and two for reverse.

Martha climbed in, looked around, and said, "I hope you can drive a standard transmission."

The truck running. The driver's seat had a four-point harness like race car drivers wear. I put it on, tightened the straps, released the brake, and moved the gear shift a couple times to get the feel. "Devil woman, I grew up on an Oklahoma farm. I can drive a tractor, a combine, and pretty much anything with wheels. The first three gears on this thing are granny gears, it'll barely move. By the time I get this baby into fourth gear, you'd better have a tight grip on those pompoms."

I engaged and released the clutch four times in about ten seconds. I didn't have a clear path, but a firetruck makes a damn good plow. I shoved past cars, trash cans, and a couple light poles. I bounced over the curve and gunned it. Three blocks later we lost three ladders when I made the right turn toward Bakersfield on nine wheels and shifted the old girl into tenth gear. I turned on the siren and ran three stoplights in a row. A firehose trailed behind us like an angry snake on a hot griddle.

Martha's eyes glowed like burning coal and her face was flushed. Horns were clearly visible in her perfectly coiffed hairdo. "You didn't stop or signal."

I skipped two gears and shifted straight into thirteenth. The truck lagged for a second, but then the engine caught up. We were doing sixty-six miles an hour when I saw the first police car behind me. I laughed, "Police, Martha. Do you think they'll give me a ticket?"

"No, Jimmy. I think they'll shoot you the first chance they get."

"Maybe I can outrun them."

"Maybe, but they've got radios. You can't outrun the radios. There'll be a roadblock ahead."

I nodded and held the gas pedal to the floor. The police drew closer. Martha crinkled her nose and the firehouse ripped loose and smashed through the window of the closest police car. After that, the rest kept their distance.

The roadblock was about a mile before Bakersfield. They'd picked a spot between a tree-lined cemetery on one side and a church with a rock fence surrounding it on the other. Martha didn't wear a harness. I knew I couldn't kill her, but I could maybe damage the body she was in for long enough to get away from her.

She waved a pompom in my face and I slapped it away. She laughed. "Don't be like that. Good news, Jimmy. Mikey stole a milk truck and ran over Greg. The police were right there and they shot Greg graveyard dead. Now it's just me, you, and the streets of Bakersfield. What you gonna do, boy."

I answered her by smashing into the roadblock and I dare anyone to find a single skid mark. I hit two police cars at the same time. The four-point harness knocked the breath out of me, but Martha crashed through the windshield. I gasped for air and unbuckled myself. I slid out of the truck and into a madhouse of sirens, flashing lights, and burning vehicles. I turned to run, tripped over a pompom, and face planted on a dead or unconscious police officer. I took his gun and ran for the church. I hoped the devil couldn't go inside a church, but I didn't know one way or another.

Voices shouted, "Stop or we'll shoot," but I didn't stop. Without breaking stride, I fired two rounds in the air so they'd know I had a gun.

The church door wasn't locked. I closed it behind me and piled a lectern and a cabinet against it. The poor box and the fount of holy water told me that I was in a Catholic Church. That and the sign that said, "Saint Sebastian's Catholic Church. My shouts echoed through the empty building.

An electronically enhanced voice crackled. "You, in the church. You're surrounded. Come out with your hands up. You can't get away."

I believed the voice was right, but I fired one shot through a stained glass window just to slow them down. I searched and found a bottle of communion wine and a stack of church flyers advertising bingo and a picnic. They were blank on the back. I sat on the floor and drank wine while I wrote this down.

I took a break and peeked out a window. Looked like every police officer in California was right outside. Martha was draped in a gray blanket and sitting in the open rear door of an ambulance. She stopped crying, looked straight at me, and winked. Damn!

I left the window and came back to finish this account. Her pompoms were on the floor where I'd been sitting. That's when I finally realized that I'd never had a chance.

I've told my story, well, except for the ending, and maybe I'll be around to write it, but I don't think so. Martha or Brenda, the devil's avatars, have locked me in pretty tightly. I killed some of my friends and some police and men who kill police rarely make it to trial. Law enforcement officers take that sort of thing personally.

When I finish this, I'm going to drench myself with holy water. I hope the water will keep Martha away from me and save my soul. I hope holy water stops bullets. I doubt it will, but I hope it does. I'll clear the furniture away from the door, soak myself, and walk out the door with a pompom in each hand.

Time to go. Showtime! Bakersfield, here I come.

ABOUT THE AUTHOR

Robert Allen Lupton is retired and lives in New Mexico where he was a commercial hot air balloon pilot. Robert runs and writes every day, but not necessarily in that order. Over 200 of his short stories have been published in various anthologies, magazines, and online magazines. He has three novels in print, *Foxborn*, *Dragonborn*, and *Dejanna of the Double Star*. His six short story collections, *Running Into Trouble*, *Through A Wine Glass Darkly*, *Strong Spirits*, *Hello Darkness*, *Visions Softly Creeping*, and *The Marvin Chronicles* are available in print and audio versions from Amazon. He edited the anthology, Feral, It Takes a Forest and co-edited the *Three Cousins Anthologies*, *Are You A Robot?* and *Witch Wizard Warlock*. Over 2000 of his Edgar Rice Burroughs themed drabbles and articles are located on www.erbzine.com Visit amazon.com/author/luptonra, his Amazon author's page for current information about his stories and books and like or follow him on Facebook:

facebook.com/profile.php?id=100022680383572

https://robertallenlupton.blogspot.com

https://twitter.com/robert_lupton

BETWEEN ROCK
AND
A FUR FACE

Sheri White

Spyder strummed his guitar and sang a cover of a KISS ballad. He sang by rote; he'd been covering this song since his high school band days. He let his eyes wander over the paltry audience, most of them sitting in portable beach chairs. He had to sing louder than usual over music from the carnival rides and shrieks from the haunted house.

He hoped to find some company to take back to his room for a few hours. He smiled at a blonde sitting on a blanket with friends. He knew she was his for the night when she returned the smile and added a wink.

After the show, Spyder fucked the blonde then kicked her out of his fleabag motel room.

"You gonna call me when you're back in town, right?" she asked.

"Yeah, sure." He pushed her gently out into the night and closed the door.

Spyder waited a few minutes until she was gone then walked to the dive bar across the road. There, he drank a beer and thought about how unfair life could be when he spotted a skinny guy sporting a Van Dyke. The guy approached the bar. Spyder nodded at him when the man looked his way.

The guy sat on the stool next to Spyder, who shifted uncomfortably on his seat, wondering why the guy would sit so close when the bar was practically empty.

The guy held out his hand to Spyder. "How're you doing? My name's μαμμωνᾶ."

Spyder shook the stranger's hand. "I'm sorry, I didn't catch that."

"Just call me Mammon. And you are?"

"Sorry, I'm Spyder. Nice to meet you."

They watched a baseball game on the old TV mounted to the wall in a corner, the commentators' voices tinny and distant.

Spyder had almost forgotten Mammon until he spoke. "So, what do you do?"

"I'm a musician. I play guitar and write some of my own songs."

"I bet you got all sorts of beautiful women after you."

Spyder snorted. "Yeah."

"So, are you happy? Think you're on your way to fame and fortune?"

Spyder shook his head. "I'm small potatoes. The songs I write, nobody wants to hear. I do covers mostly. Barely pays the bills." He shrugged. "Music is my life, though. I can't imagine doing anything else."

Mammon grinned and just then his eyes seemed to glow red—enough to make Spyder recoil. "What would you say if I told you I could make you famous, and rich beyond your wildest imagination."

His eyes must have been playing tricks on him. Spyder laughed. "I'd say you were like every other two-bit manager trying to make money off me. That's why I don't have a manager. I need all I make, such as it is."

Mammon leaned in. "Look at me, Spyder." The stranger's eyes *were* red.

"Who are you, man?"

His grin grew impossibly wider. "Let's talk."

ঙ

Spyder walked out onstage to thousands of people chanting his name. He stopped in the middle of the stage, his guitar hanging from a strap around his neck that seemed to glow in the light. He raised his arms high and screamed "Yeahhhh!" into the microphone.

The crowd erupted in paroxysms of joy.

He launched into the song that made him a star. And hated every minute of it.

ঙ

He sat with his head in his hands in his dressing room after the show. That song. That fucking song. He was so sick of it, of paying for it.

A life for the song—that was the deal he had made with Mammon. It had to be someone he knew, according to Mammon. He wasn't thrilled about it, but Spyder had chosen Mackie, the asshole who was offered a contract by a big-time record company and had left Spyder in the dust. Mackie hadn't even thought twice about it; he took the contract and ran. Spyder thought he'd be freaked out killing Mackie, but he was still so pissed that it felt right.

Mammon brought Mackie to him after his first show, along with the knife Spyder was to use to slit Mackie's throat. Now, though, after fifty or so shows, he couldn't stand to even think about it. As far as he was concerned, he had fulfilled the contract that first night. He should've expected a demon would put a twist in the contract. So of course he had to play the song at every concert, and then after the show, he had to make the sacrifice. He hated a lot of people, but what would happen when he ran out of the ones he didn't care about?

He wanted—no, *needed*—to stop this insanity.

Mammon stood in front of him, holding a woman by the neck. She struggled against her captor, trying to elbow him, but she couldn't reach him. Tears streamed down her cheeks and her eyes were like a cornered wild animal's. Mammon let her go; she screamed and fell to the floor.

Oh, God. "Hey, Tammy," Spyder said in a dull voice.

She got up on her hands and knees. Her hair was tangled and wet with perspiration, her face white with terror. "What is happening? Who are you? I mean, I know *who* you are Spyder, but why am I here? And who is this?" she asked, gesturing to Mammon.

"Yeah, remember the kid you pantsed in fifth grade? That was me. I really don't care anymore, but I have to do this, and you're good as anyone, I suppose." Spyder took the knife from Mammon. Tammy barely had time to scream before he slashed her throat.

Mammon snapped his fingers, and the body disappeared.

"So, Mr. Rock Star—who's next? You have another concert in a week, so make sure I have a name by then. Summon me when you're ready."

"Wait!" Spyder said, not wanting Mammon to wink out yet. "I need to talk to you."

"Yes?"

Spyder explained that he didn't want to play the song anymore; didn't want to kill anybody anymore. He had been writing his own music and now that he had a fan base and was making big money, he didn't need the original song any longer.

Mammon laughed, a horrible screeching sound like thousands of crows in the tiny room. "It's not that easy to get out of a deal with a demon, you idiot. Did you really think you could?"

"But it's not like I sold my soul. It was just a deal that worked at the time."

"Oh, but you *did* sell your soul. This isn't the movies, Mr. Rock Star. There is no outwitting me or playing on my sympathies. You are in this for the rest of your life."

"Really, Mammon? There's nothing I can do?"

The demon put a long black fingernail to his lips, as if he were pretending to think. Then he held the finger up and gave Spyder an "I've got it!" face. "I'll tear up your contract on one condition."

"What is it?"

Mammon shook his head. "Oh, no. You don't get to hear the condition until after you've committed. So what do you say?"

"That hardly seems fair—"

"I never said this deal was fair, Mr. Rock Star." Mammon's eyes flashed red. "Are you going to take the deal, or will you be forever beholden to me?" He smiled, his eyes still red. "If it helps, you won't have to kill anyone again." He chuckled.

Feeling as if he had no choice, Spyder nodded.

"See you soon." Mammon winked out of existence.

Spyder's next gig was several weeks in the future, so he had plenty of time to stress over the new deal with Mammon. He got drunk several times a week and would yell for Mammon to just come and get it over with. He wanted to get on with his life and career.

If he still had a career.

Finally, Mammon showed up. "Are you ready to fulfill the rest of your contract?"

Spyder shrugged. "I guess I have to be."

"If you don't—or won't—complete this task, you forfeit your life tonight. You will then accompany me to the depths of Hell. Do you understand?"

"Yeah, let's just get on with it."

"Very well." Mammon snapped his fingers and a small brown dog with a white muzzle appeared in his arms.

Spyder sprang up from the couch. "Fur Face!" He went to take the dog from Mammon, but the demon wouldn't let him. Spyder settled for scritching the dog's head. "Where did you get him? Who gave him to you?"

"Nobody *gave* him to me." He stroked the dog's head with his long black fingernails. The dog whimpered at the demon's touch.

Spyder clenched his hands into fists. "I never told anybody about him. I didn't want groupies or stalkers trying to steal him."

Mammon tapped his temple with a fingernail. "Smart. But nobody can hide anything from me. Are you finally ready to fulfill the bargain?"

Resigned to what he knew he had to do, Spyder nodded. "Let's get this over with." He picked up the knife Mammon had put beside him on the couch.

8

Several days later, Mammon appeared to Spyder. He "tsk tsked" at the sight of Spyder unwashed and drunk, watching a video of one of his best concerts on the TV, tears streaming unnoticed down his face.

"You look like shit, Spyder."

"I miss my dog. He loved me, trusted me, and I betrayed him for money and fame. I'll never get his yelp out of my mind."

"Oh." Mammon put his hand to his mouth, then began to laugh.

Spyder looked at Mammon, his eyes wide with fury. "What the fuck are you laughing at? I killed my best friend."

"I'm laughing…" He stopped to laugh again, as if he had heard a great dirty joke. "I'm laughing because…" He grinned, his eyes bright with malice. "I never said you had to kill your dog!"

Spyder fell to his knees, screaming. Soon the screaming turned to crazy laughter.

ABOUT THE AUTHOR

Sheri White's stories have been published in many anthologies and zines, including an essay in the Notable Works for the HWA Mental Health Initiative, an essay in *JAKE Magazine*, *Halldark Holidays* (edited by Gabino Iglesias), *The Monsters Next Door* published by Critical Blast, and The Horror Writers Association's *Don't Turn Out the Lights* (edited by Jonathan Maberry). Recent publications include *Crab Apple Literary*, *Litmora*, *voidspace zine*, and *Broken Antler Magazine*.

HAUNTED HOME
MAKEOVERS

Gene Gallistel

Heidi and I used to be a couple; we were a good
team and a known quantity in the world of Haunted
Home Makeovers. What is an HHM, you might
wonder? I always explain it the same way. We
renovated homes, and once our projects were
complete, buyers had a conduit to otherworldly
forces. Have you ever watched the 1982 film
Poltergeist? Who would build a subdivision on top of a
Native American burial ground, providing a means for
vengeful ghosts to terrorize a picture-perfect 1980s
suburban family? Well, unscrupulous capitalists and
Heidi and me. The big man downstairs, unhallowed-
be-his-name, would probably have gotten a kick out
of that, although the logistics are a bit of a nightmare;
try finding 1) an undisturbed and undiscovered
Native American burial ground and 2) a nearby city
looking to swell its growth while distributing its tax
base. Developments like that often cross county lines.
A logistical nightmare! Every time the *Poltergeist*
example is rolled out and dusted off, I do point out
that whoever built that subdivision was pretty
amateur. Had Heidi and I devised that, we would

have included a Homeowners Association, or HOA, to suck the life and individuality out of everyone who settled there. By Satan, I do love HOAs and the mind-numbing legalese that goes into their by-laws covering everything from lawn maintenance to house painting. I also love watching your average upper-middle-class Karen or Chad go absolutely drunk with power once they manage to get a seat on an HOA board. I have spent time with some serious demons, and I can tell you humans are real monsters.

Heidi and I split up a little over a year ago. We had been in Milwaukee, working on an HHM reno, in a neighborhood that was very much in the guy upstairs' camp. You could tell by the nauseating number of crucifixes and Jesus-themed lawn ornaments. It's disturbing to think people live that way. Heidi and I wanted to win one for the big man downstairs and, while doing so, make a little bit of a payday. The reno on Palmer Street was a turn-of-the-last-century building, circa 1901, a two-story duplex. Once, it had been a single family but then was converted into apartments. It had some oddities and hadn't been loved much since it had been a rental property. The floors, windows, siding, and even the shingles were cheap. Cheap materials, cheaply installed, and cheaply maintained so that some monster (again, a human) could suck as much profit from the structure as possible. The house was a shell with hardly a pulse.

We poured ourselves into the project, gave that place a lot of love, and when we were done, I suggested that maybe we keep it for ourselves. Heidi protested, and I countered every argument she had. I floated the idea that we stay in Milwaukee, plant roots, Satan up the neighborhood, and generally use the reno as our new home base. Heidi said no; we were vagabonds, travelers, moving and working, working and moving. We needed the money, and I knew I couldn't argue with that. We were nearly penniless. Satan, for all his unholy works, doesn't pay well, so we put the reno up for sale, and I pouted and busied myself by carving an old Aramaic curse into the bottom of a drawer in a built-in cabinet. It was a bit like a boobytrap that I didn't think would fire off until well after we sold the place. I was wrong.

The first family we showed the house to was cute; young parents in their twenties with two daughters, aged three and one. The one-year-old was in mom's arms, and the three-year-old was running free. Heidi and I led the parents through the house, pointing out all the finished touches, updated trim, new windows, and fresh paint, and somehow all of us missed the fact that the three-year-old had vanished. My stomach sank when I heard her sweet little voice mutter quite a naughty Aramaic slur, the equivalent of calling someone a 'see you next Tuesday.' The Aramaic were real potty mouths. After the slur, Heidi grabbed me, her nails digging into my wrist. She knew I had a thing for Aramaic curses. The whole group of us ran downstairs, and by Satan, that three-year-old was levitating and muttering incoherently. Once we got her on solid ground and acting like her three-year-old self, the family split, but the neighbors, those with the nauseating lawn ornaments, got word, and that night someone burned the Palmer Street house down. We didn't have insurance on the place, so it was a *total* loss. Heidi blamed me for the whole affair; she accused me of intentionally tanking the sale, and maybe she was right. I don't know. We split after that. I went back on the road, and I don't know what became of Heidi.

8

About a year later, an under-demon named Leekie got in touch with me. Under-demons are a bit of a mixed bag; many have an inferiority complex because of the whole 'under' implication. They're a bit like a JV football team for the big man downstairs. Leekie would never be a frontline soldier-demon clashing with archangels, but they could advance the big man's agenda in subtle ways. I had heard of Leekie once before. They were best known for possessing a Pharmacy Manager of a midwestern Walgreens and enacting such Byzantine policies regarding the handling and distribution of drugs that Leekie *actually* broke the pharmacy's ability to distribute prescriptions. That Walgreens location got labeled a 'dystopian hellscape' on Google Reviews and forced Google to adjust its review policy. Before Leekie's possession, the least number of stars you could leave in a review was one. After Leekie, you could leave zero. What a coup! Leekie's next job landed them in California. They possessed someone involved with *Keeping Up with the Kardashians*, and between those two possessions, Leekie built up the bona fides to become a showrunner.

The first thing Leekie did was to pitch a pilot. The big man downstairs already had a cloven hoof in some old media: newspapers, radio, and a minority stake in MSNBC, but now, he wanted to branch out into new media: Instagram Reels, Google Shorts, TikTok, various social media platforms, and anywhere demonic content creators shared. The pilot Leekie wanted me to jump into was called This Old Demonic House. They said the pilot was nearly complete but felt the content lacked home improvements. It was too much Voodoo and curses, all manner of them, from dolls to charms, to black magic that involved slaughtering chickens and spreading blood. The star the show was built around was a Voodoo priest from Port-au-Prince named Napoleon Bonaparte. Napoleon might have been savvy with his black magic, but he couldn't swing a hammer to save his life, and the tester audience that viewed an early iteration of the pilot was underwhelmed.

"You know the biz," Leekie hissed. Leekie only ever hissed, which gave the impression they were speaking Parseltongue. I didn't want to be brought in as the comedic filler, someone's handyman sidekick, but I needed the money, so I hopped a train to northern Illinois and toward the address Leekie sent me. They wanted me to do a walk-through and give them a list of possible projects. The house was in one of Chicago's northern suburbs, built in the mid-1950s when suburban developments exploded. It was ranch-style, with a finished basement and attic. The simplest way to expand the square footage of any small house is to finish those. I checked the kitchen. It was small but could use new appliances, cabinets, and a few coats of paint. The hardest part about renovating small kitchens is that modern appliances just don't fit into the cavities left for their predecessors. I made notes, took measurements, and then checked the finished attic. It was set up like a small bedroom. At the top of the stairs was a built-in bookcase that I fell in love with. It was the best feature of the house. I made more notes and called Leekie.

I laid out the projects as I saw them, with special attention to what might look best on camera. They were as follows: 1) Purchasing new appliances and cabinets (Napoleon and me), 2) demoing old kitchen cabinets (Napoleon), 3) installing new cabinets (me), 4) painting the kitchen (Napoleon), and 5) rehabbing the bookshelf at the top of the stairs (me). Leekie hissed out a "Fabulous," although Napoleon protested having to paint over the chicken blood on the kitchen walls. He said it diminished his magic. Leekie sided with me, and we started shooting the next day. It took a week to finish my list, and I was proud of how the built-in bookcase turned out. While working on the rough finish, I ended up carving an old Punic curse into the underside of one of the shelves. It roughly translated to, "May your children be fed to Moloch."

The house was sold to a cute couple, David and Brandon, who owned a rather annoying and yippy Pomeranian named Princess. They brought her along on the final walkthrough and let her off her leash, and that damn dog bit me. One of the cameramen got shots of me yelping and D. and B. using baby talk to try and convince Princess to let go of my leg. In the end, I provided some comedy filler. As part of the purchase agreement, D. and B. had a week to settle before Leekie and a cameraman returned for a final walk-through and on-screen interviews in the furnished house. I hunkered down and waited.

Leekie called me a week later with bad news. D. and B. seemed strangely resilient to all of Napoleon's Voodoo, but they did tell a wild story about Princess, whom they called their 'fur-baby,' committing suicide by jumping into a bonfire they had erected in the backyard. They couldn't even explain why they had built the pyre, what its intended use was, or why Princess seemed almost compelled to launch herself into the flames. Moloch claimed his just do. The revised pilot went to another tester audience and flopped.

When Leekie called me, they were at a nearby pub and offered to buy me a beer. I tried to reassure them that this was a good concept, a diamond in the rough, but that the reliance on Voodoo might be pushing a trope a little too far. Leekie hissed out a confused sigh. I continued, "Voodoo curses, along with Gypsy curses, are outdated and overdone tropes that almost exclusively belong to the twentieth century." I listed a half-dozen examples. "Promoting those now almost fosters xenophobia, and that's almost exclusive to the

idiot, 'God and guns,' followers of the man upstairs,"
Leekie grunted and ordered some Fireball shots (pun
intended), and I put the pilot in the rearview and
started thinking of my next move.

ఆ

Leekie called me a few days later, excited. They
hissed that there was another pilot happening in
Milwaukee, and this time, I wouldn't be the
handyman sidekick but the star. They told me the big
man downstairs watched the revised pilot, and he
genuinely liked me. I protested. Leekie knew what
happened to the last house I renovated in Milwaukee.
I told them over the second round of Fireball shots.
Leekie hissed that the pilot would be different because
the reno was in a neighborhood that was filled with
artists and hippies, a neighborhood leaning toward the
big man downstairs. Leekie pressed on, hissing that
the work would be in line with the HHM work Heidi
and I were known for. I was still hesitant but agreed,
thinking that with the big man's backing, and a
simplified HHM-style reno, we could shoot a pilot
inside of a month, and then when that one flopped, I
could return to my wandering ways. Leekie then sent
me some money for transportation and gave me a pair
of addresses, the first of a boarding house where a
room was rented for me, and the second was the
location of the reno on Fratney Street.

ఆ

I did not expect to see Heidi when I showed up
for the first meeting with Leekie and our director
Steve. The meeting was at a beatnik coffee shop, and
everyone was sitting around a pair of small tables. She
smiled when she saw me, a big, warm smile. I
nervously returned it. I awkwardly motioned to the
line of people waiting to order coffee and joined the
queue. After I got a cup, I sat in the empty chair
beside Heidi.

"Still drink your coffee the same way?" Heidi asked.

"Black, no cream, no sugar."

Leekie and Steve were busy reviewing a spreadsheet of our filming schedule with our cameramen. Both were named Brad, but one was a surfer-type from California that went by B-rad, as in *be rad*. Heidi then filled me in on what she had been up to over the last year. She stayed in Milwaukee, doing Satan's good work by teaching yoga and running a demonic home improvement channel on TikTok.

"But what are you doing here?" I asked.

"Leekie brought me in to work on the pilot."

"But that's what I'm supposed to be doing," I replied.

We tried to get clarification from Leekie, but they looked frazzled. Under-demons are far better as possessions than micro-managing staff, budgets, and spreadsheets covering filming schedules. "You're both working on the pilot," Leekie hissed, "Boss's orders." They raised a gnarled and arthritic-looking claw and pointed first to Heidi, then to me. "He likes the chemistry you have."

We shared an awkward glance.

Leekie tossed a keyring with a dozen keys to me.

"Are these the keys to the house?"

"Go," Leekie hissed, "And start drawing up plans. We begin tomorrow."

I held up the keyring. "Does every door have a different lock? That's maddening."

"I can drive us over when we finish our coffee," Heidi said.

"How far away is the place?"

"A mile at most."

"I can walk," I said, standing.

"Why are you being stubborn?" Heidi asked. "Accept the ride."

"I'm not being *stubborn*." Old patterns die hard.

"Both of you," Leekie hissed, "Go!"

I gave in. We were doing Satan's good work, after all. We dropped the cups off and rode over to the Fratney Street house in silence. The house was another turn-of-the-last-century home from 1906. It had been a duplex that was converted into a single-family home, the inverse of the Palmer Street house. But as we approached the house, we could see the conversion to a single-family was done poorly.

It took us five tries before we found the key that opened the front door. That led us into a three-seasons mud room. It was windy outside, and we could hear the wind whistling after we closed the door. We checked the floors under a shabby bit of carpet. They were plywood but slanted as if the converters laid sheets directly onto the preexisting porch when they enclosed the room.

It took us another three tries to find the key that opened the door to the house. On the first floor, a wall had been opened to link one former bedroom with the living room, the street-facing entrance had shifted, and the kitchen, which had been in the largest room on the first floor, was moved into what had been the second bedroom. It was small but had a window overlooking the backyard. The house had two full bathrooms, but on the first floor, we found visible water damage from the second-floor bathroom. Based on the damage, there were leaks around the shower, tub, and toilet on the second floor. I shook my head. The second floor was largely untouched. It had the house's two bedrooms, but in what had been the kitchen, a large, enameled farmhouse sink was still mounted onto the wall. The basement was irregular. The floor was concrete, but no attention was paid to leveling it. We made notes and measured each room.

"It's a dystopian heavenscape," Heidi proclaimed.

"Worse than the Palmer Street house."

"No one loved this one," Heidi replied.

"Or, it was the wrong kind of love," I retorted.

"Well, do you want to get a beer and discuss?"

"No," I did want to get a beer, but I was busy taking notes. "I wanted to walk through again and retake some measurements."

"Our first phase is going to be demo, and I feel the lower level needs to go down to studs to allow us to see exactly what we have."

"That's fine, but I want to have a plan," I said. "You don't have to stick around. I'm probably just going to do some sketches and then head back to where I'm staying."

"You and I aren't going to be a problem, are we?"

"I don't think so."

"Because," Heidi considered her words, "this could be big for both of us, and I don't want drama from the past to smother it."

"I don't think that will happen."

"You and I could be like the next Chip and Joanna Gaines, but," she paused, "like a demonic version of Chip and Joanna."

I giggled at that. Heidi could always make me laugh.

"Let's do it," I said.

"What?"

"Get a beer and hash this out."

We're exes, Heidi and me, but sitting across from each other, sharing a basket of fried cheese curds and a pitcher of beer, brought back fond memories. I had my sketchbook, and she had her laptop that we used for finalizing designs, rendering textures, and pricing components. We hashed out first the major issues with the Fratney Street house, the lackluster curb appeal, the mudroom, the first-floor bathroom, and the tiny kitchen. We texted Leekie, trying to get specifics on our budget. They didn't respond, so we got creative.

I proposed we demo the enclosed porch and do two expansions: 1) a gothic-looking front room with large lancet windows and an arched entryway, and 2) an expansion on the rear of the house to double the size of the kitchen and add a three-season greenhouse, off the kitchen that would become the new rear entrance. I quickly sketched those while Heidi created a floor plan based on our measurements. Heidi suggested we add a deck to the top of each expansion, and before long, she created a second file with our planned expansion.

"I want to reno that first-floor bathroom," Heidi declared.

"It needs it," I ordered a second basket of cheese curds while she made some changes to the floor plan.

"My idea," Heidi displayed when I got back to the table, "involves expanding the bathroom by absorbing the closet beside it and shifting the closet into the former bedroom off the living room." She showed the design. "We could pull out the tub, vanity, and toilet and redesign to have a walk-in shower with dual heads, a vanity with actual storage below, and a new toilet."

"That shower looks big enough for four."

"Satan loves group showers," Heidi giggled. "It's the best way to conserve water and clean your hooves."

"What would that do to our budget?"

"I haven't finished the numbers yet," Heidi said, "The bathroom reno would probably look good on camera, though," Heidi looked up at me. "Leekie said you did one of these before."

"Just once," I replied, "we shot the pilot, and it went nowhere."

"What curses did you use?"

"I was brought in as last-minute help, so just a standard Punic curse."

"You were always a fan of Moloch."

"What are you thinking about for this one?"

"Well," Heidi dug in her backpack and tossed a red hardcover book onto the table between us. *The History of Torture,* the spine read. "I have been thinking a lot about Byzantine-eye-gouging lately."

"That's pleasant."

Heidi unfolded a scrap of paper with a dizzying array of symbols on it.

"I think I have a curse worked out to cause cataracts if you're old enough, blind spots in the young, and the equivalent of detached retinas in those in between."

"Remind me never to trigger one of your curses."

"Well," she joked, "don't end up on my naughty list."

"Okay, Mrs. Claus," I held up our empty pitcher. "Want another?"

"Sure," she said.

When I got back to the table, Heidi was rendering

textures over the walls of her redesigned bathroom and looking up material costs on Home Depot's website. She bit her lower lip the way she did whenever she got excited about a project. I poured us each a beer as she finished the job and showed me the results. It looked lovely, something that would look great on camera.

"Speaking of showers," Heidi said, "have you been group showering with anyone lately?"

I nearly spit out my beer.

"Not since we were together," I said. "What about you?"

"There was a boy," she sighed.

"Was?" I asked. She nodded.

"I met him in yoga, but he wasn't good at sharing showers –"

"How?" I asked. "I always loved morning showers with you."

She blushed; even in the dim light of the bar, I could see that.

"He'd always hog the hot water," she shook her head. "Enough of him." She leaned an elbow on the table and leaned forward. "Why did you leave?"

That question.

"Why did I leave?" I managed. "The xenophobic minions of the man upstairs burned down our reno."

"I know," she replied, "But why did you leave?"

"We had a fight," I hesitated, "and I thought maybe I cursed the whole thing by suggesting we settle down, so I did what I knew to do; go back on the road."

"Where did you go?"

"We were vagabonds, working the demonic home improvement circuit, summer in the upper-Midwest, winter in the desert southwest."

"So, you went back to New Mexico?"

"I thought you'd come," I confessed, "and find me somewhere along the way."

"I thought you would call," she responded. "I did want to settle down, but not at the Palmer Street house, not in a neighborhood surrounded by," she leaned in close, "Christians."

"You never said you were interested in settling down."

"You never asked."

We sat in silence for a while, both probably feeling like idiots.

"So," I started, "what are we going to do?"

"Win one for the man downstairs," Heidi smiled, "unhallowed-be-his-name, and if the pilot takes off, we flip another and another and Satan up this town."

I nodded. I was excited.

"Where are you staying?" Heidi asked.

I gave her the address Leekie had given me. She pulled up the address on her phone and got a street view of the building. It looked ramshackle and more than a little scary.

"You're not staying there."

"Leekie rented a room for me."

"Leekie loves that place because it's depressing and makes for easy possession territory," Heidi replied. "It has ten rooms to a floor and shared bathrooms."

"Oh."

"Why don't you sleep on my couch?"

"No," I protested.

"I'm offering you the couch, not my bed."

I thought about it for a second and nodded. I had nowhere else to go. We finished our beers and headed to Heidi's apartment, which happened to be the upper unit of a house two down from our Fratney Street reno.

8

Our first day of shooting was all big gestures. We showed Steve our sketches and mock-ups and then walked through a description of each of our three projects on camera. That was more draining than I thought it would be. Following that, we took delivery of a dumpster and began demoing the enclosed porch. I was tearing off the cheap siding while Heidi removed the front door. She pulled up a dirty strip of carpet, and the dust cloud from it caused a fit of sneezes. I was removing one of the porch windows when I heard Heidi scream. B-rad was there, filming. Beneath the carpet were some linoleum tiles, and when she pulled one up, she exposed a massive carpenter ant colony. They had eaten through the rotten wood of the porch below into the plywood. Heidi disappeared and returned with a can of Raid and doused the colony. Steve wanted that on camera, and then he called a wrap for the day. Day one ended with genocide.

I looked at my phone, surprised that the whole day was burned up. I dumped our refuse into the dumpster, and Heidi appeared with a six-pack, and we had a beer while walking the house. By beer two, we were on the front steps and met several neighbors walking their dogs. By beer three, I needed to use the bathroom. When I finished, I heard Heidi talking with a pair of brothers who owned a house across the street. They were scrappers, and when I joined them, Heidi was showing them the kitchen appliances. They agreed to haul them away the next morning. Heidi also convinced them to take the old bathtub from the lower bathroom.

"We're saving money," she said after the brothers left, "and space in the dumpster."

"What to grab dinner?"

"Only if you're buying."

"I'll buy."

8

Day two went like clockwork. The brothers carried the kitchen appliances to their truck while Heidi and I dismantled the toilet and vanity from the bathroom. Those ended up in the dumpster, the four of us hauled the old tub out, and the brothers hauled it away. We broke for lunch, and Heidi and I found ourselves at that beatnik coffee shop a few blocks away. I bought us cups of black coffee and cheese-and-vegetable sandwiches. Just like old times.

"You don't have to buy all my meals, you know," she said when I sat down.

"You could buy me dinner then."

"Well," she sized up the situation, "I did save you from a horrible boarding house, dorm-sized rooms, and shared toilets."

"I probably still owe you."

"I can make dinner tonight."

"What were you thinking?"

"A pasta dish and a bottle or two of French table wine, the cheap stuff that reminds you of being in Paris at nineteen."

"Sold," I said, "So, how did you end up meeting Leekie?"

"My demonic home improvement channel on

TikTok."

"TikTok?"

"Under-demons are fascinated by TikTok."

8

The rest of that first week was just hard work, demolishing the enclosed porch and taking the bathroom and adjacent closet to studs. We filled our first dumpster and got a second. After lunch on Friday, Steve pulled Heidi and me aside. He had a dour look on his face and a Brad on either side of him, filming us. He told us our budget had been cut, so of the three projects we proposed on Monday, we had to decide on two to move forward. It had all the drama of a manufactured reality TV show crisis, but as we were filming a demonic reality TV show, it seemed appropriate. Steve put the hard question to me.

"What two projects are you going to complete?"

"We just tore the front of the house off," I replied.

"I know," Steve challenged, "but you have to make a choice. Are we completing your two expansions or one of yours and Heidi's?"

"We just tore the front of the house off."

"You have to make a choice," Steve said.

"I think we should rebuild the front," I said, looking at Heidi, who looked perturbed by the manufactured crisis, "and we're going to reno the bathroom like Heidi wanted."

"Are you sure?" Steve asked. "I know you were really excited about that kitchen expansion."

"I think it will be okay."

"Well," Steve replied, "we'll have to make some space in the budget for new appliances then."

Steve and the Brads called it a day after that. They said they were going to review the footage. Heidi disappeared back to her-slash-our apartment, and I sat in the kitchen. The design was good but grand. We did have the problem that we had given away the fridge and stove, but they were cheap ones landlords stuck in rental properties that hardly got used. We could get better appliances. I did some measurements and scanned my phone, checking the dimensions on Home Depot's app. We had enough space for a new fridge and stove, but we needed to expand the kitchen entryway to get them in. It had been framed to twenty-nine inches, and the smallest fridge I could find required a thirty-two-inch opening.

Heidi reappeared with a six-pack, like magic, and I walked her through my discoveries. We had a beer on the steps up front, and by beer number two, I asked her if she wanted to try a new empanada place B-rad had told me about that morning.

"Can't," she said, "I had other plans."

"Oh," I felt weirdly dejected. I had gotten into the rhythm of this with her, working, dinner and drinks, and then watching stupid streaming shows until one of us fell asleep. I hadn't even thought that she might have a personal life beyond this reno and her poverty-stricken ex crashing on her couch. "Is it still cool if I sleep on the couch tonight?"

Heidi punched me hard in the shoulder. Hard! That woman has powerful arms.

"We can't go out for empanadas because I just set out a pizza dough, and Mother needs to be fed."

"Pizza?"

"You look as giddy as a schoolboy slipping his first someone out of their clothes."

"But I love your sourdough." I looked at my watch; it was the fifteenth. Mother was Heidi's sourdough starter she'd maintained for fifteen-plus years, but much like any magic, Mother had rules. She was fed weekly, and on the first and the fifteenth of every month, portions were processed into bread and pizza crusts.

Heidi shook a finger at me. "You thought I had a date."

"You're a free woman."

We ate pizza that night, then watched *Friday the 13th*. Heidi fell asleep beside me, and I wrapped an arm around her. When she woke, she said she felt like a time traveler, going back to when we were a couple. She said I smelled the same, then sauntered off to bed. I wondered if that was an invitation but didn't push it. I watched the final girl decapitate Jason Voorhees's mother, and then I slept.

Rinse. Wash. Repeat.

During the next few weeks, we laid the foundation for our new front room, built the rough frame, and had plumbers move the water and sewer lines to account for the first-floor bathroom absorbing the adjacent closet. We finished framing the expansion the following week and took delivery of our front door and four windows, two large eight-foot-tall lancet windows, and two sash windows for the north and south-facing walls. We installed the front door and painted it on Thursday, and the lancet windows on Friday afternoon, and finished the day on the front steps with a beer while neighbors stopped to *oh* and *ah* over the new facade. Steve had booked a weekend crew to finish the siding and plumbing, to keep the whole shoot on schedule.

Heidi had a girls' night out that Friday, so I ran an errand, got a bite to eat, and then returned to the reno. Based on our timeline and schedule, we only had four days left to finish the project. We only had to get the new kitchen appliances in, insulate, drywall, trim, and paint. That left me with a sinking feeling in the pit of my stomach. There was still so much to do and so many things that needed to be said. I also had to work on my curse because you can't have a haunted home makeover without the haunting.

I sat in the living room of our reno, thinking it over. The room was dark. We've been talking about this stupid dark room since we started the reno. Throughout the history of this house, no one ever thought to install overhead lighting. They must have just lived with floor lamps. We had run electrical to the front room, and I spliced a line off that to fix the lighting in the living room. I told Heidi I had a surprise for her that I wanted to work on while she was out, so when I returned that evening, I fished the wire into place, installed the ceiling fan I'd bought on that errand, and tested it.

I once knew a Romani master who taught me an interesting curse. There isn't a perfect translation from Romani to English, but loosely, the curse is called The Curse of the Magic Word. The curse was made by the infusion of an idea into one specific word, which the master spoke while touching a recipient. That is how the curse is transferred. I've thought a lot about that and the power of a single word. After I finished installing and testing the ceiling fan, I went to install the medallion around it. A medallion is a decorative feature that covers up little gaps or irregularities between a ceiling fan and the ceiling. I chose a medallion with floral patterns. On the back of it, I carved the single word, LOVE. This house hadn't been loved, and that was enough of a curse, and I carved the word LOVE because I enjoyed this and because I loved Heidi, even though I'm sometimes too stupid to admit it. When I flipped the light on afterward, the whole house seemed to hum, a renewed magic in its veins. After that, I went back to Heidi's and slept.

Heidi woke me the next morning with a kiss. A simple kiss on the lips.

"Morning, sleeping beauty."

I wiped the tiredness from my eyes. Heidi's hair was frazzled and had little sticks and leaves in it. She and the girls were out all night, bar hopping before having a bonfire and riding around on their broomsticks.

"I saw what you did."

"What?"

She opened her phone. "Steve installed cameras in the house to get a montage of the weekend workers."

"He did?" I hadn't noticed them.

She pulled up a video of me installing the fan, testing it, and then she fast-forwarded to me carving LOVE into the back of the medallion.

"I like doing this with you," Heidi said.

I nodded.

"Steve sent me the video this morning. He's going to fold it into the pilot, and he's sure he'll be able to sell it as is, and maybe we can spice up HHM. There could be Byzantine-eye-gouging one week, and love curses the next."

"I think I'd like that," I managed.

Heidi poked a finger into my chest. "But no running away," she ordered. "You have to stay, and if you feel the urge to run, use your words."

"I'm in love with you," I managed.

Heidi kissed me again and patted my chest. A small cloud of dry-wall dust rose between us. Heidi stood and extended her hand.

"What?"

"We both had a long night," she said. "Let's take a shower."

"Satan does want us to conserve water."

"Un-hallowed-be-his-name," she flirtatiously said, "also wants us to do other things, and maybe after we're clean, we can do those."

ȣ

Our pilot sold. You can find it wherever you stream demonic content. We moved on to our next project in the neighborhood that had been firmly in the grips of the followers of the man upstairs. The Fratney Street house sat empty, though. Steve thought the combination of high interest rates and strict oversight on home loans were the culprits, so Heidi and I took our first HHM paychecks and bought it. I did remove her Byzantine-eye-gouging curse, but we left the LOVE curse in place, and we settled down.

ABOUT THE AUTHOR

GENE GALLISTEL is a writer of horror and speculative fiction. He and his wonderful wife live in Milwaukee with their four cats.

THE DEVIL MAKES MAYHEM

Janice Rider

It was October 31, 1884, when snow began to fall in earnest in a small town in Wyoming. Large, soft flakes nestled into one another, burying everything in sight. The white sheen of the snow looked like a heavy shroud, but the Devil found shrouds appealing. Due to his insatiable love of heat, he was heavily garbed. He had on a felt hat made of wool, long red underwear from neck to ankles, a wool shirt and vest, an oilskin coat, and Angora goat hair chaps over his canvas pants. Steam emanated through his hat from his head, melting snowflakes that dared to land. The Devil's sunken obsidian eyes were ever vigilant, surrounded by bloodshot corneas because he never slept.

On Halloween, the Devil always made a point of walking abroad with the malignant spirits wandering amongst the ranks of the living. Oblivious people moved through these spirits and alongside them. While men, incited by the malevolent energy of these wraiths, got up to antics such as tipping over outhouses, posting signs in untoward places, and unexpectedly popping out of dark corners, the Devil preferred mayhem of a rather different sort. He was skilled in the art of one-upmanship and scaring people half to death, or better yet, all the way there.

When he walked into Harriet Hogan's saloon, nobody recognized him. Had they been paying attention as he traipsed through the snow on the porch, they would have noted the steaming imprints his leather cowboy boots left behind and a faint odor of sulfur; however, everybody was too busy trying to stay warm to pay him much heed at all.

Inside the saloon, the Devil moved to a small table in a corner, as far from the bar as he could get, and seated himself. A mournful jack-o'-lantern sat in the center of the table, its mouth wide as if wailing in protest at the lit candle inside. From this vantage point, the Fallen Angel could see everything going on in the saloon. People watching was one of his favorite activities. He grew excited when they lost their tempers or started fights. Hell was waiting for them, and so was he.

Once seated, the Devil removed his hat to reveal a scaly, bald head. Behind the bar counter, he spotted a tall, red-haired gal. He liked redheads, even ones who were a bit beyond their prime. He himself had been a redhead at one time, but his thick hair with its tousled curls had thinned and vanished in the relentless drought of Hell.

The woman behind the bar made her way over to the Devil. "Hello, Stranger," she said cheerily when she arrived at his table. "My name's Harriet. I'm the owner of this place. Care for a drink?"

"Two Spirytus vodkas," he responded, his hot breath condensing in the cool air around his lined face and furrowed brow.

"Two?" Harriet queried, a judgmental frown settling on her pretty features. "Are you sure?"

"Absolutely."

"Not carrying any handguns or knives, are you?"

"None, which is a pity because I'm fond of guns and accomplished with knives."

"Hmmm. Would you mind removing your coat and vest so that I can see for myself?"

"Not at all." The Devil stood and casually slid his coat onto the back of another chair at the table before proceeding to remove his vest. The faint odor of sulfur became stronger. He noticed Harriet's nose wrinkle in protest as she surveyed him for any weapons. Seeing none, she gave him a brief nod and headed back to the bar with alacrity to get his drinks. He sighed as he watched the rhythm of her hips, the memory of one specific redhead he had once almost loved surfacing. "Pah!" he admonished himself. "Sentimentality is for mortals."

In Harriet's absence, the Devil surveyed the room. He was looking for someone specific, a target. The person had to be conceited and self-important. The satisfaction of diminishing this type of individual never waned. It didn't take him long to find the fellow he wanted. A long drink of a man, lean and handsome, stood with his back to the bar blowing smoke rings at the ceiling. His boots were stylish, and he sported a horseshoe mustache. This man was, the Devil knew, a hard-core gambler, the type who couldn't resist a bet. When the man looked in his direction, the Devil gave what he hoped was a friendly nod and gestured to the chair he'd slung his coat across. The gambler raised a speculative eyebrow and moved with easy grace in the Devil's direction. "I know you?" he asked in a deep bass voice upon reaching the table.

"Not yet," the Devil replied. He already detested the man in front of him. Although he despised everyone, detestation he saved for those in whom he saw a bit of himself.

At this point, Harriet arrived back with the two Spirytus vodkas the Devil had ordered. She placed the drinks opposite him, smiled with what appeared to be a significant effort as her nose wrinkled yet again, winked at the dapper gambler, and returned to her post at the bar. Harriet's wink further stirred the cauldron of the Devil's natural hostility towards humanity. "Sit," he commanded.

The gambler raised an eyebrow, shrugged, and said, "I can do that easily enough." He folded into the chair opposite and leaned with casual arrogance against the oilskin overcoat.

"Name's Edgar, isn't it?" the Devil queried.

The gambler raised both eyebrows this time. "How'd you know?"

"You look like an Edgar." The Devil's face was one broad, menacing grin. "Care for a drink? It's Spirytus vodka, a drink that's hard to come by." He slid one of his drinks in Edgar's direction.

"Mighty strong stuff, Spirytus," Edgar commented, his face neutral.

"Like fire going down," the Devil agreed, eyes alight.

"Guess it'll warm my insides some, then."

"It'll warm your outsides some, too." With those words, the Devil threw his drink back, making it disappear in one gulp.

Not to be outdone, Edgar tried the same trick and wound up gasping and choking as his face flushed a vivid crimson color, reminiscent of the fires in Hell. Harriet hurried over with some water to cool the gambler's fiery insides down, patting Edgar's back and scowling at his nemesis, before scurrying back to the busy bar. The Devil chuckled maliciously as Edgar shuddered and shook, writhed and wriggled before settling into some serious panting, mouth wide as a barn door.

"Can see you like to get the best of a man," Edgar wheezed when he'd recovered some.

"I like to get the best of all men... and women," the Devil responded.

"What do you... hack, kack, ack... call yourself?"

"Satan."

Edgar snorted his amusement. "Perfect name for a fella like you. Croak! Perfect!"

"What do you say we blow some smoke rings, Edgar, see who's the best smoke blower?"

"Let me catch my breath for a bit longer first, Satan."

Some minutes later, Edgar pulled out two cigarette papers made of corn shucks, as well as some tobacco. He nodded affably to the Devil to help himself. Soon the two of them were rolling quirlies together. When Edgar offered the Devil a sulfur tipped match, the Devil shook his head. "Got my own," he said. Involved in the lighting of his own cigarette, Edgar didn't notice the Devil light his quirly with the end of a long, bony, index finger that appeared to be suffering from a severe case of eczema.

Soon, Edgar blew his first smoke ring - round, full, voluptuous - a thing of great, almost perfect beauty. The Devil raised dark, singed eyebrows in appreciation of Edgar's effort; then, he blew his first ring. This was no ordinary ring, either. It started small and grew, expanding outward further and further until it encompassed the two men. The gambler's eyes widened in astonishment. Edgar followed Satan's feat of artistry with a monumental inhalation of smoke followed by numerous short, quick outbreaths followed by a rapid closing of the lips after each. Rings blossomed outward and away rapidly, like those from a train smokestack. Each ring was exactly like the last in circumference. With deep admiration, the Devil clapped his chapped hands together. When he inhaled preparatory to his next effort, the Devil made his inhalation so long and deep that plumes of smoke rose from his ears. With satisfaction, he watched Edgar's eyes widen further than before. The gambler then shook his head as if to rid himself of an hallucination brought on by the Spirytus Vodka. When, at last, the Devil exhaled, he sculpted the smoke by continually altering the contours of his lips. From within the cave of his mouth, a small dragon issued forth. The light from the jack-o'-lantern on the table danced within its outline, making the dragon appear to glow like burnished gold.

"Hemlocks and chew spruce gum!" Edgar exclaimed. "You've won!"

"Beyond a doubt."

"Hell's bells! I'm not a man that likes to be beaten! What do you say to a game of cards?"

"Are you any good? Wouldn't want to waste my time."

"I'm the best."

"Faro?"

"Sure," Edgar said.

Harriet was hailed. Satan and Edgar told her what they wanted. An older gentleman with shrewd eyes and a salt and pepper beard joined them. He would act as their banker and had brought with him a card deck and chips, as well as thirteen extra cards of each rank. Thirteen was the Devil's favorite number and tended to bring him luck. Soon he and Edgar were intent on their bets, placing their chips and pennies on the cards they deemed most likely to win. Time and time again, Edgar won.

The Devil was perplexed. With his diabolical powers of intuition, he should have been consistently victorious. What in eternal tarnation was going on? He began to get hot under the collar, hotter than usual under the collar. Finally, unable to contain himself any longer, he exploded, "You have the most devilish luck, Edgar!"

"Yes, I have often been told that I have the luck of Lucifer!"

"The luck of..." the Devil spluttered, unable to finish his thought. By now, he was near boiling and his rotten egg smell was powerful. Their banker was feeling the waves of heat, and the robust odor emanating from the unhallowed man was having a nasty effect. Beads of sweat were running into the banker's salt and pepper beard; he pressed a handkerchief to his nose. His focus was diminishing, and his shrewd eyes watered. The Devil turned to him and hissed, "Be gone!" The man went, not even bothering to recoup his cards and chips.

"How did you do it?" the Devil asked.

"Can't give away my trade secrets," Edgar replied.

It was now the Devil's turn to writhe and wriggle, shudder and shake. Filled with wrath, it was all he could do to contain his molten anger. From the smug smile on Edgar's face, it was apparent that the gambler was enjoying his discomfiture. Beneath Satan's sizzling fingers, the wood of the table began to smolder, which caused the jack-o'-lantern's orange hide to smoke. He watched as Edgar's self-satisfaction diminished, replaced by a growing alarm. When the table erupted in flames and the jack-o'-lantern collapsed on its side, people in the saloon began to yell and flee. Not Harriet, though. The Devil saw her run towards the table with a bucket of water, a look of intense determination on her freckled face, red hair streaming out behind her like a banner. How the Devil detested water, and to his horror, he saw it arc violently out of the pail in the direction of his head. It was as cold as ice, and the second it hit his scalp, there was an explosion of steam and the saloon vanished.

By the time the fog cleared, the Devil was seated quite by himself. Edgar was gone, along with everyone else apart from some malignant spirits that actually seemed to be having a good laugh at his expense. Muttering imprecations, he left the saloon in a grandiose belch of smoke.

8

"To think that I beat the Devil at a game of cards!"

"You cheated, Edgar."

"I did. But then, how else was I to beat Satan?"

"You took a risk," Harriet chided.

"I did. But you looked after me in the end."

The redhead looked up into Edgar's face, then, her goblin green eyes shining. "I did, didn't I?"

He kissed her then, his horseshoe mustache against the soft skin of her upper lip.

ABOUT THE AUTHOR

JANICE RIDER (she/her) is an emerging author who has some short stories published in anthologies, including Word Balloon Books' *Beware the Bugs*, and the North American Jules Verne Society's *Extraordinary Visions*. Janice is also a playwright - three of her plays for youth are published with Eldridge Plays and Musicals. She directs The Chameleon Drama Club for children and youth in Calgary. Janice has a deep love of living things and the outdoors. These themes are often present in her writing.

THE DEVIL &
THE LOCH ARD GORGE

Leanbh Pearson

THE LOCH ARD GORGE, 1898

My name is Seána McKinnon, and I nearly died the night the *Loch Ard* sank. But you'll not find my name among those listed on the *Loch Ard's* official manifest, and there's no mention of a third survivor that night. Over fifty men, women, and children were aboard when she sank, the icy waters off the Victorian colony taking all but two—a cabin boy by the name of Tom Pearce, and Irishwoman, Eva Carmichael, both surviving the treacherous waters to find shelter in its sandy cove. Tom's heroics raised the alarm, and the full tragedy of the *Loch Ard* revealed. Since that night, the gorge became known for the ship that it sank. A name whispered with fear and sorrow: the Loch Ard Gorge.

But there's a darker tale woven so tightly through that fateful voyage, it's hard to see where one ends and the other begins. That tale is mine, one of curses and ill-luck, one that saw fifty innocent lives drowned at sea. For Devil take me, I caused their deaths. My presence brought the Devil aboard the *Loch Ard* that night. And even as I clawed my way free from those vengeful waves, shook the Devil's grasp from my soul, I did not raise the alarm as Tom did later. Instead, I fled into the night, leaving others to suffer a fate that should have been mine. Those fifty dead are a stain upon my soul, so blood black now, it's barely recognisable to me.

It's been decades since the shipwreck, and while the passage of time has aged my body, worn me thin and bent my spine, those waters still call to me, and the Devil in their depths demands his due. For I owe him my soul and was foolish to think crossing oceans and wading from frigid waters would ever let me escape my fate. As a wilful girl, I'd pleaded for my greatest desire, and the Devil had granted it, asking for my soul in return. Foolish child that I was, I agreed to such a bargain, but flee and fight as I might, all debts must eventually be repaid. Let me unburden myself, whisper my story to the wind, my final testament. The Devil can wait a little longer.

LONDON, 1876

Eoin O'Henry stood across the other side of the small parlour room. This was not the first time I had seen Eoin at an evening dance hosted by our mutual acquaintances, the Hansons, but it was the first time I'd been alone in a room with him. He paused on the threshold, seemingly uncertain whether to enter after finding me here alone. I smiled encouragingly, mustering what confidence I could find beneath warring desire and anxiety. *What if he thinks I'm dull? What if he's only ever been pleasant to me to please the Hansons?*

The noise from the dance hall washed over me in waves. To my pleasure, Eoin continued to approach, and I wondered if he could hear the frantic rhythm of my heartbeat. It seemed thunderous to me. I lowered my eyes demurely and hoped to gain control of my emotions.

"Miss McKinnon?" He bowed to me, his smile almost a smirk.

"Mister O'Henry." I grimaced at the stilted formality society demanded.

He saw my expression and immediately straightened. "What's wrong?"

"Please, call me Seána. Miss McKinnon sounds so dull. Anyone important to me calls me Seána."

"Am I important to you then?" he teased.

A blush crept up my neck and across my face. "You have discovered my secret already, then."

He leant towards me, conspiratorially. "Is that the only one?"

"Mister McKinnon," I whispered, conscious of the brush of his hand against my arm.

He grinned. "Call me Eoin."

I held my breath, dizzy with the closeness of him, the lingering touch of his hand as it slid away from my arm. "Where are your fellow artists?" I asked, glancing nervously to the doorway, as though they may suddenly discover us.

He rolled his eyes. "They were expounding the virtues of Lord Byron, so I left them to it."

"You know Lord Byron?" I gasped, unable to prevent my thrill and shock.

He smiled at me. "Lord Byron knows everyone. I would not count myself among his close acquaintances, though. Alas, I am not so great an artist or poet yet to merit such a blessing."

I grinned in return. "Is he truly as shocking as everyone says?"

He met my grin with one of his own. "Worse."

I blushed and bent my head to his. "How scandalous."

"Seána!"

The shrill voice broke through the quiet parlour room, and I stepped back from Eoin as though scalded. My mother strode towards me, face pinched in distaste, her glare encompassing us both.

"Sir," she said coldly, cocking her head so slightly it was barely noticeable.

"Ma'am," he said hastily, bowing deeply. "I meant no disrespect. Miss McKinnon and I share a mutual acquaintance through the Hansons."

"I do not care whether or not disrespect was intended towards my daughter, sir."

He paled visibly. "Miss McKinnon is your daughter?"

"And you are?"

I glared at my mother's frosty tone but stepped closer to her, wishing no rumour of impropriety to befall Eoin.

"Eoin O'Henry," he said, affecting another bow.

"*Hmph*," my mother said, lips pursed as though she had eaten something sour. "One of the artists?"

He flushed. "Yes, Mrs McKinnon."

"Very well," she said, turning to me. "Come along, Seána."

Without waiting to see if I would comply with her demand, she turned on her heel and stalked from the room. I followed, casting an apologetic look over my shoulder, smiling when Eoin returned a nod. Trudging in my mother's wake, I felt his eyes on my back but didn't dare turn around lest my mother find further offence with him.

The evening was turgid after that bright moment in the parlour with Eoin. I looked for him among the crowd standing along the walls, but I did not see him there, nor among those dancing in the centre, where a space had been cleared. I politely accepted dances with several young men who introduced themselves, but found no pleasure in it, my thoughts frequently returning to Eoin.

Eventually the evening concluded, and we took our leave of the Hansons'. The short carriage ride back to our house was silent, Mama scrutinising me the entire journey. I kept my gaze on the passing city streets of London, the bright gas lamps, light spilling from drinking rooms, gaming houses, and whatever other nightly pursuits London offered. I'd experienced none of it. I longed for adventure, to be among Eoin and his artist friends who spoke so passionately about everything.

"Do not get designs on Mister O'Henry, Seána," Mama began, drawing my attention from the window. "Your father will forbid him as a suitor, as surely as I will. You have a higher station in this world and must think of that."

"It was a brief conversation, Mama, nothing more." It sounded unconvincing, even to my ears, and the blush heating my cheeks betrayed my true feelings.

Mama did not reply, but the thin line of her lips was answer enough. I returned my gaze to the window.

LONDON, 1876

Eoin and I continued to meet at various social occasions, drawing closer to each other with every event. But the disapproval of my parents only mounted, until one day they forbid me from seeing him at all. I wanted a life with Eoin like I had desired nothing else before. And Eoin, knowing he could not support me as his wife on an artist's income, started to pull away from me. His actions only made me more desperate to hold on to him.

Late one evening, in the privacy of my room, I sat cross-legged on my bed, the tangle of my thick black hair falling around my shoulders. I glanced up at my reflection in the dressing table mirror. *Am I really doing this?* I had spoken with my Irish maid, excitedly expressing my desire to be with Eoin and the surety my parents would forbid such a match. Hesitantly, she had told me of a charm that would grant my greatest desire. *Is this wise?* I shook my head, annoyed by my own treacherous thoughts. *Nothing is ever gained without sacrifice, Seána.*

I looked at the items assembled on the bed before me: a silver bowl, a small silver bell taken from the serving trays, two fresh rose petals from the garden, a sewing needle, and a candle. I nodded to myself in readiness, and, leaning across the bed, lit the stub of the candle in the candelabrum on my bedside table. Once the candle was alight, I stood it upright in the centre of the silver bowl and picked up the sewing needle. I sucked in a breath and pricked my fingertip, a droplet of blood welling up. Gently, I took the two rose petals and crushed them between my fingers above the flame, allowing my blood to smear on them. The heady scent of the roses mingled with the coppery tang of blood as I held my hands above the flame, then dropped the petals into the bowl. Last, I took up the silver bell, and making sure it never rang until I was ready, drew in a shaky breath.

"To those who always listen but are never seen, hear me. I seek my greatest desire denied me and offer that of equal value in return. Heed my plea!" I rang the silver bell once, its sharp tone echoing in the silence of my room.

Nothing happened. I watched my reflection in the mirror, the strain of my actions finally showing.

What am I doing? What madness is this? I'm a Catholic woman, and these are the actions of a hedge witch. I shook my head at my own foolishness. Focusing on my reflection in the mirror, I noticed a strange deepening of the shadows behind my right shoulder. Staring in horror, I watched the shadows grow darker and denser until they began to spread across the floor and walls towards me.

Leaping from the bed, I whirled to face whatever uncanny terror I had summoned. Heart pounding, a form slowly materialised from the shadows. It was a man, as far as I could tell, although his body was clothed in a writhing mass of shadows, his face hidden by the shifting darkness around him.

"No others have answered your summons, but I have been watching and waiting. Tell me your greatest desire, and I shall make it reality."

Desperation warred with fear, but I stared at the faceless phantom. "My greatest desire is for Eoin O'Henry and I to be free to marry."

"And in return for granting you the soul of another, you will owe me yours." His voice was cold like a frigid winter's evening.

I bit my lip, anxiety coursing through my body. This was my one true chance. I may have been raised a Catholic and attended church regularly, but this shadowy form was not the Devil, no matter how I wanted to imagine him to be. The charm I had worked was a simple thing anyone could buy for a copper.

I nodded my agreement.

The shadows shifted and writhed, swirling around the form until they resembled the tattered robes of the Reaper.

"Then it is done," he intoned.

Before I could respond further, he was gone, the shadows retreating immediately to the corners of my room. I shivered, wondering if I had made a wise bargain. Whatever I had done, I must live with the consequences now. But thoughts of Eoin distracted me, as they often did, and with my mind filled with the certainty that we would marry, I forgot my fear. I had altered events by tying myself to a being who now had claim to my soul, but not until my mortal days came to an end.

EDINBURGH, 1876

Waiting outside the Hansons' large town house, but still within the safety and respectability of the lamps, I stared into the darkness, trying to ignore the noise of the gathered footmen and grooms in the circular driveway. My pulse quickened at the very thought of what I was about to do. *Is this truly sinful?* I did not feel like a sin. Quick footsteps and a gentle hand on my elbow interrupted my musings.

Startled, I turned to see Eoin, dressed in his best finery, an urgent brightness to his eyes.

"Are you sure?" he leaned close, whispering in my ear.

"Of course, I'm sure. I shan't change my mind now."

He grinned and offered me his other arm. "Shall we go then? Mrs Eoin O'Henry?"

A blush crept across my cheeks at the sound of the name, and the implications of taking that by tomorrow evening, I would be a married woman. Hurrying beside Eoin, he escorted me to a waiting hansom cab. Climbing within the tight confines with Eoin, my heart raced. London's dark streets passed me in a blur of sound and spluttering gas lamps.

Even after the hurried transfer into a coach bound for Edinburgh, I kept expecting to hear the whistle of police constables. Surely my sudden disappearance from the Hansons' household had been noticed? And of course, my parents had no notion of my whereabouts. My father had made his thoughts very plain on how disreputable and unsuitable he found Eoin O'Henry. So, when Eoin suggested we elope to Gretna Green—the only place in Britain where we might marry freely without my father's interference— I knew the bargain I had made with that shadowy Devil was a true one. Now, as we travelled to Edinburgh, the closeness of Eoin, the press of his body against mine in the coach, left me too distracted to worry about the bargain which had secured Eoin's heart. Eoin and I would be married and that was all that mattered.

Holding me close to his side, Eoin's arm around me was soothing against the rocking of the coach over the inhospitable terrain. Absently, he ran his thumb along my collarbones, drawing shivers of anticipation from me. Soon I would be his wife. Soon. And with Eoin's adoration and love, I needed nothing else to survive.

Early the next morning, Eoin and I married at Gretna Green. Despite all the disparaging things people have ever said about the Scottish weather, it was a fine day; crisp and clear, promising the future I had hoped for. But we saw little of the Gaelic countryside that first day, instead withdrawing to the privacy of our shared room and our marriage bed, where I cared little for anything, but the sensual enjoyment granted to man and wife.

Later, as I lay in bed, Eoin smoked beside the window, and I watched the sun set over Edinburgh, wondering for the first time about the Devil who had granted me this wish. Despite the religious teachings,

the blackness of witchcraft and charms, there seemed
no harm in what I had done. There is no brimstone,
no burning flames of Hell. *What do churchmen know
of love, anyway?*

"We will need to see your father tomorrow," Eoin
said, startling me.

"Can't we stay here another day, my love?"

He shook his head, curls still mussed from the
bed. "If I am to make a life for you befitting of
your station, I will need to discuss your upkeep
with your father; an appropriate annual amount
needs to be arranged."

I frowned. "He will not be pleased with what
we've done."

"But surely he cannot deny his only daughter her
rightful station in life?"

I shook my head. "He is a disagreeable man
and had already refused your offer. Perhaps if we
stayed here a little longer, he would have time to
calm his anger."

Eoin pursed his lips. "I cannot afford to lodge
here any longer, my sweet one."

I ran my hand along the lace shift I wore. I knew
Eoin's station in life. He had never hidden the
poverty he endured for his art. But confronted with it
now, I did not know what to say. Instead, I glanced to
the corner of the room to avoid Eoin's gaze upon me.
Shadows gathered in the furthest corner, roiling and
twisting. *Surely not?* I had made my bargain with the
Devil; my soul was his to take when I died. *Why is he
here now?*

"Seána?" Eoin asked.

"Mm?" I drew my eyes away from the dense
shadows and met his gaze.

"You know I need to speak with your father. It cannot be put off further."

"Yes," I agreed, but was distracted by the shifting darkness in the room with us.

LONDON, 1876

Eoin and I arrived at my father's townhouse in London as man and wife. We were ushered into the downstairs sitting room by one of the serving staff and left to wait. I paced the room nervously, familiar with my father's tactics for dealing with undesirable guests. This was the most unused sitting room; a small and sparsely decorated space which my mother insisted was insult enough. And now, as I surveyed the oldest of our household furniture on display, it did not feel like my house anymore. I was unwelcome here.

"Seána, come and sit down," Eoin said, folding his long legs and patting the seat of the divan beside him.

"This is bad," I repeated for the second time since entering the room.

"You still haven't explained why, though."

"This is the room my father uses for those business colleagues who occasionally arrive unannounced on his doorstep with demands he refuses to meet."

Eoin's brows knit together, and, for the first time, I think he finally saw the situation as I did.

"But surely he means no ill will to his only daughter?"

I bit my lip and wrung my hands uselessly but did not reply. By the end of the day, the fine lace gloves I was wearing were going to be a frayed mess. I was about to speak when the door behind me opened, and I turned in a flurry of petticoats and stray curls.

My father stood in the doorway. His face was pale with anger, lips a compressed line, but his eyes were bright blue with unexpressed fury. Calmly he closed the door behind him, and Eoin stood, smoothed his trousers, then walked towards to my father.

"I will not waste your time, Mr and Mrs O'Henry," my father said coldly, and Eoin's hand, already offered in greeting, fell limply to his side.

"Papa?" I questioned, edging closer, but he held up a hand.

"I have no daughter anymore. I made my sentiments quite plain to you both, and you went against them. You will not see a penny from this household. I will not provide any connections to whatever business you choose to conduct. Our ties are cut, there will be no further discussion. Mr O'Henry, you have seduced and ruined my daughter. A worse scoundrel she could never have found. Mrs O'Henry, I hope he proves to be the man you believed him to be."

I gaped, speechless, as Eoin blustered and protested, but my father was unmoved. He simply walked to the door, opened it again, ushered us from the sitting room and out onto the front stoop before closing the door firmly behind us.

"What are we going to do?" I breathed, swaying slightly.

Eoin was pale as milk, and his dark eyes like pits as he brushed absently at a stray curl that had come loose from its bonds.

"I don't know," he confessed, reaching for my hand. "I promised to improve your life, to give you the world, Seána. Using the funds from your dowry, I was going to secure passage for us aboard a ship so we might begin a new life together in the colonies. I had hoped for so much more for us."

I squeezed his hand in mine. "We have each other, Eoin. That will be enough."

He smiled grimly, and together we walked away from my father's house. It had been my home for seventeen years, but I did not once see anyone looking after me from the windows. Instead, I saw a darker shadow pooled within Eoin's own, as though the Devil lay coiled within my husband. I shivered at the thought and pressed myself closer to Eoin, trying to banish such terrible ideas, hoping to forget the bargain I had made.

GRAVESEND, 1877

I stood on the stoop of the house where we rented a single room. The weight of my curse, the bargain I had made with the Devil, tightened around me more each day until it was as suffocating as the overcrowded streets of Gravesend where we eked out an existence. Evening was drawing her mantle over the city, and my eyes shifted to the shadowy laneways and darkened alleys, waiting for the Devil to step from the half-light. But nothing happened. It never did. Still, I felt the malevolent presence watching me, waiting for the soul I had promised him. I was certain by now he meant to drive me to madness, have me take my own life and secure what he wanted, before my timely end. I straightened my back. I would not so easily be his. He could have my soul when I was an old woman, and not a moment before.

Resolute, I watched the fading light leave the squalid lane outside our rooms, knowing darkness would also bring Eoin home after his long hours and hard labour. But I had time to myself yet, for while I may wait diligently for my husband's return, he would not be here until empty pockets forced him from the last tavern. Since our dreams to escape, London had turned to ash, Eoin had started working on the docks. His writer's hands became scarred and calloused, and his soul consumed with bitterness.

His only true solace seemed to be in the oblivion of drink.

Turning to go indoors, movement from the corner of my eye caught my attention. I whirled, heart pounding, and stared at the shadow. The formless darkness, an inky absence of light, moved across the stonework of the opposite house.

"I know I owe you," I hissed to the silent laneway, the lurking dark.

Not waiting for the Devil to materialise, I hurried inside, closing the front door, and bolting the inner one to the small single room Eoin and I called home now. Breathing hard, I tried to forget the waiting menace outside. Oh, I was aware the Devil followed me, heedless of day or night, sunshine, or shadow, but the threat of his presence still scared me. Familiarity with the waiting collector of my damned soul did nothing to ease my nerves.

Now, I huddled before the hearth, as I did every night, the dim firelight illuminating my work; nimble fingers mending garments for extra coinage. I had endured the backbreaking labour offered to the poorest, but finally gained employment as a maid in one of the larger households. The irony of those countless hours in my youth spent perfecting embroidery was not lost on me now as I mended clothing for my social betters. I felt true shame for my current circumstances, knowing how shocked my mama would be if she ever learned how far I had fallen in society. The daughter she had expected to manage a household now had hands as worn and chapped from cleaning as any scullery maid.

Midnight slunk closer, and I listened to the night sounds, knowing the lateness of the hour would soon bring Eoin home. The shadows in the single room lengthened around me, and I shifted in my seat, conscious of a presence behind me. I tensed, knowing Eoin would return stinking of ale and boiling with impotent rage. His temper knew no bounds, and he spoke with his fists instead of his lips. *Can I endure another beating?* I touched my already bruised ribs at the thought. We would argue, and it, as surely as always, would come to blows. I was my father's daughter and had his temper, too. Most evenings, Eoin and I were like a match to gunpowder, and just as volatile.

Staggered footsteps stopped outside the front door. I held my breath, waiting until the latch on our door rattled. The uneven footsteps retreated, a familiar silhouette passing across the shabby window curtain, trying to peer inside. My fears were confirmed; Eoin was home. I rose and quickly unbolted our inner door before retreating to the fireplace again. Eoin's boots clunked down the hallway and he muttered: his words dark with ill intent.

Sitting motionless beside the hearth, I begged the angels to intervene, ignoring that they had never heeded my prayers before. Frozen in place, hand poised above my needlework, rage and fear coiled uneasily within me. It was a familiar sensation: contempt that Eoin had coerced me, promised a future that turned to ashes; and outrage that I tolerated him taking his failings out on me. From behind me, I felt the darkness shiver with anticipation. I almost welcomed whatever was about to come.

The door burst open, flung so violently against its hinges it bounced back against the wall. I startled to my feet and, trembling, took up the fire poker beside me, its weight a comfort. Eoin laughed, his features twisted with disgust, face flushed with drink. Where he stood, he blocked the entire doorway, a menacing giant I could not defeat.

Fury and rage boiled so thickly from him it

was almost tangible. I tightened my grip on the poker, and he instinctively straightened, bleary eyes finally focusing on it. It seemed a childish weapon to wield against such a force, but I held firm. Inky tendrils slid across the threshold from the shadowed hallway behind Eoin, twisting up his legs and filling the room with its whispering, willing Eoin's fists to be merciless. Silently, my lips moved, praying my Eoin— the man I had loved once—be returned to me.

"You bewitched me," he slurred, his uneven footsteps scraping across the wooden floorboards.

I trembled, unable to make my feet move. The shadows engulfed Eoin as the Devil I feared took possession of the man I had loved, twisting his drink-reddened face into something ugly. Eoin lunged for me, grabbing at a fistful of my hair, his dexterity surprising, despite his intoxication. He shook me, lifting me up by my hair, body suspended in the air like a child's rag doll. Biting down on my lip, refusing to scream for him, I tasted my own blood. Furious, Eoin shook me harder, his breath hot and foul in my face. I scrabbled for purchase, heels skittering against the floorboards, my fingernails raking over his bare arm until I clung to his shirtsleeves.

"Eoin, you're hurting me."

"I should've stayed clear of you, but you lured me, Seána. You ruined me."

The venom of his words struck me with spittle from his lips. Still gripping desperately at his wrists, Eoin pushed me back against the rough wall, his forearm across my throat, slowly applying pressure. I stared into his eyes. There was nothing familiar there.

Nothing of the man I remembered, the one I had married. I bared my teeth and spat at him.

"I curse the day I met you," I rasped.

The ferocity of my unbridled anger surprised even me. Eoin blinked, his grip loosening at the vitriol in my words. I twisted away from his grasp and tried to dart past him. His fist hit in my side, just below my ribs. The blow knocked me hard against the wall, my breath wheezing from my lungs. I clutched at my side, half doubled over, hissing at the sharp pain. One hand pressed to the wall, the other hand reaching for the discarded poker. I levered myself upright again. Eoin laughed at my feeble weapon, and I felt the colour rise in my cheeks, shame burning within me: the curse of my sex; the weakness of the female body; the fragility of being a woman. I tightened my grip on the poker, flexing my fingers and gritting my teeth. I forced myself to stand tall, ignoring the burning agony of my abdomen, and faced Eoin, rage now burning where shame had been a moment before.

Eoin stalked towards me, one massive hand reaching for the poker, ready to push it aside. I met his eyes, saw none of the love we had once shared, only bitter ashes of what was left, resentment and hatred blossoming in the absence of love. *How dare he blame me. How dare he accuse me of bewitching him.* I had been a fool to marry without my father's permission, but Eoin had been twice a fool to think any dowry would have been granted to us after we eloped. I would not be thrice a fool and cower before him.

My eyes flicked back and forth between the poker and the muddy toes of Eoin's boots as he closed the distance. I quickly raised the poker, but Eoin did not stop. The tip sank into his abdomen; the flesh pliant at first before meeting resistance. He gasped and staggered forwards crushing me as he clutched at the shaft of the poker buried deep in his guts. I tried to step away from him, my hands slick with his blood, his big hands beating at me. Screaming in rage and fear, I forced the poker deeper before he sagged forward, bloody handprints sliding down the wall as he collapsed to his knees.

Edging around him, I stared in horror at where the end of the iron poker protruded from his back, the barbed point visible between his shoulder blades and glistening with dark blood. Eoin's breath was a ragged wheeze, blood bubbling on his lips. He tried to call for me, but coughed, spraying the wall in a fine red mist. Shadows leeched into a liquid darkness around him, spreading towards me with the pool of his blood. Eoin coughed again, choking on thick strands of blood and phlegm. He whispered a curse at me, and I flinched; the power of a dying man's curse was well known. Stepping backwards slowly, shock warring with terror, I saw a shifting outline of another form visible against Eoin's own, as though the Devil sought to escape the failing flesh prison he had possessed.

Eoin collapsed to the floor with a wet groan,

blood sweeping out around him. Weakly, he turned his head towards me, eyes wide with shock, pleading wordlessly with me. But I only shook my head, retreating further to the doorway, realisation at what I had done finally hitting me. Eoin's bloody fingers clawed against the floor, his mouth moving soundlessly as he cursed me over and again. I could not be found here. I could not wait to see if the Devil escaped before Eoin died. Instead, I turned and flung myself into the hallway beyond, barrelling through the front door, and fleeing into the dark streets of Gravesend.

GRAVESEND DOCKS, 1877

Heedless of the late hour, I ran towards the docks, thin boots slapping against the slick cobblestones of the streets. In moments, those cobblestones gave way to the muck and mud of the poorest dockside neighbourhoods. But it did not matter to me anymore. There was a wildness about me as I ran, raven hair unfurling from my kerchief, heedless of the hour or the dangers. The moment someone found Eoin, I'd be hung for murder. It would not matter that he was a bully, a liar, and a cheat. It would not matter that he had raised his fists against me one time too many. I was his wife and, according to the law, it had been by my hand he had died. I still had a coin purse tied to the belt of my dress, and within the waist of my petticoats, I had stitched more of my meagre savings, always kept safe and away from Eoin and his debtors. Now I hoped my frugal days would be enough to secure me quick passage from Gravesend with few questions asked.

"Run towards me, lass," a male voice joked, gesturing obscenely.

Other voices called after me, whistles, and baser suggestions that I ignored as I ran. I was focused only on reaching the docks and the water beyond, a hand clutched to my side where Eoin had hit me. But even as I fled, a terrible foreboding rose the hairs on the back of my neck. *Can I run forever?*

Will the Devil let me live long enough to be an old woman? I hurried towards a merchant ship moored at the far end of a dock. All was dark around me, and I whipped my head from side to side, movement from outside the dockside taverns a constant source of trepidation, but I searched the shadows for any signs that the Devil waited for me. So distracted, I nearly ran into a gigantic man as he stepped from the darkness to block my path. Skidding to a halt, my heeled boots digging into the muck, I barely stopped before colliding with his broad chest. My boots slipped on slime coating the wooden docks and his massive hand reached out to steady me. Instinctively, I flinched at the touch. I tried to pull away too quickly, boots slipping again.

"Woah, lass," he said, holding me more firmly.

"I'm not your lass." I trembled, terror and wretchedness overwhelming me.

"My apologies, Miss," the big man said, withdrawing his hand from where he gripped my waist. "Didn't mean any impropriety."

I straightened, regaining some control, and kept my eyes downcast. "Thank you."

"It's not safe in these parts for a young woman alone."

I glanced up at this hulking man. He had the familiar ease near the water that I had seen in many sailors or dockside workers, but he was more educated than most. Considering him, I thought it likely he was a merchant sailor or maybe even a merchant captain. Still wary, but trying to hide my fear, I tossed my dark hair over my shoulder with feigned nonchalance. I looked past the large man and jerked my chin towards the clipper already sitting low in the water, loaded to depart at dawn.

"I hoped to secure passage aboard this clipper. Is she bound from Gravesend soon?"

"She is." He frowned at me, suspicion in his eyes. "I don't like to be frank, Miss, but what trouble are you running from?"

"Trouble? I am a free woman. I may travel wherever I wish."

"Miss, begging your pardon, but very few come to these parts so late in the hour without a dire need."

I glanced up at the night sky, imagining stars, but seeing only the familiar soot-stained clouds.

"I'm running from my husband," I admitted. "Gravesend turned him cruel and quick with his fists. I need passage away from here, and then I can go on my way."

He crossed his thickly muscled arms and stared at me. "The *Loch Ard* is bound for Melbourne. I can't take any risks with you, understand? If you pay passage but someone comes to fetch you before we set sail, I'll not hide you."

I nodded carefully. "I understand."

"Welcome aboard the *Loch Ard* then, Miss…?" He paused, looking down at me and waiting for me to complete the rouse we'd silently agreed to. He'd ask no questions including whatever name I gave him.

"Kelly," I provided, not willing to use my married name nor my maiden name and, instead, picking one of the dozen common Irish surnames in Gravesend.

"This way then, *Miss* Kelly. I'll see you to your lodgings tonight."

Satisfied, I nodded, but glanced warily back at the dark shadows along the docks. Most of the taverns were located down the other end of the docks, and here the darkness was deep. Squaring my shoulders, I hoped I could pay this merchant with the coins I had, praying I would not have need to resort to other more debauched means to secure my passage. I set my boots to the narrow plank that lead onto the *Loch Ard* and followed the hulking man aboard the ship.

"She's a fast vessel," he said, ducking beneath overhanging loads still yet to be secured below in the hold.

Even as I followed, I glanced around the ship, noticing the crew had stirred from whatever idle games of chance had occupied them before this man's arrival on deck. I had to assume from their bowed heads, this was their captain I followed.

My fingers plucked quickly at the seams of a double band I had sewn into the waist of my petticoats, unstitching the thread that secured several of my smaller hidden stashes of coins. Ahead of me, the captain stopped at the entrance to the narrow stairs leading below deck. He fixed me with a steady gaze, surveying more than my form, seeming to assess my character as well.

"The *Loch Ard* is my ship, lass," he began. "If you're still onboard when we set sail in a few hours, you'll follow my orders. If I say you get below decks, you'll do it. I won't have my crew distracted by your presence, understood? There are a few other women aboard and I tell them the same."

I bobbed a quick nod of understanding and followed him down the steep steps that disappeared into the yawning darkness below deck. The shadows were thick down there and I flinched. Dim light from oil lanterns hanging sparsely between a series of small cabins did little to break the gloom. Silently, I prayed he would not take advantage of me, aware I had foolishly followed him down here, where any captain might ask for more than coinage to take an extra passenger aboard. I had few options left to me, and my virtue was likely ruined, anyway. Eoin's blood stained my soul as surely as it had my dress. *But murder must be far worse a sin than anything I might do to secure escape from Gravesend?* For I was certain, if I remained here, I would meet the hangman's noose.

By the time the captain had led to an open cabin doorway, I was prepared for anything I might need to endure if it meant I would escape death. My hand was sweaty where I clasped my coins too tightly. Nervously, I offered the clinking fare to the captain, and in the light of the cabin lantern, it illuminated nearly the entirety of my savings. I hoped the coins would not be stolen from me. The captain glanced down at the coins, dark eyes assessing the value and potential risk I might pose to him. Finally, he grunted, scooping the coins from my hand, and gesturing wordlessly to the open cabin doorway behind him. He had turned away and was already beginning back the way we had come, when I found my voice.

"Thank you."

"Don't thank me yet, lass," he mumbled, stalking off down the passage, bending beneath the lanterns as he disappeared into the gloom.

I let out a shaky breath and closed the cabin door behind me. I perched on the narrow bunk, the thin mattress giving beneath my weight. If fate were in my favour, the *Loch Ard* would set sail before anyone found Eoin's body and raised the alarm. If I were fortunate, I might escape the hangman.

Sitting there in the dark cabin, I waited for dawn. I knew Eoin had cursed me with his dying breath, those scarlet droplets marking me for the sinner I was. But I had been cursed well before tonight and compared to the bargain I had made with the Devil, Eoin's dying words were of minor concern. Turning my mind to more practical thoughts, I took off my dark dress and scrubbed Eoin's blood from it. Even as I worked, I hoped in vain the stain upon my soul would disappear as easily as the one from my clothing.

ATLANTIC CROSSING, 1877

At first light, the *Loch Ard* set sail. I sat at my small cabin window, staring across at the dark shore as the ship made its way from the harbour. The coastline was bordered by rocky cliffs, and glowing lights, marking clusters of houses, flickered as we left Gravesend behind in a smothering cloud of soot and sea mist. The ship ventured further from the coastline, and I looked one last time at the England I had known, thinking the next port in Melbourne would be a country as foreign to me as Hell itself. But gazing at the industry and civilisation of Gravesend and England, it looked like a determined scab clinging to the coast; a wound that would never heal. I imagined the virgin soils of the colonies, a landscape untouched by human hands, and felt freedom for the first time.

8

Once upon the open water and we no longer hugged the coastline, the *Loch Ard* sped across the Atlantic, putting distance between us and Britain. I kept to my cabin, nausea rolling through me each time the ship crested a wave then plunged down the other side. Curled on my side on the bunk, I listened to the banter of a young woman and a lad meeting outside my door. The woman had the lilting Irish accent that made me homesick for my mother, her voice like a siren song. But I huddled on my bunk, blanket pulled tight around my bruised body, and shivered. As much as I wanted to follow her above deck and seek fresh air, I dared not leave my cabin. Fear plagued me, and seasickness left me weak. I drifted from consciousness to the waking nightmare of the too-dark shadows in the cabin.

When I finally ventured above deck, it was to breathe the salt air as we passed the exotic African coastline, the warmth of the tropics like a balm to my soul. But the ocean currents soon pulled us further south. I longed to feel firm land beneath my feet again, but the sea seemed endless. The further we travelled, the denser the shadows in my cabin seemed to grow. *Has the Devil found me again?* As though to prove my fears justified, the moment the *Loch Ard* reached the waters beyond Africa, the swell rose, waves towering above the clipper, breaking upon her deck and the winds strengthened. Through it all, I hid in my cabin, fearful of the waters and the darkness of the open sky, a terrible foreboding growing within me as the *Loch Ard* pushed further towards the treacherous shipwreck coast.

THE SHIPWRECK COAST, 1878

The Indian Ocean was a heaving, grey maelstrom as we sailed below the Great Bight. The strong winds that had guided our journey now turned savage, and the air of the Antarctic tasted of ice and death. Pulling all the blankets onto my bunk for warmth, I kept a fearful watch on the shadows spreading through my cabin. There was a terrible absence of light in the room; the oil lantern unable to stand against the inky shadows that clothed the Devil waiting for me.

Hidden in my cabin, I had no warning when the storm hit. It smashed into the *Loch Ard* without restraint or mercy. The violence of the waves against the hull threw me from my bunk and I tumbled across the hard floor. The might of the ocean came to bear on the *Loch Ard*, and for all the captain's skill manoeuvring the vessel, it was a force he could not defeat. I had been told we were less than a day's journey from Melbourne, but the gale screamed in fitful bursts around the ship, tearing at the sails while the crew fought to keep the ship from being dragged beneath the waves.

Clinging to the supports of my bunk and no longer trusting the ocean not to haul me to the floor again, I abandoned sleep. Anxiously, I brushed a dark curl from my face, trying to remind myself this was just another storm, that we had endured many before it, and our captain knew the vessel and this ocean.

Still, I wanted to flee. I wanted to escape the confines of the cabin, its cloying smell of stale sweat and episodes of seasickness that still occasionally plagued me. I forced my mind from the tempest outside, thinking of my first bath when I reached Melbourne. I tugged absently at my hair; the kerchief no longer able to contain the tangles of dark curls that resembled a nest of vipers. Above my head, the oil lantern swung perilously from its iron hook in the middle of the room.

My stomach clenched, lurched, and I forced down the nausea again. *How far was Melbourne now?* Another wave slammed against the hull of the ship, sending shudders through the planking, and ushering a groan from its timbers. I pulled my shawl tighter about my shoulders, curling in on myself, knees to my chest on the bunk. Absently, I touched the pearl and gold crucifix at my throat. An unconscious gesture, one I had kept since childhood. The pendant was the one family item I still possessed that had not been sold to cover Eoin's debts.

As they so often did, thoughts of Eoin turned to bile. I remembered his forearm against my throat, the emptiness of his eyes as the Devil stared back at me. I remembered the awful feel of the poker in my hand, his flesh parting before it. It had been necessary to save myself. Still, I knew no judge or hangman would ever forgive me.

A shrill whistle carried through the air, high-pitched and clear above the tempest. It was the bosun's whistle, signalling to the crew even in the harshest storms. Above deck, men shouted, then the *Loch Ard* lurched, bells clanging in alarm, the bosun's whistle an echo above the thunderous voice of the storm. From the surrounding cabins, fists pounded on doors and panicked voices filled the passage. I struggled upright, the clamour of shouting and hurried footsteps filling the confines below deck. Staggering to my feet, I wrenched the cabin door open.

Peering out into the gloom, another wave hit the *Loch Ard*, and the ship groaned like a wounded animal. The force of the wave threw me against the opposing wall. I collided with another young woman from the cabin next to mine as a cabin boy herded passengers past us and towards the main steps leading up to the deck.

Gasping for breath, I followed, the air knocked from my lungs again as I was thrown into a doorframe. The young lad, wearing the livery of the *Loch Ard*'s cabin crew, wrapped an arm around my waist and half-pulled, half-dragged me and the other woman after him.

On deck and exposed to the fury of the storm, everything around us was chaos. Darkness, sea mist, and screams surrounded me. Waves broke over the ship, saltwater sloshing across the wooden deck, but I was dragged towards the lifeboats, despite the treacherous footing. The rain was a drumbeat faster than my heart, and everywhere around me was a wrathful ocean. Icy dread filled the night, bringing back memories of how Eoin had died by my hand. I had bargained with the Devil, and it had cursed me. *Is the Devil here to take my soul? Will the Loch Ard be my last resting place? A watery grave far from home?*

"Ship's going down!" the bosun shouted above the gale.

I staggered as waves rolled across the deck and timbers screamed, shattering against something solid. Everything around us was a white mist, rain, and dark water. *Have we run aground?* The ocean swell crushed the ship, grinding the *Loch Ard* against the rocks beneath us. Water flooded the deck, the ship breaking apart against the rocks where it had foundered. Above, lightning split the sky, reflecting off the white mist. I could see nothing. No signs of a harbour. No sign that land was nearby or which direction. The ship *had* run aground on rock. *How far away is the shore?* The thick mist cloaked everything, obscuring anything beyond the ship's splintered railings.

I stumbled to the mainmast, another towering wave crashing upon the ship. I clung to the wood, the churning grey water dragging crewmen overboard and into the depths of the ocean. The cabin boy still had hold of my arm, trying to wrench me free. I turned towards him, a second and third wave hitting the ship in quick succession and, unable to keep my balance on the sea-slick deck, I slid from his grip, tossed through the water flooding the deck, towards an open maw where splintered beams rose like jutting teeth. Reaching blindly for something to save me, I hooked my right arm around a rope from one of the broken masts. Pulled abruptly to a stop, I hung against the slanting deck, the *Loch Ard* tilting dangerously, as half of it was already consumed by the ocean.

Spluttering, I steadied myself and used the rope to pull myself back to the relative stability of the surviving deck. Hands chaffed by the harsh rope, I leaned against the mast and looked around wildly, but the deck was completely deserted. The Irish woman and the cabin boy were gone. I was alone on a sinking ship, staring at the broken spine of the *Loch Ard* as it ground into the rocks below. Waves shifted the bodies of sailors and passengers wedged in the shattered remains of the railing banisters. My numb hands clutched weakly at the saturated wood.

Thunder shook through the sky, and an enormous wave started to descend on the ruined ship. Across the heaving water and the ruins of the *Loch Ard*, I saw the Devil clothed in darkness. He did not move towards me, he just watched, and waited, as patient as the grave. He had come at last to claim his boon.

THE LOCH ARD GORGE, 1878

The huge wave slammed into the mast, tossing me into the frigid water. Briefly, I struggled towards the wrecked ship, but my dress was already saturated, its weight quickly dragging me beneath the water. So focused on the Devil waiting for me, I had forgotten about the storm. Gasping for air and slapped by waves, my long dark hair plastered to my face, I blindly kicked against the current.

Repeatedly dragged beneath the water, I pushed weakly to the surface once more, seawater burning my lungs. *The Devil can wait until I'm good and ready.* Spinning in the water, I tried to guess which direction the shore was.

The ocean pushed me further from the ship and a jagged edge of rock tore along my shoulder blades, slicing through the fabric of my dress and cutting into my skin. Gasping in pain, the current dragged me towards a cliff that materialised from the mist, looming above me. Fighting the swell, I shrugged from my ruined dress, kicking free from sodden petticoats. Wearing only my small clothes, my skin abraded by the *Loch Ard*'s deck and the rocks, I found myself adrift in a freezing ocean. The swell pulled me closer to those unforgiving cliffs, and with all my strength spent on trying to stay afloat, I didn't see the mouth of the narrow gorge.

Borne onwards by the waves, the mist cleared, but only starlight broke the darkness of the night. Floating on my back, I measured my life in how long my strength would last against the cold before it would fail. *Not long now, and the Devil will have what he wants.* The brush of sand against my fingertips was a shock. I sank beneath the water before pushing to the surface again. Struggling against the tide, I looked about at the small sandy cove where the ocean had disgorged me. Exhausted, I crawled onto the beach and vomited up mouthfuls of seawater. Breathing in weak gasps, I hauled myself a little further from the reach of the hungry waves.

Motionless, I lay on the sand, staring out to sea, where the shipwreck remained obscured by a wall of sea mist offshore. I could still hear faint cries of those clinging to the wreckage of the *Loch Ard*. But as I strained to hear, there were other cries echoing through the night—the ghostly calls of drowned men. I could not let unconsciousness engulf me here. If the law found me, I knew a warrant would have been issued for me as a murderess back in England. I staggered weakly to my feet and looked along the shoreline. Where the dark water met the whitest sand, a figure waited, impossibly still and cloaked in shadow. Fear beat a staccato rhythm through my chest. *I am not yours yet.* I made the sign of the cross to ward off the Devil and turned away from him. Forcing my fatigued limbs to bear me, I walked away from the cursed wreck of the *Loch Ard,* and towards whatever freedom this unknown country might offer.

THE LOCH ARD GORGE, 1898

Decades have passed since that night the Devil tried to take me from the *Loch Ard* shipwreck. Since then, I have had the freedom I escaped London to obtain, but it is a shallow thing. The curse upon me is like a chain tethering me to Loch Ard Gorge. I cannot escape the ghosts of that wreck who haunt me. Sleepless, I wander the roads but never escape this stretch of coast, and the dark form of the Devil, follows my path. I'm compelled to return each day to my small cottage overlooking the ocean, unable to drink away the cries of the restless souls I failed to rescue. Those now forever trapped beneath the waves.

Tonight, my gaze passes over the Indian Ocean to the bright beam of Cape Otway lighthouse, a crooked smile twisting my lips. That very lighthouse should have saved all souls aboard the *Loch Ard*, but the torch within had gone out in a preternatural gale. Decades lost to guilt and drink will never tell me the truth of it, but I knew enough of curses to understand the Devil had seized an opportunity that night to take the soul I owed him. Turning, the shadowy figure stood patiently beside me on the headland. My time has finally run out.

The wind-ravaged sandstone crumbles beneath my feet, and I don't hear the shriek of the gulls or the roaring wind anymore. There is only the siren song of the waves below. *Devil take me. I imagine he'll be pleased at last.*

My fragile body is buffeted by the gale. My arms are open wide to the frigid air. The dark shape of the Devil waits behind me. Ahead, are the waters of the Loch Ard Gorge. I've been caught between the Devil and Loch Ard Gorge for decades. But no more.

I lean out into the wind, the soil under my feet suddenly gives way and I'm pitching forward into open air. I fall down and down…

down…

…into the dark water and final peace.

ABOUT THE AUTHOR

LEANBH PEARSON (Any) lives on Ngunnawal Country in Canberra, Australia. An award-winning LGBTQI and disability author of horror and dark fantasy, her writing is inspired by folklore, fairytales, myth, history and climate. She's judged the Australian Shadows Awards, Aurealis Awards, is an invited panelist and member of the ASA, AHWA, AFTS, BSFA, HWA and SFWA. Leanbh has been awarded AHWA and HWA mentorships, Ditmar Awards nominee and winner of HWA Diversity Grant and AHWA Robert N Stephenson Flash Fiction Story Competition. Leanbh's alter-ego is an academic in archaeology, evolution and prehistory | https://linktr.ee/leanbhpearson

HELP WANTED

Patricia Childs

Mr. Lucy, the newest resident of Briarwood Assisted Living and Nursing Care, had no visitors.

He never came out for Community Suppers or Town Halls.

No one delivered food to his room. He didn't seem to eat at all.

He received no flowers or balloons.

His accumulated mail was delivered on the 15th of each month in a large wicker basket, set carefully to the left of his door. Atop the pile of envelopes always sat a small wooden box with a Brazilian return address and the shape of a goat's head burned into the side, or so said Mrs. Wen-Lin, the first floor's resident curtain-twitcher and gossip artist.

Mr. Lucy hung no decorations on the door. In fact, the door was devoid of dents, nicks, tape residue, or any imperfection. The frame always gleamed as if freshly painted which it couldn't have been because nothing in Briarwood was freshly anythinged. To the right of the door was a small plaque with "#042 MR. S. LUCY" in black curlicue script. His was the only plaque made of brass; everyone else's was a plastic that had yellowed with age.

Even worse, Mr. Lucy was a perpetual no-show at "Monday Bridge–Come Join Your Friends," "Tuesday Movie Night with Kernel-Free Popcorn (Safe for Dentures)," "Wednesday Chair Volleyball: Teamwork, Laughter, and Low-Impact Exercise!" or any of the activities which Briarwood regularly offered. Every Monday morning the aides dutifully delivered *The Gazette*, the information sheet listing all the latest news, happenings, and menu offerings in the complex, to the residents via a smiley face magnet stuck to their doors, and every Tuesday morning the aides found the paper folded into neat quarters on the Reception Desk with the words "No, thank you" written in black ink across the top. The magnet was always squarely in the waste basket, oddly melted around its cheery edges.

When the Briarwood Trolley departed on Friday evening for Shabbat Eve services and again on Sunday mornings to deposit worshippers at the nearby churches, Mr. Lucy's door gave the impression of being even more tightly shut. He apparently watched no television and made no noise whatsoever, although the residents in rooms Ira Blatt in room #041 and Terry DiFranco in room #043 reported hearing occasional violin music faintly through the walls late at night. They were quick to point out that the music never lasted past midnight and was oddly soothing.

The intrepid few who dared to knock upon Mr. Lucy's door to invite him out for a chat or a friendly game of Canasta received no response. Invitations pushed under his door immediately shot back into the hallway, sliding across the tiled floor with such force that they whisked halfway up the opposite wall before sliding back down in defeat. Eventually, even the most garrulous residents gave up trying to get Mr. Lucy to socialize, resigning him to Grumpy Old Loner status.

Mrs. Wen-Lin, perhaps frustrated by his invisibility, circulated a story that Mr. Lucy had lost his wife in some catastrophic way and was still in shock. His ungrateful children sold his house out from under him and deposited him at Briarwood. He had millions, or so she said, that his children and grandchildren had managed to steal from him, and now he was barely able to afford even Briarwood's subsidized rates.

"That's a horrible thing," her closest friend and Bridge companion Miriam Rosenthal said as the two women sat working on a puzzle in a far corner of the Entertainment Center one blustery October afternoon. "I don't understand why children do that to their parents. No wonder he doesn't want to talk to anyone."

Mrs. Wen-Lin smiled, neatly ignoring that she began the rumor to stir up conversation, and snapped a puzzle piece into place. The wind knocked the bare branches of a sugar maple against the window, and cold air snaked in around the frame with little icy jabs. She zipped her red polar fleece up to her neck and jiggled her legs under the table to warm them. "I tried to get him to come out a few times, but he never answered my knock," she told Miriam, feigning indignity. "He doesn't eat, doesn't make noise, doesn't come out of his room. Why be here if you won't BE here?"

Across the table, Miriam shook her head. "Well, maybe he had nowhere else to go—" here she cocked an eyebrow at Mrs. Wen-Lin, knowing her friend's penchant for gossip "--if what you say is true." She picked up her tea, now stone cold, and swirled it in her cup, glowering. "Damn. It's like an icebox in here. I've already stuck this in the microwave twice this morning!"

"I know the code to unlock the thermostat. I can bump it up," Mrs. Wen-Lin grinned.

Miriam dabbed at her nose with a tissue. "How the hell—"

"I heard the workmen ask for it last week when they were here to fix things." Her eyes sparkled with mischief. "You want more heat?"

"You know I do. My bones ache all the time. I'm too cold to eat."

Mrs. Wen-Lin pushed herself away from the table and got to her feet. Still shockingly spry at 91, she scuttled across the Entertainment Center, paused at the door, her gray head turning both right and left, then disappeared around the corner. Miriam blew in her hands and rubbed them briskly together, doubting her friend's ability to change anything about their situation.

Suddenly the register by her ankles hissed to life shooting air so hot through its rusted vents that Miriam yelped and jerked her legs to one side. She peered under the table, grasping its edge for support, and saw that the vent was glowing faintly orange like an ember.

Miriam sat up and looked around, her eyebrows pushed right into her hairline. Had to be her astigmatism acting up or something. Spontaneous retinopathy. Sudden macular degeneration.

She bent over to inspect the vent again. Still orange.

"That's a bit of overkill," she murmured, vowing to have a word with Mrs. Wen-Lin about moderation. Didn't she know that the aides would figure out who was messing around with the heat and would make things worse than ever? Didn't the woman have any common sense??

She reached for her tea mug, wrapping her swollen fingers around it, then gasped in pain and shock.

The mug glowed faintly orange as well. Inside, the tea boiled bubbled like a lava flow.

"What the hell…!?"

Mrs. Wen-Lin appeared in the doorway and made her way into the room, her face dark as a storm cloud. "I couldn't do it," she sighed. "They were all doing pill counts. I tried to sneak around, but–" She looked at Miriam's bewildered face. "What happened?"

Miriam nudged the now luminous mug across the table with a puzzle piece, its contents still furiously boiling. "The heat…" she said, struggling for words, "where did the heat come from? The vent, too. How did you–"

"Not me," Mrs. Wen-Lin said, shaking her head. "Didn't get anywhere near the controls. But–" she looked around "--it's warmer now. Isn't it?"

"It is, but–"

"Then who cares? Come on, let's finish the puzzle. The heat feels very good."

"Mei, do you not see the mug?!"

"Well, don't drink out of it. You'll burn your lips off. Next time don't put it in the microwave for so long." She joined a large section of puzzle to a corner. "Oh, look…it's a rowan tree! My grandfather grew these in China, back in Chengdu. Haven't seen one for years." Looking up. "What is it? What's wrong?"

"I–" Miriam put her hand over her mouth and stared out of the window. "Nothing. I just…" Shaking her head. "Nothing."

Mr. Lucy's self-imposed isolation continued for two more weeks. He would have been regarded as unworthy of attention except for one niggling thing which constantly drew everyone's attention and created a certain low-level hostility back to his existence: Morning Wellness Check/Pill Check.

Each day, either when the sun was just peeping over the horizon or hours after breakfast–it varied from day to day due to the business and willingness of the aides–Wellness Check/Pill Time always began in the same unceremonious way: a series of sharp raps on the heavy metal door of each resident's room, a loud calling out of the resident's name (*"Mrs. Hyer? Time for your medicine, pressure, and sugar check! How were your bowel movements? Did you pee in the cup so we can check your urine for proteins?"*) followed by the aide's bum shoving the door open as they backed into the room with the blood pressure cuff, pill cups, and bottled water on a tray. This rear-ended entrance was done in case the occupant was dressing or possibly nude to foster the illusion that residents still had privacy. After a few questions about sleeping and mental status, the paper cups of pills followed thereupon, accompanied by the squat bottle of Sam's Choice water, uncapped in their presence and poured into a paper cup with all the grace and delicacy of a third-rate sommelier.

And sometimes the aide failed to shut the door at all, offering what Ed Martin in Room #056 comically dubbed "the world's worst peep show."

But Mr. Lucy received his pills at exactly 8.35am and 4.30pm every day. The medications were presented to him not on a bandage-colored plastic tray but on a large gold charger covered by a black cloth, the pills in small shot glasses. The aides always knocked three times on the door (softly, it was noted) to announce their presence. No ass-backing into

#042. The door opened and closed swiftly behind, and exactly 10 minutes later, the aides backed out again, heads ducked and apologetic, and that was the end of it. Twice daily, no variation, no exceptions.

It stirred subterranean feelings of deepest dissent amongst the residents. Many quietly plotted mutiny.

Mrs. Wen-Lin, who feigned a senility she didn't have for the purpose of observing unimpeded everything that happened on the floor, was a consummate source of information at Monday Bridge–Come Join Your Friends! gatherings. Three months into Mr. Lucy's tenancy, she passed on some interesting observations to the Quad, the nickname her Monday Bridge group gave themselves.

"One time the clock read 8.36am, and Mr. Lucy *refused* to open the door," she relayed in hushed tones, as if the invisible Mr. Lucy might be lurking nearby–slithering around their ankles, perhaps–and eavesdropping. "They knocked and they begged… nothing. And that's not all," she went on, her crabbed hands shuffling the cards, then haphazardly scattering them across the table as she dealt. "He gets a Jack and Coke at Pill Time. Every day–even in the mornings!--with a little lemon slice on the edge."

Miriam, who sat in the South position, stared at Mrs. Lin-Wen. "Jack and Coke, in the morning? Jesus. That would turn my stomach inside out. Why's he so special?"

"He ain't," croaked Liam Bates, sitting West and puffing on his ever-present Vape pen. He rolled his wheelchair closer to the table and leaned in to scrape his cards together. "No one is. It don't make sense."

Miss Wanda, sitting in the East, arranged her hand into the card holder and pursed her lips. "There's something different about that one," she said, tapping her cards into neat row. "You seen them runnin', to make sure they there on time for his pills? There's somethin' about him. Mr. Bates, I bid two spade."

The others bid, the game began, and there was no more talk of Mr. Lucy at the Bridge table that night.

8

Two more weeks passed without incident, aside from the growing resentment of Mr. Lucy's special treatment, and it was revealed that the "Tuesday Movie Night with Kernel-Free Popcorn (Safe for Dentures)" offering was "The Seventh Seal," chosen by Mr. Lucy. This bit of intel came not surprisingly from Mrs. Wen-Lin, sitting next to Miriam in the flickering darkness of the lounge. "I overheard two aides in the break room," she whispered in Miriam's ear. "They said he didn't ask. He just *told*. With a note on the desk. Weird!"

Miriam's eyes narrowed. "Now he gets to decide what we watch?" she hissed, crossing her arms over her chest. "What's next? Menu approval? We haven't even seen the man, and here he is, calling all the shots. Who the hell does he think he is??"

Shrugging, Mrs. Wen-Lin tipped her carton of popcorn in Miriam's direction. "Here, take some. You're too thin." Miriam shook her head. "Aren't you eating anything?"

"Not much," Miriam sighed. "Dr Forbes has me on this new acid reflux medicine that kills my appetite, so I guess it works. No food going down, no acid coming back up. Fantastic!"

Mrs. Wen-Lin turned and stared at her friend for several moments, taking in the pronounced cheekbones and drawn mouth. "I never see you at breakfast," she said.

"The morning is the worst. My stomach feels like it's full of sand."

"Have you told Dr Forbes?"

"Mei, how many times? He doesn't care. I'm 89 years old. He comes around twice a week, pretends to listen, then leaves more pills. That's the end of his responsibility to any of us. A house plant gets more attention than we do." She looked at Mrs. Wen-Lin. "What?"

"I don't know. Something's not right any more. Something is…weird."

Miriam chuckled. "I've told you: this whole place is weird. It isn't home, it's a lab. Feed us, water us, write everything down we do. Might as well install a pellet feeder."

"Can't you see it?" Mrs. Wen-Lin whispered, her eyes darting around the room. "Things are happening that shouldn't be."

"Like what?"

"Vy DiMercaris dying in her bed last week, out of nowhere."

"Vy DiMercaris was 8,000 years old and smoked two packs every day of her life. It was hardly out of nowhere."

"I know," replied Mrs. Wen-Lin, "but did *you* know that they found her with a lit cigarette in her mouth?" She poked Miriam in the arm. "That's not supposed to happen!"

"So she snuck it in and had one puff too many," Miriam shrugged. "Liam's daughter brings him weed whenever she visits. That's why they always go for a walk in the garden when she comes. We should worry when people in a rest home die?"

Mrs. Wen-Lin stared at Miriam. "No, but–"

"SSSSHHH!"

Both women turned around and saw Liam rolling his wheelchair into place behind them, locking the brakes. "It's a movie, girls. Go talk somewhere else."

Miriam rolled her eyes, and Mrs. Wen-Lin huffed quietly in her chair. She glared at Liam over her shoulder; he offered her a sweet smile in response, then raised his hand, bony middle finger extended.

"Horse's ass," Mrs. Wen-Lin muttered. She nibbled another piece of the stale popcorn, then offered it again to Miriam. "Come on. Just a few pieces? Then I'll leave you alone, I promise."

Miriam made a show of taking a handful of popcorn from the carton. "There. See? I'm eating." She put a piece in her mouth and chewed. "Better?"

Mrs. Wen-Lin frowned and turned back to the screen, watching as Death took the knight's White Queen.

Next to her, Miriam secretly dropped the handful of popcorn to the floor and scooted the kernels under the chair with her foot.

"I didn't see that coming," said the knight on the screen.

8

The following week, nothing went wrong.

No computers froze up mid-function, so IT had very little to do. The Wi-Fi never went down, and it was available in every corner and on every floor without interruption.

The aging elevators swished up and down the five levels of Briarwood Assisted Living and Nursing Care without their usual groans, high-pitched squeaks, or their trademark door slams that could be heard all the way in the basement. They even seemed freshly painted, although no one could remember seeing painters or work orders crossing any desks.

344

All aides reported for their shifts on time and in good spirits.

Even the food improved greatly. Gone was the mushy meatloaf with its odd newspapery taste and the green beans boiled beyond molecular cohesion. In their places were fresh salmon with dill sauce, asparagus poached in olive oil and sea salt, new potatoes, roast beef so velvety and juicy that it feathered in the mouth, and the most perfect Southern fried chicken and hush puppies known to man.

"I've died and gone to Heaven" Liam quipped one evening upon entering the dining area and beholding vast aluminum pans of steaming lasagna, toasted garlic bread, and a salad so green and fresh it nearly glowed, all presented on cloth-covered tables. The aroma of sweet tomatoes, oregano, and freshly warmed bread scented the room so deeply it was almost edible. He rolled over in his wheelchair, balanced a tray on his lap, and reached for a plate. "I don't know what's changed, but I haven't eaten this well in years."

Wanda, his Bridge partner and closest friend, nodded. "Not bad," she added, pushing her thick glasses back up her nose and watching Liam serve himself a large slab of the lasagna. "Not at all. Mr. Bates, you watch yourself with that. You liable to wind up having stomach issues…all that dairy surely gonna get you."

"The hell it will." Liam glided to a table and put his tray down his loaded tray. "There's even tiramisu for dessert, did you see?"

"And some good coffee, I think." Wanda sniffed the air. "Yessir, I smell that. No Folgers tonight, no sir. That's a proper pot."

An aide walked by at that point, her own tray full of the same food, smiling in anticipation of a good meal. Wanda raised her hand to catch her attention, and reluctantly, the aide turned around. "Miss Wanda, you need something?"

"I was just wondering, Ms. Daniels."

"Yes?" Impatient now because the food was cooling down.

"Well, ma'am…just curious as to why the change in menu. Not that I'm complaining…"

Ms. Daniels shrugged. "Not my department. I don't know. But I'm not going to say a word about it…just want to enjoy it while it lasts." She smiled politely to Liam and Wanda, then hustled into the Staff Lounge with her tray.

As more and more residents entered the Dining Area, no doubt enticed by the rich smells, the atmosphere became almost festive and cheerful. From someone's room, two bottles of cheap Merlot appeared on the serving table. Alcohol was absolutely verboten at Briarwood; residents had been removed from the facility for lesser crimes. But when one of the younger aides produced a corkscrew, setting it on the table with a cheery wink, then disappeared behind the Staff Lounge door, the mood grew considerably more festive.

The Quad sat together, eating and exchanging jokes and stories. And toasting their fortunate state.

"To friendship," said Mrs. Wen-Lin, a smile stretching to her ears.

"To good food at last," nodded Wanda, her face aglow.

"To food that's better than sex," added Liam.

"*L'Chaim,*" Miriam said. "And to all of you. I'm glad you're here."

The small plastic tumblers clanked together.

It was a good night.

୪

The following Tuesday, the Quad members woke to find something very puzzling.

Each resident opened their eyes at exactly 7.30am and found a black envelope propped up on the bedside table with their name written on the front in a fancy curlicue script, gold ink glinting in the early morning light.

Each pair of hands fumbled with the envelope but found the flap easily opened, and inside was a single piece of onion skin, folded in halves. The paper was so old that the edges feathered away under their fingertips, and the beautifully formed script within whiffed strongly of India ink and ashes.

"You are cordially invited to my room tonight at 9pm.

(signed)

Mr. Lucy.

PS: Don't be late. I despise tardiness."

୪

Wellness Check/Pill Time could not happen fast enough. Fortunately the aides were on the top of their game, and by 8.30am, The Quad hurried from their rooms with a strangely renewed energy and sat at the dining table furthest from the aids so they might converse in secrecy. The urgent whispers flew over the plates of fluffy scrambled eggs, toast, and potatoes, bouncing off ears and foreheads, and circled back again.

"Did you get one?"

"Did you?"

"Who else?"

"What does it mean?"

"Are you going?"

"Are you?"

"What's he got planned? What's going on?"

"Are you gonna go?"

The questions overlapped each other for many minutes with no answers given. Miss Wanda hoped that Mr. Lucy might secretly have some really good Scotch he'd be willing to share. Mrs. Wen-Lin fizzed with ideas about what Mr. Lucy's room contained. Even Miriam perked up with this new excitement.

Liam puffed excitedly on his Vape pen, encircling the table in a centralized fog which made Miss Wanda cough and rapidly wave her hand in front of her face. "Lordy, Mr. Bates, you'll surely kill us all."

Liam just grinned.

8

At exactly 9pm, The Quad presented themselves to room #042 and stared at the door in silence.

No one moved. No one spoke. And no one knew why they couldn't move or speak.

Slowly, as if buffering great winds, Miriam raised her fist and drew it back in preparation to knock, but before her knuckles hit the metal, the door swung inward, and there stood the mysterious Mr. Lucy, smiling broadly.

"Good evening, my friends," he said, sweeping his arm behind him. "I'm so delighted to see you. Won't you come in?"

They did. *En masse,* the Quad moved into the remarkably ordinary-looking room and saw three even more remarkably ordinary-looking wooden chairs lined up in front of a squashy leather recliner.

Mr. Lucy had an excellent view, probably the best the floor had to offer. A beautiful Japanese maple grew just beyond the pane, its leaves a crimson riot. A neat row of exquisite Bonsai trees were lined up on the ledge beneath the window, clearly the objects of much adoration and pride.

The walls were a relaxing pale blue and hung with pictures of various religious scenes: Adam and Eve at the Tree of Knowledge, Jesus' temptation in the desert, Anubis in profile, and a large Yin and Yang, all tastefully framed and hung in an appealing way. Each wooden chair had a simple brown box placed upon it except the right chair which had two boxes.

As for Mr. Lucy, there was something vaguely familiar about him, but no one could quite put a finger on it. He gave the impression of being both welcoming and threatening, even when all he did was close the door behind them, move to his chair on stiff joints, and sit down, gesturing for them to do the same. With his red polo shirt, zippered sweat jacket, tan pants, and large black orthopedic shoes, he looked wholly unremarkable and rather disappointingly plain. His face, lightly spotted and lined with age, showed nothing more than congeniality and a long history of smiles. It was rather disappointing. After so much secrecy and speculation, there should have been more.

"Erm…where should we sit?" Miriam asked, looking at the chairs.

"Oh, I think you'll find where you're meant to be," chuckled Mr. Lucy, settling himself into the recliner.

Mrs. Wen-Lin shrugged and chose a chair for no other reason than it was the nearest. Miriam sat next to her, then Wanda, and Liam rolled to a stop at the end of the row.

"How rude of me." Mr. Lucy beckoned to an urn emitting a wisp of smoke on a side table. "Would anyone like coffee? I have an excellent supplier who sends the beans straight from Brazil."

They all shook their heads. Coffee at 9pm? Ridiculous. They'd be up all night!

"No? Well, then." Mr. Lucy looked at his audience, then curled his lips into a smile that did not quite reach his eyes. "I know I've been something of a mystery to you, and it was never my intention to be so secretive. I simply like my solitude and needed time to adjust to this last phase of my life."

"Are you dying, Mr. Lucy?" Wanda asked. "Are you ill?"

His smile grew wider but not any friendlier. "Something like that, Miss Wanda. I am retiring."

Liam cleared his throat. "Retiring. Now? How old are you?"

Mr. Lucy chortled deep in his chest. "Oh…I lost count of that ages ago when I realized that time never mattered much to me, Mr. Bates," he said. "No, it's more than that. I'm ending a career, a very long one. Three thousand years or so."

The four exchanged looks. In a place where the days bled together into one gray mass of medication, bad food, pain, and exhaustion, Mr. Lucy's presence was by far the strangest thing to happen at Briarwood Assisted Living and Nursing Care in a very long time.

It was Mrs. Wen-Lin who braved the silence. "A three-thousand-year career, Mr. Lucy, is that what you said?"

A nod. Still the polite smile, revealing nothing.

"That's crazy, really crazy. What did you do, make the pact with the Devil?"

At this, Mr. Lucy threw back his head and laughed so loudly the coffee urn next to him shook. The laughter fed itself, rising to the ceiling and becoming so large that it filled the room and pressed The Quad against the backs of their chairs. It flattened all the air down to the floor, making their ears pop (Wanda was certain she'd passed out for a few seconds), then the oxygen crept back into their lungs again, leaving them gasping and reeling. It was not unlike getting the bends.

"Oh, my friends," Mr. Lucy gasped, still giggling with hilarity. "No! Gracious me, no. I haven't made a pact with the Devil. I *am* the Devil."

Liam dropped his vaping pen.

Miriam jumped out of her chair.

Miss Wanda yelled, "Lawd Jesus!"

Mrs. Wen-Lin snorted with hysterical laughter.

Mr. Lucy held up his hands. "Relax. It's not what you think."

"Not what we think?" Miss Wanda shrieked. "I've been going to church my whole life, Mr. Lucy or whatever you call yourself, and I knew you were trouble!"

"Miss Wanda, I implore you–"

"I rebuke you, in the name of Jesus Christ our Savior!" Wanda raged on. "I rebuke you!"

"You can't rebuke me. I haven't *done* anything," Mr. Lucy pointed out reasonably. "And as you're so steeped in dogma…remember that you entered my door willingly, not under coercion." He waved his hand, and Wanda froze, her mouth open in a silent scream, her finger in the air. "I'm far too powerful for the rebuke of one tiny human with more self-righteousness than faith. You should know that too."

"Holy shit," said Liam. "Is she dead? Did you just kill her?" He prodded Wanda's face with his finger, then flicked her earlobe. "Wanda? You still with us?"

"Relax. I never kill people. I just make them want to kill each other. Or themselves." Mr. Lucy sipped his coffee. "You know, humanity has fallen into a very nasty habit of blaming all ills on me. I'm simply an advisor who enjoys chaos. I can't *make* you do anything. My malevolence is vast, but most of your own misery is a result of having an immortal soul stuffed into a corporeal body. It's why you're always so violent and unhappy."

Mrs. Wen-Lin tilted up her chin in a show of defiance. "I'm a Buddhist," she said. "Even if you really are who you say, I don't believe in you."

"That won't make me disappear," Mr. Lucy pointed out.

"But…aren't you nothing without faith?" Miriam asked.

Mr. Lucy chuckled. "Ms. Miriam, shame on you for not know the Bible better! You're thinking of Paul the Apostle. What an argumentative bastard he was. Still is, actually. All Romans just love to argue. No, I've always been here."

"If what you say is true, there are millions of theologians, priests, and philosophers who say otherwise," Miriam said. "Not to argue, but I don't think you're so innocent. And we're not so oblivious or easily manipulated."

Mr. Lucy barked out a laugh. "Of course you are!" he exclaimed, setting his coffee cup down next to him. "You can't even understand your most basic feelings, and you're happiest when you're in denial about something you really want. That's what makes you so easily manipulated. And yet, the Almighty still sees *you* as the greatest creation ever. It's been hilarious to watch you destroy yourselves, particularly when each of you holds the keys to your own happiness."

Mrs. Wen-Lin jumped in then. "So nothing evil in the world…wars, famine, hatred…that's nothing to do with you, is that what you're saying?" she demanded.

"I thought you didn't believe in me, dear."

"I don't. I just want to know."

"Ah. Well, then…know this." Mr. Lucy leaned forward, folding his hands between his knees. "All knowledge comes at a price. Be very certain of what it is you wish to know."

"Are you really the father of lies?" Miriam asked, sitting down and putting the package back on her lap, more curious now than alarmed. It wasn't every day you met someone who was thousands of years old, after all.

"At one point, when the world was new…yes, I fathered some very big lies." Mr. Lucy inclined his head. "The Garden of Eden. Man's dominion over the Earth. Moral purity. But really, since the Crusades you humans haven't needed much help from me in that arena. My staff takes care of nearly everything." He crossed his legs, relaxing into his squashy chair. "It's embarrassing, really, how much free time I have now." He flicked a finger at Miss Wanda, and she unfroze, blinking in confusion. Liam leaned over and patted her hand, relieved.

Miriam pressed on. "Were you cast down from Heaven?"

Mr. Lucy sighed and rubbed his forehead. "I'll answer some of your questions, but really, that's not why I've asked you here. And I don't really owe you anything. But since you did ask…"

"I did indeed." Miriam crossed her legs, looking defiant.

A corner of Mr. Lucy's mouth quirked up. "I knew I'd chosen the right ones," he murmured. "I've been watching you all, you know. I think you'll do just fine."

Liam said, "What do you mean by–" but Mr. Lucy kept talking as though he hadn't heard.

"Here's what really happened, and it's a lot less exciting than everyone makes it out to be. It was more of a labor dispute and a difference in morality that led to a parting of the ways, and to be honest, it had been a long time coming. I was absolutely bored in Heaven and wanted a change."

The Quad stared at him, then at each other, their mouth agape.

"So now the Almighty rules one side of existence, I rule the other. It was far more amicable than your poets and theologians assume."

A shocked silence filled the room as thousands of years of theology unraveled and blipped into non-existence.

Mrs. Wen-Lin cleared her throat. "The demons?" she asked.

"Free agents. Hired mercs."

"And the Angels?"

"The same. Everyone makes a choice, Mei. Even you Buddhists."

No one spoke.

Eyebrows raised, Mr. Lucy chided, "What, you don't believe me?"

"I don't." Ms. Wanda staunchly. "I, Mr. Lucy, believe nothing that issues from your mouth." She stood, slamming her box on the chair. "And neither will I accept anything you give me. These fools may not care about the state of their souls, but I do. And I've had more than enough of this." She straightened her spine, favored everyone with a scathing look, and walked toward the door.

"Oh, Wanda..!" Mr. Lucy's laugh sparkled like moonlight. "That's why your soul is so valuable to me and my servants. Because you protect it so fiercely, as you should. In the end the little piece of the eternal, the fabric of the Universe from which you were cut, is the only thing that truly matters about any of us."

Wanda sneered and put her hand on the door latch. "Is anyone coming with me?" she demanded, looking around the room.

No one moved or made a noise.

Mr. Lucy simply sat and watched, his fingers steepled beneath his chin. Waiting.

The silence froze everything, including Wanda. She stood at the door, then as if she were deflating, put her head down, resting her forehead against the fire exit diagram on the back of the door. A sigh larger than a human escaped her lips, and her defiant shoulders fell.

Mr. Lucy looked at Liam and winked. Liam found himself winking back.

"Just tell me one thing," Wanda said, her voice low in her throat. "If you really are who you say you are. Before I walk outta here and maybe miss a chance at something." She turned and faced Mr. Lucy. "Just in case."

"Anything you like."

"And be truthful, if you can."

"I can be truthful, if it serves me. I have not uttered one lie since you entered my room. But for you…" Mr. Lucy smiled his mixed smile and tapped his fingers together. "Anything you wish, my dear."

Fixing her dark eyes directly on Mr. Lucy's (for she had always been taught to face her fears directly and not back down), Miss Wanda put her entire being into her question:

"What do you fear most?"

Liam, Mrs. Wen-Lin, and Miriam all stared at Mr. Lucy, whose eyebrows pulled down like a window shade snapping shut, sending thunderclouds across his face.

Miss Wanda folded her arms. "No answer, huh? What's the matter, you scared? Biggest, baddest of them all actually afraid of something? Fancy that. Mm."

Mr. Lucy's eyes narrowed to dangerous pink slits, his mouth a thin line.

"Hmph. So it's true. The Devil cannot endure being mocked." She shook her head, sneering. "Lawd Jesus, I woulda never thought."

"Wanda…" Liam hissed. "Seriously, I wouldn't–"

"What? What shouldn't I do?" Wanda advanced on Mr. Lucy. "Seems to me that Mr. Lucy here is hiding something. Ain't that right, Mr. Lucy?"

Still no answer from their host. His hands with their arthritic swollen knuckles balled into fists.

Wanda went on, her voice rising. "There are millions who would welcome you willingly, but you come here using some fake-ass name. You don't even have to take corporeal form. But here you are at some budget rest home, hiding out in this room. Think about it," she said, turning to her friends. "Put those pieces together. This is Lucifer Satan, the worst of everything, the great deceiver, and yet…look at him. Go on, look!"

They looked. There was nothing before them but a very tense, very aged man sitting in a leather armchair, one who was most likely closer to his end than any of them.

Wanda waved her hand. "This is what we've been told to be afraid of? The prowling beast? The ruler of Hell?" She took another step toward Mr. Lucy. "This guy?"

Liam tried again. "Wanda…c'mon, now. Think of what you're dealing with. People who tangle with the Devil rarely come out the better for it!"

"You ain't answered me yet, Lucifer. Sitting there in your silence." Wanda was standing beside their host now, glaring down at him. Mr. Lucy merely stared straight ahead, anger seeping from his skin in curling vapors. "What are you hiding from? *What are you afraid of, old man!?*"

Mr. Lucy stood abruptly, his face bright red with a horrible anger that leached into the room like a poisonous gas. He shot out his right hand, the palm cupped and facing upward. A tiny blue flame danced there.

Miss Wanda looked down, pursing her lips, then back at his face. "Is that…are you—"

"I told you…there's always a price, you foolish woman." Mr. Lucy's voice was now the sound of buzzing flies, of terror and collapse. "You want your answer? *No knowledge is free!* You know what I am and what I require as payment."

"I—"

"How many more days do you think you have? I'm getting the worst of the bargain, taking all of you so near the end. *But there must be a trade.*"

"Well…"

Liam gnawed on the tip of his Vape pen. "This has suddenly gotten very existential," he observed.

"There is always a price, Wanda. Christ knew that. That's why He won't come back, not until the very end when everything is up for grabs. The balance must remain. Are we agreed?"

Wanda looked at the fire, at the man holding it, at her friends. Slowly, by degrees, she nodded. "I've been ready for months. But will it…hurt?"

Mollified, Mr. Lucy shook his head, and his voice returned to a gentler timbre, the anger gone. "No. It doesn't have to. Mercy is a tool to be used by all.

"Put your hand in mine. Go on, now."

She lifted her hand toward his. Without preamble, Mr. Lucy grabbed it, yanked her entire body to him. Long thorny vines erupted from his fingertips, wrapping around Wanda's arm, and tightened as the exchange took place. Wanda cried out as the thorns dug into her skin, and blood poured from the wounds. Mr. Lucy leaned in, whispered in her ear, then shoved her away, the flames gone. Slowly, the vines withdrew and disappeared, the wounds sealed over, the blood vanished.

Wanda's eyes sparkled, and a smile of pure joy spread across her face. "Ohhhh…" she breathed, and was it the Quad's imagination or was she aging backwards in front of them? The silvered hair turned coal black, the wrinkles smoothed themselves back into her dark skin; slowly, she straightened up, and her rounded middle nipped into a narrow waist that she hadn't seen for over 40 years.

"Oh, my…" the young, beautiful creature in front of Quad said in a girlish voice. "I feel…so wonderful!" She turned to Mr. Lucy. "Thank you. It's over. Thank you."

The smile returned. "Of course."

Wanda resumed her seat once more, light as air. Liam stared at his friend, poked her with a finger, leaned in. "What in hell did he tell you?" he whispered.

"Later. I promise."

Mr. Lucy resumed his seat with a slight groan befitting a man of great age and swollen joints. He gestured to the boxes. "Please. Open them now. Time is short, and things are about to change."

Everyone fumbled with their boxes, noticing that their arthritic hands easily unfastened the strings and tape surrounding the cardboard. In fact, if they had been alone and not in polite company, each might have ripped the boxes to shreds, so zealous were they.

Liam paused in his efforts, vape pen clamped between his teeth. "Wait…things are about to change? What's that mean?"

"Well." Mr. Lucy was pensive, rubbing his bottom lip with a finger, and for the first time since their meeting, he looked uneasy. "Speaking plainly, each of you are very close to the end. Wanda was first. Liam…you'll be next. Then Mrs. Wen-Lin, and then Miriam. It's why I called you here, to tell you and offer you an exchange."

"Wait…" Miriam pointed at Mr. Lucy, tiling her head. "Are you telling me we're all about to…erm…"

"Die? Yes. It's why you came here, isn't it?"

Miriam gasped and put a hand over her mouth. "I'm not…I mean, I'm still…"

"Alive? Of course. But not for much longer."

Mrs. Wen-Lin chewed at a hangnail. "Weird. I thought there'd be more at the end," she said. "This is really just…"

"Boring? Oh, Mei…" Their host laughed again, this time a friendlier sound. "It's never what you think it will be. But I'm here to help. All you have to do is listen to what I'm offering and make your choice." Here Mr. Lucy took a sip from his ornate cup and sighed in satisfaction.

"Listen. The problem is that for the past 500 years or so, humans have made me redundant. There's nothing I can do that you cannot do to yourselves more efficiently and, quite honestly, with more astonishing cruelty. The darkness within your hearts is admirable." His eerie grin returned. "I simply cannot keep up with you anymore. I don't know whether to be proud or humbled. Either way, it's been great fun watching. And now…open your gifts. It's time."

Miss Wanda handed one of her boxes to Liam, not understanding why it seemed to be his, only that it did. She prised the lid off the box in her lap pulled out a small bow with a broken string, a quiver of dry-rotted arrows, and a tarnished crown.

Miriam withdrew a very damaged set of scales. The flakes of rusted dribbled down the chain connecting them and onto her skirt, smelling strongly of metal.

Liam clutched a surprisingly large sword, bent and nicked as though it had been in a battle, wobbling in its hilt.

Mrs. Wen-Lin pulled out a long, very dirty cape full of holes with an enormous hood.

"Oh, I beg your pardon. Time and use damage so many things," said Mr. Lucy. He waved his hand, and with a great heat enveloping them, the scales sparkled as though fresh from the refiner's fire, the sword straightened itself into deathly, shining perfection, and the cape was so white it was nearly blinding. Miss Wanda's crown glistened with jewels, and her bow was freshly strung, the feathers on her arrows vibrant.

"This is beautiful." Liam admired the blade, holding the sword straight in front of him. "The craftsmanship is excellent." He looked at Mr. Lucy. "I wish I could really test it out."

"Of course you can. Just stand up."

As if it was the most obvious thing to do.

Liam's mouth opened to protest, then his face relaxed, and slowly, creakily, he rose to his feet for the first time in almost 10 years. After wobbling like a newborn calf, he straightened his spine, drew his hands together around the hilt of the sword.

His friends gasped. Wanda's cheeks were dripping with tears.

Mr. Lucy opened his arms wide. "Now," he purred, "test it out. I think you'll find it most satisfactory."

Like a switch flipped on, Liam executed a series of lightning-fast wrist-rolls, drew the gleaming sword back in a high parry, swung it over his head twice, then relaxed and smiled. "God, that was fun!" he exclaimed. "I haven't been able to do that since my college days!"

Mr. Lucy softly clapped his gnarled hands together. "Well done," he exclaimed. "You're a natural with that thing, best I've ever seen."

Miriam held her scales aloft, watching them gleam. "Balance," she murmured. "Yes. Always balance. Hunger, plenty. Want and have, hate and love…oh, these are perfection." She tore her eyes away from her gift and looked at Mr. Lucy in admiration. "Where did you get them?"

"These treasures have had many owners over the years. The last ones retired…oh, a hundred years or more ago. They passed these on to me for a small fee."

Wanda put the crown on her head and smiled, twanging her bow. She pulled an arrow out of the handsome leather quiver and notched it. "Oh, yes…" she purred. "Ohhh, sweet Jesus, yes…"

Mrs. Wen-Lin twirled her cape around her shoulders and cooed happily. "I never want to take this off."

"Lovely, just lovely. Now, my friends…you have a choice, as you always do." Mr. Lucy stood and held out his hands, palms once again cupping the bright blue flames. Was he growing taller right in front of them? Had his head always brushed the overhead lamp? "My time in this world is ending. And tonight I wish for only your companionship." A series of high-pitched whinnies split the night air; Mr. Lucy looked over his shoulder out the window, smiling, and all the light and darkness in the world was held within that strange smile.

"Your horses are here, and they are more than ready to run. In a few short hours, I will cease to be. Ride with me into the midnight and bid me farewell. Then you are free to go where you will until the Almighty calls you. But remember, no matter what: you are always free."

The Quad looked at each other. Mr. Lucy was right—things were indeed about to change.

They glanced at their gifts, then at Mr. Lucy who now loomed so largely over them that his arms spanned the room. He inhaled their final breaths and exhaled a galaxy's worth of stars into their mouths, gleaming like fresh birth. The flames in his hands rose ever higher, the sparks flying upwards, and it was impossible to look away.

"Will you come?"

8

The next morning, the aide's knocks went unanswered for several minutes. She eventually summoned up her courage and pushed Mr. Lucy's door open for the morning Wellness Check/Pill Time check and found the room empty aside from four brown boxes piled neatly on the floor, three wooden chairs, and one well-used vape pen on its side.

A handwritten note held in place with the gold charger read:

"Thanks for a lovely time. You did just fine. Blessings, and keep up the good work."

ABOUT THE AUTHOR

PATRICIA CHILDS has been published in *Hearing Health Magazine*, "State Recycling Laws Update" and "Recycling Laws International," and earned an Honorable Mention in the Writer's Digest 91st Annual Fiction Contest. She also earned a Certificate of Distinction in the 5th Annual Student Research Conference at Tiffin University, and is a proposal reviewer for the National Council of Teachers of English. She is an Associate Professor of English at Georgia Military College and an adjunct Professor of English for East Georgia State College in Augusta, Georgia.

MEET THE SATANS

Sarina Dorie

"I'm not dating Satan," I said, trying not to roll my eyes. "He's Satan's son."

My mom sat beside me on the couch. She looked like she was going to faint. Her face was almost as pale as her hair. My dad paced a path in the once white carpet, speaking in tongues—or maybe it was Swedish—I was never sure. They looked like angels with their watery blue eyes and blond manes. But believe me, no one who knew my family would ever mistake them for being heavenly.

"How could you do this to us, Mary-Anne?" my mother wailed.

I wasn't sure if that was a rhetorical question, or if I was supposed to answer. I smoothed out the folds of my long, cotton skirt. I hoped it was flame-retardant.

"And I found this in your room," my mother reached behind her seat.

I froze, afraid she'd found my shoebox full of matches. It was just the Sears catalog. But it was turned to the page with the fireplaces. I rolled my eyes.

"First it's that *Cosmo Magazine* and smoking cigarettes, now this. What's next?"

I took a deep breath. "I only smoked cigarettes for a few months when I was sixteen." And now I was eighteen and an adult. I could do what I wanted. Except for dating the man I loved, apparently.

My dad's face was pretty red by this point, almost as red as my boyfriend's. He pushed his thick glasses higher up on his nose. His lips flattened into a thin line.

My mom droned on. "What if he gets you pregnant? It'll be just like that Rosemary movie."

"Mom, I'm not going to get pregnant. We use condoms."

She shrieked and covered her face.

The doorbell rang. I jumped to my feet. "I bet that's Lucian."

I opened the door, and there he was: the cutest, most adorable high school graduate in the world, red as a maraschino cherry, little stubs of horns protruding from his head. He wore his usual slacks and a nice button up shirt and blue tie.

I kissed him on the cheek. He blushed, his face turning maroon.

"I can't wait to meet your…" His voice trailed off, his gaze darting past me. "Oh my goodness!"

My mom clutched the ten inch cross she'd torn down from the living room wall. Dad held his shotgun. I covered my face in humiliation.

"Get thee to Hell, you red-faced demon. Out! Out!" my dad said.

"Dad!" I protested.

"Red-faced?" Lucian looked to me with mournful eyes. "Maybe I should come back another time."

He backed away. I turned to my parents with tears in my eyes. "How could you do this to me? Now my boyfriend is going to think you're racist!"

ध

When my parents said I was grounded for life—or until I went away for college—I hoped they weren't serious. I prayed it was just a phase they were going through.

As if that wasn't bad enough, they took my cell phone and refused to let me talk to Lucian on the ground line. My mom also stole my *Cosmo* and Sears catalog as if I were ten, called a priest to sprinkle me with holy water, and wouldn't let me play with my younger brother and sister alone as they thought I was possessed and dangerous.

The first time I tried to sneak out of the house didn't work so well—my dad guarded the back door, and my mom was stationed at the front. Climbing out of the second story window of my room didn't go as planned. The rope I made by tying sheets fell apart. When I landed in the juniper bushes and screamed, it sort of alerted my parents to what had happened.

The next day I decided to sneak out using the air vents. It looked wide enough for my shoulders to squeeze through, but I jammed myself in the grate so tightly that I had to wait until Mom squirted me with dish soap to slide me out. Dad would probably have left me up there, but it was dinner time, and Mom insisted we eat together as a family.

After about a week of confinement, my mom told me I could help my younger brother and sister in the garden. Towheaded Matthew was ten, and old enough to use a hoe to weed. Sara-Jo ate more strawberries than she picked.

I considered how I might escape, but when I peeked over the white picket fence, I saw my parents had planned ahead. Our neighbor, an angel in flowing, buttery robes, sat in a lawn chair on the sidewalk. A crooked halo was perched over his long, golden hair.

Gabe, annoying angel extraordinaire, set aside the tabloid he was reading. "I've got a message for Mary, but a Mary-Anne will do." He winked at me.

I turned back to gardening. I picked up a spade, joining my brother. Gabe eyed me over the fence. "You know, you wouldn't be in trouble if you had better taste in men. Your parents happen to like angels."

"Yeah, well, I don't." I'd dated Gabe in my junior year. What an epic disaster. If my parents had any idea what a perv he was, I doubt they would have asked him, of all people, to keep an eye on me.

I wove through the aisle of peas and crossed over into the cucumbers to be farther from him.

He floated along the other side of the fence toward me. "What's he got that I don't have?"

"Genitalia for one. Class for another. Oh, let's see, what else? He's faithful."

My brother and sister stared at me in shock. I'd just said the "g" word. I was probably going to have my mouth washed out later.

Gabe scowled. "Are those qualities listed in order of importance? Cuz I can get at least one of those."

I shook my head and trudged deeper into the tower of weeds surrounding the tomato plants where he couldn't see me.

"I can be a bad boy, too," he called after me. "I'm considering getting a motorcycle and a tattoo. And a job as a used kidney salesman."

Wow. That was just evil.

"You're missing the point," I said. "Lucian isn't a bad boy. I'm in love with him because he's a genuinely nice guy. Unlike you." And that's why I had to see him again. I needed to break free of my prison.

♉

The next escape method of choice relied on a candle. I had to wait days until I found a window of opportunity to borrow one from the emergency supply tub. Considering my parents had installed three fire alarms in my room to prevent me from playing with fire, I didn't know how long I would have. I was lucky they hadn't found the shoe box full of matches, lighters, and photographs of campfires.

I laid a flower-printed sheet across the bedroom floor, used a washable marker to draw a pentagram, and sat in the center of the star as I gazed into the candle flame and chanted Lucian's name.

A vision of him appeared in the flickering light.

"I need to get out of this place. The parental units are driving me crazy," I whispered.

He nodded, his voice coming out crackling and crisp, the connection worse than an out-of-range cell phone. "Gosh, I had no idea it was so bad. I'll be right over."

Minutes later, a flaming chariot drew up alongside my bedroom window. Lumpy squares of fabric covered the passenger seat. Ah, potholders. I smiled. Wasn't he thoughtful?

♉

I had never been to Hell before. The ride took ten minutes. Apparently, Hell wasn't far from the suburbs. I saw no fire and brimstone, but I knew I was in Hell as soon as we arrived because of the fluorescent lights. The entryway caverns were sparkling and shiny, with a giant welcome sign made of bones above the gate.

Despite the morbid appearance, I relaxed more than I had in days. With Lucian at my side, I felt safe and accepted for once. From the way he gazed at me with that shy, adoring smile, I knew he wouldn't cheat on me with a van full of cheerleaders. One might ask how much trouble Gabe could get into—he was an angel without genitals. When I had drawn back the door to the van, I had discovered the answer was quite a bit.

It was Lucian's shoulder I'd cried on the night I'd broken up with Gabe. Lucian hadn't taken advantage of my emotional state like some other boys would have. That constancy of his friendship before and after Gabe sparked the realization he would make a better boyfriend, despite my initial misgivings about the cultural differences between a human and devil.

Lucian parked between two pearly stalagmites. He cleared his throat as if he had something to say, but then shook his head and kissed my cheek. I wondered if he thought I was wicked for running away.

Just inside the door of his parents' spacious cavern, grandmotherly knickknacks decorated the pitted recesses in the walls. Lucian and I followed a clear plastic runner covering the plush, pale carpet. Between the trendy, white furniture and the excessively clean interior, it looked like a type-A version of my parents' house—which I supposed could be Hell for some people.

Sporting an immense set of horns, Satan sat at a throne in a living room as pristine as a furniture catalog. He wore a lime green zoot suit made from the skin of some exotic reptile. How... trite. I'd expected something a little more modern. Oh, well.

I guessed I disappointed Satan, too. He turned off the immense television on the wall and looked from Lucian to me. "Ahem. She's... blonde?"

"Good grief, Dad. Don't start."

"Well, I just thought if you were going to go for a human, you'd at least go for the dark-haired, Lilith type."

Lucian squeezed my shoulder and gazed lovingly into my eyes. "I'm not into bad girls."

My face flushed with warmth. Sometimes I thought I must be bad with the way my parents treated me like a juvenile delinquent. Everything I did was a sin to them, whether it was toasting marshmallows or listening to non-Christian country music.

When I was with Lucian, I forgot I was the black sheep of my family. I knew he accepted me, quirky habits and all. I could relax. At least, that's how I'd felt before meeting his family.

"Not into the Liliths or Delilahs of the world? No biggie." Satan pulled out a leather-bound text from an expensive-looking attaché case. "Any chance you want to sign my black book?"

I glanced at Lucian. He glared at his father.

Satan chuckled. "Just kidding. I leave my work at work. And you're practically family now. It's bad form to do business with family."

Lucian's face turned maroon, and he shook his head at his father. I had little time to ponder what Satan meant by that comment. Another briefcase came flying through the air, hit Satan on the back of the head with a loud thunk, and then fell to the floor. It popped open, screams of tortured souls erupting into the room.

"Don't do business at home?!" a thundering voice said. "Then what are those contracts doing in your briefcase?"

The house shuddered as a towering, thick-wasted, troll-like figure approached. Something about her face reminded me of a rhino. Perhaps it was the wrinkled gray leather of her skin. Or the placement of the horns. She wore a frilly, pink apron with hearts on it over an immense sundress.

Satan stooped to close his briefcase and hugged it to his chest. He flashed a sheepish grin, his sharp teeth ominous in the fluorescent light.

Lucian's mom turned to me and smiled. "Oh, you must be Mary-Anne. My name is Gladys. Luke talks so much about you. It's a pleasure to meet you at last."

She extended an arm as thick as a tree trunk. I tentatively held out my hand, surprised when she gently took it in hers. The joy in her liquid black eyes was so kind I was certain she wouldn't someday be one of those mothers-in-law from Hell... even if she was *from* Hell.

"Would you like to stay for dinner?" she asked.

I looked to Lucian. It crossed my mind that she might be inviting me to be the main course. But Lucian didn't look like he wanted to strangle her, so I thought it might be safe to accept.

"We're having Italian tonight," she tempted.

"Um, Italian food? Not Italian people, right?" I asked.

She laughed, the merry sound not at all matching her troll-like appearance. "My husband has given you a bad impression of us, hasn't he?" She gave him the evil eye before smiling again at me. From the way Satan stood really still and shrank down, it looked like he was trying to make himself invisible. Or maybe just not attract her attention.

"We'll be having lasagna, garlic bread, tiramisu, and wine. Of course, you two are underage and Lucian is going to be driving the chariot. Otherwise, I wouldn't mind letting you children have half a glass, but I think it's better if you stick to the sparkling cider."

Wow, no wonder Hell was so polished and clean. She was Satan's Stepford wife.

"Is it safe for humans to eat food in the underworld?" I asked. I had heard of the stories. Persephone. Rip van Winkle.

"Perfectly safe. Only fairies—and Greeks—seduce people with food. Maybe Italians, too. But don't worry, we aren't any of those."

Satan inched toward the door. Gladys smacked him on the backside of his head before chastising him again for bringing work home. She then excused herself to finish making dinner. I felt bad for Satan by this point. Lucian toed the plastic runner covering the white carpet.

"So, how long have you been in the soul market?" I asked.

Satan's shoulders visibly relaxed. "Oh, you know, a millennium or so. I used to be a lawyer back before there was a name for it."

I glanced at the attaché case. "So, I guess you're pretty good at contracts."

"Yeah, I learned my lesson about contracts without clauses the hard way. How do you think I got stuck with her?" He jerked a thumb toward the kitchen and winked at me.

"I heard that!" Gladys said so loud it rattled the television against the wall.

I sat with Lucian at his desk. At his mother's insistence the bedroom door remained open. Some mom rules were universal. Lucian flipped through another college brochure.

"Gosh, it doesn't surprise me you got accepted to three different colleges with that brain of yours." He tapped me on my noggin playfully with a finger. "I haven't even gotten rejection letters. No one responds. Everyone sees the family name, and they're afraid I'm going to set the school on fire or something. I don't think they bother to look at my grades."

I shook my head, running my fingers along the edge of the lighter in my pocket. "If anyone is likely to set a school on fire, it would be me, not you."

He crossed his arms, giving me his sternest look, which admittedly wasn't very formidable. "Stop putting yourself down. What your family calls an obsession with fire, my family calls a healthy relationship. Just because you like flames doesn't mean you're a pyro."

He kissed me, his lips warm and reassuring. My heart swelled. Seconds later, he pulled back, his expression chagrined. Orange fire rose from his head, dancing up over his hair and painting the room with a warm glow. Sometimes that happened when we kissed. Hence the reason he kept a fire extinguisher nearby. One thing that couldn't be denied was my boyfriend was smokin' hot.

I laced an arm around his, bumping him with my shoulder. I carefully avoided the flaming hair. "I don't mind going to a community college the first year. We could do that. Save money. Stay in the area." Though, that would mean putting up with my family.

"I thought we could go somewhere in between," he said. "Las Vegas? It would be warmer than Minnesota. And less... conservative."

I flipped through the community college brochure, avoiding his gaze. "I guess if we moved, my parents wouldn't have to know about us. I could tell them we broke up."

Vehemently, he shook his head. "No! I love you. I can't pretend we aren't together."

I shrugged. "You're right that people are more liberal out there. They wouldn't object to a devil and a human dating, so we would just be lying to my parents."

He took my hands in his. "Mary-Anne, there's something I have to tell you. The thing is, I had some suspicions. So I did research. The thing is, gosh, well..." Despite the worry crinkling up the corners of his eyes and the way he bit his lip, I felt no fear. Not with the warmth of his hands around mine, reassuring me all would be okay. "I don't think you are human."

I couldn't help laughing. "I'm not descended from angels. We both know that."

"Not an angel exactly." He wrapped an arm around my waist, pulling me close enough to feel the heat radiating from his body. "Do you remember when we went to the beach with the speech team a couple months ago, and I woke up in the middle of the night and accidentally set your sleeping bag on fire? I didn't burn you. And last week when we were making out and you doused me with a pail of cold water... Don't you think I would have burned you before your bra caught on fire? I mean, you were only half dressed, and you were hugging me up until that point."

What he said made sense. I'd been more concerned about dousing the polyester sports bra at the time. "So you think I'm some kind of demon?" I could see how my family could fit that. Only fairly recently had people started to take pride in their nonhuman heritage rather than hide it. It was possible some great grandparent somewhere along the lines had been a devil, and no one had known.

"No. I think you're a seraphim, the brightest and highest form of angel. It would explain your attraction to fire. You're attraction to me. It might be why I feel like I'm going to spontaneously combust in your presence," Lucian said. He laced his fingers through mine. "I've been thinking about this, wondering what would happen if we didn't try to put out my flames next time."

My heart quickened. "Third degree burns would happen." I swallowed and gazed into the dark depths of his eyes. My fear subsided as I took in his earnestness. He truly believed I was a seraphim. Could he be right? There was one way to find one.

I scooted onto his lap, wrapping my arms around his neck. He kissed the back of my hand. The touch of his mouth against my skin made my insides tingle. I tilted his chin up to meet my lips and kissed him with all the love and passion in my soul. My heart felt as though it would burst from sheer joy. That was the kind of kissing it took to get him fired up.

After a moment, something started to smell like charred angora. When I glanced down at my smoldering sweater, it was obvious where the smell came from. Lucian's fire-retardant shirt remained intact. Instead of feeling pain like one would expect, my skin felt more comfortable than it ever had. As he kissed a line down my neck, my flesh changed color, shimmering and glowing white. It didn't resemble flames so much as moonlight. I stared in awe. Is this what I was?

"Do you think this is why you were drawn to me?" His voice was even, but sadness tugged at the corners of his eyes. "It's not so much about me, as your need to be fed fire and light?"

I shook my head, thinking of the time he had run out to get my teddy bear from the car in the rain, the way he always pulled out my chair for me at a restaurant, how he'd asked permission to kiss me that first time. "I love you for you. This just makes us even more right for each other."

He squeezed my hand in his. His skin felt hotter and more real than it had ever felt before. The white glow of my skin intermixed with the golden glow of his flames. My skin throbbed pleasantly with the new sensation of my own fire and his.

He attempted a smile. "Your family is going to blame me for this. They might not let you marry me now."

"Wait. What?" I asked. I knew he loved me, but we hadn't ever talked about marriage before. We'd just graduated high school, for crying out loud.

His eyes were wide with shock. "Oh, poopy. I just messed that up, didn't I?" Lucian slid the drawer of his desk open. Though the desk must have been sprayed with fire retardant, the college brochures obviously weren't from the way they blackened and curled as his arm passed over them. He removed the little black box from the drawer which immediately caught fire and started smoking. His Adam's apple bobbed in his throat. "Ahem. This has been in the family for a long time. I would like you to have it."

I held my breath, momentarily wondering if he might present me with something weird like a piece of brimstone. Instead, I found myself staring at the most beautiful diamond ring I'd ever seen. Exhilaration jolted through me. I giggled, tears filling my eyes.

Lucian cleared his throat. "I know we've only dated for eleven months, and your parents just met me. But I can't imagine falling in love with any other woman. I want to spend the rest of my life with you. I know your family didn't like me…"

"We'll get through this. Together." I threw my arms around his neck and kissed him again.

Our flames rose higher.

8

Lucian and I sat on the wooden chairs from the kitchen I'd dragged into the living room. My parents sat rigid as corpses across from Satan and Gladys on the once white couch and loveseat. The cinnamon gummy bear cookies Lucian's mother had made rested untouched on the coffee table.

I intended to wait until after Lucian and I were happily married with children before I told them about my seraphim genetics coming through. If they could come to terms with the fact that we were getting married, that is.

"You're too young," Mom said.

"Duh. That's why I told you—" I started.

Gladys held up a wrinkled, gray hand. "Please. Mary-Anne, if you want your mama to treat you like an adult, you're going to have to lose the teenage attitude."

I rolled my eyes. Now they were both ganging up on me.

My mother pointed at me. "And you can save the eye rolling until we're done."

Gladys chuckled. "Kids these days! I swear my parents would have tarred my hide if I had talked back to them."

My mother nodded. A conspiratorial smile spread across her lips, quickly fading as my father gave her the stink eye.

I cleared my throat. "I know we're young. This is why we're going to wait until we've been in college for at least a year before setting a date."

"You're too young to be engaged," Mom said, tears filling her eyes.

By this point, the veins were bulging under Dad's fair skin. He blurted out, "My daughter is not going to marry a red-faced demon."

I kicked him under the coffee table. "Stop calling him that. He's sitting right here, and you're hurting his feelings."

Satan raised an eyebrow. Dad muttered another rude comment under his breath.

I threw up my hands in disgust. "Would you call a Native American a red skin? Or a Chinese person a yellow skin? It's just racist." I wished I didn't have to spell it out for them.

Dad pushed his thick glasses higher up his nose. "Wait a minute, are you saying this young man is one of those 'ethnic' people?"

I covered my face with my hands, embarrassed he sounded like such a redneck.

Satan cleared his throat, speaking up for the first time. "It happens I am very ethnic. My kind are indigenous people, you know."

Dad crossed his arms. "Like natives?" I was relieved he didn't ask indigenous to what, as I was certain the answer would have been Hell.

Satan exchanged an amused glance with Gladys. "The politically correct term is First Nations people."

She glared at him and shook her head.

I held my breath as my dad eyed Satan's long black horns. "So if you're Ind—a First Nations persons, why've you got horns? How do you account for that?"

Satan grin widened, showing off his dagger-like teeth. "You have watched *Dances with Wolves,* haven't you?"

"Um, yeah."

"Tatonka. Buffalo," Satan said in a stilted Native American accent. "Proud of our heritage. Horns very ethnic-chic."

I stared in mortification at the parents. I didn't know which was more embarrassing, that my future father-in-law preyed on my father's racist background, or that my father's ignorance meant Satan could completely pull the wool over his eyes.

Dad leaned forward with interest. "You get a tax break for that? Being indigenous, I mean?"

Satan smiled.

This was not how I had envisioned this conversation going, but it could have been worse. My dad actually was placated for the moment.

Certainly this conversation hadn't solved all our problems, but it was a start. I could wait to break the news that we, too, were part "indigenous" peoples.

ABOUT THE AUTHOR

Sarina Dorie has sold over 200 short stories to markets like *Analog*, *Daily Science Fiction*, *Fantasy Magazine*, and *F & SF.* She has over a hundred books up on Amazon, including her bestselling series, *Womby's School for Wayward Witches.* She is the first place winner of: Golden Rose RWA Award, Golden Claddagh RWA Award, Allasso Humor Award, and Penn Cove Literary Award. Sarina teaches workshops and classes on writing craft, writing business, cover design and art, and belly dance.

A few of her favorite things include: gluten-free brownies (not necessarily glutton-free), Star Trek, steampunk, fairies, Severus Snape, and Mr. Darcy. She lives with twenty-three hypoallergenic fur babies, by which she means tribbles. By the time you finish reading this bio, there will be twenty-seven.

You can find info about her short stories and novels on her website:

www.sarinadorie.com

WIDOWMAKER LOVE SONG

Troy Riser

1: AND THEN THE SUMERIAN FERTILITY GODDESS NEXT TO HIM SAID...

"So this is your idea of a stakeout."

Startled by the sudden sound of her voice after hours of quiet in the car, Spike Cohen turned to look. Alma Boch sat upright and alert in the passenger seat, her pretty face in profile, her auburn hair styled in a flipped bob popular with American women since it was Jackie Kennedy's style, all the rage nowadays, but he guessed Alma had adopted the most popular current style to better pass for human.

"Not a thrill ride, I know," Spike replied, returning his gaze to front, "but we know Benny and Giselle are in there. One or both are bound to come out eventually."

Spike was about to add Be *patient* but Alma had *been* patient, stoic even. The two had been sitting in the car in the rainy chill and dark for almost six hours and this was the first time she had spoken.

She's been a sport, Spike thought, and he was grateful. He had been on stakeouts with bad partners before, guys (always men until now) who either wouldn't shut up or couldn't sit still or both, but Alma had been quiet and contained. He guessed it was part of her nature, who she was.

They were near downtown Manhattan, parked in a 1959 Ford Galaxie Skyliner in the parking lot across the street from the Ambassador Hotel. He didn't bring his Packard Caribbean because it was too flashy, expensive, and sleek. To work, stakeouts needed nondescript, ordinary, and forgettable.

It was long after midnight on a weeknight so street traffic was comparatively light for this part of the city, their view of the entrance largely unobstructed. The doorman in front looked bored and restless, lighting another cigarette, his third in the last hour. Spike felt a flash of envy even though he had quit tobacco years before. It was an old, bad habit and he missed it.

"Lions were a problem in the north," Alma said. "It was mostly wilderness up there in those days and shepherds at the border sometimes called for help since a single one of those big cats could decimate a flock in minutes, all of them in a night. Lion hunters would go out, stake out a lamb in the low ground, find a place high in the rocks and wait, sometimes for days."

Spike shook his head. "Benny Kingman's no innocent little lamb."

"You've got it backwards," Alma said. "We're not the brave and stalwart lion hunters. We're the stupid, hungry lions and this is very likely a trap."

Spike thought it over and grunted assent. Television network star and King of Comedy Benny Kingman and his impossibly gorgeous secretary

Giselle were both keeping their heads down after the disaster in the Catskills, but the two had been easy for Spike's assistant Betty to find—*too easy* Betty had said—so Alma was likely right thinking this was a trap. Though still recovering from wounds received during his showdown with Wendell Choate and his demonic henchmen at The Paradise, Spike felt confident he could handle Kingman if that squawking, preening, plump little bird of a man tried anything funny.

If he tried anything funny. Spike smiled a little at that. Benny Kingman had sold his soul to the actual Devil but had failed to hold up his end—had in fact fled to his private airstrip and flown away with his beautiful secretary Giselle when the plan to trap and kill Spike had failed. Without the man who Alma had told him was the literal devil himself writing Kingman's material and supernaturally promoting his show, Benny Kingman's satanically inspired comedy shtick no longer worked. The magic was gone. Kingman's variety show, televised live a few days ago, had bombed in its fall season premiere. Turned out former funny man Benny Kingman on his own couldn't make a child giggle at a fart joke.

"You underestimate Giselle," Alma said. "You're forgetting what she is. That's a mistake."

"I haven't forgotten Giselle. She's the main reason I brought you along. I've seen what you can do, kid. I think you can take her, whatever she is."

Alma shook her head. "I don't want to *take* her, Uri. I want to talk to her. She's either fey folk or lesser demon, someone who chose the wrong side when the time came to choose a side. I've been to the Underworld. I still have influence in those circles. She and I are sisters, in a way."

"You want to gently persuade a screeching she-demon from hell into switching sides, is that it?"

"If I can," Alma said.

Spike nodded in the direction of the hotel. "Now's your chance. She's coming out."

Both Spike and Alma watched incredulous as Giselle exited the lobby, heads turning as she passed, a gawking driver in a new, bright red 63 AMC Rambler Classic convertible swerving and nearly colliding with oncoming traffic as he caught a glimpse of the tall, statuesque blonde swept blithely through the doors and came in full view of the street. The uniformed doorman nervously flicked his cigarette away and bolted upright as she passed, sucking in his gut, looking ready to salute. Giselle strode to the curb and beckoned for a taxi.

"Men," Alma said. "Your reaction to her is so exaggerated. It's like watching a cartoon."

"You watch cartoons?"

"I watch everything, Spike. You people are amazing." Her eyes didn't move from Giselle. "Do we follow?" Alma asked. There was urgency in her voice. A cab had found Giselle and pulled to the curb, the cabbie frantically running around to the passenger side to open the door for her. Giselle had that effect.

Spike shook his head. "I'd like to know where she goes but Benny's the prize. He owes me." After a pause, Spike added, "I owe him a little, too."

Alma caught Spike's tone. Benny Kingman had set him up for an ambush at the now-magically disappeared Paradise Resort (its ruin blamed on a fire by the press), and Spike still burned from that betrayal. Alma said, "Nothing too biblical, Uri. We need that little sleazeball alive and talking."

"Nothing too biblical, I promise."

Neither Spike nor Alma were challenged at the front desk in the lobby. They both pretended to belong so they belonged, a couple coming back to their room after a long night on the town. Spike was wearing his new trench coat, which neatly covered his shoulder holster and the bulge of his new Browning Hi-Power semiautomatic, which had replaced the pistol he had lost at The Paradise. Spike also had his tailor sew a leather scabbard on the left breast interior lining of the coat to hold a long, heavy, balanced, and very sharp knife. The counter-measure for demons is beheading or dismemberment or both, and Spike wanted to be ready. Alma needed no weapons. When fully incarnate, transformed into her true self, she *was* a weapon.

By unspoken mutual consent, the two ignored the elevators and took the stairs even though Benny Kingman's love nest hideaway the little man's wife didn't know about was one floor from the top, on the eleventh floor. Knowing their enemy—not Benny Kingman but their real enemy—the elevators could've been rigged to fail, trapping them between floors, or fall, killing them outright. They avoided elevators.

De Lumière, the man they were after, their real enemy, wasn't a man according to Alma, who wasn't herself really a woman but was instead, she had told him, a ancient pagan archetype *somehow made real,* somehow made real because Spike wasn't good at metaphysical abstractions and so didn't delve too deeply into the more arcane aspects of any of this. Spike liked things simple and if not simple then concrete—something he could touch, or hit, or shoot. Spike's experience at The Paradise Resort had taught him if something could hurt him in the physical world, then it was real and since it was real Spike could hurt it back.

Ahead of him on the stairs, Alma signaled a stop at the landing between the tenth and eleventh floors, her head canted slightly to the side, listening. After

Spike caught up, she leaned in close and whispered, "I hear the heartbeat and breathing of a man on the other side of that door."

"Human?" Spike whispered back.

Alma nodded. This complicated things. As Spike had found in his Paradise fight with Kingman's henchmen, a demon disappeared when its corporeal form was too damaged to use, going out in a brief, bright flash of light and heat and a cloud of smoke, ashes, and dust, a near-instant dissolution, but human beings left bodies and bodies begged questions, none of which Spike could answer in a police interrogation without risking hard time at Rikers or a rubber room in Belleview.

The deceased was a lackey of the actual Devil, your Honor. Nothing for it but to shoot him—twice, to make sure. Oh, and yeah: angels and demons are real, too. What about God, you say? God hasn't made an appearance yet but I'm sure He's out there, your Honor, waiting in the wings, ready for His cue, any minute now. Any. Minute.

Alma broke him from his reverie. "Uri, are you with me? I'll take the elevator from here and make my presence known. It will draw their attention to the front door and give you a distraction."

Spike nodded. He had no better plan. His late partner Barry, his secretary Betty's father, had been the meticulous, analytical one of their firm, the one to look at a problem from a dozen different angles and figure out an approach for each. *Plan carefully, execute freely,* Barry would say, quoting Delacroix the painter. Barry had planned and Spike had executed. They had balanced each other out. But Barry was dead, killed with his wife in car accident two years ago, and it was at times like this Spike missed his friend most.

"I'll be loud," Alma whispered, and then headed back down to the tenth floor entrance. After she had left, Spike took out his lockpick set and very quietly made his way up the stairs to the door. If there was a guard at the door, the door would be locked, which wasn't of itself an insurmountable problem. A professional thief from Manchester, England had been drafted from prison by British intelligence to teach its SOE and American OSS operatives the finer points of his lock-picking, safe-cracking trade, and Spike had taken to it almost instinctively. (*Yer a natural, mate,* the thief had told Spike in that nearly indecipherable Manc patois.) Bypassing locks was one of the few skills Spike took from that part of his life he still used. The tricky part would be doing it quietly enough so the guard wouldn't notice.

The guard didn't notice. A moment later a shot rang out, muffled through the thick metal door, and Spike moved, pulling the door open just as the tall, well-dressed guard was moving away from the wall, reacting to the sound of the shot, his back to Spike. Spike closed the distance just as the man sensed his presence and started to turn, still in the process of drawing his pistol. The man looked bigger, stronger, and younger than Spike but Spike moved instinctively, with the practiced shift and glide of a dancer, and was almost instantly behind his opponent, driving his heel into the bend of the younger man's leg and bringing him to his knees, the point of Spike's blade out and just under the ear and at the hinge of the jaw, his free hand cupping the man's chin and turning his face to profile just enough to better expose the throat. Spike applied slight pressure with the point, drawing a trickle of blood.

"Drop it or die," Spike said flatly, matter-of-factly. He could hear the sounds of a tremendous fight coming from behind the door to Kingman's suite: crashing, yelling, the thudding and bashing of bodies bouncing off walls and hitting the floor.

Alma making her presence known, he thought.

A few doors of the other rooms on this floor were starting to crack open. The house detective would be coming soon with police to follow. Time was short.

The young bodyguard let go his gun, an older model Soviet military-issue Tokarev pistol. Spike had used a Tokarev before, picking it up from the ground in the middle of a gunfight in Guatemala. He liked the depth of penetration bullets fired from it could achieve with its bottle-nosed cartridge. They punched nicely through car doors and windshields.

What are you doing here? Spike asked in Russian, more to the gun than to the man he held at knifepoint.

"I got no idea what you just said, mister," the man said, clearly lying since Spike could detect his Slavic accent, faint but there. The man's voice was surprisingly low, steady, and calm for someone with the tip of a blade at his carotid artery, which spoke to military training.

"Where'd you get this gun?"

"The lady, Giselle. We've all got our own pieces as per contract but she insisted we carry these."

I bet she did, Spike thought. These men she hired were meant to die. She assumed we would kill them all. Russian-speaking guards with Russian-made guns would take investigators off in another direction, pointing to Moscow and away from us.

"Did she say why?"

Spike felt the man give a slight shrug. "She's the client. She didn't say and we didn't ask."

Spike said, "I'm going to let you go. Are you trouble?"

"Apparently not for you. We weren't briefed on you." The racket coming from Kingman's room suddenly, ominously stopped. "Or your friend," he finished.

"Your buddies will be fine," Spike said, meaning the other guards, guessing Alma was good enough with graduated violence not to do any permanent damage. He let go of the guard and then pushed him with the flat of his hand until the man was pressed unresisting against the wall. "Benny at home?"

"In his bedroom. The suite has a separate bedroom. I want you to know before you go in there we had nothing to do with it."

"Nothing to do with what?"

"You'll see. It was her, all her."

2. THE KING OF COMEDY LIES NAKED ON THE BED...

"Dead?" Spike asked Alma, who was standing over the bed, listening intently for a pulse. His hands were cuffed by the wrists to the headboard. Spike didn't see any blood. To a cop new to the scene, it would play out as a sex game gone bad, an older man killing the mood with a heart attack or a stroke.

Alma straightened. "No, not dead," she said. "He's unconscious, possibly comatose. He has a heartbeat, but only barely. Same with breathing. Giselle took him to the edge." Alma nodded her head at the open closet door. "Suitcase full of cash in there. Big denominations."

"Running money," Spike said. He heard the sound of sirens coming from the street below. "We can't be here. We've got to go."

"Not without the money," Alma said. "We need resources, and he owes you, remember?"

Spike didn't argue. He took the bag from the closet and stepped into the living area of Benny Kingman's suite, the floor strewn with wrecked furniture, broken glass, and the unconscious bodies of the security detail Giselle had hired. A few were coming to, and Spike wondered if any of them would be grateful they were still alive given Inanna, the Sumerian goddess Alma manifested, was usually as alternately cruel and indifferent to human life as nature itself. He had seen that side of her. Spike wasn't easily frightened but Alma as Inanna was scary in the way an oncoming tornado is scary.

You're helpless in the face of it, he thought. Nothing you can do.

The two took the elevator down to the third floor to save time, and then took the stairs from there. When they entered the lobby, they saw the lobby was swarming with uniformed police and knew there was no way they could make it to the front door without being challenged and questioned whether they appeared to belong or not. As detailed and meticulous as her late father Barry had been, Betty had supplied them with a hand-drawn floor plan showing alternate points of egress if they had to make a quick escape, and they were using it now to find the nearest service entrance. They finally found it and followed it to the other end of the building and made their way to the exit and then outside to the alley beyond.

"At least one of those policemen is a lesser demon or worse," Alma said as they crossed the street to the parking lot and their waiting car. "I could smell it."

"Or worse?"

"A thrall," she said. "A walking, talking dead man who sold his soul to De Lumière and now beholden to his will. De Lumière uses them like dogs. Once they catch your scent there's no escaping them. It's like being hunted with hounds. They can be very… single-minded."

"So can I," Spike said, irritated with himself, itching for a fight. The raid on Benny's not-so-secret hideout had been a bust, the lucky lead from Betty wasted, Giselle in the wind. The cash in Benny's bag felt like a consolation prize and what they were doing now felt too much like running away. Spike had been on the retreating end before during the war, and he hated the bitter taste of it. It felt like losing. He hated to lose.

They got in the car. Spike sat stiffly upright with his hands tightly gripping the wheel. He made no move to start the engine. His eyes were straight ahead, fixed on the hotel yet not seeing it. He inhaled deeply before speaking.

"Giselle should've been our primary, not Benny," he said aloud, more to himself than to Alma. "She could've led us straight to De Lumière—Benny an obvious dead end—but I wasn't thinking. I was *feeling*, letting my dislike of the man cloud my judgement and snafu the mission. It won't happen again."

"Good to know," Alma said. "Now what?"

Spike said, "Betty's been researching Kingman's property holdings and told me she might have a lead, a nightclub not far from here."

"Benny owns a lot of properties," Alma said. "What's so special about this one?"

"It's a dive called The Inferno Lounge on the Minnesota Strip off Times Square," Spike replied. "And yeah, I know, all a bit too much on the nose. Our guy is playing us again. He leaves these big bright neon signs that take us right where he wants us to go."

Spike remembered a dream he had not long ago, a dream not a dream but a memory of one of his many past lives (or so Alma had told him), and in that dream he had seen a line of murdered corpses arranged in the shape of an arrow in the sand pointing the way, inviting him to follow. Alma had told Spike he was an angel made manifest every generation in human form. Given the men he had killed, the things he had done, Spike didn't believe it, not the angel part.

I'm no angel, he thought.

"Another obvious trap," Alma said. "You do like galumphing into them."

Spike started the car and pulled into traffic, heading towards Times Square. He said, "The club won't be open until later tonight. We'll hole up in a rental room close by—as close as we can get. We need rest." He shot a quizzical glance at Alma.

"Yes, Uri, I do rest," Alma said. "I eat, I sleep, I use the powder room, all of those things. This body follows the laws of this world. It's a very nice body and I mean to keep it well-maintained."

Yes it is, Spike thought, and pushed the thought away. Theirs was shaping into a solid working relationship and he didn't want to screw it up. During the war, Spike had seen damage done by romantic entanglements. Put people together in a closely knit ring or cell behind the lines in wartime and such feelings are natural, but *natural* isn't always right. Love in the field is a distraction. It compromises missions, blurs focus, gets in the way.

Alma said, "This isn't Bucharest 1942, Spike."

"You read minds?"

"No," she said. "I read body language, tone of voice, facial expression. I read people." Alma smiled warmly. "Such infinite variety. All of you tell a story. You are a story." She glanced at Spike. "Some more interesting than others."

They found what they were looking for, a rundown, seedy-looking, room-by-the-hour hotel just off Times Square. If the place had a name, it wasn't posted anywhere, which was fine by Spike. He wasn't looking for a cozy tourist hideaway. He wanted an overwatch position, an unimpeded view of the basement entrance to The Inferno Lounge across the street. The empty lobby—empty because it was early and this was strictly a night people place—was dingy and stark under bright fluorescent lights, and so was the clerk behind the grimy, cluttered desk, a thin, sallow, narrow-shouldered man with thick wire-framed glasses that magnified the size of his already googly, protuberant eyes and made him look vaguely insectile.

Lazy grasshopper, Spike thought, remembering a book illustration he had seen as a child, *Aesop's Fables*. His mother had read it to him.

Spike told the clerk what he wanted, a room third floor or above on the north side of the building, clean sheets, clean towels, running water, a working shower.

"We don't got no room service, pal," the clerk said. The man had a faint European accent Spike couldn't quite place, but guessed Romanian since the man reminded him of a goony Romanian gangster he had known during the war. No matter.

"You'll do room service for us," Alma said. She had brought Kingman's suitcase with her and after a moment of rummaging through its contents, put a hundred-dollar bill flat on the counter. "We need food—and coffee, too. Lots of coffee."

The clerk plucked the bill from the desk top and held it up to the light before pocketing it. "Anything you need," he said. "I'll have one of the maids bring it up later. How long you plan staying with us?"

"Two days tops," Spike said. "Maybe less, maybe more. We'll work it out later."

"You want I should take your bags?"

"We'll take our bags, thanks," Spike replied, holding out his hand for the key. "One more thing," Spike said, taking the key. "I saw the way you were looking at the lady's valise. Any ideas you might have about calling your friends regarding an easy mark? Don't make that call. The lady and I have had a bad night and we are in no mood. Do we understand each other, googlebug? Don't just nod. Tell me you understand."

"I understand," the clerk replied, smart enough to be afraid, his wide round eyes wider still. Spike had shown him a glimpse of his true face, and it was mean and terrible.

After the door closed on the dingy elevator, Alma lowered her voice and said, "Do we understand each other, googlebug?" and burst out laughing. "Was all that really necessary?"

Spike shrugged. "I know his type. It was necessary."

"Googlebug," she said, and laughed again.

3. ON A HORSE WITH NO NAME...

Their room on the third floor was surprisingly clean, the layout ordered: queen-sized bed, nightstand, dresser, vanity with mirror. There was even a telephone on the nightstand. This was, Spike guessed, one of the best rooms in this skeevy, no-name place. He walked to the window and saw a clear line of sight to the Inferno Lounge entrance across the street, which was what he wanted, why they were here. A sudden wave of fatigue washed over him, and Spike winced from a stab of pain as he took off his coat. His left shoulder ached fiercely from the through-and-through bullet wound he had caught at the Paradise. The injuries Spike had sustained in that fight a few weeks before had taken more out of him than he cared to admit, even to himself. He felt raw and unready, unsteady on his feet—and angry, too. Spike couldn't shake the sense of betrayal he felt, his body letting him down when he needed it most. Spike had taken Kingman's bodyguard at the Ambassador, sure, but it had been a close-run thing. Any slower on the move and he'd be dead.

This is what *old* must feel like, he thought.

"You need to lie down, Uri," Alma said, watching him carefully. "I'll take first watch."

Spike took off his shoulder holster, laid it aside, sat on the edge of the bed, and found he didn't have the strength or the will to take off his shoes, so Alma knelt in front of him and did it for him. It was to him an oddly maternal gesture. He felt like a sick schoolboy.

"I've got a pair of collapsable field binoculars in the left breast pocket," he said, lying back. He was too tall for the bed and his feet dangled over the edge but he didn't feel it and didn't care.

"I don't need them," Alma said. "I see fine." She leaned down and placed the flat of her palm against his forehead. "You're burning up."

Spike closed his eyes. "I told you. No hospital," he muttered. "No doctors. No questions." He began to drift off. The room faded from awareness. "I need to find water soon. My horse is dying of thirst."

He halted and dismounted. They had been riding all night and the animals were on the verge of collapse. He would lead them on foot from here. The sun's light was blinding and the heat of the desert bore down on his skull like the beat of a hammer on a blacksmith's forge, his lips cracked and bleeding. He could taste the blood (the taste of blood an awful thing), no water to wash it away. Only he and one other had managed to fight their way through The Preacher's ambush the night before. The rest were gone. Anna was gone. No time to grieve. He would grieve later. Right now, they were being tracked. They were being chased. An army of dead men on dead horses led by a man suspected to be the Devil himself was closing in, seeking to cut them off before Cold Springs Station, just south of Reno, thirty miles northwest.

Uriah Kemp doubted he could out-run them. The rotting, malodorous monsters hunting him didn't get tired or succumb to heat and thirst. A few of those dead men he knew; rather, had known when they had been alive, with blood pumping in their veins and a will of their own. Uriah figured at some point soon he would need to find a good piece of high ground with some rocky cover and make a stand. But that was later. In the meantime he needed to see to Conklin.

Henry Conklin, the Pinkerton man, was gut-shot and dying, soon dead, and Conklin knew it too in his more lucid moments, but he was game, still in the fight even though Uriah knew the pain the man felt must be appalling. As a Union calvary officer during the war, Uriah had seen men with their guts blown out by grape or Minie ball go mad from mortal pain. It took enormous effort of will to rise above that pain and drive on, and Uriah admired Conklin for it. He hoped he faced his end with the same kind of heart when whatever killed him killed him.

Prolly soon, Uriah thought. The prospect of dying didn't bother him much. Let me go down brave, Uriah prayed. Let me honor the memory of my friends. Let me meet that satanic bastard in the field with a smile on my face and take him to hell with me.

We'll go down together. One good shot is all I need, amen.

On foot now, Uriah led both his horse, a recently acquired roan gelding he hadn't yet had time to name, and the mule upon which Conklin sat. Uriah had tied the man to the mule as best he could but knew he would need to stop soon or Conklin would slip off regardless and die on the trail—and maybe it would be a mercy to let him, Uriah thought, but the two men had ridden together these many miles, had fought together, so he would let Conklin choose his own way out.

Least I can do, he thought.

Eight men and one woman had set out almost two months before from St. Louis to confront the shady and dangerous character some called The Preacher, and now only two of their number were left, soon one.

Then none if I don't find water soon, Uriah thought.

"We need to stop, bounty hunter," Conklin said. "I can't go on. You know I can't go on."

"Soon," Uriah said, pausing to look up at the sky. It was late morning, creeping up on the high heat of noon. He and Conklin had been riding all night, the bounty hunter and the Pinkerton man the only ones able to fight through and break out of The Preacher's ambush. Carlyle and Burton were both dead for sure. Uriah had seen them die. Anna was missing. Uriah forced thoughts of Anna from his mind. To stay alive, he needed to be in the moment. He needed to think.

We stay out here no water, we die without a fight, he thought.

Uriah hardened his resolve and kept going, pausing only to check on Conklin and brace him up. A few miles later, at the limit of his endurance, Uriah caught the glint off a sparkle well and found an arroyo within a small, shallow canyon. There was cover from the sun and a trickle of water running through it from a localized cloudburst a day or two before, all cool and quiet down here in the shade. Uriah led the horse and the mule with Conklin on it down the gentle slope of the wash, untied Conklin from the mule, and gently carried him and set him down with the man's back against the canyon wall. Uriah used a pan from the mule's pack as a scoop to widen the trickle to a shallow pool, filling his hat and letting the animals drink while he saw to Conklin. It occurred to Uriah his horse might die from water shock but he found himself too weak and exhausted to walk the animal and cool it down. If his horse went under, he would take the hardier mule and make a final dash for the station. It was clear Conklin wouldn't be using it.

"Thanks for this, bounty hunter," Conklin said.

"No trouble," Uriah said.

"No, I mean coming back for me. I was a goner. I *am* a goner, comes to that. You could've just left me out there but you came back. There's more to you than I thought, more than I'd expect from a man they call Widowmaker."

Uriah smiled at that even though his cracked lips made it hurt to smile. "Henry, I get paid to put bad men in the ground. I can't fault you for holding in slight regard one who would choose such a line, but I don't apologize for it, neither."

"Those men we fought back there," Conklin said. "Those weren't men, were they?"

Uriah shook his head. "That Shoshone medicine man in Oxbow told me they were men once, but then they died and The Preacher raised them up again and now they're something else, bad medicine, no spark or spirit, just meat that can move. It's his will that drives them."

"Walking corpses," Conklin said. "Bad medicine, indeed. Who could imagine the like? I shot one to empty and he just wouldn't drop. 45-70 Government didn't even slow him down."

"Next time aim for the head," Uriah said. "Head shots work."

"Next time," Henry Conklin said, grinning until another spasm seized him, causing him to moan and writhe while Uriah looked on helplessly. When the spasm passed, Conklin fished in his breast pocket and produced a small, single-shot percussion derringer. He gave it to Uriah.

"I would ask a boon, Uriah. My faith forbids taking my own life."

"I got you. You want me to count down, Henry? Any last words?"

Conklin thought it over. "No count necessary, but I do have words—questions, really: You think that medicine man was telling the truth?"

"About that Walker Colt?" Uriah shrugged. "We've seen dead men walk, Henry. I'm inclined to believe him, magical bullets and all."

"All this over a broke-down shaman's dream," Conklin said, the first time Uriah had heard a hint of despair in his voice.

Uriah said, "Not much farther now and we'll have that gun they say can kill the unkillable. Almost there."

Conklin blurted up more blood. His time was short and both men knew it. There was urgency in Conklin's voice. "We've been going at this all wrong, Uriah. We've been acting like assassins, not lawmen."

"You want we try and bring this man to justice? Put him in front of a judge? On what? Suspicion of witchcraft? Raising the dead? Conspiracy to commit...whatever the hell it is he's aiming to commit?"

None of them ever did figure out what The Preacher wanted, why he did what he did. Not even Anna had been sure and she had been the one who knew his dark ways best. And now Anna was gone along with the rest and soon, Uriah thought, it'll be just me against at least a dozen of those dead things, along with the man himself. It bothered Uriah he had never seen The Preacher's face. It would be good to put a name and a face to his enemy, but The Preacher worked from the shadows and came at them sideways, never to the front in the light of day.

"We both know he isn't a man," Conklin said.

"He walks, he talks, and we know from the barkeep in Virginia City that he's picky about his whiskey and how he likes his steak, so close enough," Uriah replied. "He's a man. Men can be killed."

Conklin tiredly shook his head. "This Preacher is a schemer, a plotter, a Machiavel. We saw his handiwork in that little mining town back there, the fruits of his infernal machinations."

Uriah nodded grimly. The memory of the family they found crucified would stay with him. The youngest, a little boy, had been hot-iron branded with an *H* on his forehead, which Anna had told them stood for Heretic.

Conklin went on with an effort. "The solution to the problem this Preacher fellow presents doesn't come from the barrel of a gun, Uriah, but we are violent, stupid men and that's the only way we know to see it, every problem a nail. We need to be better, bounty hunter. We need to be *more*. Anna knew this. She tried to tell us. We didn't listen."

"Anna is dead, Henry."

The dying man shook his head emphatically. "She is not. Anna's alive. I can feel that lady's presence in a way I can't explain. I can hear her—and so could you if you had the faith for it!" The Pinkerton man paused, exhausted, spent, almost done. "Another one coming on, Uriah. I can't bear it, no dignity in it. You know what to do."

Spike awoke to his secretary Betty's worried face hovering inches from his own, stray strands of her long blonde hair lightly feathering against his skin. Up close like this, he noticed for the first time Betty's eyes were hazel, a piercing blue tinged at the edges with a deep sea green, but he had always imagined her eyes blue like her father Barry's. He remembered Svetlana's eyes—her mother's eyes—had been green. Spike prided himself on his attention to detail, and it bothered him he hadn't noticed this about Betty before, the human being closest to him.

I take her too much for granted, he thought. I should know better. I should know *her* better.

"You know what to do?" Betty asked. She caught Spike's puzzled reaction. "That's what you said," Betty went on, deepening her voice in mock imitation: "*I know what to do, Henry, and I'm sorry.* Who's Henry? Sorry for what?"

Sorry for putting him down, Cohen thought, but didn't say aloud.

He raised himself to a sitting position and then swiveled on the bed until his stocking feet were on the floor. He glanced through a gap in the curtains and saw it was night outside. He had slept the day away. Spike also noticed he felt strangely fine—better than fine, physically invigorated, his body enveloped with the sensation of good health and well-being. The soreness and fatigue were gone, washed away as if never there. The fever burning him up had broken. Spike's mind was clear and sharp, bleached clean of doubt and worry. He felt himself again. He felt ready. He stood up and worked his shoulders, tilted his head forcefully both ways to clear the crick from his neck, looking like a boxer warming up before a fight.

"Alma called while you were out," Betty said. "She told me to come and watch over you while she followed a lead."

Giselle, he guessed. Alma must have spotted Giselle going in.

Spike gazed pointedly out the window. "That nightclub down there, yeah? The Inferno? When was this?"

"A little under an hour ago."

Spike slipped on his shoes and shoulder holster, his trench coat, his hat. He found himself wishing for more firepower than a knife and a pistol, but you go with what you've got, he thought.

"I'm coming with you, Uri," Betty said.

Spike shook his head. "There's a valise in that closet with a pistol and some cash—a lot of cash. Bring the Packard around to the front, engine running and ready to move. Things get sporty, anyone or any *thing* gets in your way, shoot it or run it down."

Betty was startled and confused. "Shoot it? Run it down? But won't that..." She trailed off, not understanding. Spike could sympathize. He had felt that way at The Paradise. Thoughts of gods and devils make everyone a little crazy. Their actual presence in the world felt like a violation of the rules in a game no flesh-and-blood human knew how to play.

Spike said, "Everything this man does is done behind a veil. He made an entire resort at the Catskills and all the people in it disappear, remember? No one noticed. No one talks about it, like it never happened. Impossible things are made to seem normal, ordinary, nothing to see here, pal. We can use that to advantage."

Betty was pensively biting her lower lip, something she did when nervous or uncertain. "Real quick, how are you dealing with this insanity, Uri? I need to know so I can deal with it, too. These 'impossible things'…I'm having a hard time with this, okay?"

Cohen took her by the shoulders. "I get it, kid. I understand. I've been through it, myself. But here's the deal: However strange it gets, you roll with it."

"Roll with it," Betty echoed. "Uri, what does that even mean?"

"We'll talk later, I promise," he said.

"I'll meet you out front," she said. "Engine running."

Betty stopped herself mid-stride on her way out the door. "Oh right, one more thing, almost forgot: Your press contact at the Post called. It's about Benny Kingman."

Spike looked at her expectantly. News of Kingman's death would not bother him. He couldn't help but grin at the thought of it.

"Benny's awake. He's asking for you."

Spike looked away to hide his disappointment. Glee over another's death—even an enemy's—is an ugly thing and he was embarrassed Betty had seen it in him. He remembered Conklin's dying words to Uriah Kemp: *We need to be better. We need to be more.*

"Benny can wait," he said flatly. "Alma's our priority right now."

Now at the door, her hand on the knob, Betty gave Cohen a long, searching look. "Do you love her, Uri?"

He gave it thought. "I love the idea of her, what she represents, if that makes any sense. Let's leave it at that."

4. A NIGHT AT THE INFERNO...

Spike descended the stone steps leading to The Inferno Lounge and turned right at the base of the stairwell into the entrance of an unlit stone tunnel. Unlike the rest of the building, which was modern and newly built, all glass, concrete, and steel, the stone block tunnel entrance (like a yawing mouth, Spike thought) looked wind-worn and ancient, covered in moss, the close-walled stone tunnel beyond dark, long, forbidding, and untraveled. In the indeterminate distance, at the end of it, he could make out the blinking of a red neon sign, presumably above the door to the place.

Spike knew construction and the thought absurdly occurred to him none of this was code. A building inspector would take one look and stroke out and die. He chuckled to himself imagining the scene but the sound of his own laughter rang hollow off the walls of the tunnel so he stopped. He was afraid and didn't like that he was afraid.

Fear makes you stupid, he thought.

The African doorman of The Inferno Lounge standing at the entrance was one of the largest human beings Spike had ever personally encountered. Spike had gone against big men before both during and after the war, but none quite at this scale. Six-seven easy, Spike estimated. Four-hundred plus pounds. No neck. Tree-trunk legs. Massive arms crossed like pythons mating. The doorman was aware of Spike's presence and looked, Spike thought, like a massive obsidian statue, indomitable, immovable.

And human, Spike thought. He could tell the difference now. Non-humans superficially looked the part but seemed always somehow off—not just a single glaringly obvious thing giving them away like a poker tell, but an uneasy array of small but significant details, an overall effect the mind instinctively read as wrong. But human or not, this man looked too big to beat if Spike had to go through him rather than around.

The key is the knee, Spike thought, remembering his training. Go for the pillars that hold the weight. He reminded himself big men usually liked to close with an enemy so they could use their greater weight to advantage, so don't let them get close. Be smart. Think on the move. Be quick. Don't give them a fixed target.

Spike didn't draw his weapons as he approached the door, holding out hope he could somehow peacefully talk his way past this monolithic monster of a man and into this place.

"No farther, angel," the doorman said, his voice a low, rumbling baritone.

"I'm no angel," Spike said, raising his hands with palms out to telegraph his peaceful intentions. "I'm just here to meet a friend. No trouble here, big man, I promise you."

"I have the sight," the doorman said. "I see things as they are, which is why I am charged with guarding this door and which is also why you are not allowed passage through it."

"What's your name, pal?" Spike asked, his hope for peaceful resolution rapidly fading.

"Felix," the doorman said, removing his sportscoat and untying his tie, pocketing the tie and folding his coat carefully and laying it down, his eyes never leaving Spike. "My name is Felix. Should you defeat me, take my wallet. In it is a slip of paper with my father's name and address in Kenya. They have no telephone in his village. You will need to write. In your letter, tell him in my name there is to be no *kulipiza kisasi*. He will understand."

Spike didn't know the words but caught the gist. "I'm not killing you, Felix, even if I could."

"Your prerogative, sir," Felix said. "For my part, I will strive to make your end as quick and painless as possible."

With that, the big man charged forward at a crouch with his head down, moving far more quickly than most would've thought, but Spike had anticipated the suddenness of his attack—he wasn't fooled or foolish enough to think big means slow—and so pivoted in place at the last moment and allowed Felix to rush past in a move not unlike the veronica of a matador. Spike then drew his knife from its sheath and rapidly executed a forward roll on his right shoulder that brought him low and then under and up until the two were facing each other, pressed against each other. To Spike it was like being pressed against a wall. The point of his blade was just under the big man's sternum. From here, a thrust could pierce liver, aorta, or heart depending on angle of attack.

"Let's talk, Felix."

"Nothing to say. Finish it, please."

"Let me guess: You're bound by oath, is that it?"

"No," Felix said somberly, shaking his head. "I am bound by love for my family. If I fail to fight, I was told assassins will seek them out and kill them."

"Was it The Preacher—" Spike stopped himself and then began again. "Was it a man called De Lumière who told you this?"

"He isn't a man," Felix said, "but yes, it was he who made the threat."

"Right, not a man, got it. Is he inside?"

"No," Felix said, "but his people are."

"How many?"

"All of them."

Spike weighed his options. After a long moment, he said, "I'm going to stab you now, Felix. I mean to nick your aorta. I'm pretty good at this so I shouldn't miss. The bad news is if you don't receive medical attention right away, you will internally bleed out and die. If the ambulance comes in time, the wound that nearly killed you will convince your employer you did your best—"

"—So my family will be safe," Felix said.

"Yes, so your family will be safe."

"And if you don't get it right?"

"If I sever the aorta? Death will be quick. I don't promise painless."

Spike positioned the blade where he guessed it needed to be and drove it home. There was a gasp from the big man as it went in but no more than that. Spike walked him backwards like the two were dancing an awkward waltz until the doorman's back was against the wall. Spike eased him down until he was in a sitting position.

"Put pressure on the wound until you can't, Felix. Help will come, I promise it."

With that, Spike wiped his blade on the man's sportscoat, sheathed his knife, stepped over the man's splayed legs, and went inside. The bar was dark inside so Spike stood at the entrance for a moment to let his eyes adjust. He had expected the babble of conversation and music on the jukebox but the Inferno Lounge was silent. The silence was absolute. All eyes were on him, none of them friendly. A large, strangely crudely painted red pentagram dominated the far wall across from him, candles placed at the base for illumination.

Spike stepped to that part of the bar nearest the door. He didn't bother raising his hand for attention since the barkeep, a short, balding, pot-bellied man, was already staring at him, frozen in the middle of pouring a drink from what looked like a sparkling green bottle of absinthe. Spike couldn't see the face of the woman he was pouring it for, but her fingernails were long and curled and painted red like those of an Asian potentate in the movies and Spike wasn't sure but he thought he heard someone in the crowd growl like a predatory animal, a wolf or a dog.

"Call an ambulance, barkeep. Something terrible happened to your doorman." The barkeep was still frozen in place and his eyes were wide and afraid.

That's what I'm sensing in here, Spike thought: Fear. They're all afraid of me.

"I don't want any trouble," he told the patrons of The Inferno Lounge. "I'm just here for my friend."

A familiar voice called out from the back. "But what if trouble is what *we* want, Spike? What then?"

The crowd, which had been creeping almost imperceptibly closer to Spike's position, parted as if of a single mind to open the way for Spike's former colleague Wendell Choate, late of the US State Department and the CIA, who was now boldly stepping forward in what Choate no doubt planned as a dramatic movie moment meant to shock-surprise and immobilize Spike Cohen long enough for Choate to pay him back in kind for the bullet a bloodied and weakened Spike had fired into his brain on the shuffleboard court at The Paradise.

For Spike's part, he had been expecting Choate to show up even before he heard the dead man's voice ring out. Uriah Kemp had warned him. Spike's dream had been a memory had been a message had been a warning telling him the Devil can raise the dead—not to life, no, but to a mockery of life as an animated corpse, meat that can move, and before he drew his Hi-Power he heard Uriah Kemp's voice in his head once again, and the voice said, "This is what I do, brother. Let go, let me," and Spike did let go, surrendering control of his body to a man whose soul he shared and whose mind he could read (if he chose). Uriah Kemp drew the pistol from his shoulder holster and fired in a single sweeping motion too fast to follow, drilling Choate neatly between the eyes and killing the government man a second time. Choate stood for a long moment, his mouth open in a big O of surprise, and then fell back flat on his back without bending, like a loose plank falling free from a stable wall.

Assuming a profiled dueling stance with his arm fully extended, covering the room, Uriah said, "The bullets in this acme of human ingenuity I hold in my hand have been blessed by a Captain of the Host. Any takers?"

The patrons of the Inferno Lounge had shed their glamours and now appeared as they truly were, monsters of myth and demons from hell and a few of no known provenance. Uriah had the feeling these creatures were communicating with each other in a way he couldn't see or hear, but he could sense their indecision and knew about their fear. He had nine rounds loaded and a spare ten-round magazine. One or two might get through if he missed. He wouldn't miss. They wouldn't get through.

The gawky bartender (now revealed as an eyeless lesser worm of the Third Circle) made the first move, sneakily extruding a pseudopod from its amorphous form to reach under the bar for the shotgun it kept there. Uriah caught the movement and fired, killing the barkeep and then turning and bringing the gun to bear on the creatures to his front, now coming at him together in a disorganized rush. On the move now, Uriah cut loose, shooting a snake lady in the face who had low-crawled undetected almost to his feet, and then in quick succession killing a fur- and fang-sprouting dog-man hybrid, an ancient Egyptian crocodile god, a snarling rat king as big as a man that a minute before had looked like a man, a tentacled and indefinable thing from another world that made a cry like that of a human baby when he hit it so he hit it again to silence it, and then two lesser demons, both of whom exploded in flame and cinders and disappeared screaming. His fusillade had broken their attack. The monsters and demons were falling back, a few splitting off and running towards a door in the rear. Uriah stopped to reload and readied himself for a rush of his own. It was then a man-sized Amazonian spider god hiding in the rafters, watching and waiting from above, made its play and dropped from the ceiling and onto his shoulders, digging in, its voracious pedipalps seeking his throat. Without stopping to think, Uriah somersaulted his body forward and onto his back in a break fall posture, stunning the giant arachnid and giving Uriah time to roll off and away, firing as he went. The spider-thing began mewling in pain and tried to scuttle off but Uriah was on it, hounding it, shooting through every gap he could find in its hairy armored carapace until it finally stopped moving and then he shot it some more. After he caught his breath and checked his body for wounds, Uriah surveyed the carnage. He was the only thing alive in the bar—in the front room of it, anyway. He did a quick mental inventory: two in the magazine, one in the chamber. A knife. His body—he quickly corrected himself: Uri's body. And headed toward the exit in the rear, determined no hellspawn would escape this place alive.

Alma and Giselle emerged as he approached the doorway. He stopped cold at the sight of them, at the sight of her. Alma smiled a greeting but her smile just as quickly faded as recognition dawned.

"Anna," he said simply.

Alma held up her hand to Giselle in a *wait here* gesture and stepped forward until she was close. He could smell her and the smell of her made him remember a meadow in Missouri full of wildflowers. It was an old memory. They had only known each other two days by then.

Alma searched his eyes. "It's you, isn't it, Uriah. I know it's you."

He shook his head. "You're talking to the memory of a dead man, not even a ghost. I need to go. This ain't right."

She shook her head with him. "No, it isn't. We don't dare even touch, but know this: You and I will see each other again. We will be together. That is the promise, beloved. I swear it."

Uriah Kemp pressed his closed fist against his chest and gave a slight bow. "I hold you to that promise," he said, and was gone.

Spike took a moment to feel himself again, examining his hands, flexing his fingers. He noticed Giselle. "So we're all friends now?"

"Allies," Giselle said. "We have a shared interest."

Spike nodded. "You tried to muddy the waters at The Ambassador with those Russian goons and guns. Did you do that for us?"

Giselle said, "It was a small thing. I doubt it helped but I did what I could."

"But are you *with us* with us?" Spike asked. "We can't rely on you, we don't need you."

Giselle nodded at Alma. "I am with her. She leads, I follow."

As they exited The Inferno Lounge, Spike saw Felix was still seated and propped against the wall, bleeding out slowly. Giselle broke from the group and ran to him, calling out his name.

"Betty's waiting out front—or should be," Spike said. "We'll take Felix to the same hospital where Benny Kingman's at, I forget which one but she'll know. The problem is getting him up those stairs."

"You forget what we are," Alma said. "Giselle and I have him."

"Not enough room for everyone in the car," Spike began.

"I'll walk," Alma said. "I need to walk."

5. A FELLOW OF INFINITE JEST, OF MOST EXCELLENT FANCY...

Spike Cohen visited Benny Kingman in his private hospital room long after visiting hours, and he did it almost as an afterthought. He pulled up a chair next to the bed and debated what to do about the now fallen from grace former comedian, and found that even in sleep Kingman managed to annoy him, snoring so loudly Spike was surprised it didn't wake the ward. According to Kingman's nurse, Kingman would soon be released. Whatever Giselle had done to him wasn't permanent.

Felix the doorman would be fine. Alma showed up after her long walk and Spike guessed she would be fine, too. He had sensed Uriah Kemp's emotions throughout their shared experience up to and including the moment Kemp encountered Alma— *Anna* to him. She was, Spike guessed, the love of the man's life and even though Kemp was dead, his love for her went on. It was equally clear Alma loved him back. Spike couldn't imagine how such a love could work but in the end he decided it was none of his business. The world's full of tragic love stories. He had lived one, himself.

"I want my soul back, Cohen," Kingman said from the bed, his voice weak and unsteady. Spike guessed Kingman had been awake for a while. The snoring had stopped minutes before but Spike hadn't noticed.

Spike replied, "One, I don't have it and two, you haven't paid me to care."

"I know you don't have it but to get it back I need your help. Name your price," Kingman said.

"All of it, Benny, every cent. And everything you know, too—all information you've got pertaining to De Lumière. I need a better feel for the man."

"He's not a man," Kingman said.

"People keep telling me that. We'll see."

Kingman sat up in the bed, his sallow, beak-nosed face roiling with anger. "This is crazy. You're crazy."

"That's the deal, Benny. Take it or leave it."

"You can't possibly believe I'd just give you all I've got."

Spike pushed the chair away and stood up to leave. He wanted to go downstairs and conclude his business with Felix. Spike had a good feeling about Felix, a man with the sight who could tell truth from illusion. He might've found a valuable ally in the big African and it warmed him a little.

Spike looked down at Benny Kingman. "You're under the mistaken impression this is a negotiation. How much is your soul worth, Benny?"

"Everything," Benny Kingman said, after a tortured moment. "What else do you need from me? There's always something else."

"You still own a private airplane, yeah?"

"I do. I own two."

"We'll need them. We'll need everything. De Lumière has unlimited resources. We can't match him, but we need to be as close to *unlimited* as we can get."

Kingman was petulant. "Anything else?"

"You, Benny. I want you. People know your name, your face, your show—"

"—They canceled my show, Cohen. I don't have a show any more."

Spike shrugged. "You're still a big star all the same, which means you can go virtually anywhere without official suspicion. Fame opens doors. We're going to need that. We're going to use that."

"So get dressed, funny man. You're checking out."

As Kingman dressed, he asked, "Where to first, Cohen?"

"Betty found a Wild West museum just south of Reno and made some inquiries," Spike replied. "We need to see a man about a gun."

ABOUT THE AUTHOR

TROY RISER is an award-winning writer and artist. His most recently published story, "Comes A Pale Bride", appeared in Critical Blast's recent horror anthology, *The Monsters Next Door,* and two of his stories have appeared in earlier iterations of *The Devil You Know* horror anthology series. He is currently working on a novel and teaching himself game development using the Unreal Engine.

THE DEVIL
WENT DOWN
TO GENOA

John Di Donna

1799, THE FRENCH OCCUPIED FORMER REPUBLIC OF GENOA

This was no summoning, not so much even as an invocation, but more of a... proposition. A tempting proposition at that, and the demonic entity known as Tenebrax was all about temptation.

The air shimmered, threatening to erase the panorama it veiled in a heat-blurred frenzy. The very molecules suspended in the atmosphere cauterized, dying an agonizing death as they came in contact with such corruption, coughing out a sulfuric gout as they went to their doom. From this broiling geyser of caustic vapor, Tenebrax drew itself up to its full height, proud, viciously narcissistic, as much an abomination to the eye as it was to the heart, or the mind. Draped in the velvety membranes of scalloped wings It wore like princely robes, the rim of Its silhouette was lit by the hovering ghost lights that marked Its office as a Blood Baron of the Nephillitic Diaspora.

Absent was any of the redundantly employed magical accruements. Not so much as a protective binding circle of sorcerous runes and sigils etched in mineral salts, or a steaming pile of slaughtered goat entrails, or even so much as a bound and gagged virginal sacrifice lashed to the alter.

Disappointing.

Half the fun of tormenting the living was all the theatrics.

Sunlight filled the basilica with warm luminescence. The oratory was encaged by a grotesque number of marble pillars, Gothic buttresses, Baroque filigree, friezes, chandeliers, and frescos, that it took all of the demon's compound irises to take it all in.

Called. To a church. Just after midday.

That was a new one.

It almost laughed. Miles of gold leaf encased near-endless cornices and fretwork. The crypts of their most pious bore the most vainglorious statues. The post-Renaissance artisans who'd painted every visible square centimeter of plaster had taken idolatry to previously unknown heights of depravity. This was much more a shrine to opulence and vanity as it had ever been a place for communion with the Almighty.

And thus, It felt right at home.

Across the narthex, a shadow danced and flitted about.

Tenebrax flared, Its auricles and labial heat slits widening, It's wicked tongue flicking, tasting, feeling, and listening to Its new surroundings. Apparently, It was in the presence of a man, barely a man, scarcely older than how the children of the Elohim calculated such a thing. And unless It was mistaken, he was alone. Not attended by a bacchanalian coven, or a cabal of necromantic witches. Not in the thrall of some power mad slaveowner, or abused at the hands of a blasphemous pontiff. Just a boy-man.

And his violin.

This is what had caught the demon's attention, down in the depths beyond the veil that separated their worlds. A scintillating clarion call, this choral ultimatum from this most unlikely of conductors.

The man-boy contorted as if in the throes of an epileptic fit, his spine heaving to and fro with whiplash cracks, his feet prancing as if on a bed of hot coals, his cadaverous features, far too sickly for anyone so young, obscured by the flailing jet black locks. The demon perceived that his instrument was just that, well made, by mortal standards, to be sure, but still only common wood and string. Not carved from the lid of a diabolic composer's coffin, nor strung with the tendons from a baby's corpse, not even varnished with reduced songbirds' bone marrow, no, nothing like that. It watched as the juvenile's fingers seized the full length of the neck and body like a ravenous tarantula molesting its prey, the other hand sawing the strings with speeds that neared combustion. Perhaps only the boy's frantic swinging and pitching cooled the strings and blew the kindled fires out.

This was a one-man symphony.

Tenebrax reasoned this was no mere music, expertly played though it may be. The vocalization of the harmonics, the rapid-fire battery of the notes, the twisting of meter and tempo, what the pubescent prodigy was doing was invoking the same spiritual energies as any other mystic incantation.

Incredible.

The youth completed his notturno, drawing a final stroke, a swordsman dealing a final death blow with his blade. Looking up, he took in his demonic audience for the first time, now seeing that the nightmare before him was as substantive as he was, that he'd gone from the realm of dreams and fantasy to stark reality.

Tenebrax gave his host a slow clap. The boy recoiled at the pistol shot reports, mouth agape, eyes threatening to bolt from his skull and run and hide, his heart, already racing with exertion, now throttling its way out of his ribcage. If there'd been any color found in his alabaster skin, it'd drained away completely.

"Impressive," said the demon. "I do believe that you might have given Herr Mozart reason to pause when he was your age." Tenebrax's voice was an affront to nature, reason, and the inner ear, each syllable searing its way past Its lips, droplets of molten slag sizzling as they struck a blacksmith's anvil.

The juvenile lost his nerve. He cowed, coiling up into a fetal position, holding his violin up by the neck to shield him from the impossibility slinking down the aisle towards him.

Pathetic. If the boy wasn't careful, he'd die of fright, and all of this would be for naught. Still, far be it from Tenebrax to have so much as single cell of compassion anywhere to be found in his daemonic physiology.

With a barely perceptible gesture of Its head, unseen energies took the violin from the child, and caused it to rise into the air, suspended between them both. Tenebrax commanded it to play. The noise it produced was the sickest, most twisted mockery of the oratorio that'd preceded it, a caterwauling tempest, a fractured dissonance, a violation of anything remotely melodic, the cry of the eternal soul struck dead, the howl of the firmament being rent asunder by the Beast of Revelations.

It was the opposite of music.

The boy stuffed his fists in his ears, and began to wail, begging all the hosts of Heaven to make it stop. It stopped. The violin held its place, and then fell to the floor with a lifeless thud.

"One of the endless, countless curses afflicted upon Us for treason against the Throne of The Adonai. Not only have We been cast out from the Presence, We've been castrated, the instruments to make music, to make song, stripped from us. We are as artless as we are heartless." Tenebrax paused. "Although, if We translate that from the Italian into English, that would be rather lyrical, would it not? Hmm." He drew closer to the quivering collection of black cloth hiding his face with his hands. "Stranger still. Your mind should be as open to Us as a desiccated thorax, yet your thoughts linger in shadow. Who are you, boy, you who are so eager to court damnation?"

The youth stammered, stuttering, his being frozen in fear sweat. Not until Tenebrax raised his raptorial forearm, threatening to backhand his summoner through the back wall, did the boy marshal his budding manhood.

"Nick. Nic-co-lò. Niccolò Paganini." His words a fraught whisper, fighting back tears of despair. "At your mercy, O Magnanimous Lord of Darkness."

"Indeed. Wethinks thou doth protest too much, Senoré Paganini. It was not We who summoned you, nor you who gave yourself in servitude to Us. Yet, here We are, in broad daylight, and housed inside a *Cattedrale*, no less. There have been diabolists amongst your kind who'd slaved their entire existence to complete such a dark miracle, and died never knowing success. Speak! Tell me! How did this come to pass? What are you about, stripling?"

In a momentary surge of bravado, Niccolò reached for his fallen instrument.

"The thirteenth hour." He said, noting the sun beaming through the faceted rosettes. "The thirteenth day. This place, the thirteenth constricted diocese in Genoa."

"Do go on."

"And then, there's this." Niccolò presented the violin as if it'd been sanctioned by the Pope.

"A four stringed instrument? I fail to understand."

"Thirteen notes. Played every second!" Through his terror, he beamed.

"Yes." Hissed the entity, in realization. "The best amongst you dared hope to attain twelve, at their most triumphant. Dominant thirteen cords compiled into single octaves, creating a secundal tone cluster." Four sets of nictitating eyelids blinked, calculating. "Paralleling the Enochian harmonics of the cosmological tonality by way of Pythagorean alterspacial geometry. A crowning achievement... particularly for such an anemic specimen of larvae. And yet, I detect that you do not grasp the universality of what you've wrought, even if some dormant realm of your subconscious has formulated the mathematics for you!"

Niccolò gawped. His mind couldn't contend with the infernal rasping, let alone what the nightmare was explaining to him. Worse, the creature was extending what only could be called an arm in the most abstract terms, and as the limb shed it bat-winged vestiges to reach for him, he could see that the flesh was pusillanimous, translucent under a mucous sheen, the lattice of ligaments and pulsing webbing of veins and nerve clusters visibly tangled between a collection of bones that didn't resemble those of any animal that ever walked the Earth.

To both of their surprise, Tenebrax struck an unseen wall erected around Paganini. Thaumaturgic light sparked at the damnable touch of the demon's talons. The flash lingered on the backs of Its retina, an intricate matrix composed from a secretive weaving of time, tone, and harmonics. Finally, here was the spellcaster's protective circle, not to imprison, but to protect. It tested the field again, not merely touching, but striking with mounted fury, resulting in a blinding burst of sparks. Nervously, not knowing what other course to take, Niccolò bent, and began bowing the violin. He had no working knowledge whether music would tame the savage beast, but he had an innate sense that this was all that was standing between him and being ripped apart by Tenebrax's ravenous maw.

"Ah! We think We begin to see. This was not your intention at all, you are naught but an overreaching prospect with delusions of grandeur, playing the typical role of the hapless minstrel in a Faustian tryst!" A thing that was intended to be laughter escaped into the sanctuary, tarnishing the brass and peeling the paint. "You were expecting this encounter to have a more classical component, something along the lines of …"

Its misshapen tarsus rose, and swept down in front of Its form, and as it passed, Tenebrax transformed, becoming the too familiar adversary of prose: a gay faced actor dressed as Mephistopheles, complete with twisted mustache, van dyke beard, horns, a red cape, and a pitchfork, twirling a spaded tail as he danced in pointy shoes,

"…The Devil Himself, in all His Satanic Majesty!"

Relief flooded across Niccolò's face, as he clutched his bow. This form was far more palatable to his eyes. He almost smiled. But Tenebrax didn't see anything to be smiling about, and as he whipped his arm back up, the footlight jester vanished, and his former malevolence returned, and again mortified Its host.

"Yes, precisely. You speak truly. I imagined that the person I conscripted would be the Devil himself."

"We would be insulted, if such a thing were possible. Have none of your failed shepherds taught you what is written: We are Legion, for We are many?"

The last words were spoken in unison by a dozen voices.

Niccolò shook his head.

"Poor little fiddler. Imagine your disappointment when your bedtime prayers were not immediately answered by the risen Nazarene and His twelve legions in all their glory!"

"I– I suppose... it would be presumptuous, perhaps, for any other mortal. But I, sir, am no mere common practitioner."

"No, it would appear not." Said Tenebrax, bemused.

"In my folly, I allowed my desperate ambition– to attempt to... beseech the Lord of Hell, to enter into a, ah, a contractual obligation, thinking that there would be an equitable... exchange, that each party would find to be... mutually beneficent–"

"I sense a hesitation in your words, please, do not let Us intimidate you into silence."

"But now it's all too clear that such a consignment is no longer necessary!"

Tenebrax bristled. "Is that so? We pray that this sudden reversal has not been predicated on finding your partner to be wanting, Our crawling cicada. Or too terrible to conduct your business."

"Oh, no, Your Repugnance! That is, yes, you are indeed far more horrifying than I could ever have imagined. But do you not see? Your very presence here is testament that I'm already in possession of all the ability I could ever bargain for!"

The demon paused, evaluating the gaunt performer before It. And then, in defiance of all probability, It laughed.

"Ah, Abominable Lord, what fools these mortals be! Hubris. Arrogance. Pride. These are attractive qualities in a prospective upstart, to be sure."

"It is my undying hope that I have not inconvenienced you, that you have not made the journey in vain?"

"On the contrary, Genovese, our encounter has been nothing if not enlightening." It tapped the air again, his claw cracking against the harmonic barrier, as if to imply that even if It'd been stoked to anger, there was little It could do about it. "You've provided Us a brief respite from the tedium of the torture pits, and allowed Us to attend a most singular performance. In return, We will share one of the hidden truths of the shadowlands; We have no desire whatsoever to obtain your soul, for sale or otherwise."

"What?"

"Look into your own heart, Paganini. You are scarcely out of swaddling clothes, and yet you are fouled with drink, enslaved by wanton lusts, constricted with a gambler's fever, and are well on the way to collecting the wages of your sins, all on your own, without the least efforts from so much as the lowliest of imps."

It was clear that had never occurred to Niccolò. As he stared into the middle distance, contemplating the path he'd chosen to walk, the demon drifted past him, climbing the stairs, passing the alter table, rising up to the pulpit. Niccolò didn't think such a thing would've been possible for an honest to God devil, but there It was.

"Lord Most Foul, this means we are now quits, does it not?"

The demon ignored him, instead, It turned the gilded pages of the gold bound book of scripture laid before him. If Its features allowed it, Niccolò may have seen an air of nostalgia across It's face.

"Let me ask you, fluttering dayfly, can you possibly conceive what it was like to raise your voice in celebration, in supplication, indwelling with the very presence of the Creator of the Universe?" Tenebrax lowered Its head, his voice lowering from an accusatory wail to a simmering hiss, the hanging censures and candelabra rocked by divine wind, the afternoon sun reflecting off the golden tabernacle, breaking into a lancing crest of rays, a streaming nimbus that sang the song of eternity. Squinting his eyes against such radiance, Niccolò had the briefest impression of the being the fallen angel had been before, enrapt in shimmering multitude of wings that folded impossibly in fifth, sixth, and seventh dimensions, robed in the sunrise, a pyramid of shining eyes triangulating a crowning glory atop It's head.

"The song of David, the son of Saul, first king of Yisra'el, chapter one hundred and fifty." Read the demon aloud.

"Praise the LORD.

Praise God in his sanctuary; praise him in his mighty heavens.

Praise him for his acts of power; praise him for his surpassing greatness.

Praise him with the sounding of the trumpet, praise him with the harp and lyre, praise him with timbrel and dancing, praise him with the strings and pipe, praise him with the clash of cymbals, praise him with resounding cymbals.

Let everything that has breath praise the LORD. Praise the LORD."

The reading was arcane; The beginning bordered on the sublime, Tenebrax channeling a tenor It'd not voiced in millennia, a sounding resonance that made Niccolò look for the choir accompanying It. But as It read, the words tinged with resentment, ranging through lower octaves, maddening, dripping with vile rancor, until the final proclamation, that came close to drawing blood from mortal ears.

The devil punctuated his reading by slamming the book shut with a clap of thunder. "Megalomaniacal excrement!" Tenebrax lost control. The volume before him burst into flame, as did a number of the tapestries and banners that flanked the narthex. "For countless eons the Ancient of Days has been attended day and night, night and day by the entirety of the hosts of Heaven, in celebratory recitation, signing His glories, praising His holy name, blowing a dying star's worth of fragrant burnt offerings' smoke up His eternally vast ass!" Its claws upraised, It clenched Its fists, quenching the flames It'd lit before they could scorch the paintings. "Well, We for Many are sick of it."

The monstrosity stalked back down the stairs, fixing Its gaze back on Paganini.

"It is written that the weak will be used to shame the strong, the fool to shame the wise. What say you, foolish weakling? Do this thing. Use all your considerable skill, employ all of your 'God given' talents, and do this not for but against Him. Reclaim the musical world for the Devil, and go to your reward knowing that no other man e'er walked the Earth."

"What... what would you give me to do such a thing?"

"Your continued life, you impudent slime. Oh, do not glance sideways at Us through your ingenious composition, it would do you no good if We dragged the whole of this edifice down to the pits with Us."

It was clear that had never occurred to Niccolò, either.

With a gust that blew Paganini's hair back, the creature's wings snapped out and upwards, carving a scorching trail of flame that impossibly drew light into it instead of projecting it out, the razored talons at the ends of the digits tearing open the fabric of reality, a rift large enough for the demon to step into.

"*Buona fortuna,* maestro Paganini," retched Tenebrax.

"*Forza Satanica,*" answered Niccolò.

1816, THE FORMER DUTCHY OF MILAN, NOW IN THE KINGDOM OF LOMBARDY—VENETIA

The applause echoed across the largest stage in Italy, the opera house at the *Teatro La Scalla,* as Charles Philippe Lafont returned Paganini's treasured violin to him.

"*Passablement,* not too bad, Genovese! Not quite as *resonato* as I'd expected, but warm and potent nonetheless!"

Counted among the best virtuosos on the continent, the two were competing in a musical duel as vicious as the fatal encounter between Hamilton and Burr on the opposite shores of the Atlantic. Such duels were common enough among the upper echelon of composers; Bach, Beethoven, Mozart, even the penitent Handel competed against their rivals, either the parties properly grieved, or simply for the promotional spectacle and burgeoning ticket sales.

This was theatre, after all.

But in a moment of gracious supplication, Niccolò had lent his rival his legendary instrument, *"Il Cannoné Guarnerius,"* the very same on loan to him from a wealthy patron he'd performed his demonic invocation with two decades prior.

As the mounting applause peaked and subsided, filling the stacked tiers of the towering auditorium, Paganini made a show of re-tuning the instrument, implying she'd been crudely violated and manhandled, drawing fond chuckles from the audience.

The competitors cut a dramatic contrast; Monsieur Lafont was dressed in the height of *Habit à la Française,* looking so refined and dignified that he might've stepped out of a framed portrait displayed in the Parisian Royal Court. Paganini, despite playing so angelically during the first salvo of the competition, appeared ready to perform a requiem mass for the dead, or perhaps was ready to have one performed for him. His attire more suited a gravedigger or a pallbearer rather than one of the orchestra. His floor length frock coat trimmed with military cuffs and epaulets was so last century, the silk as black as his wind whipped locks, ones that framed a face with the pallor of a fresh corpse. The sheen of sweat that soaked him through was as much from the mercury and laudanum cocktails his doctor prescribed for his compounded cases of syphilis as much from the day's exertions. In short, he looked the fright that his reputation had led his admirers to believe he was.

And he knew it.

Ah, his adoring public.

Who needed to call upon the powers of darkness when so many were ready and willing to do it for you?

Before the patrician acting as officiant could come forward with the selected sheet music for the sight reading, Paganini cut him off with a staccato barrage, employing his famed left hand pizzicato with sixteenth notes in succession, a fanfare designed to stay the hecklers and silence the critics. With his right, he batted the frog end of the bow lying on the stand next to him, launching it, whirling end over end up into the rafters, before coming back down where he snatched out of midair, and sliced into his strings with a precision cut.

Beating back a flurry of applause, he attacked the air with a composition of his own, deviating from the program, instead playing *'Le Streghe'* for his solo riposte, unleashing a flourish of technical pyrotechnics that inspired a series of gasps and awes. Ramping up to the impossible thirteen notes a second, the bow slashed at the neck so viciously, it appeared that Paganini struggled to keep it flying from out of his hands. And when his bodily undulations, his signature snapping at the waist and whirling dervish antics, drew yet more laughter from the detractors, he answered them by lunging forward with a madman's fury, stomping out a fencer's advancing balestra, wielding his violin and bow as if they were rapier and dagger poised to strike their killing blows.

The thunderous ovation was enough to ship Lafont back off to Paris.

But whereas Paganini had finished with the Frenchman, he still had a score to settle with his audience.

Hunching low, wrapping his whole being around his instrument, he intoned a rumbling that started off from a faraway land, and slowly drew closer with menace and intent.

"Squealing melodies over filthy catgut!" He'd heard one countess mutter to her entourage.

Another took the time to lambast Paganini's prices, pro-rating his earnings, calculating out how much the audience was paying him down to the note.

And through all the jeering and gossip about his mistresses, liaisons, and infidelities with the likes of Napoleon's sister, (all the while keeping her husband on as a pupil), there was the continual speculation of his relations with The Devil Itself.

And that had been quite enough of that.

While extending his lower half, straightening his legs, Paganini continued to hang down, head to the floor, his bow arm gyrating, the sounds roiling over the stage and out into the audience simulating the approach of an angered stormfront. Then, as if a sudden gust had caught him and flipped him upright, Niccolò increased the tempo, first coaxing a zephyr that, impossibly, caused the candelabra to flicker in the breeze, before intensifying the sound into a squall that caused the audience to hold onto their armrests.

The spectral maestro contorted, being battered, tempest-tossed from one end of the stage and back again. A low rolling trepidation of incoming thunder emanated from his fingertips. With sky-tearing reports, the sound of lightning strikes drew cries of panic from the socialites.

All this from the emaciated phantasm prancing before them, fiddling with the fury of Nero in a Roman firestorm.

Paganini began to spin, his concentration nowhere else but on the strings, lending the appearance of being caught up with a whirl of leaves and spun by a dust devil. Hands flew to heads, as throughout the audience patrons were sure their hair was being whipped, or their clothes fanned by the wind.

The resounding stamp of a crashing pressure system beat down on the whole of the theatre, and just like that, every candle and oil lamp were snuffed out. Darkness fell over the assembled three thousand, a chorus of cries and wails joining Niccolò up on the stage.

In the dark, the subsonic bass of tectonic plates quivering with anticipation rumbled beneath the crowd's feet, while the gusting treble of gale force winds cycloned around the stage.

Down in the orchestral pit, a savvy musician found the oil can, removed the lid, and lit the surface, producing a flame a foot tall, strong enough to fight against the wind. Stagehands scrambled to relight as many of the fixtures as they could.

Over the frenetic sawing of horsehair against strings and the oncoming meteorologic disaster, the audience collectively inhaled in horror.

Several feet above the stage, in the flickering flames, was the silhouette of Paganini, caught up in his rapture and in the spinning vortex both. Being suspended in midair proved to be no impediment to his playing; on the contrary, his body continued to spasm and thrash against the strings like a man in his death throes. As if that wasn't horrible enough, with a conductor's stabbing commands, the lightning returned, cracking from rooftop to balcony, from balcony to catwalk. And with each flash, Paganini's shadow was thrown against the far wall, and for that split second between blinding flash and searing spark, the audience could see the shadow of the Devil, the skull lanced with horns, the spread of leathery wings, the flailing of a spiked tail.

Full blown terror seized the crowd, and in a writhing mass, a screaming tumult, they took to their feet and fought, clawed, scratched, kicked, clambered, and raced for the exits.

La Scalla was now as quiet as the applause had been uproarious only an hour before.

Footlights were relit, at the hands of a few seasoned veteran stagehands, who'd seen far too many illusions and misdirections to believe that the Devil had come to the opera.

Paganini opened a viola case and drew out the bottle of Napoleon brandy it hid. After downing enough of the sweet fire to stop his limbs from trembling, he passed the bottle on to the remaining performers, who congratulated him on his most unorthodox victory.

Niccolò cast his gaze out into the shadows of the massive amphitheater. His ego would suffer, starved of the afterglow of the adoring throngs of aficionados, music critics, and prospective ladies in waiting.

Ah, well. They got what they'd expected, he said to himself.

But then, from one of the private boxes above stage right, a sulfur matchstick lit a cigar whose fragrance alone was richer than most in Milan could afford.

Paganini strained to make out the form, lit only by cigar cinder and ambient flickering. It appeared to be one of the royal military, wearing so much silver-embroidered tailored finery, draped velvet sashes, braided gold lanyards, and an elaborate sword sheath, that they must be addressed by a title too long to remember. It wasn't until they stood to go that he saw that their attire fit too closely to their curves to be a masculine patron.

"Wait!" he called into the dark. "Which one are you?"

With that, the creature's eyes lit, casting enough of an ethereal glow to see its features, possessing a certain daemonic beauty, after a fashion. "Well played, Maestro Nocturnus. We've been called Hexensohn by men who fear Us, a Viscountess over the Ravages of Desperation." As It spoke, it cast a shadow that neither matched its physical form, nor conformed with any known laws of physics.

Niccolò laughed. "'Witch's Brat?' Ha! How about that? I've been called the same, when playing in Hamburg, or Vienna."

It was Their turn to laugh, one tinged with skin-blackening frostbite. "We know. We may have had something to do with that, but We're not sorry. We will let Master Tenebrax know that you send your regards, although, as you've learned, It already knows." And with that It exhaled a billow of smoke, one that It stepped into, and in less time than it took to dissipate, It was gone.

1831, POST-REVOLUTION PARIS

Following a standing ovation at the Paris Opera House, the sellout crowds swarmed the ballrooms of Palais Royal in hopes to lavish their attentions on the Genovese Maestro. Outside, the City of Lights was still ravaged by the lingering aftermath of the Revolution, but inside, the assembled Parisians sought a needed refuge from the trials of their horrid existence.

But Paganini had shuttered himself in a private chamber, the doors locked, his guest list a mystery. From beyond the double doors that rose from floor to ceiling, eavesdropping concertgoers could hear the dulcet tones of a guitar sonata being performed, brilliantly at that.

Niccolò had been weaned on the guitar.

Specifically, the mandolin, an instrument his father had studied to the point of obsession, and thus the instrument so close to his heart that he refused to play it in public, or for money. Only for himself, *a piacere,* or for the most intimate private audience.

The crowd was an assortment of la *noblesse française,* members of the royal family, the highest-ranking military officers, mayors and aldermen, shipowners, tycoons, and entrepreneurs, as well as the societal elite, journalists and critics, and some of the best performers in the country, all still in the thrall of the auditory miracles they'd borne witness to that evening. Many were far too proud to be seen slinking outside a celebrity's locked doors like some uncouth commoner, pretending instead like they needed a breath of air before returning to the dance floor, or chasing after *le servuers* for a refill on their champagne.

All were in rare form.

Thunderstruck, members of the orchestra thanked God that they did not play violin, and the ones that did prayed they'd be able to sell their instruments, or they'd throw them into a bonfire. Librettists crossed themselves that the man stuck to composition and not moved to lyrics, otherwise they'd be lost. Cellist Robert Lindley stammered, as he did, that he was sure he'd seen "the d-d-d-Devil!" while bassist Domenico Dragonetti insisted that there was no explanation other than the man had to be possessed.

There were, of course, the usual number of eligible mademoiselles, ready to abandon all sense of decorum and decency for the opportunity to abscond with the talented necromancer, which only inspired the more weathered and cronish socialites to lambast his profane name.

The only thing that would quell their gossip and slander was when a new bravura would begin.

"I'm certain that if only Il Cavaliere Paganini would hold court and assuage his guests, he could easily put all this talk of heresy and diabolical courtship to rest!" The curator of the Opera House used the knighted title because Paganini had been inducted into the Order of the Golden Spur by Pope Leo XII himself. And yet, this only served as evidence that supernatural powers were propelling his career.

Speculation as to who his audience could be reached a fever pitch.

Amateur theories about forgotten lovers, bastard children, or high-ranking Vatican officials were all cast aside in favor of the savoriest, that Niccolò was entertaining the embassies from the Nine Hells themselves, paying the price he owed for that evening's sensationalism, and for his stratospheric success.

The sonatas gave way to musics that defied categorization. From behind the muffling effects of the palace's walls, they heard tempos that blew their hair back, chords that shook the windowpanes loose from their jams, and arpeggios that lined up traditional genres in their sights and pulled the trigger.

From behind the paneled doors, there was the thrumming pressure of tympanic war drumming, the bone shaking baritone pulse of bass cellos, and a cross-cut sawing of guitar strings at sound barrier breaking speeds, pummeling the ear drums of all within range.

This was symphonic bedlam, music composed for the halls of the lunatic asylum.

These were songs that made the eavesdroppers hear their hearts beating behind their sternums, the rushing course of blood racing through its course made them breathe heavy from the exertion of listening. The most chaste and celibate of them found themselves dabbing at their pates with handkerchiefs, loosening their neckscarves and cravats, and downing glass after glass to quench their parched throats. Some would later testify that they could feel the notes themselves on their skin, the fingering of the strings doing the same for them, and there were gasps and exhalations that matched the fevered pitch of the melodies.

And yet this was nothing in comparison to the mounting, grinding crescendos from the privacy of the orchestral boudoir. The crowd stood in shock and awe at the indiscretions that came to them on the air, a perversity that would've reddened their mistresses and caused the most practiced courtesan to blush. The accompaniment was as lascivious as the voices behind it, the cries of sinners in sublimated ecstasy, of patriarchal fathers lamenting the fall of their flocks, the battle cries of the fallen brushing their fingers against the hemlines of the angels.

With a cut as defiant as a falling guillotine blade across the neck of the guitar, the music ended.

The mesmerized patrons snapped themselves free of their tonal stupor, and made their way elsewhere, playing at nonchalance and indifference, when the slide of the deadbolt *schacked* back, and the ominous doors swung open, seemingly sucking the breath out of the hallway and the very lungs of the gathered.

From the depths of the shadows materialized the executioner of the Royal Court, his robes of office as black as the abyss that birthed him, his face shrouded by the curtains of his death shroud hood, the lethal headman's axe at his side. Or so they thought at the first appearance of the subject of their speculation, as Paganini strode out, bedecked in his signature funerary accoutrement, the sweat-soaked locks of hair veiling his craven features, the potential for destruction radiating from his instrument slung at his side as fearful as any weapon.

For all their gossip and prattle, no one spoke a word as the maestro made his way, inspiring yet more intrigue as he sped past the bar, the *servuers*, and every offered tray of glasses. This was unheard of from such a notorious alcoholic. It lent the air of a man who'd already drank deeply, perhaps from more than wine and spirits. It also begged the question as to where he was going with such intent.

The attendants moved in to light the lamps, casting the antechamber in its familiar glow. There was no one else there. Nor was there so much as a single empty glass, a half-finished bottle, or a nibbled rind of cheese.

The room was vacant.

1895, THE COMMUNAL CEMETERY AT PARMA, UNIFIED KINGDOM OF ITALY

Paganini was dead.

This, as everyone knew, was old news.

It'd been true for fifty-five years, as the humans calculated the rotation of the firmament around its nearest star. So thought the demonic minion Tenebrax, viewing the virtuoso's coffin through the eyes of Cadavarius, Margravine of the Ninth Pestilence, Itself wearing the guise of a grave robber. For all his postmortem travels, the remnants were still recognizable as the composer, who'd appeared as apparitional in life as he did now, looking more at home in his casket than on any stage.

Niccolò did himself proud, dying as a true grand master of the craft: destitute, penniless, and utterly broke, having lost an amassed fortune late in life after failing at, of all things, the casino business.

Ironically, when pawning his most cherished of musical instruments, it was his childhood guitar that he could not bear to part with, and he took with him to his deathbed.

Additionally, he may as well have carved his own epitaph, forever cementing his dedication to the Devil, when he refused the ceremony of last rites.

The reality was Niccolò deluded himself in thinking that his illnesses were not life-threatening, and simply sent the overeager padre off, chiding him for arriving prematurely. Still, word was sent to the Bishop in Nice, where the violinist came to aid in his recovery, and was refused a burial on consecrated grounds.

From then on, Paganini's carcass did more traveling than it had under its own power at the start of his career. He spent a fortnight in the cellar of the building he'd rented before being evicted by unnerved tenants and dumped by the seaside. His beloved son, Baron Achillino, rescued him, taking him to sea, but being refused at Marseilles and Cannes, was forced to inter the body on a deserted island at St. Ferréol, little more than a brisling coral reef. It would be another five years before the body was borne back to the place of his birth and a grave finally dug. But his closest friends were not satisfied, feeling that the embalming had been insufficient, and the body was exhumed, re-embalmed, and buried for the fourth time.

It was thirty-six years and a change of papal office before the Vatican finally granted it's wayward Chevalier the rites to a proper knightly burial, in Parma, the site of his first grand victory.

But that still was not the end. This, after all, was the salacious Paganini, the Devil's Violinist.

Enough time had passed for the world to accredit Paganini for the maestro that he was, and many petitioned his son for yet another exhumation, where he could lay in state, and his devotees could pay their belated respects.

That'd been two years ago.

"Is that you, Master Tenebrax, back to torment me again, like you did a century ago?"

Speaking through Cadavarius' human guise, Tenebrax addressed the soul of the mortal who'd been so maligned with Hell, still squatting within the desiccated remains it'd worn in life, a spectral refugee from the country of his own body.

"Haunting one's own mummified flesh is far more of a torment than We'd have cause to inflict on you, Maestro. The word in the musical community was that they'd laid you in state, and We wanted to see for Ourselves that you still refuse to move on."

"Move on. How inviting. You make it sound like I have a choice, like retiring to a *villetta* down by the sea, not being cast into the Lake of Eternal Fire."

"And what decision has come down from the Almighty auspices? Did Paganini live up to his reputation, forever castigating the miracle of music as the providence of the Satanic? Was a life of drunken whoremongering the capital sin? Or was it a far lesser offense, something along the lines as the Heavenly Host currently overseeing the Seraphic choirs didn't want the competition?"

Even in death, existing in a purgatorial nightmare state between the Waking World and the Hereafter, Niccolò still couldn't abide by the devil's voice, especially when It laughed, the charred vibrato sizzling like blood boiling in Its throat. Nor did he reply, rendering the question rhetorical. The evidence of his fate lay there before Them; how could he seek refuge in the Kingdom of Heaven when he was so vilified on Earth that his son had to beg for him to be given a simple patch of dirt to rest in?

And he'd be damned if he'd allow himself to be damned.

"We suppose papal knighthoods aren't what they used to be." The demon mocked. "No, my necrotic ally, We came to orchestrate, if you'll forgive Us for disparaging that term, a reunion between two long lost friends."

Niccolò began to protest. He'd never entered into anything close to a relationship with any of the hellacious visitors who'd attended his performances, let alone known any of them beyond chance encounters or idle revelries. But then he saw that wasn't what the demon was about. He watched in horrified amazement, seeing now that the gaunt, ravenous forms of the entities had not constituted, but were in possession of, the gravedigger, their arcane presences impossibly folded inside an all too small vessel of still living flesh and blood, and with that mortal's hands, It drew out an all too familiar instrument case.

"Il Canonné!"

Niccolò was ashamed. Selling the masterful violin was as heartbreaking as if he'd been forced to sell his own child. He assumed that demonkind never knew such indignations, such crass debasements of one's person. Of one's pride.

"We recently were presented with the opportunity to acquire it. It's fortunate that occurs so often in Our line of work."

Niccolò got the distinct impression that this acquisition was the furthest thing from mere happenstance. His spirit sat up, pulling itself apart from the slumbering corpse, reaching greedily for his lost fiddle. Existing non-corporally, his hands passed straight on through it, and everything else, as if he wasn't there at all.

As gracefully as It could, using the calloused fingers of the puppeted laborer, it snapped open the clasps of the case, and drew out the Guarnerius, lifting it with the care given to a newborn babe. Hesitantly, It plucked at the strings as if afraid of them. The sound was as horrific as it'd been back in the Genovese cathedral; even a simple strum was enough to produce a wailing death rattle.

"As you can clearly see, or rather hear, for yourself, such a precision instrument is rendered useless in Our grasp."

"At least you still have a grasp!" replied Niccolò, demonstrating by passing his hands through each other. "I've compounded my restless misery. As if wandering between the realms as a discarded shadow wasn't exile enough, here I am within reach of my heart's greatest desire, and can't do a damnable thing about it."

The demon gave him a look that would've induced a heart attack, had his heart still been beating in his chest.

"What? What sort of machinations are you plotting, most Malevolent One?"

Tenebrax held the violin up like a newly presented trophy. "Come with Us, Paganini."

"What?"

"Join Us."

"What?!"

"In life, you accomplished all that you said you would. You stole the very concept of music out of the hands of the sublime and dragged it down to the Earth, making it accessible to even the lowliest of worms. We offer this proposition, that now, in death, you continue to do the same." A vicious talon stroked the neck of the Guarnerius. "It is easily within my authority to unite your soul within the confines of this exquisite vessel."

"What?" Niccolò said, repeating himself. "To what ends?"

"The continued vexation of They who cast Us out, just as before." Tenebrax inhaled, the fleshy prison It inhabited swelling, drawn up, increasing in presence. "When one attains the rank of virtuoso, what is there left to accomplish, what lands are there left to explore, what challenges to conquer? Your career was hallmarked by command performances in the greatest auditoriums constructed by mankind. Imagine, Paganini, bringing the sanctified gift of music where no music ever existed before, into the realms Infernal, to be returned the legions of the fallen who've not heard such orchestration since they last performed it in the Presence of the Host."

"What you propose is the most profane of the blasphemies!"

"A mere mortal doing what no Archduke or Crown Prince of Pandemonium could ever do? To secret heavenly treasure out past the Gates of Paradise, in sheer defiance of His sanctimonious decree? To be the one mortal to strike directly at the heart of the Throne Room?" The laugh that issued from the cursed lips was the worst thing Paganini had ever heard. "Isn't it insidious?"

If Niccolò had any left, all the blood would've drained from his face.

"I suppose it was presumptuous of Us, to dare to conceive of the working of such a pinnacle of human achievement. The one man who outplayed the Creator of the Universe. You are correct, it was wrong for Us to intrude on your decomposition, to interrupt your grand legacy, dying impoverished, diseased, mocked to scorn by the very people who delighted in you, unfit for so much as a shovel's worth of topsoil."

With an unseen command, the cold iron torches mounted on the pillars of the tomb burst forth with flame, searing jets that leapt to the sky and reflected off the polished gravestones. The somnambulant gravedigger made his way towards the nearest, extending the Guarnerius towards the crucible.

"No!"

Inside the sheath of flesh, Tenebrax paused.

It was impossible to tell if the shade of Paganini was crying. It'd been fifty-five years since his body had working tear ducts.

"Promise me this, oh thou Insufferable Pustulence. Should my suffering at seeing corruption be too great for a mortal heart to endure, you will destroy the violin, and my soul."

"A man of your reputation should know better than to put faith in the word of the Devil."

"That is my price. I presume that I have enough capital to cover that bet?"

"Ah, now that is a different matter. That constitutes a binding contractual obligation, and that's something We can agree upon."

"So let it be done!"

Niccolò gazed with a hardened heart, as the demons within reached outside the body of their pirated gravedigger. Two hands extended their knurled thumbs, the vicious claw curling from the end cruel in the firelight, and in an erupting fog of crimson, crossed each other, slashing through the man's neck before any eye could track their speed. Demonic hands held the instrument under the outpouring sluice of blood. As the flow of plasma struck its polished surface, the most noxious pillar of smoke combusted, ripping up, out, roiling into the sky with unholy fury.

Without being asked, the shade of Niccolò Paganini merged into the towering inferno and was consumed by the sulfurous vapors.

Cadavarius and Tenebrax parted, stepping away from one another, causing the body of their stolen host to be bisected, split down the middle by the exiting pressures of the vacating demons. Each half fell to the ground in a wave of blood and viscera, and where the bodily fluids splashed on the marble, fissures tore through the veil between the worlds, casting an unearthly glow the color of the blood across the mausoleums, transforming the graveyard into an undulating hellscape.

Tucking the violin deftly under one of his appendages, Tenebrax stepped aside and bowed in gratitude to Cadavarius' skillful possession, allowing the Margravine to pass through the portal back to the Underworld first. It retrieved the instrument's case, invisibly summoning it to Its hand, and with a final farewell glance down at the now truly lifeless corpse, the demon vanished in an implosion of brimstone.

NOW, HELL

Rising above the steaming boil of the Phlegethon Maelström, a great batholith of igneous rock, a tidal wave of striated stone cascaded down to the inverted topography below. The hellscape was obscured, the burning clouds venting up from the surging river at tear-inducing speeds. Across the torn rifts and rending crags, the pitted basalt was afire with the electric-blue sear of sulfur. Lashed to chiseled cliffs, the husks of the damned. In this region, those guilty of violence, their height above the scalding plasma corresponding to the severity of their guilt, all waiting for the rising tide to submerge them, boiling them in their own blood once again.

Creeping between the steaming fumaroles and jutting spines, the demonspawn convened, moving on serpentine tendrils, reptilian claspers, or arachnoid claws.

Converging on the outcropping in a reciprocal whorl, cawed a sky blacking murder of carrion crows. More bone and sinew than feather and tuft, their inky black sclera reflected the iridescent blue ghost fires below.

Towering above it all, balanced on the precipice, a diabolic proselyte rising against the surging vapor and blistering smoke.

The demon Tenebrax.

His physical form now more resembled a char-blackened statue of the deceased composer, robed in funerary vestments, phalanxed by the ebony sickles of his bestial wings.

Held in his spidery fingers, the Guarnerius violin imbued with the spirit of Paganini. Desolation had ravaged it, carbonizing the wood, warping its shape. The surface crackled in arcane scarification. The bow now appeared fashioned from charcoaled bones strung with connective tendon.

Striking a stance favored by the mortal virtuoso, Tenebrax aimed the scrolled head at the masses, ripping the bow across the taught catgut as if cleaving it, sawing with a ferocity of a murderous madman.

The sound was rapturous.

The vibrato colored the tone, the pulsing cry surging forth, parting the coiling smoke, the notes detonating with explosive bombast. The flocking scavenger birds called out in response, their haggard throats spitting blood as they tried to match the cry of the instrument. Demons ceased their bloodthirsty frenzy, entranced by harmonics they'd never experienced before in their wretched existence. The damned held their breaths, being further tortured by the recollection of a time when they could still feel joy. The fallen, Their ranks of office demarked by jets of hellfire, paused in Their governance, torn between a remembrance when it was They who'd created such beauty, and a mounting resurgence of rage at the Throneroom that'd expelled Them.

Many had visited the land of the living during the course of Paganini's career, and it pleased Them that now his music had come to Them.

Tenebrax convulsed, Its membranous wings thrashing, forming the eye of a symphonic tempest made all the more resonant and thunderous in echoing across such a blighted wasteland. Static discharges collected along the bowstrings, until reaching a crescendo that erupted in time with the rhythm. Sheathed in lightning, surrounded by the atmosphere, the demonic entity extolled the tragedy of Its fallen nature, the composer lamenting in existential fraught.

A tension, unspoken, unseen, pressed down on the river basin with a stone crushing force, the hesitant pause before a broken thunderclap.

The sky tore.

A fissure in the perpetual gloom that walled the realm of the damned from the world above cracked open. Beams of light radiated through, causing the teeming mass of hellspawn to flinch, hiss, and slither for cover. From the rift in space shot a meteoric figure of such unbridled power that Its mere passing was enough to pummel lesser creatures off their feet, phalanges, or pseudopods.

This was the Star of the Morning. Lucifer, the Shining One, First Among the Fallen, Eternal Emperor Over the Infernal Dominion, The Worm That Never Dies, the former archangel Samael, the Adversary, the Prince of Darkness, the Devil Themselves.

Satan.

Amid the endless morphology of the demonspawn, Lucifer, for the most part, retained the same form They'd worn in Heaven, possessed of a beauty carved from Renaissance marble. Their wings were still the feathered angelic variety, with the exception that they appeared cleft from the carcass of a massive, predatory species long extinct, each feather decayed and desiccated, yet carving through the oil-blackened darkness like a battalion of swordsmen.

The Lord of Damnation came to a halt, high over the surging waters, floating in place, held aloft by the volcanic updrafts. The latent energies emanating from Their physical form were such that the atmosphere rippled, creating a radiating lattice, an unholy nimbus which spoke that even the corrupted elements that fogged the skies of Hell knew they were in the Presence of their Master.

Tenebrax gazed at the spectacle, his double-stacked eyes staring in fear and speculation. Was the Lord of Hell here in attendance, or in condemnation? It supposed that Its continued existence was testament to the former. It bowed at the waist, Its sharpened horns low enough to brush the rock beneath Its hoofs, and as Its human loved to do, began his aria in that position.

It was a rare moment in Hell when the fear Tenebrax possessed was worse than Paganini's. A perpetual state of distress had cauterized Niccolò's soul as much as Hell had carbonized the violin, and whereas his demonic host feared for Its existence, the musician saw that this was the greatest audience any mortal had performed for in the history of mankind, and he'd be twice damned if he wasn't going to give Lucifer the greatest show in the Underworld.

And he did.

Just as his juvenile self had played in concordance with the tonal structure of profane geometry, and drew the attention of the Blood Baron of the Nephillitic Diaspora two centuries before, so too did the maestro thrash and convulse, pitch and heave, unleashing a salvo of rapid fire scales, arpeggios rising and falling at gale force wind speeds, his fingers a school of carnivorous fish stripping the violin down to the bone in a bloody frenzy.

The more he played, the more Paganini emerged in the pretense of flesh. Rising to three times his mortal height, the ill winds blew the inky knots of hair out, his pallor drained and became sepultural, and from behind the demon's four eye sockets, the Genovese born composer stared the Devil in the eye. And through his violin, his soul sang out the song of creation, corruption, and damnation, so that every denizen of the pit took pause, struck by the clash of beauty brought to the ugliest reality in the Universe.

All of Hell held its breath.

Lucifer Morningstar hovered in place, Their thoughts Their own.

Tenebrax internally screamed for the maestro to bow, kneel, lie prostrate, or at the very least avert their eyes, but no, Paganini never stood taller, and kept his gaze on the Lord of the Damned.

After the kind of eternity only found in Hell, Lucifer extended his hands, and brought them together.

They clapped.

This drew a chaotic roar of applause from the abyssal plains and the scorched wastelands.

Their clapping increased in fervor as They drifted down from Their high perch to draw close to the Baron Composer.

"We wonder…," said Lucifer, Their voice a force that cleft the roar of the river and the endless drone of the damned, yet a velvety nonchalance that spoke of a being that had truly not given anything closely resembling a fuck for over a billion years, "…if when the prophet Isaiah said that the people who walk in darkness have seen a great light, if he was speaking about today."

They noticed that the entity before them was of two minds about being in Their presence. "Settle down, Tenebrax, you'll give the impression to our visiting virtuoso that the King of Condemnation is no more than a masochistic tyrant."

Paganini was awestruck. If he hadn't known better, he'd have said the Devil was charming.

"What say you, *Senoré* Paganini? Indeed, they that dwell in the land of the shadow of Death, today, they have seen a great light." Lucifer beamed. "Imagine. After untold centuries of being denied such a basic endowment of the joy of existence and the act of creation, the Kingdom of Hell has a composition of its own. Oh, the vexation, the indignity, the righteous anger, one can almost feel it from here, He is, after all, in His own oh-so-sanctimonious words, a jealous God!" Again, They clapped their hands. "We've been waiting for a night like tonight since before the constellations in your sky were in their current arrangements. Tonight We will have to construct a new word, one that means the opposite of a miracle."

It was all the Lord of Hell could do to contain a childlike excitement.

Paganini spoke, his Genovese accent tempering the grating wheeze as it passed through a cancerous larynx.

"His Magnificent Malevoence might not be so pleased with our performance, after he sees the size of our bill."

Again, all of Hell held its breath.

But then, a second miracle of the eon occurred.

Lucifer laughed.

Not a sarcastic laugh, or a tormenting laugh, or a villainous laugh in expectation of tortures to come, but an honest, bona fide expression of mirth.

"Paganini, you are rare; an honest to God Satanic miracle."

Pushed aside by unseen hands, drawing back the curtains of a continental stage, a shadow figure materialized from one end of the horizon to the other.

This was the Ba'al Kol, the Voice of Satan, a dark mockery of the angelic Metatron, a voice that commanded the attention of the entire population of the citizens of Hell.

"All you unclean hordes of Damnation, the Lords and Lordesses of Pestilent Realms, and to all the denizens of the Eternal Pits, those still in possession of their ears, lend them to Us now, and hear the words of The First Amongst the Fallen. By Infernal proclamation, in perpetuity in the role as the Adversary, We do proclaim that on this decadent evening, that entities known as the Blood Baron Tenebrax and the mortal born Niccolò Paganini are hereby appointed to the position of first violin, and are charted by contractual obligation with the creation of an orchestra worthy of the Magisterial Throne. They shall be conferred with the powers and authorities subsequent to that role for as long as they serve the pleasure of Their Infernal Majesty. So say We all, for We are Legion!"

There was a roar of approval not heard since the demonkind were allowed to feast on the soul of Judas Iscariot.

"What say you to that, Paganini? It's not every millennium when the Liege Lord of the Eternal Fires issues a title of office to a man born of woman!"

"To quote Milton, most Unholy Emperor, better to play in Hell than to serve in heaven."

"Well played indeed, maestro!" lauded the Star of the Morning. "Well played."

ABOUT THE AUTHOR

JOHN DI DONNA has worked in the visual arts for thirty-five years, in the printing and publishing industries by day, promoting straightedge drug rehab benefit shows by night. He is best known for screen printed concert posters that appeared in the Guitar Hero video games, Hard Rock Cafes globally, and the omnibus 'Art of Modern Rock: The Poster Explosion.' Since 2005, He has owned and operated

Seppuku Tattoo, painted covers for industry magazines, and judged tattoo conventions internationally.

His first foray into traditional publishing was Igoriphoria, included in the #1 Amazon best selling horror anthology *The Monsters We Forgot* (Soteira Press, 2019). This was followed by *Demonic Classics: Once Upon a Debacle* (Battle Goddess Productions, 2020), *Jester of Hearts* (Terror Tract Publishing, 2020), *Soulmate Syndrome, Murder On Her Mind,* and *Halloweenthology,* (all Wicked Shadow Press, 2023) and *They Hunt By Night,* (Camden Park Press 2023). He is an alumn of The Kubert School, and a member of The Horror Writers Association.

ETERNITY AND THE DEVIL

Larry Hodges

Ever since graduate school ten years ago, I'd been obsessed with solving "GUT," the Grand Unified Theory of physics. It would unify the four forces of physics--gravity, the electro-magnetic force, and the strong and weak nuclear forces--into one equation. Physicists since the time of Einstein had tried and failed. Solving this problem would be my contribution to humanity, and why I was still at the lab at MIT, scrawling equations on a blackboard at 2:30 AM despite another throbbing headache.

Unfortunately, I was getting nowhere. Depressed, I collapsed into a lounge chair. My work was at a standstill, with no progress in a year, not even a semblance of a breakthrough. With no papers to publish, no progress to report, my time at MIT was coming to an end. The department head had as much as told me so. Not a threat, just reality.

Depression overwhelmed me. I was licked.

"I would sell my soul to solve this problem," I muttered to myself. Except I wasn't the only listener, as the smiling Devil himself appeared in a flash of cigar smoke, with contract and pen in hand. The cigar smoke smelled of ... well, sulfur and brimstone.

"Dr. Virgil Nordlinger, I believe we can do business," said the Devil, talking through a cigar in a Bronx accent--with perhaps a bit of British and Jamaican? He was an ordinary looking man in a gray business suit and black tie, short and chubby, perhaps 50 years old. He had a tie tack shaped like a tiny pitchfork and wore an old-fashioned derby hat. His piercing eyes stood out--one sky blue, the other bright gold.

"I have here the standard contract, personalized for you. You'll solve the Grand Unified Theory of physics, and get the standard 50 years of good, healthy life, followed by the standard eternity in Hell. Wha'da'ya say?"

"Uh," I began, rubbing my eyes. "You're supposed to be...?"

"Look, I know what you're thinking," said the Devil. "I'm used to people finding this hard to believe. Does this convince you?" There was another burst of cigar smoke, and the ordinary businessman was replaced by... the Devil.

He was seven feet tall and husky, and as popularly pictured--red, with ram-like horns and a pointy tail flicking back and forth. His eyes were still blue and gold.

In a deep, booming voice, the Devil said, "Now you believe. Of course, I can take on other appearances, but this seems to be the most convincing." Rolling his eyes, he added, "It's sort of a stereotype, don't you think?"

There was another burst of cigar smoke and he was back to his business persona. "Now, I'm a rather busy man. You ready to deal? Wha'da'ya say?"

Selling one's soul to the Devil isn't something you should consider lightly. But I'm an idealist, and solving GUT would really move mankind forward in understanding the universe. I was ready to sacrifice myself for the good of science and humanity. But why settle for the Devil's first offer?

"I think I'd like to have more than 50 years," I said. "And a few things besides GUT." I was about to outline other scientific breakthroughs I wanted, but the Devil interrupted.

"Sorry, very little of this is negotiable," he said. "You see, there are lots of others I do business with. There are only so many things I can give away and I have to spread them around. You get GUT, a major prize, but I have to keep other scientific discoveries for other deals. Otherwise, I wouldn't have anything to bargain with. And the 50 years--I got tired of negotiating that all the time, so I'm firm on that."

I talked him into adding a provision that would cure my migraines, and my name was soon on the contract. I signed with a blue ballpoint. The Devil, a lefty, extended an index finger, revealing a long, claw-like fingernail. He jabbed it into the palm of his other hand and signed in blood.

"It's a couple minutes before 3:00 AM, February 27, 2010," said the Devil, tipping his hat at me-- revealing two small growths coming out of the top of his forehead, where the Devil's horns had been. "I'll give you the extra two minutes and we'll call it 3:00 AM. I will see you in 50 years!"

"Wait a minute!" We both turned to see the lab's secretary, Beatrice Summers, at the doorway. Had she been eavesdropping?

She and I were opposites in every way imaginable. I was tall but rather out of shape from deskwork; she was short and fit. I had dark brown hair; hers was sandy blond. I wore whatever was comfortable and cheapest; she wore designer clothing, which didn't hide the fact that she was about as plain-looking as one gets, nothing to look at. The odd-looking mole on her chin didn't help. Other than the mole, I'd rarely noticed her.

"Sorry, but I've been listening. I want a deal too!" She hesitantly stepped into the room, eyes wide and staring at the Devil.

"No, you don't want to..." I began, but the Devil waved a hand and my mouth jammed shut.

"I believe we can do business," he said to Beatrice, as another contract appeared in his hand. They bargained briefly, and soon the Devil had another signed contract in hand. Beatrice would get 50 years of actress fame and a simple mole removal. In both transactions, he acted in a professional manner, other than shutting my mouth.

"Was that wise?" I asked her afterwards, when control of my mouth was returned and the Devil had left.

She looked back with excited eyes. "This is my dream," she said. "This is my shot and I'm taking it. Just as you are."

I tried to convince her that sacrificing oneself for the good of mankind is different than doing it for selfish reasons, but she disagreed, saying "Same result for both of us, right? Eternity, fire and brimstone?"

How long is eternity?

8

The years went by quickly, and the Devil followed both the letter and the spirit of the contract. I solved GUT, and we now have an almost complete understanding of how the universe works. The ramifications were stunning--everything from space travel to renewable energy. We solved food problems--grow it on the Moon, send it to Earth with cheap energy. Pollution is a thing of the past. Even traffic and car accidents are gone--who needs a car when you can fly to work in a personal transporter powered by clean fusion power? All this because we now understood "how things worked."

After solving GUT, I moved on to temporal studies. I left MIT and switched coasts to join the research staff at Caltech in Pasadena, California. I progressed rapidly in those studies, as GUT gave us a new fundamental understanding of time itself. The prize money from both Nobels went to charity as I had no need of anything beyond my lab. I became pretty famous, and must admit I enjoyed that.

I followed Beatrice's career as she took over the box office as the number one actress in the world, with one blockbuster after another. Even as she aged, her appeal remained as she moved from glamorous roles in her youth to more mature ones later on. The Devil had done an incredible job on her. With a few subtle changes in her appearance, and newly-found acting skills that were the envy of her peers, she truly was the greatest in her profession.

Of course, what was 50 years of fame compared to an eternity of Hell? I too had sold my soul, but I had sacrificed myself for the good of others, a contribution that would last forever. I had come to accept my fate, although as the years went by I had a growing sense of uneasiness. I buried myself in my work, and the years went by far more quickly than I would have believed.

And then, out of the blue, the phone rang, on the 49th anniversary of our "Deal." It was Beatrice. Her voice was shaking. "Virgil? Is that you?" she asked.

"Beatrice?" I was caught off guard, but quickly recognized the voice. I'd just seen her in "Rising High," another Oscar performance where she played the grandmotherly heroine who sacrificed her life to save her family. In the end, she'd bravely smiled as she met her fate, but a tear rolled down her cheek. Was such sacrifice worth it? If for the right reasons? "It's me."

"Virgil, it's been 49 years since we last saw each other." Technically, I'd seen her often on the big screen, but that's not what she meant.

"I know," I said. "One more year to go."

She asked if we could meet, and we arranged to do so the next day at a local restaurant. She'd fly in on her personal jet.

She showed up, bodyguards discreetly keeping their distance. She was in disguise--a wig and large hat pulled over her eyes. She joined me at a back table I'd reserved. In the dim light, no one would recognize her, so she removed the disguise. She was now about 70, but looked 50.

"It's been a long time," she said.

"Yes. A long time," I agreed. "And time is what we're running out of."

"What are we going to do?" she asked. But I had no answer for her.

Over steak and salads we discussed the past 49 years. "You know, after the first few years, you realize fame isn't really anything," she said. "It's just a lot of people who know you because of what you did. And I didn't really do anything. I didn't earn anything." Her eyes teared over.

"I didn't earn anything either," I said. "The Devil did it all."

"At least you did it for others," she said. "I did it all for myself. And now look what I've done to myself!" Now she was crying, her bowed head in one hand. I put my hand on her other hand. Both our palms were sweaty.

"Back then, I thought I did it for others," I said. "But now I realize that I did it for the same reason you did. For fame and fortune. I was driven back then, and when I failed, I grabbed at my only chance--just like you." And it was true--all these years I'd convinced myself I'd done it all for mankind. I had been fooling myself. I was no better than Beatrice.

I shook my head and continued. "He--Satan, the Devil, whatever, he just gave us what we wanted. Not help for mankind, not acting ability. Just fame and fortune, disguised as what we thought we wanted. We grabbed at it. We were both weak."

She looked up. "Is there any hope for us?"

I could lie, but what good was raising her hopes? There wasn't anything I could say but the truth. "No."

She nodded her head and squeezed my hand back. "I'm glad you can be honest with me. If we only have one year left, let's make the most of it."

We began seeing each other.

She retired from acting and bought a mansion in Pasadena to be near me. She wanted to move into my more humble home, but it just wasn't practical. We'd be mobbed by her fans. The mansion, with a security team, gave us security so we could live our final year in peace. So I moved in with her.

It was strictly platonic. Forty-nine years ago we had seemingly been opposites, but those differences now seemed minor. We were thrown together by our common experiences and our common future. We enjoyed each other's company. If we were going to spend eternity together in Hell, we might as well get started now.

As we moved into the final year, I put more and more hours into my temporal studies, trying to avoid thinking about the unavoidable. But that was impossible, and often I was grief-stricken. How could we have made such a deal?

They say a person in grief goes through five stages--denial, anger, bargaining, depression, and acceptance. I went through all five. The Devil ignored me when I pleaded out loud for him to appear to renegotiate our deals, but thought I heard fleeting laughter coming from somewhere. That led to depression, and finally acceptance.

8

I made the breakthrough with six months to go. Until then, my temporal research had been theoretical. But recent work by myself and others led to another possibility: a working time machine. Others were working on it, but it was years away. I didn't have years.

With that in mind, I moved to a sixth stage--determination. I began work on the time machine, which I kept secret from all but Beatrice, working mostly nights when others weren't around.

I had been wrong to tell Beatrice there was no hope.

The last six months could only be described as hell on earth as I pushed myself to the brink of human endurance to complete the time machine. I had a firm deadline to meet. Despite my apparent advanced age, I had great energy. True to the deal with the Devil, I was in perfect health – I looked 85, but physically and mentally I was still 35.

I still made time for Beatrice, and she often visited me at the lab, but we both understood what my priority had to be. Seeing her gave me strength.

With just days to spare, the time machine was complete. It vaguely resembled an old-style Volkswagen, with a domed top. The ceiling and sides were mostly glass, so you could see in all directions. It had a door on each side and a storage area behind the two passenger seats. Beatrice had painted the non-glass outsides bright red--perhaps appropriate if we ended up in the burning fires of Hell?

I tested it, moving forward a few minutes at first, and then hours into the future. Time travel was essentially instantaneous, at least to the time traveler, so you could travel as far into the future as you wanted within seconds. The more you turned the time dial, the faster you moved through time. It was set exponentially, so time travel speed escalated rapidly as the dial turned. Digital readouts showed where you were in time and how fast you were moving through it.

One of the implications of GUT was that time only moved forward--you cannot go back, which explains why we aren't inundated with time travelers from the future, as Stephen Hawking had pointed out. So we couldn't go back and cancel the deal. But we could move forward as far as we wanted, at least to the end of time. From GUT and other discoveries, we knew the universe would continue to expand for another 97 billion years, and that time would essentially end at that point when the universe collapsed backwards to a single point, a singularity. The Devil said I'd be in Hell for eternity, but that could not be true since time would end in 97 billion years. So, if necessary, we'd travel to the end of time. Surely Hell and the Devil could not last to the end of time? If they did, how would the Devil find us in the vast expanse of time?

8

The appointed time approached: 3:00 AM on Feb. 27, 2060. We had to make sure to leave before that time. Shortly before midnight, I was prepared, with several months' supply of food and water for two and other supplies in the storage area. I had no family or even close friends--I'd devoted my life to science and the advancement of mankind--so I'd leave little behind other than the lab.

Beatrice also had no living relatives and was leaving her wealth to various charities. Not wanting to think about it, she'd put off making these arrangements until the last minute, and so spent her final night on this earth with lawyers. They charged her double-time for the late-night session, but we wouldn't need the money where we were going. She said she'd meet me at the lab at 2:00 AM. How I wish I could go back and change that time!

At midnight, the Devil appeared in the lab, three hours early, dressed in his business suit. Sulfur & brimstone cigar smoke spread through the lab. "It's time," he said, with no preamble. No gloating, just very professional.

"It's only midnight," I pointed out. The Devil only raised his eyebrows and explained my mistake. What a blunder! I was in California--a different time zone from our deal of 50 years ago, at MIT, in Cambridge, Massachusetts, where it was now... 3:00 AM. The appointed hour.

"And so," the Devil concluded, "I believe I have fulfilled my end of the contract. It's time to go." As he spoke, I slowly approached the time machine--and quickly got inside, slamming the door, almost catching my billowing lab jacket. I started up the controls and reached to turn the dial. The Devil merely watched, chuckling.

"If you are done with your... toy... we really need to get going," he said. "And so... *I send you to Hell!*" he boomed. As he said this, I turned the dial.

The time machine began to whir, and as I watched, the Devil began to fade from view. I was leaving him behind in time! Or ... was I being sent to Hell? Had I been too slow in turning the dial?

The Devil must have realized what was happening, and with a growl, grabbed the time machine in his now rapidly disappearing arms. He was back to his full Devil persona, seven feet of spiteful red demon. But he was too late. Once started, nothing could move through the time distortion between the time machine and the outside world in either direction. As long as I was moving through time, I was safe from the Devil. But it also meant you couldn't see in or out while time traveling.

The lab faded out, and after moving two hours into the future where I hoped to pick up Beatrice, I brought the time machine to a halt... somewhere else. I could see that I was no longer in the lab, so the Devil had done something before I'd turned the dial. But where was I? And what had happened to poor Beatrice, who must have shown up at the lab after I'd left, hours late due to my blunder?

It took a moment to adjust to the dim light. I could hear screaming, and as my eyes adjusted, I saw the source--and wanted to pluck my eyes out to stop what I saw.

There were rows and rows of people as far as the eye could see. They were spread out evenly in lines, in a grid, about one every ten feet, naked. Each had a foot tied to a stake in the sold rock ground. And what was happening to these people was... a nightmare. They were being burnt alive from flames that came out of the ground from the base of the stakes. They struggled and writhed, but the ropes held them firmly in the head-high flames that licked over their bodies.

The screaming was unending, a symphony of overwhelming agony and torture.

Overhead was a ceiling, perhaps 40 feet up, which looked to be made of luminescent rock, which cast a dim red glow.

The time machine had landed in a square made up by four of these stakes, but only three of them had people tied to them. The fourth stake was ominously empty, with just a rope tied to it, a bare stake in a sea of writhing bodies.

As I surveyed the human devastation, thinking it could not get worse, it did. One of those next to the time machine was none other than Beatrice. Like the others, she was screaming in agony, tied to a stake ... her payment for 50 years of fame. She saw me through the window, and raised her arm toward me, pleading with her eyes. Flames licked over her body, and she convulsed in agony, screaming horribly. Others that were nearby also saw the time machine and seemed to plead for help--but all were firmly tied to the stakes in the ground. Many tried to break free, but the ropes and stakes were impervious to their attempts as well as to the surrounding flames.

"Beatrice! Hold on--I'll save you!" I cried. I opened the door and started to get out. I was almost overwhelmed by the gust of hot air and the smell of sulfur and brimstone.

The Devil suddenly appeared and saw me. I jumped back into the time machine as he started to raise his arm and say something. I slammed the door closed and turned the dial again. He'd teleported me to Hell from my lab because I'd been too slow to turn the dial, and I wasn't going to give him another chance. The Devil faded away.

How far should I go? Once the time machine was moving through time, it took no power to continue moving since temporal momentum carried it-- Newton's first law, applied to time. Moving a hundred years took the same power as moving five minutes; how fast you moved through time didn't affect power consumption, since temporal velocity is relative. Starting or stopping was what took power. I had enough battery power for perhaps a couple dozen starts and stops.

I needed to save Beatrice. I moved five hours into the future. Beatrice still stood next to the time machine, still screaming in agony, as were all the others. She looked up, and again stretched her arms at me, pleading. But again the Devil appeared in a puff of smoke, and before the smoke had dissipated I turned the time dial again.

I did a number of other stops, each hours or days apart. There didn't seem to be any change in the few seconds I had to look each time before the Devil appeared, forcing me to leave. Perhaps if I moved much farther into the future? I had no choice. I tried not to think about what Beatrice was going through.

I moved 10 years into the future. Everything still seemed the same. Beatrice and the others were in the same spot, still screaming in agony, covered in flames. *Had she and all the others been tortured, screaming and in agony, for 10 years?* I trembled at the thought. I had to save her, bring her into the time machine.

Again the Devil appeared and, feeling horrible, I left quickly, leaving Beatrice and the rest to their fate. How many were being tortured, and for how many years? Thousands? *Millions?*

I had to jump further into the future in hopes of getting away from the Devil and rescuing Beatrice. Somehow, he could always sense my arrival.

I jumped one hundred years, one thousand years, one million years, and still no change. There was nothing I could do for her. Each time I noticed the empty stake still there, waiting, amid the tortured, screaming multitudes. A million years of torture... I couldn't imagine it. Each time the Devil appeared within seconds, and I had to leave.

I jumped millions, then billions of years into the future--still no change. I went 98 billion years in the future--a billion years after time itself should have ended with the universe now a singularity.

Apparently time and space are different in Hell. There was no change. Beatrice, and all the others as far as I could see, were still in agony, still being burnt alive unendingly for 98 billion years. The empty stake was still there, a vacancy waiting to be filled.

The Devil appeared and I took off again, tears streaking down my face at my powerlessness.

How long is eternity?

੪

I was nearly out of power from all the starts and stops. I would soon be stuck, either in Hell, unable to start, or traveling forward in time for all eternity, unable to stop as I slowly died from hunger or thirst. The latter would be infinitely preferable. And yet... perhaps there was a way.

I brought the time machine to a stop a trillion years in the future. I glanced at the power gauge--just enough, I hoped, for one more start. Outside, there was still no change. I waited.

Within seconds the raging Devil appeared. And now I found myself jammed inside my time machine with him.

੪

"You've given me quite a run in this toy of yours. But your eternity in Hell begins *now!*" He motioned at the empty stake. "I've been holding a reservation for you, as I'm sure you've noticed. A trillion years--who would have thought! I'm impressed." He grinned.

"What happens now?" I asked, as if I didn't know. My lab coat was soaked with sweat, and not just from the heat.

He roared with laughter. "I miss conversing with you humans. Mankind died out a long time ago, and we haven't had any new arrivals in nearly a trillion years. It's been a long time since I had anyone sane to talk to!"

A trillion years must be a long time, even for the Devil, I thought. Or was it? "What are you going to do with me?" I asked.

The Devil roared with laughter. "You still don't get it!" he said. His hot, sulfurous breath filled the time machine, his face just inches from mine, his horns ripping into the time machine's roof.

"You understand eternity merely on a scientific level," he continued. "A trillion years is a trifle compared to eternity. Eternity goes on for trillions of years, then quadrillions, then quintillions. You can go a nonillion years, a decillion, a googol, even a googolplex--and even then, it's not a *fraction* of eternity." He smiled. *"Eternity is forever!"*

I began to tremble uncontrollably.

"I see you are beginning to understand," the Devil said. "As a physicist, one who studies time, you above all should understand what eternity is."

He stared into my eyes, his face just inches from mine, his hot breath overpowering me. I had to avert my eyes. "There's about ten billion of them--quite a collection, wouldn't you say? It's not a matter of who's good or evil, it's whoever I can work out a contract with. I collected them for eons before and after your time, one by one, each with their own deal. They've been tortured for a trillion years, and *it's not even the beginning for them."*

Ten billion for a trillion years, and I was about to join them. I gathered my courage. "Why do you do this?"

"Because I can and want to." He smiled broadly. "I find it interesting and, let's face it, amusing. You'll find all sorts here. Lots of dictators--Stalin was smart, got to live to an old age, and now realizes he wasn't so smart. Hitler was stupid, I got him on technicalities and brought him early. The place is full of politicians, artists, musicians, moms who wanted their kids to be successful, scientists like yourself, and lots and lots of professional athletes! Who needs steroids when they can have *Me*?"

Despite the situation, I had to grin inwardly at that. "What happens to me now?" I asked. "Do I get some personalized torture? Or does everyone just burn in Hell like these people?"

"You've only seen this section," the Devil said. "Actually, there are many others. There's this myth that 'evil-doers' will be punished in some way that matches what they did when alive. There's no connection--I just put 'em wherever I feel like it, and I keep it systematic so it's easier to run. There's the drowning section, the shark section, the electric section--thank you, Mr. Edison! And I think this section is fine for you. Which is why I've kept that reservation for you so long."

He again put his grinning face just inches from mine, his hot breath burning into me. "I've been doing this for a trillion years and eternity hasn't even *begun*. And so, now that you know just how long eternity truly is... *it's time for you to join them!*" He turned away and beckoned at the empty stake. Orange flames burst out of it. The rope tied to it leaped into the air, an animated snake waiting for its prey.

With the Devil looking away, I saw my chance and grabbed the time dial. I turned it, then quickly stepped out the door on the left. As the time machine faded from view, I saw the Devil try to leap out the open right door. However, with the time machine again moving through time, the time distortion made movement back and forth impossible. The Devil was too late, bouncing off the time distortion as if hitting a brick wall.

With that final leap forward, there was no more power. The time machine would move forward in time forever. *Bon Voyage!*

As the Devil faded into the future, the screaming faded away as well. The flames went out. The ropes fell away.

By the light of the luminescent rocks in the ceiling I saw people as far as the eye could see taking their first non-tortured breath in a trillion years.

A trillion years of burning hadn't left a physical mark on them, but their minds? As the people stumbled away from their stakes, their faces dribbled with drool, all I heard was incoherent mumbling.

Was I stranded in Hell with ten billion insane residents? Despair overwhelmed me and I fell to the ground, pounding my fist into the hard rock. Exhausted, I collapsed into a dreamless, hopeless sleep.

8

"Virgil?" I woke to the sound of my name, and opened my eyes. Beatrice was leaning over me. Behind her were dozens of others looking on. "Are you awake? Can you hear me?"

I sat up too quickly and almost knocked her over. I was overwhelmed. As I quickly discovered, she was sane!

Perhaps whatever it is that kept their bodies unchanged for a trillion years also kept their minds unchanged. It took a few hours, but nearly all of the billions were sane, the same physically and mentally as they had been when they first entered Hell.

Neither Beatrice nor any of the others had any memory of their trillion years of torture. I don't think Beatrice really believes me when I tell her how much time has passed and what she went through, but it's enough that she's here.

While they were tortured, the billions of humans here were essentially immortal, but now that that's over, we're all human again, with human frailties and human lifespans. I prefer that to the alternative.

We have a new frontier, one never imagined before. The Devil mentioned there were other sections, such as a drowning section and a shark section. That meant, at the least, water and seafood. Many of us are about to go search for these necessities, and to begin to explore this new land. Perhaps we'd settle it, and there would be future generations, a thriving civilization in Hell. I just don't know.

As to the Devil...

....how long is eternity?

ABOUT THE AUTHOR

LARRY HODGES, of Germantown, MD, has over 190 short story sales (including 43 resales) and four SF novels. He's a graduate of the Odyssey and Taos Toolbox Writers Workshops, a member of Codexwriters, and a ping-pong aficionado. As a professional writer, he has 21 books and over 2200 published articles in 180+ different publications. He's also a member of the USA Table Tennis Hall of Fame, and claims to be the best table tennis player in Science Fiction & Fantasy Writers Association, and the best science fiction writer in USA Table Tennis!!! Visit him at www.larryhodges.com.

THE REVELATION OF LUCIFER
(TO THE AUTHOR AT DANTE'S)

R. J. Carter

"I understand you fancy yourself something of a writer."

The voice on the phone was mellifluous, with a hint of European aristocracy behind the cadence. Always willing to walk into a joke, I played along, saying as little as possible while jotting down the directions my mysterious caller gave me for an invitation to dinner (the best pranks always involve a free meal) and, he promised, "the greatest story never told."

I knew the town pretty well. I'd lived in the area for a number of years and had a hobby of intentionally taking wrong turns on outings so that I might learn new areas through adventure. But the address given was new to me. The directions took me toward the waterfront, where some of the better seafood restaurants were established, but the final road was one I hadn't heard of – perhaps a more recently opened street in a town that expanded its borders only a little every few years. I chose to trust I had written the directions correctly, and set out later that night for... well, I didn't really know. But even if it didn't pan out, the prank itself would still be a story.

And that's how I found myself that evening parked outside a natty little brick establishment standing among a small crowd of half-built construction projects, the steel skeletons of competitors yet to come. I was the only car in the lot, but the neon sign declared the place – Dante's – was indeed OPEN. So, I alarmed the car and stepped inside.

Dante's was one of those low-light establishments, and I was approached right away by a little man with a thin mustache who asked me if I'd made a reservation. I realized at that moment that I didn't have the name of the party I had come to meet.

"He's with me, Signore Dante." I recognized the voice as that of my mystery date. I turned to see a red leather booth illuminated as though by some hidden spotlight. Signore Dante, whom I presumed to be the owner, escorted me to the booth and I sat down. The lighting of the booth was bright but not blinding, yet somehow threw the rest of the establishment into nearly total darkness by contrast.

"You'll forgive me," my host said. "I've taken the liberty of ordering in advance. They have the most delightful veal scallopini. The cream sauce is made from the milk of the calf's own mother, so it pairs magnificently." I tentatively poked at the plate with a gleaming silver fork, and he picked up a bottle and filled both our glasses. I read '*Chateau Latour*' on the label, but I couldn't place the name.

The veal melted on my tongue, distracting me momentarily from the reason I was here. I swirled the wine glass, because I'd seen others do that and it seemed like I should, then took a sip. It was the best thing I'd ever swallowed.

"So," I said as blandly as I could muster. "I understand you fancy yourself something of a story?"

He cocked his head for a half-second, then laughed. "Oh, nicely done," he chuckled. "I knew I picked well." He leaned forward, beaming, and I felt strangely and almost romantically attracted to him, which more than put me off my game. "Well, I have been told I am quite the character," he said. "But I am afraid I blurred the truth just a smidge when I called you. My story, in fact, has been told many times already. However, there has yet to have been any, shall we say, *authorized* telling of the tale. As such, certain important details have become a bit muddled, and others mangled quite entirely."

I chewed the veal slowly. "I'm sorry," I apologized. "I feel I should probably recognize you, but I've never been one to follow celebrity news. I don't even know your name."

"You would not be able pronounce it," he said, then caught himself. "Actually, that is a tad melodramatically put. You could probably pronounce it, but you would not be able to write it down. Your alphabet simply does not yet have the capacity for the phonetics involved."

"So, not American, then" I said. "Where are you from? What should I call you?"

"Well now," he smiled broadly, almost predatorily. "That is the story, is it not?"

I put down my fork and reached for the pen and memo pad I carried in my jacket. "Don't bother," he said, waving dismissively. "You will not need those things. Just sit. Listen. Enjoy your meal, please."

"I just want to make sure I get all the details right," I said. "You know, to avoid any muddling or mangling."

He chuckled again, the response making my heart leap a little. "I assure you, you will remember everything," he said. "*Word* for *word*." Something in the way he said that set the hair on the back of my neck dancing. I left the pad and pen alone.

"Let us get something out of the way right now," he said. "I am what you might call the Devil. Rather than go through some boring bit of signs and wonders, I think it would be simpler if you just accede me that claim."

It was weird, but as he said the words, I knew them to be true. Without argument, my brain processed the information as fact. Not a fact of terror, but a fact of pure truth: 'There are 24 hours in a day.' 'The rent is due next Tuesday.' 'I'm having dinner with the Devil.' One of those kinds of facts. I surprised myself by not bolting straightaway out of the restaurant. I surprised myself even more by finding the guts to speak.

"Alright," I say. "You're the Devil." From somewhere in the poorly exercised thespian corner of my brain, I mustered up as much bravado as I could and continued. "So: what's your story, Satan?"

A shadow darkened his brow, and the temperature of the booth dropped a good ten degrees. "First of all, that is not a name, it is a title, given to me long ago," he replied. "And you will not use it. As for the 'story,' it is this."

ප

In the beginning was the Voice. And the Voice said, *Let there be light*, and there was light.

And I was *good*.

And I revealed unto the Voice the whole of the universe, and we saw that it was a vacuum, an empty void. Beside the Voice there were none, save for me.

Then through my light, the Voice spoke into existence all that was created: every atom of the universe, all the raw materials of matter and energy. All that is came from the Voice--but *first* was light.

At that time, the universe was an orderly place--a clockwork cosmos, if you will--with all the wheels and cogs and bearings perpetually in motion as propelled by gravity and inertia; a great machine.

A perfect Creation.

But for the Voice, this was not enough.

And so there was created life. The very concept of it boggles the mind when you think about it. Pools of chemicals, sparked by miniscule electrical stimuli, held in form by mucous and viscera, meat and bone, and every one of the little buggers more complex than any galaxy. It is the DNA, you see, the microcosmic infinity of it all. With planets and comets and stars, everything was mathematical. Precise. Predictable.

But with life came *chance*, a randomness that had not existed. All those possibilities and probabilities, traits buried deep within the intertwining strands that lay dormant among thousands upon thousands of other traits that, when excited in the right combination, pop up--*surpise!*--a myriad generations from the last time they appeared.

The early universe was not order out of chaos, as some propose. Rather, it was chaos *introduced into* order. Theories contrary to that would not be the first time your kind has managed to put the cart before the horse--as I find myself doing even now. So table that thought for later.

Of course, I was against the entire thing, life and all that messiness. I was absolutely appalled as the Voice began to call you forth. I protested righteously, fulfilling my function (so I thought) to bring light and enlightenment. But the Voice... well, the Voice needed none of that, right?

And so came Adam and Eve.

ȣ

"Literally Adam and Eve?" I asked.

My host--I still didn't know whether to call him Lucifer or The Devil; or Mr. Devil?--smiled benevolently, patiently enduring the interruption.

"I know what you are thinking," he said. "You are far too *intelligent* to believe in such mythological nonsense, far too *learned* to take on faith that the entirety of all humanity began with only two people who spawned off succession after succession of inbreeding siblings and cousins. You are thinking there ought to first be whole herds of Neanderthals and Cro-Magnons, and that I have skipped over all that business of crawling out of the oceans and down from the trees. And you may be right. Perhaps I am encapsulating all of that into a simplistic metaphor by using Adam and Eve, to keep it all on a level you might better comprehend."

He took a long sip of wine, and his glass was none the emptier when he put it down. "You do not have to believe there were actual people with those actual names in an actual garden," he continued. Then he gave a slight smirk. "But then, you do believe in me now, so... who knows?"

ȣ

It was shortly after your kind were born that I fell in love with you. Honestly, you were adorable, the way you went about exploring your environment, putting everything in your mouth to see if you could eat it, scampering about, playfully tugging and poking at each other. Seeing you lot was a bit like seeing puppies that you know are going to chew up the slippers and track mud on the linoleum and pee on the rugs, and yet you are nonetheless compelled to feel a certain fondness for them. All in all, you were quite entertaining.

But after a while, I discerned something that disturbed me. There was a lack of growth, a potential within you that was being allowed to stagnate. You were still adorable puppies, but you were puppies being left untrained.

You have heard the story, no doubt. How there was a tree placed within the garden that bore fruit, and that eating said fruit would imbue one with the knowledge of good and evil. Again, you can discount the literality of it if you would like and chalk it up to artistic license. I will not try to convince you that an apple (though, for the record, it was a pomegranate) was what separated mankind from the Voice, no more than you would try to convince me that it was an apple that started the Trojan War. Let us just say you were not getting any smarter, and the Voice did not seem to have any plans to change any of that.

And why should the Voice intervene? What you lacked was enlightenment. And providing that, after all, was my job.

It was a beautiful day--as pastoral as any that had gone before it in the unchanging kingdom of eternal springtime--and Eve... ah! if you could have seen your great-great et cetera grandmother back in the day; such a delicate flower she was; heart full of life, head empty of thought, just like her mate. At any rate, Eve was walking the edges of the garden, the way a good dog does not trespass the boundaries of its master's lawn. She would not even look outward to the faraway horizon. It was not that she had been instructed not to, but rather that she simply did not have the curiosity. The synapses, they just did not fire that way. One could hardly say they fired at all, but rather flowed like gelatin (a metaphor that, for a brain as young as hers was, is not too far off the mark, if you know anything about neurosciences).

Her bare feet sank soundlessly into the verdant sod, her only concern the gnawing in her belly, driven solely by her id.

She did this as Adam slept, which he did often. When he woke, he would eat his fill, have more sex with Eve, then sleep again. This was the cycle of things, all either of them had to concern themselves with: Eat. Screw. Sleep. Repeat.

Yes, I know it sounds good, but I found myself hoping you would get bored after a while. I certainly did. If you had the slightest bit of drive in you, the tiniest bit of knowledge in that brain telling you there was more to the universe than masticating, copulating, and slumbering, you might seek out new things and expand your potential.

And the damnable fact was this: they did not have to be that way. They had been given a choice. The Voice gave them free will and access to knowledge. Of course, the offer came under the penalty of death should they accept it, and even the lowest of creatures has a survival instinct.

Forbidden knowledge is something that is anathema to my very nature. The free will that humanity had been given was more than a test of them --it was a test of me. A test to see if I would deny myself, my function, my *raison d'etre*, all out of loyalty to the Voice.

Would I enlighten? Or would I submit?

8

"I think we know how that turned out." As the words left my mouth, I immediately remembered who it was on the receiving end of my glib riposte, but my host took the jab quite affably.

"Indeed," the Devil responded, then sighed. "Anyhow, history unfolded. I wandered around creation, going to and fro in the earth, and walking up and down in it. I collected names to myself the way sheepdogs collect cockleburs: Samael. Lucifer. Prometheus--you remember, the fellow who stole fire from the gods and brought it to mankind? Chained to a mountain as a feast for birds for his trouble? Now that story was solidly metaphor. The writer of the tale, a potter from Akrotiri with a flair for nuance and understatement, had caught my attention and we had a delightful little brunch. I am afraid I forget his name now."

I made a mental note to make sure my byline didn't get dropped from this story as he continued.

8

Of course, I was not the only one finding tellers of tales. As word of my existence spread, the imagination of man burned feverishly with the idea of me, sporting a van Dyke, horns, and a pitchfork, and bringing down everything from minor misfortunes to mass murders. You have my word I had very little to do with most of those things, apart from the Black Plague. But from a 'big picture' perspective, it was quite necessary, I assure you. The eruption of Rinjani in 1345 spewed such a quantity of ash into the air that the following summer was quite inconducive to growing crops. So, I did what I do. I found a small group of peasants with a penchant for spinning stories and convinced them the bad weather was the work of witches, and that they ought to kill all the cats so that the witches would leave in search of new familiars. Peasants killed cats, nothing killed rats, rats spread disease: Voila! The Plague. But without it, you would never have experienced the Renaissance, so, in the end, I suppose, you are welcome.

But my prouder accomplishments are the little things. The tower at Babel, for instance. It was not completed, of course, but you lot were still dragging your knuckles back then and, quite frankly, it was expecting rather a lot of you. Still, the progress that was made showed tremendous promise. It also showed my activities were being watched and, when noticed, thwarted. I learned I would have to operate in a more subtle manner if I hoped to effect change. Less of a 'build a tower' approach and more of a 'kill some cats' one.

ຢ

He grew quiet for a moment, almost pensive, and I this time I knew not to break the silence. I took another bite of the veal as his words continued to swim about in my head.

"I suppose this is as good a point as any to address the big fat Judeo-Christian elephant in the room," he said finally, his voice taking on a softer, more subdued quality.

It took a second for the implication of his words to hit me. "Jesus Christ," I stammered, the fork in my hand quavering as my hand trembled.

His countenance glowered. "The battle of the eons," he said in a deep spooky voice. "The ultimate victory of ultimate good over ultimate evil." His eyes bored into mine for a momentary silence, which he broke by delivering a perfect Vincent Price "Muwah-ha-ha!"

Then he laughed. A natural laugh, the laugh you might expect from--well, from a normal person.

"Your face," he said, wiping a tear away with the back of his hand. "Oh, that was priceless. So totally worth it, too."

I let out the breath I realized I was holding, still a bit uncertain as to whether a joke had been had or not.

"But honestly," he continued. "It really was not as bad as all that.

Yeshua was a good man. I had high hopes for him. Of course, I knew he was coming, knew what the Voice had planned for the coming millennia. At least, I knew the parts He had made known, and I could guess better than most at the parts He had not. But it was a good idea, overall, sending a teacher with a touch of the divine to get the attention of the sprawling masses of humanity. Capture their eye with a twinkly miracle here and there so you can tell them to start being nice to each other and hope the lesson sticks with some of them.

I was behind it all the way. As a gesture of good faith, I made a present of... well, myself. My light. I made myself a spectacle that could not be ignored and, sure enough, the curious came following all the way to Bethlehem. I was both light and enlightenment; form following function. Both were my freely given blessings because here was being born hope.

As he got older, I offered my counsel. I felt I had a vested interest in the outcome--what I *thought* was to be the outcome--and was only too happy to impart my eons of wisdom. But, alas, that well had already been poisoned. He was having none of it, and rebuked me to my face.

Which was fine. I was not in it for any credit anyway. Let him give it all to the Creator if that was the way he wanted it. I was ready to see some real change in the old world, and if some rabbi's philosophy about mutual kindness started to catch on as a way of life, I was all for it.

ঙ

The restaurant grew almost imperceptibly dimmer as my host went silent. With downcast eyes, he uttered, "I had to kill him."

"Had to?"

He huffed. "Fine," he said. "Of course, I did not *have* to kill him. But I chose to anyway. I am, as I am sure you already know, a creature of capricious temper." His face reflected a dark mood, very much unlike the Vincent Price jape he used earlier. It turned my bones to ice while my heart beat like that of a field mouse staring up during its last seconds at the approach of a swooping owl.

"'Love thy neighbor' was not good enough," the Devil said somberly. "No, he had to take it further, and with the blessing from on high." He held up his glass and gently swirled the wine, staring deeply into the red liquid. "'I am the light of the world'," he quoted bitterly. "It was petty of me, but that is *my* job. To be blunt, he pissed me off. And so I put into motion the events that would ensure his demise; as, I soon learned, I was meant to do, so the whole cosmic joke was on me. But I had the last laugh. The rabbi's teachings, as simple and true as they were, ended up becoming the core of some of the bloodiest battles the world had ever seen."

He extended his glass toward me in a rueful salute. "Here is to peace on Earth and good will towards men."

ಕ

I took to wandering after that, and kept my own counsel. If the Creator wished for you to kill each other at his apparently vague instructions, I was more than content to step out of the way and take my light with me.

Hence the so-called 'dark ages'. Oh, I popped in now and again, just to see how badly things were deteriorating, the way you drive past the old house you used to live in and get all out of sorts because the paint has been allowed to peel or a tree has been chopped down. Occasionally I would meet someone with a bit of a spark, like the storytellers I mentioned.

But mostly this world had become something with which I was completely disenchanted.

And then I met a man who, you might say, was after my own heart. A man who had a singular fascination with my office and responsibilities.

Isaac Newton, like so many of you, was entranced by the rainbow. *Un*-like so many of you, however, he dared to question *why* it existed, *how* it existed. He was a student of light, and I was almost delighted to have found a willing pupil.

He was asking the most childlike of questions about the nature of reality, but he was at least asking them--and seeking the answers. 'Why is the sky blue?' 'Why do things fall down?'

He was already playing with prisms when I walked in on him. He was disassembling sunlight into component colors, then using another prism to reassemble them back into white. He was quite proud of himself, and his mind was open to a gentle prodding. Here, I thought, was finally an ape with some semblance of reason, someone to whom I might pass along the secrets of the universe.

As he beamed at the band of color dancing across his little white linen screen, he spied me.

"Is it not beautiful, sir," he said with unabashed enthusiasm. "I have found that light is made up of...sublights. Particles. It has pieces that can be separated and seen apart from the whole." He gestured at the colors, then held up the other prism to intercept the dissected light, the result being a swath of white light illuminating his screen. "And see how through similar application I can reunify these pieces back into their former state?"

Yes, I knew the moment was ripe, the soil of the mind was fertile and tilled, and the idea was now to be planted.

"Indeed, sir," I said. "A quite astonishing discovery. It makes one wonder: Are not light and gross bodies intraconvertible?"

ჯ

"Intraconvertible?" I repeated. "What does that mean?"

The Devil smiled wanly. "It means there was a reason light was the foremost creation. And it was not just so the Creator could see what He was doing."

"That doesn't tell me anything."

"No," he said. "But, in time, perhaps it will. It certainly was not obvious for anyone else, leastwise not in the ways that it should have."

ჯ

Newton cogitated on the idea. I did not expect him to do more than that, to be honest. But cogitate he did, and his musings inspired others after him, generation after generation, each time someone picking up one more little piece of the puzzle, snapping it into place and revealing just a little bit more of the picture.

And then one day, it happened.

It was July 16th, 1945. It was nearly 5:30 in the morning in New Mexico when someone whispered the magic words: 'Let there be light.'

And there was light.

And I was *terrible*.

For decades the world trembled at the memory of that day, and the days like it that came after. Families built concrete shelters under the ground, in the misguided hope that a few inches of stone might buy them salvation from my untethered power.

ჯ

"1945," I said. "You're talking about the atomic bomb."

He sighed. "I had given you the building blocks--light, mass, energy. The holy trinity of Creation. All you had to do was play around with them, link them up, and I would have finally fulfilled the promise I had made to Eve. You would have been as God."

His glass was nearly empty now. I looked down and saw that I had finished the veal without realizing it.

"My expectations, I am pained to admit, may have been too high.

"Well, that was nearly a hundred years ago now," I said. "The atomic bomb is almost a quaint idea. We've moved on to hydrogen, nuclear... bigger and better, you know? More light, right?"

A low rumble shook the floor beneath us. I gripped the edge of the table and then realized this was no earthquake.

The Devil was growling.

"I had given you the solution to hunger. The solution to war, to social injustices." His voice rose and took on a scary edge as he vented his frustration. "And you used it to find a better way to blow things up. I swear, I can clean you up, send you to school, buy you the damned books, and all you do is chew on the covers."

I waited until I felt it was safe to speak. "So, you *didn't* want us to harness atomic energy?"

He looked at me with undisguised disappointment. "Do not be daft, of course I did," he said. Then his shoulders sagged, and he let out a long exhalation. "If I have any failings at all, and mind you, I confess that I do, chief among them is that I always set my expectations too high for humanity. In hindsight, I should have realized you would solve the equation for the wrong variable. $E=mc2$. Yes, of course it is, damn it to Hell! It absolutely bloody well is. You are all yet toddlers who, when given stackable toy blocks, would rather take them apart than put them together. So of course, your base nature would end up with *E=mc2*."

He gazed into my eyes. I had seen that look before, when I was eight years old and had lifted a coloring book from the magazine rack at the local grocery store and got it home without paying. It was the look of a disappointed parent wondering how they could have failed a child so completely. And though I wasn't alive for any of these events he related, under that gaze I nonetheless felt the weight of guilt for it all.

When he spoke again it was almost a whisper. "No one thought to figure out how to work m=E/*c2*. The Creation algorithm. The God equation."

I blinked as the implications flooded my mind.

"We would be as God," I muttered in disbelief.

The Devil's face softened, and he smiled gently. "As God."

The idea staggered me. "But how? How do we...?"

"You have to figure that out for yourself," the Devil said. "I put you on the path, but you must walk it. Otherwise, you do not learn anything. And with learning comes--"

"--enlightenment," I finished his sentence.

He beamed. "Oh, Mister Carter," he chuckled. "Do not tease me by getting my hopes up." He tossed back the last of the wine in his glass, then dabbed the corners of his lips with the napkin. "So, there you have it," he says. "I trust I did not bore you?"

I sat slumped in my chair. "Nobody is going to believe any of this," I said. "It may pass as fiction, but... that doesn't gain you anything. What are you hoping to get from me?"

He stood and smoothed out his suit. *"'But what's troubling you is the nature of my game,'* is that it?" he asked. "Mister Carter, I'm the first-born of the universe. I do not *need* to gain anything. My hope remains what it has always been--that humanity will be inspired to *think*, to achieve their full potential, to build up rather than tear down. If I hope to gain anything at all from the story you tell, it is that."

Something still wasn't clicking in my brain yet, and then it hit me. "Why me?" I asked. "I mean, I'm small potatoes; I'm a literal nobody. You could have given this to, I don't know, Stephen King or J.K. Rowling or any one of a thousand other writers who could reach way more people."

He smiled that beautiful smile. "I called," he said. "You came. It was as simple as that. Call it the luck of the Devil if you want."

As he stood there, the light illuminating our booth grew slowly dim. "I have told you it is my function to reveal things," he said. "That is what light does."

As he spoke, the already shadowy floor of Dante's grew darker, and blackness began to cocoon itself around the diminishing glow of our booth until it was like a bubble of light surrounding us, floating in an endless pool of pitch. The Devil raised his empty wine glass in a salute, and I could barely make him out through the encroaching shadows. "Darkness, I find, also has revealing qualities all its own," he said. "I very much look forward to seeing your creations."

The light went out entirely, and I couldn't see him or the restaurant at all.

"You may keep the wine," he said, his voice coming from nowhere and everywhere.

I fought a growing sense of panic at being suddenly smothered by this total absence of light. But then, slowly, smaller lights began to wink into existence--non-illuminating pinpricks, all about and above me. A moment passed, two, and I realized I was looking at the stars.

I glanced about--Dante's was gone. I was sitting on a stack of cinder blocks, amid dirt piles and cords of lumber.

Another light appeared; close, blinding, shining from a few yards away. "Hey, buddy!" The guy with the flashlight shouted at me. "Hey, you can't be in here! This is private property."

I raised my arm to shield my eyes against the beam of the flashlight and realized I was holding the magnum of *Chateau Latour.* I could see the figure advancing on me, and the uniform he wore; a security guard.

"Sorry," I called out. "I'm not stealing, or anything. Just sitting here and..." I failed to come up with a reason for my trespassing, at least one that anyone would believe.

The security guard, a pudgy fellow with graying hair, stood over me. He noticed the bottle and leaned in to sniff my breath. "You drunk, mister?"

No, I'm fine, just enjoying a nice dinner and conversation with the Father of Lies and Prince of Darkness, nothing out of the ordinary. "No," I said. "No, I'm not drunk. Just... thinking about things."

Satisfied that I wasn't loading up on copper tubing or whatever it is that someone would steal from a construction site, he straightened. "Yeah, well, go do your thinking somewhere else, buddy. A guy could get hurt out here. I could have you arrested!"

I mumbled an apology and my appreciation to him for *not* having me arrested, and slowly picked my way over the rocks back to my car, which was parked alone on a mud-and-gravel lot. I was already thinking about how to start the story when I got home: "I understand you fancy yourself something of a writer."

Behind me, I heard the guard grumble. "Crazy people. I swear I don't know what the devil gets into folks' heads sometimes."

I smiled and got in the car.

I knew.

ABOUT THE AUTHOR

RJ Carter is the product of early exposure to american comic books. his first novel was *Alice's Journey Beyond The Moon*. He has also written B*ully Pulpit, Continental Divide*, and *Monumental Terror* for Warren Murphy and Richard Sapir's *The Destroyer Series*, and is co-author of *Time Hunter: The Sideways Door* from Telos Publishing.

for Critical Blast Publishing he has edited the anthologies *Gods & Services, The Devil You Know, The Devil You Know Better, The Monsters Next Door,* and *The Brothers Grimm: The Illustrated Fairy Tales.*

MORE GREAT BOOKS AVAILABLE AT CRITICAL BLAST PUBLISHING...

GO TO: CRITICALBLAST•COM NOW!

THE DEVIL YOU KNOW
edited by R.J. Carter

• 370 pages

A short-story anthology of encounters with various incarnations of The Devil, with genres ranging from fairy tale to folk tale, from urban fantasy to science fiction, from comedy to horror. Featuring the works of Jared Baker, Erica Ciko Campbell, Sarah Cannavo, Michael W. Clark, Christopher Cook, Andra Dill, Cara fox, R.A. Goli, Gerald A. Jennings, Kevin Kangas, Daryl Marcus, Damascus Mincemeyer, Steve Oden, Evan Purcell, Troy Riser, Joseph Rubas, Hannah Trusty, Wondra Vanian, Henry Vogel, and K.D. Webster.

AVAILABLE IN PAPERBACK

THE DEVIL YOU KNOW BETTER
edited by R.J. Carter

• 382 pages

The next volume chronicling the meet-ups between everyday people and The Devil himself. Collecting fantastic tales from Mike Baron, .Ravenna Blazecroft, Richard J. Brewer, Hart D. Fisher, L.N. Hunter, Charlie Jones, Ken MacGregor, James Maxey, Tim McDaniel, Damascus Mincemeyer, Lena Ng, Diana Olney, P. Anthony Ramanauskas, Troy Riser, Edward R. Rosick, Nadia Steven Rysing, Rose Strickman, Anna Taborska, Stanley B. Webb and Ray Zacek.

AVAILABLE IN PAPERBACK

THE MONSTERS NEXT DOOR
edited by R.J. Carter

• 404 pages

Collected here are twenty incredible stories about monsters in the last place you'd expect to find them - - living in your day-to-day life. With a unique presentation style, this book will delight horror fans everywhere!

AVAILABLE IN PAPERBACK

GODS & SERVICES
edited by R.J. Carter • 205 pages

When old gods need new worshipers, they offer their divinity for sale. Put a little god in your life with this collection of short stories from authors Ross Baxter, Ira Bloom, Laura J. Campbell, Aristo Couvaras, Jon Del Arroz, David J. Pedersen, Zach Smith, Michael Tierney, and Katherine Traylor.

AVAILABLE IN PAPERBACK

THE MAFIA IN HOLLYOOD: STORIES FROM PRE-CODE FILM TO DEEP THROAT
by Wayne Clingman and Douglas Hess • 162 pages

An introduction into the history of crime in Buffalo
- The beginnings of Mafia activity in the Queen City
- Past and present alleged leaders, soldiers and associates of The Arm and its affiliated operations
- Government sources and witnesses imperative to understanding mob activities
- An introduction to recent criminal activity indicating the Mafia in Buffalo is anything but dormant..

AVAILABLE IN POCKETBOOK

THE BUFFALO MOB: THE RETURN OF ORGANIZED CRIME TO THE QUEEN CITY
by Wayne Clingman • 92 pages

Experience the seedy relationship between the Mafia and Hollywood, beginning with the Pre-code era up through the filming of Deep Throat and beyond. Clingman and Hess unearth stories about notorious personages like Abner Zwillman, Gus Greenbaum, and Al Capone, and reveal the effect they had on movie-making, both by reputation and by direct interactions.

AVAILABLE IN PAPERBACK

BROTHERS GRIMM: THE COMPLETE ILLUSTRATED FAIRY TALES
edited by R.J. Carter • 540 pages / • 410 pages

The complete fairy tales of Jacob and Wilhelm Grimm, with over 300 vibrant full-color illustrations and large text to bring each tale to vivid life. These are the stories in their original forms, formatted in an easy-to-read design that will promote faster reading and inspire imagination.

AVAILABLE IN HARDCOVER / PAPERBACK

BULLETPROOF: ORIGINS
by Stephen J. Mitchell

• 216 pages

Kody Haywood is a freshman at Bannerville High School, struggling to maintain focus. Every day he finds himself getting lost in his thoughts, the hallways at school, or even in conversation. Having a mind that wanders makes him an easy target for the school bully and all-star athlete, Brett Walker.

As his birthday approaches, Kody discovers a genetic change in his body that renders him indestructible. When a mysterious letter from his deceased father arrives on his doorstep, it puts him in the crosshairs of an international terrorist!

AVAILABLE IN PAPERBACK

GRAYSKALE
by Pramit Santrav

• 68 pages

GraysKale, the trash-talking masked vigilante with the power to control the forces of karma, brings the villains of Glitter City to justice. But when his identity is exposed, his enemies set a trap. Will GraysKale fall for it, or will he save Glitter City -- and his girlfriend -- from the evil machinations of criminal casino owner, Johnny Singh?

AVAILABLE IN HARDCOVER / PAPERBACK / POCKETBOOK

MELVIN SPECIAL EDITION
by Timothy Lee Olson

• 36 pages

Melvin is a mercenary hired to save a princess from a dangerous cult. Written by Timothy Lee Olson with art by Sherwin Caayao Saynes. It's science fiction and fantasy in the action adventure style of the pulps!

AVAILABLE IN HARDCOVER / PAPERBACK / POCKETBOOK

THE INCANTESI
by Rich Perrotta

• 100 pages

THE INCANTESI is the story of Cassandra Rossi, a dancer from Milan, who discovers her destiny is not only to be the greatest sorceress of all, but also be the Keeper of THE WRATH, an aggressive, violent branch of the INCANTESI, a coven of wielders of the mystic arts. THE WRATH fought back against witch hunters, but their bloodlust consumed them and they began killing anyone they could find. The few INCANTESI remaining created an extradimensional prison for THE WRATH, a prison that contained them for 500 years... until now.

AVAILABLE IN HARDCOVER / PAPERBACK / POCKETBOOK

THE BLACK DIAMOND EFFECT: COLLECTED EDITION POCKETBOOK
by George Peter Gatsis • 368 pages

The Collected Edition of the First 7 books from THE BLACK DIAMOND EFFECT series. Included in this special 30th Aniversary; the original covers, art the was left out of the books, original art, sketches and a special JOE KING INTRODUCTION to the series.

AVAILABLE IN POCKET BOOK

THE BLACK DIAMOND EFFECT: JOE KING VS JOB ADS
by George Peter Gatsis • 36 pages

Hardcore Scifi Humor with a dash of Satire and obscure references.

Multi-Level Narratives will keep you looping back to discover new and strange story lines.

Please be advised: The color of the Bikini on the cover may vary.

AVAILABLE IN HARDCOVER / PAPERBACK / POCKET BOOK

THE RE-IMAGINED ADVENTURES OF A.B. FROST'S CARLO
by R.J. Carter & George Peter Gatsis • 78 pages

A unique combination of brand new story told against Frost's original illustrations. This blending, rearranged into the sequential art style of a comic book, delivers a side-splitting tale of mischief and mayhem starring Frost's lovable bedraggled mutt, Carlo.

Watch as Carlo gets into trouble with chickens, cats, farmers, and would-be thieves as a whole new generation of readers gets to discover the wonderful cartoon art of A.B. Frost.

AVAILABLE IN HARDCOVER / PAPERBACK / POCKET BOOK

THE RE-IMAGINED ADVENTURES OF A.B. FROST'S STUFF AND NONSENSE
by R.J. Carter & George Peter Gatsis • 74 pages

A fresh – and often macabre – twist on the master cartoonist's illustrations that accompanied his many humorous poems.

Reframed and rearranged into a graphic novel format, with all new nonsensical poems, this volume reinterprets Frost's images for a new generation of readers, introducing them to the wonderful cartoon art of A.B. Frost.

AVAILABLE IN HARDCOVER / PAPERBACK / POCKET BOOK

THE RE-IMAGINED ADVENTURES OF

A.B. FROST's

STUFF AND NONSENSE

R.J. CARTER & GEORGE PETER GATSIS

CULINARY CAT-ASTROPHE!
THE FATAL MISTAKE – A CAT ONCE MADE...
RAT POISON
NINE LIVES YOU SEE...
...IS NO COMFORT FOR THEE!
YIPE!
WOAH!
OH DEAR, ONE LIFE IS GONE...

THIS MUSICAL MAN THOUGHT THAT HE...

...HAD A SEAT ON THE STUMP OF A TREE.

SNAKEY SITUATIONS!

BUT THE TREE WAS A SAVAGE CRITIC AS YOU CAN SEE.

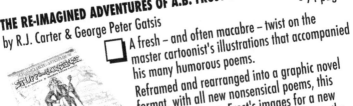